THE HYPNOTIST

A Novel
Richard C. Loofbourrow

iUniverse, Inc.
New York   Bloomington

The Hypnotist
A Novel by Richard C. Loofbourrow

This is a work of fiction. All of the characters, names, incidents, organizations, and dialogue in this novel are either the products of the author's imagination or are used fictitiously.

iUniverse books may be ordered through booksellers or by contacting:

iUniverse
1663 Liberty Drive
Bloomington, IN 47403
www.iuniverse.com
1-800-Authors (1-800-288-4677)

Because of the dynamic nature of the Internet, any Web addresses or links contained in this book may have changed since publication and may no longer be valid. The views expressed in this work are solely those of the author and do not necessarily reflect the views of the publisher, and the publisher hereby disclaims any responsibility for them.

ISBN: 978-1-4502-1494-0 (sc)
ISBN: 978-1-4502-1495-7 (e)

Printed in the United States of America

iUniverse rev. date: 3/2/2010

I am grateful for my two
beautiful granddaughters,
Colby and Riley,
and my wife, Chris,
for her encouragement and love.

"We are what we think.
All that we are arises with our thoughts.
With our thoughts, we make the world."
—*Buddha*

PART ONE:
Hypnotism and Tarot Cards

Chapter One

"It was the best of times, it was the worst of times, it was the age of wisdom, it was the age of foolishness ..." Michael Doc Mesmer had heard of Charles Dickens but never read him. The sentiment, nevertheless, fit. At thirty-five he was too young for a midlife crisis. He felt on top of his game, in control. Nevertheless, Doc was at a turning point; his life was about to change.

He tossed the final worksheet in the trash, swishing the net. "Yes," Doc blurted. He hated preparing his taxes as much as paying them, but the three-pointer closed the deal. "Finished, done, out of my hair!" Doc shouted. He had wrapped up his federal taxes a month early. *No procrastination this year*, he mused. His eyes fixed on line 28—taxable income, $75,000 and change, just for making people feel better. Not bad for an amateur.

He glanced at the Ph.D. certificate adorning his office wall; it was bogus, on sale for $69.95, purchased over the Internet. The fancy certificate issued from London College even impressed Doc, spelling his name in gold lettering followed by Doctor of Philosophy. It beat suffering through college and grad school, quicker, surely cheaper. His steadfastness in having his clients call him Doc had clearly paid off. He encouraged the nickname, a quick smile and "Oh, just call me Doc." The calculated move gave authority and credibility to his services.

His attention shifted to a second certificate, off to the right, hanging askew, directly above his well-stocked bookcase. It was no less important, sanctioning him as a minister, allowing him to perform marriage ceremonies, ordained by the Universal Life Church of Modesto. He bought it on the Internet for the discounted price of $39.95. It was a great investment, helped spread the word, and let people in on his hypnotherapy practice. He glimpsed the antique wall clock. "It's on!" he shouted, springing to his feet. As he hastily filed the tax form, the nineteenth-century clock chimed, filling his small office with the sounds of Westminster. The clock, a gift from his mom, gave him solace. "God bless her soul," he muttered as he gazed at the clock's hands, wishing he could reverse time. *I miss her.*

Reverend Michael Mesmer, better known to his clients and friends as Doc, was a hypnotist, a vastly under-regulated profession. He followed California guidelines, dodging controversial areas, never offering advice concerning emotional or mental disorders. He was skilled at reading people, sweet-talking gullible neurotic types out of their hard-earned cash; he literally mesmerized them with his charm. His ex-wife, when first married, called him charismatic, but later, after a contentious divorce, a charlatan.

He could easily fit in with any crowd. His quick wit, boyish looks, and penchant for laughter made him immediately likable. The empathy expressed for his clients was real, only the credentials were phony. Anyone knowing this would instantly call him a quack. The State of California, however, considered him a hypnotist; he saw himself as a savior of souls.

The buzzer sounded, alerting him to his next client. He waited a bit, building the suspense. *Let 'em wait,* he thought; *it makes them more appreciative.* He slowly opened the door to the waiting room, warmly greeting Maggie, a married, middle-aged woman struggling with America's biggest vice—being fat and overfed.

"Maggie, so good to see you." Doc Mesmer motioned toward the sofa, waiting for her to settle her girth before he sank into his oversized swivel chair. He liked to glide about the hardwood floor, rolling just enough to make a point. "Tell me about your week. Did our plan work?"

"Doc, I don't know what you did, but I avoided sweets all week. Gee-whiz, the mere thought of *choc-o-late* made me grimace. What's happening?" she gushed. Maggie was not only fat, but also hyper. She spoke rapidly, punctuating her speech with gee-whiz, gee, and good-golly. She shuffled about with quick, jerky movements, rapidly fluttering her eyelashes when excited. Her bleached blonde hair and pudgy cheeks reminded Doc of a female evangelist he once caught on late-night TV.

"It's working, my dear. Our last session was only the beginning. Great things are about to happen."

"I'm too excited for words," she said, rapidly tapping her right foot. She did this every session. It drove Doc nuts, but he didn't let on.

"Now the work begins. Close your eyes and take a deep breath." Doc's soothing tone cast a spell over Maggie, soon halting her tapping foot, causing her wide, heavy shoulders to sag, followed by her slumping head. He counted backwards from one hundred, and by seventy-five she was under his spell. He again offered a post-hypnotic suggestion, only reinforcing the one he planted last week. Comfort food was demonized, associated with the wicked and disgusting, nasty food forced on her in childhood by her authoritarian parents. Treats were linked to asparagus and broccoli, still on her most hated list. The induction shifted from food to images of tranquility when Doc noticed her grimacing. After forty-minutes she shuffled out of his office, wide hips swaying, contented with her session.

It was time for a break. He glanced back at his office door, grinning at the bold black print shaded in gold: Reverend Mesmer: Hypnotherapy. It was noon; his next client wasn't scheduled until two. Just enough time to visit Wally's Emporium, his favorite bookstore. He preferred reading and gossiping with Waldo, the proprietor of the San Fernando Valley's biggest used bookstore, than wolfing down a cheap burger. Waldo eked out a living, cursing the big chain operations, slamming them for their glitz and artificiality.

He walked briskly east on Ventura Boulevard, passing quaint boutiques, hair salons, and a costume shop where he once rented a Count Dracula costume for a Halloween party. After three-blocks and a long traffic light he entered Wally's Emporium, spotting Waldo leaning on the checkout counter, staring at the front page of the *LA Times*, talking to himself.

"Hey, Wally, what's new?" Doc knew if he called him Waldo, he would freeze, not thawing for weeks. His deceased wife, when pissed, called him Waldo followed by a derisive sneer.

"Same old crap. Old ladies and cheapskates camping out, reading for free, seldom if ever buying. This ain't no public library." Waldo nodded to his left where a gray haired lady wearing faded jeans and navy blue sweater reclined reading a paperback. She was stretched out in one of three easy chairs, scuffed walking shoes propped up on the coffee table, enjoying a free read. Patrons could sit and read or just gaze out the front window, watching the endless parade of humanity. He referred to it as leech's heaven. The longer a customer sat reading, the less likely they'd buy. Years ago he removed the chairs to the back room, but all hell broke loose. Within a week he reluctantly replaced them. Doc heard about it for a month. "Cheap bastards!" Waldo complained, shaking his head.

"It's far better, my man. Hidden treasures await the curious."

"Tell that to the leeches clinging to my bookshelves."

"You're being too cynical."

"Optimism is for the naïve," he snorted, returning to the folded newspaper and his ubiquitous mug of lukewarm coffee. He was never seen without the heavily stained cup, partially filled with a bitter swill he brewed in the backroom. "Coffee's ready. I just made it."

"Thanks, but no thanks." Doc knew that was a stretch. Waldo made one giant pot first thing in the morning. The industrial sized urn would simmer all day, by evening turning into something resembling Texas crude. Better fitted, Doc learned years ago, for lubricating machinery than sipping.

"Seen Gypsy lately?"

"Last night, just before closing." Waldo didn't raise his head from the newspaper, pretending to read, giving the impression he was preoccupied. He wasn't. He actually looked forward to Doc's visits but didn't want to let on. Since his wife passed, Doc was his main man. With the exception of Waldo's dead wife, Gypsy was the one woman who tolerated his gloominess. She and Doc were Waldo's only close friends, everyone else just acquaintances, passing souls in search of a cheap read.

"What's she up to?" Doc glanced about, marveling at the towering walls of books, aisles lined with old, wooden bookshelves, sturdy and substantial like old Waldo, defying the ravages of time. The store wasn't busy, maybe a half-dozen customers looking for a bargain.

"She's being evicted." Waldo looked up from the day-old paper, frowned, and dropped his head again, as if he really enjoyed savoring yesterday's news.

"What!" Doc said, slowly shaking his head.

"She's a month behind on her rent," Waldo mumbled into the newspaper. He hunched his broad shoulders, sloughed, searching for a comfortable spot on the stool. He looked the part of a burly longshoreman, on break, resting before hoisting another load aboard a waiting cargo ship.

"That's nothing new. She's always a month in the rears." Doc shrugged and went to the magazine rack, checking out the latest covers of *Time*, *Newsweek*, and *The New Yorker*. His mind was not really on the magazines, but rather on Gypsy. He enjoyed their chats, often disagreeing about how best to win over a client. She was a fortuneteller, a tealeaf reader, an avid astrologer, and a crackerjack at milking tarot cards for all they were worth.

She rented a second-story office space, which served both as a private residence and as a parlor. Gypsy chose bold decor; heavy, dark red drapes smothered all four walls, interrupted only by two doors and thin columns of pink and white wallpaper. If the incense and flickering candles didn't open portals to the occult, Gypsy would. It was over the top, too flashy for Doc, but cozy, tucked away above a busy liquor store on Ventura Boulevard, a mere two blocks from Doc's office. In the street-side window, competing poorly with the garish liquor store lights, was a small neon sign: Fortune Teller. The dimly lit device was her sole source of advertising. Beneath the blinking neon, bathing in its glow, hung a more modest sign in black script: Spiritual Adviser. Word of mouth, however, was much more effective. People liked Gypsy, and so did Doc. He'd call on her later.

Doc needed a haircut, so he bid good-bye to Waldo. "Later, Wally," was all he said before leaving, walking two blocks east, and then crossing the street. The barbershop was something out of the 1950s—a working red-and-white barber pole, three chairs, but of late, only one barber. Sammy, the owner, had recently lost his last barber to Supercuts, leaving him alone to juggle the customers. Today, there was only one.

"Sammy, what's up?"

"Hey, Doc, haven't seen you lately. Maybe three weeks or so."

"Sammy, you know my habits, Wednesdays, every two weeks like clockwork. Got to be clean-cut for my clients."

"How's the practice?" Sammy's scissor work slowed as he applied the finishing touches to a thirty-something blond wearing an expensive, dark gray business suit, hair cropped short. *All-American type, preppy, probably peddles insurance*, Doc thought, picking up the latest issue of *Sports Illustrated*. There on the front page, shoulder to shoulder, were four of the highest paid Yankees: Alex Rodriquez, 10 years/$275 million; Derek Jeter, 10 years/$189 million; Mark Teixeira, 8 years/$180 million, and C. C. Sabathia, 7 years/$161 million.

"Good, but not as good as what I see here." Doc waved the magazine at Sammy. "What's up with sports these days. No love of the game."

"Hey, love ain't got nothing to do with it. Money rules." Sammy brushed off the blond, fussing over the guy in hope of a tip.

"Thanks, keep the change." Preppy flashed Doc a smile, then turned to Sammy and said, "See you in a couple of weeks."

"It's a deal," Sammy gushed, cleaning off the chair with the flair of a bullfighter entering the ring. Sammy was Italian, through and through. He was a Dodger fan, hated the Yankees, had cringed when Doc waved the *Sports Illustrated.*

"I took the wrong turn at the fork in the road." Doc slid into the chair.

"What?" Sammy dropped a white cloth around Doc's shoulders, turned and picked up his shears.

"I was a lefty, threw a mean slider."

"Any good?"

"Maybe. I tore my left rotator cuff my senior year of high school. A Yankee scout was in the stands. Thought I had a shot."

"That was it?"

"Yep. All my dreams down the drain. Joined the army. Spent time in Germany. Good duty."

"You missed Viet Nam?"

"Yep, way too young. I'm only *thirty-five*," Doc stretched out his age, knowing that Sammy was a good twenty-five years his senior.

"Don't rub it in. Just a trim?"

"Whad'ya think, I'd go for the bald look?"

"Nah, your head's too big. Got too many hills and valleys."

"What?"

"Doc, I've been cutting your hair for at least five years. I know every nook and cranny. But I didn't know you were a ballplayer."

Sammy spun Doc around, facing him to the wall-to-wall mirror. Doc grinned and studied his image. Not bad for thirty-five. Full head of dark brown hair, easy smile, blessed with white symmetrical teeth, no doubt from his mother's side. His dad's were crooked, missing a couple from his days as a boxer. Doc didn't think he was handsome, but he did believe his small, chiseled facial features projected a boyish image. He often drew comparisons to George Stephanopoulos, always with the caveat, "a poor man's George." The quip was clear; he lacked the money, power, and polished demeanor of the famous newsman.

"Make me handsome. It'd be good for business."

"Not in my powers. If I could, I'd make you taller though. I read that a man's salary grows right along with his height."

"Well, my towering five eight frame belies my poverty. Should've played more baseball."

"Yeah, and become one of those Yankee creeps." Sammy spun Doc back around, facing him toward the muted overhead TV. It was tuned to ESPN. NBA basketball scores dotted the screen, passing in quick succession, catching Doc's eye. Lakers won again.

"I'd be a Dodger, just to please you."

"You'd better, or I wouldn't touch your unruly mop."

Doc hit it off with Sammy, but then again, he hit it off with everyone, except his dad and ex-wife. That's another story he'd just as well forget. Right now he needed to head back to the office and prepare himself for his two o'clock.

"Thanks, Sammy. You shined me up like a new penny."

"Pennies ain't worth nothing, not even new."

"You got that right."

* * *

Doc skimmed Barbara Wilson's file, an inveterate smoker without the will to quit. Her doctor recently scared the hell out of her, motivating her to seek help. That's where Doc came in, but the first three sessions went slowly. She was middle aged, graying hair, extremely thin, perhaps anorexic, tense and jittery, unable to flow with his guided imagery. Her dull smile gave vivid testimony to her nasty habit. Kissing her, Doc mused, must be like smooching a dirty ashtray. Her resistance proved stubborn, making Doc scramble for an inroad. He had an idea, but before thinking it through, the buzzer sounded, announcing her arrival. The buzzer thing was impersonal but efficient. He couldn't afford the overhead of a secretary. The lobby was shared with a psychologist, an old guy with unruly white hair. He reminded Doc of Einstein. *Make her wait a few more seconds,* he thought, standing for a moment, preparing for the seventh-inning stretch.

"Barbara, good to see you."

"I'm a wreck. Down to six a day. It's killing me." Her voice was hoarse and raspy, surely the result of her addiction.

"Excellent. Six a day for how long?"

"All god damn week! Excuse my French."

"Good. Get comfortable. I have something new I want to try."

"New?"

"New and improved. But, this isn't an ad, it's the real deal."

"Oh, I hope so."

Doc turned on a recording; soft, rhythmic sounds of a forest in springtime filled the office. The faint chirping sounds of birds, flowing waterfall, and wind chimes were barely audible. He asked Barbara to visualize the spot, walk about, see the birds, touch the water, and roll around in the grass. Doc's voice lowered, became soft, suggestive, mesmerizing, sending Barbara to a new place, a quieter existence free of tension. The induction was quick, smooth, and incredibly seductive. Here, he made the key post-hypnotic suggestion, associating smoking with disgust, literally equating it to the stench of death. He spoke of maggots, rotted flesh, puss, and the violent vapors of black bile. Her head bobbed and then lowered, lazily dropping onto her slumping shoulders. The imagery was suddenly making him feel queasy, so he carefully brought her out of the trance, pleased with the hypnotic adventure.

Doc was patient, never hurrying, allowing his words to create an inner force within his clients. He was confident, almost smug, about his ability to draw a person into his fabricated world. He almost believed it himself.

"Barbara, we are leaving the forest. We are returning, coming back with a renewed energy and resolve. We are whole again, in a safe place, ready to take the next step." Barbara gradually raised her head, gazed at Doc, eyes out of focus, gently coming back to his small office.

"Wow."

"Yes?"

"Just wow. I feel funny."

"How so?"

"Kind of out of sync. Maybe relaxed, but it's hard to remember the last time I felt relaxed."

Barbara turned before leaving and flashed Doc a rare smile, dull but genuine. "Thanks, Doc. See you next week." Her new lease on life was infectious, making the next three sessions a breeze. It was his most productive Wednesday in months.

Chapter Two

It was eight-thirty, not too late to swing by Gypsy's, catch up on the latest. He had treated Waldo to Italian, washed down the pasta with Chianti, and left him laughing from a joke about a one-eyed sailor. Waldo wasn't easily moved to laughter, but Doc had an endless supply of dated jokes from his army days in Germany.

Doc paused outside the liquor store, looking up at the neon sign, red letters circled in green, beckoning the curious: Fortune Teller. He took the stairs to the second floor and rang suite 201. He knew Gypsy was spying him through the peephole. If the neon was lit, she was there. He stood grinning, giving her a good shot of his mug. He heard a chain slide, deadbolt release. Gypsy appeared, smiling.

"Doc. What a surprise. Please, come in."

Doc smiled, gazing at the heavily draped parlor before settling into a Windsor chair across from Gypsy. A few candles burned on a nearby table, and the aroma of jasmine filled the room. The parlor glowed, bathed in shades of red and pink, creating an air of mystery, even for the most skeptical.

"I just had dinner with Waldo."

"You didn't call him that, did you?"

"Nah. It's always Wally to his face. But Waldo captures his essence."

"I saw him yesterday. He looked well."

"Wally's fine. But I'm here to talk about you."

"That's my favorite subject." Her green eyes glowed, sparked by a nearby lamp, her short auburn hair richly reflecting the parlor's rosy ambiance. Her pale, blemish-free skin seldom saw the light of day. Gypsy, born Maria Dumitrescu, lived the first half of her life in Romania and then came to the

States when she was twenty-one to find her fortune, wanting to escape the dreariness of her small village. Her distinct European accent added a layer of mystery to her profession. Her mom had taught her well. The occult had worked flawlessly back home; "Why not here?" she said aloud, gazing at her youthful reflection in the mirror. It was an exercise she practiced many times before opening up her parlor on Ventura Boulevard. After all, she'd learned much about her craft in her early years, absorbing her mom's mystique and style. *It's a gift*, her mom had often said.

Gypsy had been instantly drawn to Doc. It had been etched in the stars, she found out after doing a reading when they first met. They were born the same year, to the day: only she in Amara, he in Los Angeles.

"Wally said you're in the rears."

"What?" Gypsy blurted, shifting uneasily in her chair.

"You're behind on the rent."

"Wally talks too much."

"Are you?" Doc eyes narrowed, searching for some honesty. Gypsy was proud, self-reliant, and often stubborn.

"Just a month."

"That's what you always say. Be real, tell me the truth." Doc smiled, not wanting to be an inquisitor.

"The truth's not always what it's cracked up to be." Gypsy leaned back and crossed her arms across her chest.

"Gypsy, you're not playing fair. I thought we were friends."

"We are." She pushed back against her chair, arms still folded, protective.

"Then, be honest."

Gypsy paused, tilted her head, wrinkled her turned-up nose, and said, "It will be two months this Friday."

"Do you need help?"

"No! I can handle it." She dropped her arms, smiled, and said, "Thanks for your concern."

"I got a few bucks stashed away. How much is your rent?"

"Please, Doc. I can handle it."

"I'm here for you."

"I appreciate your concern. Say, how's that voodoo thing going?"

"Gypsy, it's called hypnotherapy."

"You do voodoo like no one else does voodoo." They both laughed.

"Wow, you make it sound sleazy. Anyway, I'm fairing well, especially lately. Some breakthroughs. Makes *me* feel good, making people feel good."

"How come it's taken you so long to drop by?" Gypsy studied his eyes, looking for something, trying to crack the protective veneer. Doc was friendly and fun, but not open. He seldom, if ever, showed emotion, and he never expressed any self-doubt. Gypsy sensed he was hiding something. He was funny, friendly, and definitely cute, yet something didn't feel right. She wanted to squeeze Doc in a hug, but feared if she grabbed too tightly, he'd burst, jet away, leaving behind only hot air.

"I've been busier than ever. I often think about you."

"How so?" Gypsy locked on his brown eyes, causing him to lower his head, averting her gaze."

"You're charming, attractive, and easy to be with. I can't get enough of your accent. It sends *s-shiverr-rss* up my spine."

"Doc, there you go again, falling back on sweet talk rather than sincerity."

"It's all true."

"I'm not one of your clients. Come clean." Gypsy wouldn't back down.

"Hey, I'm telling it like it is."

"Is this from your heart or your head?"

"Both." Doc felt uncomfortable, like some specimen in a collector's lab, pinned, squirming, but to no avail. Doc shifted the talk back to Gypsy, offering once again to help her with the rent. She politely but sternly declined.

Doc rose, pulled Gypsy to her feet, and gave her a brotherly hug. He felt protective; they were friends. "Keep in touch. I'll drop by in a day or so."

"*Promise.*" Gypsy smiled and walked him to the door.

"Guaranteed."

* * *

Doc gunned the engine and darted to the fast lane, unleashing the awesome power of his deuce coupe. The '32 Ford had been chopped and channeled, fixed up, beefed up, and raced throughout Southern California for over seventy years. The early morning sun reflected brightly off the candy-apple red paint, causing some casual Sunday morning drivers to take a second look. It was obviously not the original color, but it was his granddad's first car, his pop's sole hobby, and the only surviving heirloom of the Mesmer clan. Doc was now the aging classic's sole custodian and loving protector, successfully monitoring several restorations.

He made a hard right, exiting at Winnetka, then headed north a bit before finding Pierce College on his left. The beefed-up V8 hummed, cruising effortlessly, just like it did for his dad and granddad. The classic's functional beauty was just about the only thing Doc and his dad agreed on. It was their favorite ride.

Even though today was his only day off, he was booked solid, not with clients, but another weekend seminar. His mood was good, the morning ride fast and fun. He knew he had a lead foot, one of a handful of avowed vices, but couldn't afford another ticket, so he eased off the accelerator before pulling into the college parking area.

He found a safe spot for his candy-apple beauty, away from the careless swinging and banging of car doors. Before hustling up the hill to a small theater in the music complex, he gently wiped away the muddy effects of yesterday's rain showers, gently touching up the fenders and running boards. The panoramic view of the San Fernando Valley and surrounding mountains was spectacular, the air cleared by yesterday's downpour. It never rains in Southern California, but it did last night. He entered the building, hastily grabbed some literature from a hallway desk, put on a nametag, and signed in; he was now properly logged into HPN's Twenty-Fifth Annual Hypnotherapy Conference. He made a point of keeping current. There may be no official licensing requirements for a hypnotist, but he liked being on the cutting edge.

Doc moved comfortably among the conference participants, mingling with psychologists, psychiatrists, social workers, alternative medicine practitioners, and New Age spiritualists. Seated near the back of the conference room, he gazed at the zoo of psychobabble devotees boning up on the latest in hypnotherapy. He recognized several colleagues, instantly smiling when he spotted Gwen. *Now there's the real deal.* Most of his acquaintances were honorable types who had the best interest of their clients in mind. A few, *damn it*, were con artists, looking for any way to expand their client base, buttonholing everyone in sight, pumping them for the latest, whether it be a technique or a connection. He thought of himself as above the fray, using his natural talents and acquired skills to make people feel better. He may have bought phony credentials—*stage props*—but his heart was in the right place. He was a hedonist, dearly wanting to make his clients feel good—everybody loved Doc.

The morning session dragged on, unnecessarily dwelling on well-known self-improvement techniques. The last hour, a guest speaker hit it out of the park; a psychologist led an induction session, showcasing the latest concentration skills. "We all needed enhanced awareness," Doc blurted to no one in particular as he descended the steps of the music complex. He rushed past a couple of acquaintances, said his hellos, then spotted Gwen heading for the parking lot. He hustled, catching her before she got in her car.

"Hey, Gwen, I'm famished. How about lunch?"

"Perfect. I was just thinking about you."

Gwen was an herbalist who genuinely believed Mother Nature had all the answers. Gwen Bloomfield, a petite, pixie-like woman, had an inexhaustible passion for research and study. She was consumed with finding the correct elixir for better living. With an encyclopedic mind, able to instantly recall thousands of medicinal plants, she lovingly prescribed them for her loyal clients. Her surname fit.

Doc and Gwen found an outside table at Good Earth, just a mile from the college, a whole food restaurant—that's what she called it—serving nothing but natural goodies, untouched by Dow chemical. So she said. They studied the menu, Gwen offering a running commentary on the health benefits of selected items, or lack of, and ordered.

"So Gwen, whadya think?"

"About what?" She squinted, pushing a cluster of freckles across her nose and cheeks.

"The morning session."

"The first was a waste, too general, the worst of old school. The hour on enhancing concentration made the conference worthwhile. Of course, dining with you is the crème de la crème."

"You are a sweet-talker," Doc said, grinning into the sun.

"Not as good as you," she said with a wink.

"You getting many referrals?"

"Most of them by way of the chiropractor I now work for."

"Same guy?"

"No, I just started with Stevie three months ago."

"*Stevie*. You call him Stevie?"

"When we're alone. In the office, it's Dr. Stevenson."

"That's smart."

The waitress brought Gwen a veggie salad, tofu, carrots, celery, mushrooms, and spinach. Doc had a veggie burgher with fries. He wasn't fussy about his diet.

"Doc, you still eating meat?"

"A little, but mostly chicken, some salmon."

"You've heard the expression, if it's got a face, don't eat it." Gwen wrinkled her nose, scattering her freckles once again.

"Yeah, sure."

"It's good advice. My stomach is no graveyard for dead animals."

"Wow! *I'm eating here.*" Doc yelped, putting down his veggie burger.

"We're all so hypocritical."

"How so?" Doc resumed nibbling on his burger. He glanced about the patio, wondering if their fellow diners were as fanatical as Gwen.

"When we see a dead cow or lamb lying in a pasture, it's considered carrion, feast for a vulture. But the same carcasses dressed and hung in a butcher's shop is food for us."

"What can I say, we're all schizophrenic." Doc felt pangs of guilt. He tried being a vegetarian once, but it just didn't fit.

"Why is it that we treasure panda bears, Bengal tigers, and blue whales, but slaughter and eat pigs and cows?" Gwen was relentless. "Doc, doesn't that bother you?"

"You're ruining my appetite." He once again checked out the lunchtime crowd, feeling guilty, tiring of her rant.

"Sorry. I'm a passionate woman."

"That's why I like you. Say, how's your daughter?"

"It's been rough, single mom and all. She's a freshman at Santa Monica City College. She wants to be a nurse."

"She got the nurturing gene from you."

"Yeah, maybe. How's your practice?"

"Doing well, ever aware of crossing the line."

"How's that?"

"Staying clear of mental and emotional disorders. I'm no therapist. Self-improvement's my game." Doc smiled, causing her to chuckle.

"Best game in town. And it's not entertainment; it's life or death. Say, why don't you call me? We'll do dinner." Gwen's enthusiasm was contagious.

"I'd like that." Gwen was cute, vivacious, exuding an infectious lust for life. He liked her but knew she had her hands full with work and keeping tabs on her teenage daughter. He kissed her once. It was sweet, but he didn't want to get involved. Doc needed to focus, keep his eye on the prize. His dream had not yet been realized.

Chapter Three

I t was nearly nine-thirty when Gypsy decided to turn off the neon sign in the front window. She had a hard fast rule—*never a reading after ten*. It was simply too dangerous. Gypsy lived alone on a busy boulevard, directly over a popular liquor store. Evil things happened all too often, and she didn't want them happening to her. Not more than five seconds after extinguishing the neon light, a loud knock, followed by three taps, shattered the silence, causing her to jump. She moved to the peephole and spied a hooded figure. She didn't recognize the person. Leaving the security chain in place, she cracked the door.

"We're closed."

"I need a reading." The stranger's tone was grave, a frantic blend of desperation and urgency.

"Come back tomorrow."

"Tomorrow might be too late."

"I'm psychically more alert in the daytime."

"Please, you were recommended by Margaret Morley."

"Maggie? *She's dead.*" Gypsy gasped upon hearing her friend's name mentioned.

"I know. But I promised her I'd look you up."

Maggie was a long-time friend, a fellow spiritualist and renowned practitioner of the occult. She was tragically killed over a year ago, just outside her residence, struck by a speeding, black Lincoln Town Car. The negligent driver was Maggie's former client. Gypsy unhooked the chain, reassured by his connection to Maggie, still guarded, but sensing he wasn't an imminent threat, and said, "I must close at ten."

"I promise to leave at ten. Please, just thirty minutes."

The slightly hunched man moved slowly to the center table. His gait was uneven, noticeably limping, causing his body to shift from side to side. He paused, waiting for Gypsy to take her seat across from him. The hood, lightly tinted glasses, and gray goatee, made it difficult for Gypsy to get a read. This unnerved her, for she could easily read a person's intentions by casually studying facial expressions, animals included.

"Why do you seek my help?" Gypsy squirmed in her seat, his intrusion definitely disturbing. It was only the mention of Maggie's name that made his passage possible.

"I need to know my immediate future."

"Why the urgency?"

"My circumstances, shall we say, are life-threatening. I need access to my immediate future."

"Are you familiar with tarot cards?"

"Yes. Margaret did a reading, before her death. *God bless her gentle soul.* Her assessment was right on. She said glowing things about you. I think she loved you."

"We were very close." Gypsy reached behind her and produced a deck of tarot cards. "Do you have a specific question?"

"I need to know what tomorrow brings."

"The near future, or tomorrow?"

"Tomorrow," he said bluntly.

"Person or event?"

"Persons."

Gypsy carefully unfolded a black cloth, a dramatic frame for the tarot cards, before methodically spreading the Celtic cross. They both gazed silently at the colorful cards. Gypsy's breathing slowed and eyes narrowed as she tuned into the invisible world, the transcendent realm of truth, the only world she felt at one with. It was there that she derived her strength and resolve, the powers that gave meaning to her solitary life. Before proceeding, she waved a crystal over the cards, swinging it from a gold chain, hovering over each card, cleansing, insuring a pristine reading.

She had chosen the ten-card Celtic cross, the most common layout. Cards one through six were placed vertically, forming the upright column of a traditional cross. The immediate challenge card lay horizontally across the center card, the one representing the present. Four cards stacked vertically flanked the cross, representing four categories: factors affecting the situation; external influences; hopes and fears; and final outcome.

Gypsy worked her magic, discerning the stranger's troubled character, sensing anxiety and conflict. She slowly moved through the cards, flipping Wands, Swords, Cups, and Pentacles. When Gypsy reached the final outcome, she drew an Ace of Cups. The previous card was the Tower, indicating it was time for the stranger to move on. Gypsy avoided being too specific but insisted that the cards were right on.

"Move on?" the stranger said.

"Yes. Don't dwell on your obsession. Swords and Wands dominated your reading. There's conflict, but it resides only in your head." Gypsy's tone was soft but solemn. She allowed her European accent to flow freely, something she often did when feeling stressed.

The stranger slumped in his chair and sighed, "In my head?"

"Yes. Your troubles are within."

"Are you sure?"

"It's as clear as you sitting before me."

The stranger rose, reached in his pocket, and retrieved fifty dollars. "Thank you. I hope you're right."

Gypsy stood up and walked the stranger to the door. "May I ask who you are?"

"Vincent Salabrini. My friends call me Vinny."

The hooded man was gone, still a stranger, but one with a name.

* * *

Doc was excited, almost giddy. Juan Perez, his five o'clock, played baseball at Pierce College and was looking for an edge. Last year, Doc had helped Larry Johnson sharpen his game. Larry, a pitcher, was winning at the community college level but getting no looks from the scouts. After two months of guided imagery, he jumped to the Minor League and now played for the Jet Hawks, a Class A affiliate of the Houston Astros up in Lancaster. Larry, a former teammate, referred Juan to Doc for help with his game. Doc was psyched; he loved nothing better than working with athletes. Juan was a lefty, just like himself.

The buzzer sounded, alerting Doc to his next client. He didn't let him wait; he was ready for action.

"Juan, Doc Mesmer." Doc shook his hand vigorously, delighted to have a physically fit client.

"It's a pleasure. Larry raves about your work."

"I love working with athletes. Come on in."

Juan was a beanpole, at least six-foot four, with dark hair clipped short. Any shorter and he'd be bald. "Please," Doc said, "get comfortable."

"Thanks." Juan looked around, nervous, obviously not familiar with hypnosis. He sank slowly into the sofa, eyes wide, excited but unsure.

"Are you looking for magic?" Doc said as he slid into his favorite chair, rolling back a bit, taking in his lanky client.

"What?" Juan appeared startled.

Doc laughed. "Just kidding. So you want to improve your game."

"I love baseball. I want to be like Larry. Get some looks. Make it to the minors, maybe the big leagues."

"You're a lefty. How's your slider?"

"Decent. My curve ball is better." Juan stretched his long frame and grinned.

"What's your record this season?"

"It's early. We started conference play last week. Two starts, no losses."

"Do you know about guided imagery?"

"My psych instructor talked about it. But most of what I know came from Larry."

"Let's try an experiment," Doc said, stroking his chin.

"An experiment?" Juan tensed, but soon relaxed as Doc leaped to his feet and stood on one leg. He nearly laughed as Doc struck the Heisman pose. He never played football but could do a mean, one-armed, ball held tightly, imitation of the famous football trophy. He'd been to USC's Heritage Hall, had seen the trophies of O. J., Marcus Allen, and Matt Leinart.

"Look, it's easy, just balance on one leg. No conscious thought required."

"I'm no football player," Juan said. He stood observing Doc's antics.

"No problem. Come and join me. Just stand on one leg. Listen to all the muscles in your leg working to keep you balanced. Listen carefully, because the more aware you are, the more muscles you'll feel. Tune in, feel how they contract and expand."

"I don't know, Doc. I don't hear anything." Juan frowned, then hesitantly balanced on one leg, not sure what to make of Doc's experiment.

"Listen carefully," Doc said, holding the pose. "The balancing is accomplished automatically, unconsciously. But now raise your arm and assume the Heisman pose. This is a conscious movement, a deliberate cognitive act."

"Okay, I can see that." Juan executed the pose perfectly.

Doc dropped the pose and slid into his chair, smiling, pleased with Juan's cooperation. "Sit down, relax. The contractions and movements of the muscles in your legs are carried out subconsciously. The body is in charge. The deliberate act of positioning the arms is cognitive, involving roof brain chatter." Doc paused and took a deep breath.

"Roof brain chatter, what's that?" Juan was once again puzzled by Doc's antics. The roof brain chatter reference only worsened matters.

"We are not consciously holding our balance. We just want to be balanced. The conscious self sets goals, but the body does the work. We need to work on your inner game."

"Inner game?" Juan wrinkled his nose.

"Our main goal is to quiet the mind." Doc leaned forward, sliding toward Juan. "Set a goal," Doc said, inching even closer to his new client, "then let go, don't press, let the body take charge. We think too much. As long as the mind is in control, we'll tense up, make errors, and try too hard. The trick is to let go, get in the flow, let it happen."

"I do tense up. When I press, I bomb." Juan shrugged his shoulders and smiled. He sensed Doc was tuned in, understood the game. He realized that most of his problems were psychological, not physical. Doc was a good fit.

"Exactly! Give me a month or two and we'll send your game to a higher level." Doc smiled, trying to get a read on his new client.

"I'm in! If it worked for Larry, it'll work for me," Juan said with a burst of enthusiasm.

"That's the stuff."

After the fifty-minute session, Juan left with a promise to commit himself to the inner game. Doc was pumped, excited about his new client. Athletes were his favorites because they tended to be eager, dedicated, and ready to give it their all. He had a hankering to celebrate. *I'll give Gypsy a call.* Before he reached for the phone, his antique clock chimed six times. He flashed on his mom. They both loved antiques, although he was partial to cars. She cherished the clock as much as life itself. When alive, she had been a kind, soft-spoken woman, the only barrier protecting him from his abrasive and combative father. His dad, during his twenties, was a pugilist—it fit. What didn't fit were father and son. Doc frowned but quickly shrugged the mood off. He dialed Gypsy.

Chapter Four

Doc looked up at the neon sign; it was off. It was happening; he had a date with Gypsy. She greeted him at the door wearing a short black skirt, heels, and powder blue blouse. He took a second look, blinked, and felt pangs of lust. For years he had thought of Gypsy as a sister—not now. Tonight, they'd party, go with the flow, paint the town red. It was nine when Doc closed the passenger door of his deuce coupe, glimpsing her pale firm thighs. He was pumped. They were off to City Walk.

"We're going to howl at the moon!" Doc shouted as he pulled onto the freeway.

"We're going to do what?" Gypsy laughed.

"Well, actually, we're going to a musical revue of sorts."

"Great. I'm in the mood to sing."

"Tonight's your night."

Doc arranged for valet parking, a must for the safety of his pride and joy. There was neither a scratch nor a dent on the "Old Girl." To Doc, his little deuce coupe was female—cute, perky, always able to turn a man's head. His '32 Ford deserved the best. So did Gypsy.

The club was bustling, reacting enthusiastically to the dueling piano players belting out tunes. Nostalgic sing-a-longs energized the willing patrons as a pair of young, uninhibited piano players pumped their Baby Grands, supplying lyrics for the drunken revelers. Doc and Gypsy sang along to "Sweet Caroline," sipping their first round of Long Island Iced Teas. By the time the witty piano players sang "Devil Went Down to Georgia," they'd polished off three of the potent concoctions. After two hours of singing, drinking, and literally howling at the moon, they'd lost not only their voices but also their sobriety. Gypsy insisted that they drown themselves in coffee before hitting the road. After a rambling short walk, weaving in and out of an energetic crowd jamming the central section of City Walk, they ducked into Starbucks, ordered two large cups, black, and found a corner table away from the maddening crowd.

"Jeez, Gypsy, we're going to ruin our Long Island high."

"Better that than crashing your little old Ford," Gypsy grinned.

"How's *bus-i-ness?*" Doc slurred. His sly grin broke into a laugh. He was feeling no pain.

"It's picking up. Doc, you're cute when you're drunk." Gypsy smiled; she was having fun for the first time in months.

After ordering a second round of java, the conversation took on a more serious tone. "Are you still behind on your rent?" Doc gazed at her green eyes, looking for an honest answer.

"I'm only a month back now. By next Friday, I'll be caught up."

"Great."

"Listen, Doc, I've a problem brewing."

"Whaz up?" Doc slurred, still showing the effects of the Long Island Iced Teas.

"I had a late-night visitor last week."

"After ten?"

"No, you know I see no one after ten. A hooded man caught me just as I turned off the neon."

"Hooded man? That sounds sinister."

"Could be."

"How so?" The coffee and the seriousness of Gypsy's story kicked in. He no longer slurred his words.

"I did a reading, the Celtic cross."

"And?"

"His cards sent chills up my spine. I took liberty with my reading, told him his troubles were solely mental."

"Why the duplicity?"

"The reading was shocking. It indicated imminent danger."

"Why didn't you warn me?"

"I was paralyzed with fear and doubt."

"He's gone now, so why worry."

"I saw him yesterday."

"He came back?" Doc leaned closer, searching Gypsy's green eyes, bloodshot, showing fear.

"Yes! His reading was worse. Every sign indicated he'd face his demise within a week. His only way out was to make a radical change. He needed to be born again."

"Born again? That's sounds very Christian, ya know, Evangelical." Doc frowned his disapproval. His dad had flirted with Christian fundamentalism, and all he got for his efforts was hell and brimstone, a lot of wailing and gnashing of teeth.

"The stranger needed a new lease on life. He would die if he didn't change his attitude. He was on the wrong track. His karma was catching up with him."

"So whad'ya do?" Doc leaned back, thinking, sipping his coffee.

Gypsy hesitated, fidgeted in her seat, and then blurted, "I referred him to you."

"What?" Doc eyes widened with surprise.

"Doc, you're his only help."

"Gypsy, damn, how could you!" Doc grimaced, shaking his head, anger welling up in his chest.

"You're his last chance."

"How so?"

"You're the only one I know who could sweet-talk the devil."

"Gypsy, you're impossible!"

"No, Doc! I just call them as I see them."

"That sounds like baseball."

"This is not a game."

Gypsy and Doc shared another cup of coffee and sobered up enough for Doc to drive home. He walked Gypsy upstairs, hugged and kissed her, tenderly, but without passion. News of the stranger had aborted his lustful feelings. Earlier he was turned on, ready to take their relationship to the next level. He headed home, disappointed, frustrated, feeling like something had been stolen from him.

* * *

Doc was uptight, dreading his seven o'clock. It had been only three days since his date with Gypsy and news of his new client. "Damn it, Gypsy," he mumbled, still irked that she'd dumped the hooded stranger on him. He sat staring at his clock. *Vincent Salabrini better be on time*, he thought as he clinched his fists, ready to do battle.

The buzzer sounded, rousing him to action. He moved to the door and swung it open. There, standing in the middle of the waiting room was the hooded man, slightly hunched, leaning on a cane.

"Doc Mesmer, I'm Vincent Salabrini."

"Yes, please come in." Doc motioned him to the sofa before abruptly sliding into his swivel chair, causing it to glide across a section of hardwood. "Gypsy said you've been experiencing some difficulties."

"*Difficulties?* Much too tame for what's happening."

"Fill me in. Remember, I'm not a therapist. I don't handle emotional or mental disorders."

"Gypsy thinks it's in my head. I beg to differ."

Doc squirmed in his chair, edgy, trying to size up Mr. Salabrini. The hood, goatee, and tinted glasses created an effective disguise, making it difficult to get an immediate read on Gypsy's castaway. "What's in your head?"

"The visitations." Vincent leaned forward on his cane and continued, "They phone me, cajole me, threaten to harm me."

"They?" Doc leaned back, narrowed his eyes, suspicious and guarded, not yet feeling comfortable.

"The voices."

"Do the voices have a name?" Doc paused, then added, "Do they identify themselves?" Doc sensed the man was deeply troubled. Warning signs everywhere, Gypsy's description of Vincent's problem, his mannerism, posture, and theatrical presence, flaring like fireworks.

"They always say the same thing. *You know who we are. Now just pay up.*"

"Pay up? Do you owe someone money?"

"Not money."

"What then?" Doc was not only puzzled and alarmed, but also intrigued.

"I made a wager. They say I lost."

"A wager?" Doc rolled back in his chair, searching for a good perspective. There was none.

The hooded man leaned further forward, shaking, clenching the cane until his knuckles turned red. "They said I sold my soul to the devil."

"What?" Doc's eyes widened. He rolled about nervously, hands sweaty. *This is fucking crazy*

"I made the ultimate bet."

"How did this happen?" Doc said robotically, stunned by Vincent's confession. It seemed more like watching a movie than doing an interview.

"In a dream, but not an ordinary dream. This was real."

"This is above my pay grade. I'd advise you to seek therapy."

"No Doc. I need something you have."

"And what's that?"

"The ability to concentrate, use my mental powers to confront them. I need *you,* Doc. Teach me hypnosis, guided imagery. If I focus, concentrate my mind on their shenanigans, I could win this battle."

"What battle?"

"The battle for my soul. I'm prepared to pay you well. Money is not an obstacle. I'm prepared to pay you one hundred a session."

Doc thought for a moment as he eyed the hooded man before him. He didn't want to get mixed up with a head case; Vincent sounded psychotic. At the same time, he could simply avoid *that* area while still being willing to teach him guided imagery. One hundred a pop wasn't peanuts, after all. *Why not,* he thought. "Okay, Mr. Salabrini, but remember, I'm only going to teach you guided imagery. I'm not doing therapy."

"Great, Doc. How about we start tonight."

"That's impossible. But I can schedule you for Wednesday, seven o'clock," he said, after consulting his appointment book.

"That's two days."

"That's the best I can do."

"You're on!" Vincent stood, limped toward the door, and paused. "Can we shake on it?"

"Sure." Doc met him at the door, clasped his cold, bony hand, and said, "It's a deal."

* * *

Doc closed shop and headed directly to Gypsy's. He couldn't wait to tell her the news. He sprang up the stairs and knocked. She quickly answered, smiling. "Good to see you!"

"Gypsy, guess who I just saw?"

"Elvis."

"No, silly, the hooded stranger."

"Oh! What did you think?"

"Cuckoo. Delusional, *schizzy,* fucking crazy."

"Doc, watch your tongue."

"Come, let's sit in the parlor." Gypsy led the way to a sofa across from her consulting table where they got comfortable.

"Sorry, but I think I've blown it." Doc blurted, eager to tell Gypsy the news.

"How so?"

"I took him on as a client."

"Oh, my. Is he worth it?" Gypsy was both surprised and relieved. She knew her limits and Vincent was definitely off limits.

"One hundred an hour."

"Damn, maybe I should've kept him for myself." Gypsy loved teasing Doc.

"I'm conflicted. He wants me to teach him guided imagery."

"Right down your alley.

"To fight the devil."

"What?" Gypsy shook her head, feeling conflicted, relieved Vincent was Doc's project, but feeling guilty she had opened up the door. He was now part of both of their lives.

"He told me he made a wager, not for money, but for his soul. He wants to fight back using mental powers of concentration."

"Oh, Doc, I'm so sorry."

"It doesn't feel right."

"Take a seat. I'll do a reading."

Doc didn't think highly of tarot readings, but he kept that to himself. He joined her at the center table, took a deep breath, and played along. Gypsy spread the cards and went to work. Wands, Swords, Cups, and Plates dotted the black cloth, drawing Doc into another realm, an uncomfortable world where he felt out of sorts. After thirty minutes of mystifying questions and answers about Doc's new client, his immediate future, and the status of his mental health, Gypsy frowned, shaking her head.

"Doc, I'll be direct. There's a dark cloud hanging over you. It centers on a new acquaintance."

"That helps," Doc blurted sarcastically.

"Please be careful."

"Any positive suggestions, hints, answers for dealing with this new client that *someone* sent my way?"

"I'm sorry. Maybe you should drop Mr. Salabrini."

"It might be too late."

"How about some tea?" Gypsy smiled, stood, and motioned for Doc to join her in the kitchen. After heating some water and brewing her favorite green tea she directed Doc to a chair where he collapsed, weary. She caressed and massaged his shoulders. Doc was tense.

* * *

Doc's practice was thriving: Maggie had lost ten pounds, Barbara had cut down to two cigarettes a day, and Juan was digging guided imagery. That was all good. But a dark cloud appeared on the horizon. Doc was edgy, and the office seemed unusually gloomy, cold, and depressing. Dread consumed him. He felt numb. Vincent Salabrini was on deck.

Doc stared at the antique clock, the polished wood and gold-leaf face reflecting light from his desktop lamp. He thought again of his mom, trying to draw on her resiliency and strength. After all, she'd been able to put up with Pops her entire adult life. The buzzer rang, thrusting him back to reality. *Make him wait, by God. He's not going to be in control.* Doc was ready for battle. Like his mom, he had a penchant for diffusing stress; no problem was too big. He'd stare it down, label it, give it a nickname, and by doing so, dehumanize it and take control. *All right, Schizzy, here I come, ready or not.*

"Right on time, Mr. Salabrini."

"I'm anxious to get started," he said with a hint of optimism. His mood was not as sinister as it had been at their first meeting.

He had shed the hood, wore a fedora, chucked the glasses, and sported a black patch over his right eye. Doc was shocked. He remained standing, gazing at Schizzy, allowing him time to sink into the sofa and rest his cane. "Why the sudden change in dress?"

"I'm preparing for battle."

"And the patch over your right eye?"

"I'm sensitive to light, especially my right eye. That's why I wear tinted glasses."

"I see."

"I'm eager and willing, Doc, so let's *do it*. I want to master guided imagery."

"All in good time. But first, have you had any more visitations?"

"Visitations?"

"Yes. Dreams, wagers, encounters with the devil."

"Oh, quite right. Last night was a doozy."

"Frightening?"

"Yes, but I've got *you*, Doc. We'll beat this thing, the two of us."

"I'm here to teach you guided imagery, not to do battle with the devil."

"Gotcha. I'm ready."

Doc used a metronome, something he hadn't done in years. The prop allowed him to relax as it did its fair share of the work. A swinging watch tethered to a chain, too theatrical, over the top, but the mechanical device somehow fit. Doc had thought it through last night and was convinced it would give him an edge.

"I'll start from one hundred and count down," Doc said softly. "Close your eyes, relax, wipe your mind clean." He paused, the silence adding dramatic effect, and then continued. "Let go, drink deeply of your inner calm. Imagine a small island, white sand and crystal clear water, warm tropical breezes and the rhythmic roar of the surf." By eighty, Schizzy's body slumped; by seventy, his head dropped. Doc smiled at his apparent success and went to work.

Doc spoke of waterfalls, tropical birds, and gentle trade winds, creating a scene of pure tranquility. It was here that he planted the suggestion. "When *they* come again," he said, "demanding your soul, seek out this place of tranquility. Draw on the inner calm you now feel. When you leave my office, you will be in control."

Doc brought Schizzy back. He smiled and glided slowly in his swivel chair toward his new client. "How do you feel?"

Mr. Salabrini blinked, rolled his head, and said softly, "Relaxed."

"Good. I'll see you in a week."

"Doc, I can't wait that long. How about two sessions a week?"

Doc consulted his appointment book. "Friday evening, seven sharp."

"Excellent."

Schizzy stood and walked slowly, limping slightly. He stopped at the door, leaning to one side, propped by his wooden cane. "I feel great." His smiled morphed into a crooked grin before closing the door.

Doc took a deep breath, exhaled slowly, and mumbled, "I survived, thank God."

Chapter Five

I was eight-thirty by the time Doc dropped in on Waldo. He had survived the Friday evening session with Schizzy and desperately needed a pleasant diversion. Wally's Emporium was having a book sale; the aisles were packed with bargain hunters, young and old alike, plowing through used and discounted books, looking for their favorite author. Doc wasn't sure it was the book sale or the rain that brought them here tonight, but Wally's Emporium was crackling with energy. Emily, a twenty-something graduate student at UCLA, was standing next to Wally at the cash register, busy helping customers checkout. She waved, flashing Doc a big smile. *She's a cutie*, Doc thought, *but far too young*. The thought of dating her, however, had crossed his mind more than once. *But, no way,* he thought again now, glancing at her tall frame, *she's got to be an inch taller than me.*

After making his way to the counter, Doc said, "Hey, Wally, what's up?" Doc grinned, motioning toward the line of customers waiting to check out.

"Must be the rain. Same books, same owner." Waldo turned to the next person in line, a teenager, longhaired, skinny, wearing John Lennon glasses. "Good reads. He's one of my favorites." He rang up *The Grapes of Wrath* and *Tortilla Flat*. The boy smiled self-consciously, tucked the classics under his navy blue trench coat, and darted toward a freckled-face blonde girl waiting for him at the entrance.

Doc moved to the section on self-help, picked up a book on hypnosis, and scanned the table of contents. *All too familiar!* He changed aisles, and his eyes were drawn to a catchy but alarming title, *The Hypnotist: A Tale of*

Terror. He picked it up and slowly thumbed through the first fifty pages before uttering out loud, "Shit! A bleeping omen."

After a half hour of perusing Wally's offerings, he went back and picked up *The Hypnotist* again, then approached Waldo. He was still ringing up customers' purchases.

"Jeez, Doc, you're actually buying a book."

"Come on, Wally, I'm one of your best customers," Doc teased.

"If best means cheapest, I agree." Waldo grunted. "Say, Doc, I'm about to take a break. Join me for some coffee."

"I'll join you, but no coffee. I need my sleep."

Doc took a straight-back chair alongside the simmering urn, and Waldo collapsed into a chair. "Did you read about the escapee from Patton State?"

Doc shook his head. "No."

"Some crazy flew the coop."

"Yeah. Probably not the first time." Doc studied Waldo's face. It reminded him of a picture of an old Native America shaman he saw last summer at a Santa Monica photo exhibit he had gone to with Gwen. She had loved that particular photo; she thought the shaman's face showed character. Doc thought otherwise. The wrinkled and furrowed mug reminded him of forty miles of bad road.

"The article said the guy was schizophrenic, off his meds, prone to violence."

"Isn't Patton State in San Bernardino?"

"Yeah, that's what the *Times* said."

"Well, that's seventy miles east of here."

"Yeah, but the guy got away with some cash and a change of clothes. He could be next door"

"How'd he get by security?"

"The article didn't say. Mentioned he had roots in the San Fernando Valley." Waldo sat back, sipping and sloshing the thick swill in his trusty mug. Its stains were more like tar, caked to the sides of the cup, unyielding to soap and water. Doc once offered to buy him a new mug, but Waldo emphatically declined. "She's my baby," he had said, "through thick and thin."

"Great, all we need is one more crazy among us. What's his name?"

"I don't remember. But the nutcase walked with a limp, needed a cane, and wore tinted glasses."

"What?"

"He's probably hiding something." Waldo got up and excused himself. "I'm needed up front."

"See ya, Wally." Doc followed him to the front of the store, waved good-bye to Emily, and made a beeline to Gypsy's. First, it was the paperback he now held in his hands. The damn book even had hypnotist in its title, fucking tale of terror. And now some lunatic had escaped from Patton—one with a limp, tinted glasses, and a cane. *This ain't no coincidence.*

It was nine-thirty when he peered up at the neon sign. It was lit. He sprang up stairs and rapped hard on the door. It seemed to take forever for Gypsy to open it.

When she finally did, Doc rushed in right past her. "Gypsy, we've got to talk."

"What's up? Christ, the way you attacked my door, I thought I was under arrest."

"Do you have something to drink?" Doc paced the parlor.

"Herbal tea."

"Anything stronger?"

"A bottle of cabernet. Christmas gift."

"Good. Turn off your sign. Let's get drunk."

"Your pacing is driving me crazy. What's got into you?" Gypsy's eyes widened, surprised at his restlessness and his sudden urge to drink.

"It has to do with both of us. Bring out the bottle."

Gypsy shook her head, disappeared for a moment, and returned with the cabernet, Black Swan, and opener. "Doc, you do the honors."

She produced two wine glasses. Doc poured. After clinking glasses, he took a healthy swig. Gypsy grinned, lowered her head, and peered at Doc over the rim of her glass, taking only a dainty sip.

"Doc, you're not yourself. Let's sit and talk. Your pacing has me on edge."

"Okay." Doc sank into the sofa pulling Gypsy with him. "Listen, I've got some frightening news."

"Is it about Vincent Salabrini?"

"In spades." Doc filled her in, describing in detail the evening session with Schizzy, the fedora, black patch, and the hypnotic induction. He told her about Waldo's Emporium, the paperback, and Wally's account of the escapee. By the time he had finished, he'd downed his first glass of cabernet and was now on his second.

"Maybe we should alert the authorities." Gypsy sipped her wine, hands trembling. "This is *s-serious*," she stuttered, her voice cracking.

"It's just plain crazy. Look, we don't want to be rash." The wine was taking effect; Doc was feeling better, in control, more challenged than frightened by Schizzy.

"I'm scared." Gypsy looked pale, and her hands were still trembling.

"Let's keep a lid on this." Doc took a deep breath.

"What?"

"I need more time. Our mutual acquaintance needs further study."

"Further study. Doc, this is crazy."

"Maybe. We'll join forces. You watch my back, I'll watch yours."

"Do you think you're more taken by the money or the danger?"

"No way! It's the challenge that counts."

Doc and gypsy talked and talked, sharing concerns, conjectures, and fears well past midnight. Before parting, they agreed to be vigilant.

"I'll check with you every day." Doc hugged Gypsy. "Promise."

* * *

Doc was up bright and early, fueled with coffee, primed for detective work, not hypnosis. He was in his office an hour early so he surfed the Internet, finding the *LA Times* piece on the Patton State escapee. Waldo was right; a fifty-five-year-old schizophrenic had eluded security and was still at large. His name was Vincent, but not Salabrini. Vincent Valdez was new at Patton, apprehended a few months earlier after escaping from LA County Jail. While awaiting trial at the county facility for vehicular manslaughter, he made his bold escape. The article confirmed Waldo's account: disguised as a defense attorney, he limped out the front entrance, used a cane, and wore tinted glasses. His life as a fugitive, however, was short lived. He was apprehended within a week, evaluated, and found unable to stand trial. His psychiatric profile earned him a stay at Patton, but once again, he had escaped, leaving authorities baffled. "He's been at large for over two weeks," a spokesperson for the LAPD said. "He's a master of disguise, resourceful, emotionally volatile, and very dangerous. Please do not approach the suspect, but notify Tom Cross, Ramparts Division, LAPD, with any information regarding the whereabouts of Vincent Valdez."

The manslaughter charge was significant, but what really caught Doc's eye was the psychiatric evaluation. He dug deeper into LA City public records and soon found the original case. Vincent Valdez, speeding 70 mph in a 35 mph zone, struck and killed Margaret Morley outside her home near Tampa and Sherman Way in the San Fernando Valley. It was later learned that Vincent had been a client of Ms. Morley, a spiritualist and New Age practitioner, for several months prior to the fatal car crash. It was a hit-and-run, but within twenty-four hours, the LAPD, with the help of eyewitnesses, apprehended him at his Woodland Hills apartment. During the arrest, he assaulted two officers with his cane, and launched into a tirade about being conned by a fortuneteller. He accused Margaret Morley of evil practices, claiming she was demonic. "She was an agent of the devil!" he had screamed at the arresting officers.

Doc struggled through his morning sessions, irritated at his lack of concentration and his inability to stop thinking about Vincent Valdez. After all, he was a professional, an expert hypnotist and firm believer in the powers of the mind.

Doc skipped lunch and phoned Gypsy. Ten minutes later, he was once again frantically pacing her parlor, inundating her with his latest findings.

"Doc, calm down. Please, sit and let me collect my thoughts."

"Gypsy, Vincent Salabrini is Vincent Valdez." He sat down next to Gypsy holding a large manila envelope, hastily pulled out copies of the articles downloaded from the Internet, and spread them out on the table. "Check this out."

Gypsy picked them up and read them one by one. Key details had been highlighted in yellow, making Doc's case appear airtight. When finished, she stood, tossed the articles back on the table, and said, "That's it, we're calling the authorities."

"Authorities? I just don't know." Doc was paralyzed, not by fear but uncertainty. He felt Gypsy was too emotional, reactive. He preferred a bird's eye view of Schizzy, one not colored by panic.

"Well, I do. I'll get the phone book." She attempted to rise from her chair but was stopped short by Doc.

"Wait, Gypsy! Bringing in the authorities may harm us."

"*Not* bringing them in might kill us!" She was livid. Her pale complexion reddened and eyes narrowed.

"Having cops nosing around might hurt business."

"What?" She glared at Doc.

"It might drive clients away."

"What the hell? Doc, are you losing it?" His concern for business over their safety infuriated her.

"No, just being cautious."

"Look! You barge in here, pace up and down, throw facts around about an escaped lunatic—a shared client no less—and you want to be *cautious*?"

"Maybe *we* should do the detective work."

Gypsy grimaced. "That's crazy."

"The whole thing's crazy."

"I think you're placing money ahead of good judgment."

"What?"

"The one hundred an hour bit. That's the real reason you don't want cops involved. It's bad for business, right, Doc?"

"That's not fair."

"The death of Maggie wasn't fair. My friend was run over by that hooded stranger. All you care about is business."

"We need to take a deep breath, consider our options, and come up with a plan."

Gypsy stared at Doc, shaking her head, mumbling something about craziness, the devil, and Vincent, whoever the *hell* he is. "This is bigger than us. Please, Doc, we need to go to the authorities."

"I'll drop by at nine-thirty. We'll come up with something." Doc scooted around the table and gently hugged Gypsy. "Together we're a mighty force." Doc left, feeling better. Gypsy was in tears.

* * *

Doc's afternoon sessions went smoothly. He had two clients who were working on self-confidence issues, and a young mother fighting the battle of the bulge. His last client of the day, his favorite, had embraced Doc's strategy, faithfully using guided imagery to sharpen his powers of concentration. Juan Perez was still undefeated in conference play. The lefty hurler for Pierce College was on fire, drawing high praise from teammates and coaches. Doc grabbed a quick bite to eat, scoured the Internet for more on Vincent Valdez, and hit pay dirt with two articles about Margaret Morley. He decided he'd run it by Gypsy and get her take before confronting Schizzy.

It was exactly nine-thirty when Doc greeted Gypsy at her parlor.

"Top of the evening," Doc said. "How about some tea?"

"You're in a gay mood."

"I'm not gay."

"Oh, Doc, y'know what I mean."

"I'm ready to confront our nemesis."

"Don't count on me." Gypsy moved to the backroom to prepare the tea, leaving him alone to ponder Schizzy and Margaret Morley.

Gypsy returned, served Doc his favorite herbal blend, and sat, sizing up Doc. "So what's your plan?"

"All in good time, but first I need something from you." Doc lifted his cup, closed his eyes, inhaling the savory aroma of the tea, and then opened his eyes and took a sip.

"Okay."

"Delicious tea—thank you." He put his cup down and said, "I did some more detective work, Googled Vincent Valdez. I also found a couple of things about Margaret Morley."

"Go on."

"I found a three-year-old article about Margaret in the *Daily News*. A former customer had sued her for fraud. The article detailed a satanic scam involving voodoo curses, emotional threats, and blackmail. The case, according to an unidentified source, was settled out of court for twenty-five thousand dollars. It was Margaret Morley's second brush with the law."

"She got involved with a couple of shaky customers."

"Shaky customers! You think she was scammed?" Doc furrowed his brows.

"Maybe not, but we deal with all sorts—y'know, the needy. We attract desperate characters looking for easy answers."

"So Margaret just pushed it too far?"

"Maybe. I didn't see her as a scam artist. She was a performer, giving her clients a real ride."

"A real ride? That sounds like she was only an entertainer."

"Sometimes. She could tell if a person really believed in the occult. For the sincere, she was a facilitator."

"A facilitator?" Doc grimaced and shook his head in disbelief.

"She had easy access to the other world."

"The other world?" Doc cocked his head and starred at Gypsy. They were close, good friends, but they parted company when believing in the occult.

"My world, the real world, the transcendent world."

"It sounds like you're defending her."

"Perhaps. To me, she was the real thing."

"What about Vincent Valdez?"

Gypsy narrowed her eyes and said, "What about him?"

"He ran her down. Either he's completely mad or Margaret was up to no good."

"Damn it, Doc, Margaret was a friend. From what I know about Vincent, either Salabrini or Valdez, I'm on her side."

"So, you still think Salabrini is Valdez?"

"Yes! We should call the authorities."

"Gypsy, please. Give me one more session with Schizzy before we act."

Gypsy took a deep breath and then said, "Jeez Doc, you call him Schizzy, sense he's crazy, and cling do your doubts. You think too much." Gypsy paused, sensing she had hurt his feelings, and reached over and caressed his hands. "When do you see him?"

"Tomorrow evening."

"Fine. That's it though. If nothing's changed, I'm notifying the LAPD. Let's shake on it." They sealed the deal with a handshake. Doc stood and pulled Gypsy close for a comforting hug.

Doc knew he'd have to come up with something good by tomorrow night. Gypsy was digging in, fortified by his recent detective work, convinced that Schizzy was evil. Maggie was her friend; he'd run her over. In her mind, he was a cold-blooded killer. She was driven by her loyalties and emotions. Doc had suspended judgment, a house divided, his rational side suspicious of his feelings. He was more of a voyeur than a person.

Chapter Six

D oc fidgeted in his chair, rocking back and forth, staring at his clock. *Fifteen minutes until show time*, he thought. He felt like a prizefighter, taped, gloved, pumped, waiting for the bell. It was, indeed, the calm before the storm. But Doc was ready, breathing deeply, focusing, his eye on the prize. Schizzy was more a puzzle than an opponent. Doc was after the truth. The buzzer sounded, wrenching him from his self-imposed trance. He stretched, taking one more deep breath before getting up.

He opened the door—it was round one.

"Mr. Salabrini, so good to see you."

"Thanks, Doc. I'm eager to get started."

Schizzy had donned the same look as last time—fedora, cane in hand, limping, wearing the same black patch.

"Something's different," Doc said as they both sat, Schizzy on the sofa, Doc in his swivel chair. "Wasn't the patch over your right eye last time?"

"Excellent! I like that, a man with an eye for detail. But yes, my sensitivity to light shifts from time to time, and I've adapted."

"Are you ready?"

"Yes. Ready and willing."

Round two, Doc thought. He shunned the metronome and simply started counting backwards from one hundred, pausing every five count, inviting Schizzy to tag along. They explored Doc's secret garden, waterfalls, and crystalline pools of sparkling water. It was an enchanted place, a source of pure energy. He encouraged Schizzy to drink deeply of the experience.

"Allow it to take over your mind and body. Revel in its rejuvenating powers," Doc said slowly, lulling Vincent Salabrini into a deep trance.

Here he planted the suggestion, the knockout punch, the surefire winner. "Now, Mr. Salabrini, the next time you are visited by demons, take control, miniaturize them. When they demand your soul, reduce them to the size of a thimble. Hold them in your hand; strike the fear of God into their soulless hearts. Shrink them to child-like toys. Be as Gulliver, walking among the Lilliputians."

After a twenty-minute induction, Doc slowly brought Schizzy back to reality. "When I snap my finger, you will awake, born again, with new, limitless powers."

Mr. Salabrini sat silently, his right eye twitching, his head tilted slightly to the left, bobbing gently to and fro.

"Doc, I feel calm, somehow refreshed."

"Good. You are now empowered, a formidable foe, up to any challenge."

"Are we on for next Wednesday?"

"Yes, seven sharp. But before you leave, I have a matter I would like to discuss."

"Sure."

"I ran across an article in the *LA Times* about an escapee from Patton State, a mental facility for the criminally insane."

"*Yes?* What's that got to do with *me?*" Schizzy flashed Doc a puzzled look.

Doc hesitated, leaned forward in his swivel chair, and scooted closer to Schizzy. "The description of the escapee matched you to a tee."

"Oh! How dreadful." Salabrini laughed, finding Doc's comments amusing.

"A fifty-five-year-old schizophrenic, limping, using a cane, and wearing tinted glasses escaped several weeks ago."

"You think that's me?" Schizzy's right eye widened in disbelief.

"If it walks like a duck, quacks like a duck ..." Doc paused, searching Schizzy for a sign, a reaction. Nothing.

"Doc, for God's sake, I'm not crazy." Schizzy leaned back, smiling.

"Didn't you know a Margaret Morley?"

"Sure. She referred me to Gypsy."

"Didn't you have an encounter with her?"

"What?" Schizzy tilted his head, brows furrowed, more puzzled than frustrated.

"Didn't you sue her?"

"No way. Margaret and me, we were on good terms. I even called her Maggie. We were tight." He flashed Doc a wry grin.

"You didn't accuse her of fraud?"

"No way! She was a valuable contact."

"Are you being straight with me?" Doc inched closer to Schizzy, sliding forward slowly.

"Absolutely! So, are we on for Wednesday?'

"Yes, Vincent. May I call you Vincent?"

"By all means."

Schizzy limped slowly past Doc, shaking his head but pleased with the session. Doc smiled, feeling better, one hundred dollars richer than when the session began.

* * *

At eight-thirty, Gypsy's female client hugged her, delighted with her tarot reading. Ten minutes later, her phone rang. It was Doc. He had big news and wanted to see her in his office. By nine, Gypsy was at his office, on Doc's sofa, drained from the day's activities. She'd seen six customers, raked in three hundred big ones. Economically, she was all set, but emotionally, she was a wreck. Salabrini had her on edge.

"So what's the big news?"

She stretched her limbs before collapsing back on the sofa, crossing her legs.

"What's with the short skirt?" Doc couldn't remember the last time he'd seen Gypsy's alabaster legs, but he had to admit, they were easy on his eyes. Gypsy usually hid her body; billowy, long-sleeve blouses and ankle-length skirts draped her figure, revealing little. He'd never seen her in shorts, let alone a short skirt.

"I feel flirtatious."

"What?"

"Like what you see?" Gypsy raised her eyebrows, flashing Doc a come-hither look.

"What's got into you?"

"I thought I'd shock you, get your undivided attention, make you see the light of day."

"You look good from where I sit." Doc stood and moved around his desk.

"Doc, it's not me I'm concerned about. It's Vincent."

"That's the big news. Schizzy!"

"What?"

"I have something I want you to hear. I taped tonight's session."

"Oh my. Does he know?"

"I seriously doubt it."

Doc opened his desk drawer and removed a small handheld recorder. "Listen. It's an eye opener."

Gypsy and Doc sat together on the sofa, listening to the last few minutes of the session, the part covering Schizzy relationship with Maggie. When it ended, Doc turned off the recorder, waiting for her response.

"He's lying."

"You think so?"

"I know so."

"How can you be so sure?"

"Doc, he was laying it on thick. Give me a break! 'I even called her Maggie. We were tight.' What bullshit."

"He appeared calm, even sincere."

"And so do con artists and politicians."

"So, you want to bring in the authorities?"

"Don't you? This whole affair is creepy."

Doc reached around gypsy and pulled her close for a hug. "How can I make things right?"

"The hug will do for starters."

"You *are* flirtatious tonight." Doc smiled.

"It's either flirt with you or flirt with the devil."

Doc pulled back from the hug. "What's that mean?"

"I'm scared. What if he returns?"

"Schizzy's scheduled for Wednesday."

"But what if he visits *me*, when I'm alone?"

"You can stay at my place?"

"Is that a proposition?" Gypsy leaned her head on Doc's shoulder.

"A gesture of friendship."

"Is that all we are—friends?"

"What's more important than a good friend?" Doc was attracted to Gypsy, but it felt awkward. They'd been friends for years. She was more like a cousin or sister. If they crossed the friendship line and became lovers, it would be incest. Doc loved women, but not that way.

"I'll take what I can get." Gypsy sighed. She loved Doc, but didn't know how to tell him.

"You're welcome to stay tonight. The guest bedroom's ready." Doc hugged Gypsy, squeezing her gently. "I'm here for you."

"Thanks, but I'll ride it out for a while. However, if he returns, I'm moving in."

"The door's open, *anytime.*"

"Let's go to my place. I've got another bottle of cabernet."

"You're on."

* * *

Light showers lingered, providing enough moisture for a brilliant rainbow. The heavy rains and dark clouds had crested the mountains heading east. Doc squinted into the morning sun, dazzled by its brilliance. It was winter, so the sun hugged the southern horizon, ensuring it would be sunny but mild, not the blistering hundred-degree heat of summer. Doc loved Southern California winters, especially after a rain. Standing on his balcony, he could see Mt. Wilson, and a bit further east, he knew a snow-capped Mt. Baldy was holding court in the San Gabriel Mountains. He had inherited his childhood home from his parents. It suited Doc perfectly, less than a mile south of Ventura Boulevard, perched on a hill, overlooking an acre of orange trees. The scent of orange blossoms and the panoramic view had helped him endure the constant battles he suffered at the hands of his father while growing up. After his stint in the army, Doc rented one apartment after another, moving yearly, leading his father to quip, "Son, you got to settle down, grow up." He followed his father's advice and got married, but it didn't last.

There was no way he could afford this kind of home on his salary; just paying the taxes was a huge financial burden. The deuce coupe and his three-bedroom Encino home represented his total wealth. It had only been two years since his parents passed, first his father, then a year later, his mother. He moved in soon after his mother's death, spared the rants of his father, but missing his mother's quiet strength.

It was Sunday, finally a day off. He'd checked in on Gypsy last night again, reassuring her, telling her she was safe. He had been phoning her often and dropping by her parlor daily. He feared that if he backed off, displayed the slightest indifference, skipped a visit, or missed a phone call, she would go directly to the authorities.

The doorbell rang, slicing through Doc's ruminations. "Who could that be?" he blurted, moving to the front door. "It's not quite eight, for

God's sake." He peeked through the front window drapes, spying the profile of a tall man with a hawkish nose. He didn't look familiar.

Doc swung the door open and stared at the early-morning visitor.

"Good morning. Are you Michael Mesmer?"

"Yes, and you?"

"Leonard Eisenhower, private investigator." He opened his wallet and displayed his credentials.

Doc tilted the wallet in the man's hand, carefully examining it. "D-Day Investigations: Established in 1950," Doc read aloud.

"Yes, sir, my granddad was on the front lines, World War II. After kicking around for several years, he started up the business."

"Well, Mr. Eisenhower, how may I help you?"

"Please, call me Ike. Gramps served under Dwight Eisenhower." The stranger paused, smiled, and said, "May I come in?"

"Ike, what's this about?"

"All I need is a few minutes of your time. Please."

"Okay, but just a few minutes. I've morning plans." Doc motioned toward the living room and said, "Have a seat." Ike was tall, lean, balding at the crown, and graying at the temples. His salt and pepper moustache was clipped short.

"I've been tailing a guy for nearly two weeks. Twice last week I saw him enter your office on Ventura." Ike flipped open a notepad and continued, "Yes, it was Wednesday and Friday of last week, just before seven in the evening." Doc's heart skipped a beat, knowing who it had to be.

"What did he look like?"

"He limped, used a cane, sported a fedora, and wore a black patch over one eye."

Doc hesitated and then said, "Yes, he's a new client. I've seen him only three times."

"He's a person of interest," Ike said, flipping close his notepad.

"Why the interest, and who's footing the bill?" It looked like Schizzy was drawing a crowd.

"It's confidential. All I can say is that my client has an interest in the whereabouts of Gimpy." Ike caught himself, then said, "Sorry, I don't want to be disrespectful, but I have a habit of giving my cases nicknames."

"Why me? How can I help?" Doc said, not really wanting to help. He was looking for an opening, a chink, a crack, anything to reveal Ike's real intentions.

"Why is he seeing you?"

"I'm a hypnotist, specializing in self-improvement."

"What's your client's name?"

"That's confidential."

"What does he want from a hypnotist?"

"That's off limits. He's my client, and I value confidentiality."

"Is he seeing you for a mental problem?"

"Listen, Ike, you know as well as I do, a hypnotist can't treat mental or emotional disorders." *Is this guy checking up on Schizzy or me?* Doc thought.

"How are you helping him?"

"Again, confidentiality is the issue. Ask him yourself. He'll be at my office Wednesday evening."

"I might just do that. Here's my card. Call me if you notice anything suspicious about Gimpy. He's thought to be dangerous."

"By whom?"

"My client."

Doc walked Ike to the front door, puzzled by his unannounced visit. He watched him get in his Ford Explorer and drive down the hill, disappearing behind a grove of orange trees. He wanted to share the news with Gypsy but knew better. Ike's visit would be the last straw. She'd run directly to the authorities.

* * *

The decision was easy. Doc opted to keep the deuce coupe garaged—the streets were just too wet and muddy—and drove his seven-year-old Honda Civic to his noon lunch date. He hadn't seen Alan Workman for six months and was eager to touch base. He was an ex-client, a structural engineer and amateur philosopher. Doc had a firm rule: no socializing with present or former clients. Alan was his one exception.

As he pulled into the restaurant parking lot, he spotted a dark blue Ford Explorer, the same make and model of Ike's—*could it be?* He craned his neck, but the SUV disappeared into traffic.

Jerry's Deli was packed, humming with chatter and laughter. It featured a bakery, sawdust covered floors, and wine barrels chucked full of unshelled peanuts. The restaurant was schizophrenic, New York deli during the day, sports bar after five. The menu was diverse, the servings generous—it was Doc's favorite.

Doc spotted Alan, waved to a familiar waitress serving a nearby table, then slid into the corner booth.

"Top of the morning," Doc said, extending his hand for a quick high five.

"Doc, it's afternoon." It was twelve-fifteen. Alan was knowledgeable, intellectually entertaining, but rigid to a fault. "Precision, my dear friend, is next to godliness."

"What's new?" Doc said, ignoring his correction.

"Augmenting my world view."

"That's not new. You're always tinkering with your philosophy."

Alan grinned and said, "I've revisited a couple of old friends."

"Yeah, tell me about it." Alan was an engineer by profession but an inveterate philosopher. For the past twenty years, he had accumulated more than 500,000 words comprising the Weltanschauung of Alan Workman. It was a systematic map consisting of boxes arranged logically, symbolizing his interpretation of reality. The boxes represented portals to the real world. It was a metaphysical wonder, known about by only a handful of eccentric friends. Doc was entertained by his friend's soaring metaphysical flights but comprehended little more than the basics. It was, as best Doc could fathom, a hodgepodge of classical Greek philosophy, existentialism, Buddhism, and pop psychology. That was the meat of his philosophy. The structure was pure Kantian, rigid boxes arranged logically. The message was fluid, the structure stiff. Doc thought that it was the intellectual counterpart to Alan Workman the man.

"I've dusted off some old notes on Nietzsche and Alan Watts."

"What's the verdict?" Doc perused the menu.

"I'm stuck."

"What?"

Alan flashed Doc a Cheshire grin and said, "Nietzsche's right. We try to know the world, as it is, independent of our perception. We try to capture the 'Truth,' but it eludes us. We are deluded, deceived into thinking we can capture reality with a net of words and concepts. In the end, we confuse the label with the thing."

"So, we are victims of our own making."

"Indeed we are. Alan Watts, remember him?"

"A lover of Zen Buddhism."

"Yes, and much more. Well, Watts thought nature was wiggly."

"Wiggly?" Doc frowned.

"Sure, just look and see. The outline of hills are fluid, mountains jagged, leaves of trees irregular, and our fingerprints unique."

"Yeah, but so?"

"But we're not comfortable with the dynamic and the fluid. We want to classify, name, catalogue, and control. We live in boxes, towns laid out in tracts and grids. When we encounter an incorrigible person, we want to straighten him out. If a person fidgets, we say, 'Stand still.' If there's a wrinkle in the fabric, iron it. But this doesn't fit nature. Nature's dynamic, resistant to being pinned down. You can't step in the same river twice."

"Heraclitus?"

"Correct."

"So, what's the answer?" Doc closed the menu, happy with his selection, a veggie burger. Gwen had gotten to him.

"Jettison our language, numbers, and logic. It's too simple for the job."

"But, Alan, how can we do philosophy and science without language and numbers?"

"That's my conundrum."

"Let's eat." Doc waved over the waitress and they ordered. Doc shifted the conversation to baseball, steroids, and the Yankee payroll. They both had plenty to say. Language and numbers didn't fail them here.

Doc enjoyed Alan, to a point. He was obsessed with pinning down reality, discovering the "Truth," and completing his Weltanschauung. He lived in his head and wanted reality to conform to him. *His mind was his biggest problem.*

After lunch, Doc promised to stay in touch, jumped in his Honda, and drove west on Ventura Boulevard. Out of his rearview mirror, he spotted a dark blue Ford Explorer. Within a mile, he turned right on Van Nuys and headed north. The Explorer followed, a couple of cars back. He made a few more quick turns and ended up back on Ventura, heading for home. The Explorer was relentless. Doc made a quick right and parked in the lot behind his office, a good three miles from his place. He didn't want to be tailed back home. Doc entered the rear entrance, rushed across the ground floor, peered through a front window, and spotted the Explorer parked across the street. The driver's side was occupied. It looked like Ike.

Impulsively, Doc emerged from his office building and hustled next door to Wally's Emporium. He needed time to sort this through. After a quick chat with Waldo, Doc moved to the front window. Ike was standing at the corner, waiting to cross the street. Doc turned and dashed toward the back of the bookstore.

"Hey, Wally, mind if I use the back door?"

"Be my guest. What's the hurry?"

"I'll tell you later."

Within a minute, Doc fired up the Honda, fled the parking lot, tires squealing, and headed for home. He spent the afternoon surfing the Internet, digging up anything he could on D-Day Investigations. Leonard Eisenhower, son of Malcolm Eisenhower, grandson of "Ike," had served Southern California residents since 1950, offering a full menu of services. The agency specialized in surveillance: worker compensation fraud; missing person cases; spousal surveillance; cheating spouses; runaways; and custody cases. Ike's Web site boasted, "We leave no stone unturned."

Chapter Seven

At six, Doc checked in on Gypsy. She sounded depressed, so he said, "Put on your Sunday best, I'm taking you out." Gypsy gladly accepted. By seven-thirty, they were perusing the menu at Le Petit Bistro, a French restaurant with subtle lighting and high ceilings. Gypsy saw it as a romantic evening, full of promise. Doc's main focus, on the other hand, was to keep her from running to the cops.

They were both stressed, obsessed with Vincent Salabrini. Her obsession was grounded in fear, his in curiosity. Perhaps Alan Workman's intellectual obsession with the truth had rubbed off on him. Doc put on a show, entertaining Gypsy with tall tales of youthful indiscretions. He was covering up, testing her mood, debating whether to tell her about Ike.

After they both ordered French onion soup, Gypsy opted for roasted chicken, Doc for shrimp picante. After polishing off a bottle of chardonnay, Doc found the courage to share his encounter with Ike. By the time he got to the cat and mouse part, Ike waiting to cross the boulevard, and Doc's hasty escape out the back door of Wally's Emporium, Gypsy had retrieved her cell phone, ready to alert the LAPD.

"No, Gypsy! Not now."

"When, if not now?"

"I think we should turn the tables."

"What?"

"We should tail Ike, beat the bushes."

"Why?"

Doc cleared his voice and firmly said, "Get to the bottom of this. Expose Vincent for what he is."

Gypsy grimaced and said, "Who and what is he?"

"That's what we'll find out."

"No, Doc, we're amateurs, not fit for this."

"Together we can." Doc reached across the small table and held Gypsy's hands. "I promise."

"I'm not staying alone tonight." Gypsy pouted.

"Fine, I'll sleep on your couch."

"No. I'm staying with you, and not on the couch."

Doc felt blackmailed, compelled by circumstances to acquiesce. If he turned her down, she'd run to the cops. Besides, she was growing on him. Down deep he was soft on Gypsy, perhaps a bit smitten. But consciously he wouldn't admit it.

At his hillside home, they shared another bottle of chardonnay, and then fell asleep in each other's arms, still partially clothed. Doc had successfully avoided "incest." She was more like a sister, a partner in detective work, than a lover. That's what he thought, not what he felt.

Early the next morning, Doc made Gypsy breakfast, which consisted of orange juice, coffee, and granola, before hustling her home. By eight, she was ready to open shop, perform her magic, see into the future, and dazzle her customers. He ensured her everything was good and promised that he'd check in regularly and—most importantly—come up with a plan.

He hugged her warmly, kissed her lightly on the cheek, and said, "The mystery of Schizzy and Ike will be solved." He sprang down the stairs, leaving Gypsy comforted by the hug and kiss, but hung over. She was no boozer—last night, she had exceeded her limit.

Doc's Monday morning proceeded to be uneventful but rewarding. His three clients had left satisfied, a step closer to dumping a bad habit or reaching a desired goal. He was about to pay Waldo a visit when the buzzer sounded. *Maybe it's Gypsy, but no, she would call first*, he thought, staring at his clock. It was only twelve, two hours before his next client. It buzzed again, sending Doc to the door.

A very tall man, with a bushy moustache and rumpled trench coat, wet around the shoulder from the morning rain showers, said, "Are you Michael Mesmer?"

"Yes." Doc was taken off guard.

"May I have a minute of your time?"

"Are you a salesman?"

"No. I'm Lieutenant Fred Thompson, LAPD." The detective produced his credentials.

"What's this about?" Paranoia returned with a vengeance. First it was Schizzy, then Ike, and now the authorities.

"Please, just a few minutes of your time."

Doc motioned toward the sofa before slumping into his swivel chair. His mind raced, jumping from one haunting image to another, flashing on Schizzy, Ike, and Gypsy. Had she cracked, gone to the authorities, not trusting in their ability to handle Schizzy? Uncertainty consumed him.

Lieutenant Thompson reached into his coat pocket, retrieved three photos, and handed them to Doc. "Have you seen this man?"

Doc studied the photos, trying not to tremble. It was Schizzy. Or was it? The first photo was a mug shot of a middle-aged man with gray hair and a goatee. The next two photos were surveillance shots, capturing a man with a cane crossing the street. "Maybe," Doc answered.

"Maybe. Could you be more specific?"

Doc cleared his throat, paused, then said, "I have a client that has a goatee, limps, and uses a cane."

"What's his name?"

"He's my client. I'm duty bound by principles of confidentiality."

"I can get a warrant."

"What's this man done?"

"Let's just say he's a person of interest."

"To whom?" This was the same term Ike used.

"The LAPD."

"All I have is his name."

"Let's have it."

"Vincent Salabrini." Doc was both relieved and troubled. He was in touch with the authorities, which was sure to make Gypsy happy, but he hated the idea of cops nosing around, interfering with his practice. It could be bad for his reputation, bad for business.

"When's his next appointment?"

"Wednesday at seven."

"Evening appointment?"

"Yes."

"Do you have his phone number, address, background material of any kind?"

"No, as I said, only a name." Doc felt trapped, the walls of his reality collapsing, smothering him with doubt. "What does the LAPD want with this man?"

"Following up on a lead. A person of interest, that's all."

"I'm out of answers." Doc leaned back, opening his arms, visibly indicating he had nothing to offer.

Fred Thompson stood, retrieved a card from his rumpled coat pocket, and said, "Please call if anything comes up."

Doc walked him to the door, showed him out, and then remained at the closed office door, leaning against it for support, attempting to assimilate what had just happened. He needed a break, so he headed for Wally's Emporium, hoping Waldo might be of some help.

Sam, a part-time clerk, was ringing up a customer when Doc entered the bookstore.

"Where's the boss?"

"In the backroom." Sam was retired military, a Viet Nam vet, awarded the Purple Heart, but to this day critical of the war. He was drafted and performed his duty. From day one, he had believed in his heart-of-hearts that it was none of the United States' business, a civil war. He was a quiet man and rarely spoke of the war. "A misguided conflict," he would quietly say before changing the subject.

In the backroom, slumped over a day-old paper, was Waldo, nursing his Texas crude.

"Hey, Wally, what's new?"

Waldo looked up and barked, "Doc, where the hell you been?"

"Looking after Gypsy."

"She in the rears still?" Waldo pushed aside the newspaper, taking a noisy sip of the thick black swill.

"She's good."

"You two getting chummy?"

"What's that mean?" Doc took a chair and slapped the table.

"Looks like I pushed a button."

"She's been on edge lately."

"Because of you?" Waldo said, raising his eyebrows.

"I'm not the problem."

"Lay it on me, Doc. I ain't got all day." Waldo's eyes narrowed as he sloshed his coffee. He put down the stained mug and slowly moved his right hand as if turning a crank. "Start the damn movie."

"This is no movie. It's the real deal. Gypsy and I have a problem." Doc paused, gazing at Waldo, who just continued his cranking motion. "We've been visited by the escapee."

"What?" Waldo picked up his mug and sloshed it before taking a gulp.

"The guy you read about in the *Times*."

"The crazy guy I told you about?"

"Yeah, goatee, middle-aged, limps, and gets around with a cane."

"You sure?" Waldo continued stirring his coffee, clanking the stained and caked mug, irritating Doc.

"He's a client. Seen him several times." Doc starred at Waldo's mug and finally blurted, "Are you making butter?"

Waldo stopped his incessant stirring, put down the mug, and grinned. "Have you gone to the cops?"

"No! They came to me."

"What's your client's name?" Waldo absentmindedly picked up his mug and took a big noisy slurp, spraying coffee on his blue work shirt.

"Wally, that's confidential." Doc frowned, frustrated with Waldo's antics.

"Same name as the one mentioned in the *Times*?"

"No." Doc fidgeted in his seat, feeling more edgy than when he arrived.

"How do you know it's the same guy?"

"The description fits."

"Hundreds could fit that description." Waldo once again stirred his black concoction, clanking the spoon against the sides of his crusty mug.

"Maybe, but this guy's strange."

"Crazy strange?" Waldo wrinkled his nose.

"Schizoid. I christened him Schizzy."

"Better let the authorities handle this."

"Yeah, maybe so."

"How does Gypsy fit in?"

"He visited her first. She did a late night reading, referred him to me."

"Does she know about the cops?" Waldo frowned, narrowing his eyes.

"Not yet."

"Doc, you got to tell her."

Waldo shook his head, gulped the last of his coffee, and headed for the front of the store. He glanced back at Doc and said, "Get your ass over to Gypsy's and tell her."

Doc phoned Gypsy. She said she had a reading in an hour, but if it was urgent, she could spare a few minutes. He was seated in her parlor less than ten minutes later, dreading her reaction. He left nothing out, detailing the entire encounter with Lieutenant Fred Thompson. When he finished, she jumped up, pulled Doc to his feet, and vigorously hugged him. "Thanks, Doc. Let the authorities do their thing."

Before he left Gypsy, he kissed her on the cheek and said he'd call later. She was delighted with the news. Doc, however, was sinking into an abyss of doubt. He was losing his bearings, not knowing what to believe. His world had become a house of mirrors, reflecting distorted images. He was reminded of Pacific Ocean Pier, the fun zone, and its house of mirrors. His father took him there as a kid and laughed at his frustration as he awkwardly navigated the glassy maze. His father had laughed at him then, reality laughed at him now. Doc's reality was no fun zone.

Chapter Eight

Tuesday evening, the night before his session with Schizzy, Doc dutifully checked in on Gypsy before visiting Alan Workman. He'd called earlier, pleading for Doc's help. He was in the midst of an intellectual crisis, behind schedule at work, unable to concentrate, stumped by the most mundane of engineering problems. His crisis was not scientific but philosophical. When nodding off, he'd catch only a wink or two before the demons attacked, taunting him and accusing him of intellectual laziness. His Weltanschauung was imploding, collapsing under its own weight. He desperately needed Doc's help.

Alan enthusiastically greeted him at the front door, and skipping any small talk, ushered him directly to the study. Only a couple of draped windows, two doors, and a huge aquarium broke the floor to ceiling of books. They were crammed and stacked, arranged alphabetically, neat, tidy, and systematized, a mirrored image of Alan's goal of classifying reality. When the proper nomenclature was in place, he'd understand the world.

Alan had access to the inner workings of the aquarium by way of the closet door. There he tended to his aquatic world, meticulously balancing the miniature ecosystem, providing his creatures with loving care.

"Just look at them, all wiggly and proud," he said as Doc followed their fluid movements. Alan was proud of his aquatic offsprings, a diverse collection of exotic wonder, for he had none of his own. He often lectured Doc about their distinctive characteristics, puffing out his chest as he prattled on. Doc recognized a few, especially the fancy guppy. Alan insisted on the scientific label, *poecilia reticulata*: "A hardy and peaceful fish," he bellowed. Doc thought the guppy was beautiful, attractively colored in iridescent blue, purple, and white. Neon tetras, glowing red, white, and blue, darted about the large tank, playing a vigorous game of tag.

The books on philosophy and science peeked through a jumble of Post-it notes, clinging to the shelves like migrating butterflies. The pink, green, yellow, and orange notes contained acronyms, not the common TGIF (Thank God It's Friday), but ZEBRA (Zen Energy Brings Rare Awareness). One evening, not long ago, Doc was subjected to an hour-long survey of core acronyms. They served as signposts, he had learned, alerting Alan to the core principles of his Weltanschauung. Doc was here to save the intellectual labor of nearly a quarter century.

"Please, Doc, get comfortable. I need your help." Alan sat at his desk, Doc in a wingback chair off to the side, near the aquarium. The sights and sounds of Alan's gurgling aquarium provided a touch of serenity to the tension-filled room. His facial expressions, bloodshot eyes, and slumping posture said it all; he was stressed.

"I'm here for you, but I'm not sure a hypnotist is what you need."

"I need a friend."

"That I am." Doc leaned back and glanced over his shoulder at the aquarium, alive, colorfully radiating pure energy, Mother Nature's finest.

"I need a fresh approach, a new pair of eyes and ears." Alan clasped his hands together, prayer-like.

"I'm a good listener. Try me."

"We touched on it Sunday."

"You brought up Nietzsche and Alan Watts."

"Yes. It's the wiggly problem. We try to capture reality in a net of words. Our language and symbols have falsified things. We've become strangers to nature, cut off from the real world, a slave to our labels." Alan took a deep breath, leaning back in his chair.

"That's where we left off Sunday." Doc paused, looked about, struggling not to laugh. He'd never laugh at Alan, but all he could see were clusters of Post-its, clinging to every available shelf, pointing the way. That was their role, signs for navigating Alan's world.

"Alan, may I be honest?"

"That's why you're here. You're a straight shooter. I know I'll get nothing but honesty."

Doc waved his arms in a gentle sweeping motion and said, "You've become trapped, a prisoner to labels. Look at them; they're choking the life out of you."

Alan extended his arms openhanded and said, "They're keys to my world."

"But they've failed you. The wiggly world has escaped your clever labels. Your acronyms are invented, merely tools for tinkering with your imaginary world."

"Imaginary world?" Alan's voice became louder as he continued. "Doc, these aren't just labels, they are portals to the *Truth*."

"But last Sunday, and again earlier on the phone, you said something about a crisis. You ranted about the inadequacy of language, numbers, and symbols. They're too simple for the job."

"Indeed. We must replace them with a new means of analysis. We must let go of words and go directly to reality."

"Become a mystic, give up science and logic?"

"No! Go under and around labels."

"How can that be done?"

"That's where you come in. I want you to hypnotize me, use guided imagery, provide me with a way to beat symbols."

"I don't understand."

"You don't need to. Just provide me the tools. I'll do the rest."

"The tools?"

"Provide me with imagery to work around the problem. You get people to lose weight and stop smoking. I want you to rid my dependence on language and symbols. Show me the way, Doc."

"I think you need a Zen master."

"No! Doc, they're much too slow. You've got the quick fix."

"This doesn't feel right."

"How so?"

"It's much too large a problem. It's metaphysical. I'm just a practical guy, a guy who fixes little problems."

"Doc, you're my last chance, the only person I trust."

Doc shook his head, stood, and approached the aquarium, gazing in wonder at the fluid movements of Alan's tropical fish. They were as exotic as his towering philosophy. Doc immediately felt their presence. They weren't tidy snippets scribbled on a Post-it. The wiggles have it; they were real.

"Okay. But we should make this a professional venture. We need to schedule you at my office."

"I agree. But how about we get started tonight, a preview of things to come."

"I need time to develop a strategy. Call me tomorrow. I'll work you in."

"Evenings are best for me. The engineering department has me swamped."

"I think Wednesdays at six are available, but let me check." Doc knew that Schizzy was booked Wednesday and Friday at seven. Alan scheduled right before Schizzy could work. Alan was plagued by wiggles, Doc by Schizzy.

* * *

It was the dawning of a new era. Alan was excited, pumped with a renewed vigor, ready for the next stage in his philosophical odyssey. His Weltanschauung would survive. "A celebration is in order," he announced to his tropical beauties, swimming, chasing one another, delighting in their wiggly world.

Alan uncorked a bottle of champagne, first chilled more than a year ago, a holdover from a cancelled New Year's Eve party. Alan was no teetotaler, but booze seldom graced his lips. The sounds of Wagner's *Tristan and Isolde* filled the house as Alan danced, sang, and skipped through his empty residence. Doc was gone, but Alan was sure he had been sent by unknown powers to save his unsteady world. He hoisted the bottle of champagne, swigged the last drop, and eventually collapsed on the study's hardwood floor. There he was visited by otherworldly events and vivid images reminiscent of *Alice in Wonderland*.

Things suddenly became divorced from their names. Books, Post-its, and notepads danced around the room while computer printouts, files, and charts flew about, driven by some unseen, unfelt vortex, dislodging them, spinning them faster and faster, leaving only a blur of color. The Post-its, now freed from the shelves of books, flew out the open window, on the wings of a silent wind.

Fancy guppies and neon tetras danced, frolicked, and partied, beckoning Alan to join in. "Join us," the fancy guppies chanted. "Be one with us; join the wiggly world, the real world, the only world."

Books fell, one by one, from their mighty perch, alphabetically marching, parading, the classics strutting, the offbeat dancing. In groups of three, the animated books broke off the chorus line, again alphabetically arranged. Aristotle, Francis Bacon, and Joseph Campbell bowed before flying out the window. They were followed by more sets of three; Nietzsche,

Onora O'Neil, and Plato curtsied and made a lazy loop of the room before disappearing out the window. It was a Broadway show of philosophical talent dancing, singing, and flying about. Richard Rorty, Jean-Paul Sartre, and Alan Turing said their good-byes. Ludwig Wittgenstein closed the show. The bookshelves stood empty, their tears of sorrow splashing the floor, striking Alan on the face.

Books, Post-its, and Alan's precious manuscript were gone. All that remained was an acronym, printed in black letters, boldly displayed on a yellow legal-size pad, centered atop his once cluttered desk. It read: WIGGLY (When In God's Glorious Land Yield).

Alan awoke in the dead of night, his head pounding, and his mouth as dry as the Sahara. He looked about in astonishment. The books, Post-its, and manuscript were all there, untouched. The images of dancing books and talking fish flooded his sluggish thoughts. "It was just a dream," came a voice from some distant part of his subconscious mind. "But one you must heed."

* * *

Gypsy bid good-bye to her last client, switched off the neon light, and started toward the kitchen to make tea when her doorbell rang. Thinking it was Doc, she opened up, skipping her ritual of first spying visitors through the peephole. She jumped, startled at what she saw. It was Vincent Salabrini, dressed as Doc had described—fedora, black patch covering his right eye, leaning to one side, braced by his cane.

"Gypsy, may I please come in?"

"It's late. I just shut off the neon sign."

"It's an emergency."

"That's what you said last time."

"I need a reading."

"Come back tomorrow. I'll be fresh, more attune to the spirits."

"I can't wait. I need to see you before I see Doc."

"Don't you see him tomorrow night?"

"Yes, but I need to know something. Something Doc can't help me with."

"I don't think I'm up to it."

Vincent suddenly brushed past Gypsy, nearly knocking her down. "Please excuse my abruptness, but this is a life and death situation." Vincent pulled a chair away from the center table and sat, waiting for his reading.

Gypsy stood frozen in time, weak-kneed, finding it difficult to navigate her own parlor.

"They're coming tonight."

"What?" Gypsy lowered herself, cautiously taking a seat across from Schizzy. Doc's unique reference had now become a part of her vernacular.

"Demons, minions of Satan," he said.

"Mr. Salabrini, you're jesting."

"I'm not joking. They're right from hell."

"What do you want from me?" Gypsy sat on her hands, trying to stop the trembling. *Where's Doc when I need him?*

"A reading."

"Tarot?"

"Yes. I need some answers before I see Doc."

Gypsy sighed, giving in to Schizzy's demands. Wands, Swords, Cups, and Plates were deftly dealt and fanned out, picking up the soft light of the tableside lamp. The colors were uncommonly bright, casting a mesmerizing feel on the reading. She wanted Schizzy to narrow his question, focus in on the visitors, and pose an answerable question, one that would placate the intruder. To Gypsy, he was neither a client nor a customer. He was an intruder.

"Will they take my soul?" Schizzy's tone was emphatic.

After fifteen minutes of manipulating the cards, asking and responding to Schizzy, Gypsy suddenly saw his problem. He was in the grips of something evil. Any way she looked at it, the answer was demonic. She pulled her hands away from the table, clasping them tightly, but was unable to stop the trembling that had suddenly set in, moving from her hands to her shoulders, shaking them violently. Schizzy's head was lowered as he gazed at the cards, missing Gypsy's convulsions. She felt the presence of evil. She was speechless.

Gypsy took a focused, deep breath to calm the shaking.

"Well, what do you see?" Schizzy raised his head, searching Gypsy's eyes.

She sank back in her chair and covered her eyes, wishing Schizzy would just puff up and blow away. She dropped her hands and said, "Vincent—may I call you Vincent?"

"Of course, please do."

"You must seek out help."

"I have. Doc is in my court."

"Vincent, you need a different sort of help." She was hesitant, voice breaking up, causing her to forcefully clear her throat.

"How different?"

Gypsy paused, looking Schizzy directly in the eye. "You need a priest."

"What?"

"Please, I'm being straight. You are in imminent danger. You need more than Doc and I can supply.

Schizzy leaped to his feet, tossed a fifty-dollar bill on the table, and limped to the door. He glanced back, his face ashen, his eyes full of fear. As quickly as he appeared, he was gone. She immediately phoned Doc. He wasn't home, but she left a terse message. "Schizzy was just here. The devil's got him by the tail. Call me!"

* * *

It wasn't a lie, but merely a strategy to buy time. Doc was on the phone late Tuesday night for an agonizing hour, consoling Gypsy, promising her he would talk to Lieutenant Fred Thompson about Schizzy's tarot reading. She trusted Doc, thought it was a done deal. He decided, however, it was best to see Schizzy first before talking to the authorities.

Doc was distracted the whole next day, doing his best to serve his clients, more observing the hypnotic sessions at arm's length than conducting them. He convinced Alan to wait until Friday for their work on his Weltanschauung, freeing up time to prepare for Schizzy. He glanced at the clock every five minutes, obsessing, both dreading and anticipating his Wednesday evening session. His thoughts were a jumbled mess, jumping from strategy brainstorming to doubts about Schizzy's mental health. Was he crazy or possessed? Doc was in over his head, not qualified to handle either.

His clock ticked away in agonizing slow motion until it finally reached seven. "It's game time," Doc blurted as he stood and stretched. As the minutes ticked by, Doc began to pace. By ten after seven, he was in full stride, manically circling his small office. The buzzer sounded, and Doc froze. He took a deep breath and threw open the door.

"I'm sorry for the interruption, but we need to talk." It was the lanky LAPD detective.

Doc stood still, staring at the lieutenant, still in shock.

"Please, may I come in?"

Doc blinked several times before replying, "Yes. We do need to talk."

"Did he show?" Detective Fred Thompson walked about the office, examining Doc's phony certificates, before settling down on the sofa. "I thought you had a seven o'clock with Vincent Salabrini."

"I did. He didn't show."

"What a pity. Perhaps he's running late."

"Maybe, but that's not his pattern." Doc again glanced up at his clock.

"Anything new?"

"Yes." Doc ran down Gypsy's late-night tarot reading, the priest reference, her insistence about contacting the LAPD, and his decision to wait until after his session with Schizzy.

"Maybe I should talk with Gypsy. She recommended a priest?"

"Yes. According to her tarot reading, he's possessed. She's scared, firmly believes in her readings. In her mind, both of us are powerless to help Vincent."

"What's your take on Vincent?"

"I'm just a hypnotist. I'm neither trained nor qualified for what's biting him. He's mad. Self-improvement's my specialty."

"How were you going to help him?" The lieutenant took out a notepad and pencil, quickly scribbling.

"I started with guided imagery. I was upfront with him. I could only offer visualization strategies for his problem."

Detective Thompson stood, offered Doc another business card, and said, "Please call if he shows. It's imperative."

Doc was once again alone, both puzzled and troubled. He phoned Gypsy at eight. She'd turned off her sign. They needed each other.

Chapter Nine

Father Gallagher said good-bye to what he thought was his last parishioner. The evening mass was over at Saint Vincent's.

Father Gallagher turned off the main lights in the chapel, leaving on the altar lights and sidelights. He was looking forward to some down time, a good book, and a glass or two of wine. "A wee bit of heavenly nectar," he'd say in an Irish brogue, "the LA Lakers and murder mysteries make my nights." He was old school; he admired the pope and stood firm against abortions, mercy killing, and wayward priests. His theology was strict, but his heart as soft and warm as a baby's kiss.

"Father, may I see you?"

Patrick Gallagher flinched, snatched from thoughts of his favorite pastime—thrillers and cabernet.

"Who goes there?"

Vincent Salabrini emerged from the shadows, illuminated only by the soft lights bathing the sanctuary. Stained glass windows and colorful murals depicting church icons and saints dominated the steep walls of the chapel. He paused between Saint Augustine and Saint Thomas Aquinas and said, "I need a moment." Vincent then slowly approached the priest, limping and hunched slightly, reminding Father Gallagher of a fictional character from one of his favorite thrillers.

"I need your help." Vincent stopped about three feet from the priest, leaned on his cane, and said softly, "I'm in serious trouble."

"Is this an emergency?" Father Gallagher said, gazing at the man.

"I've been visited by the devil himself."

"What?"

"May we talk in private?"

"Trust me, we are quite alone. Come sit with me." Father Gallagher motioned to the front pew and waited for Vincent to be seated."

Vincent cleared his voice and began his tale of woe, chronicling the visitations by demons, the taunts and accusations, and the demand for him to pay up and give over his soul to the prince of darkness. He spoke of Gypsy's tarot readings and Doc's guided imagery plans to fight the dark side.

Father Gallagher stroked his bearded chin, gazed into Vincent's eyes, and said, "Perhaps these are just dreams, or cries of frustration from your subconscious mind."

"Father, it's real. I assure you."

"Have you seen a mental health professional, a psychologist or psychiatrist?"

"No. I'm not crazy!"

"Perhaps a confession is in order."

"Father, it's not about sin. It's about a wager with the devil."

Father Gallagher leaned back and then calmly said, "Come back tomorrow at two. My calendar is open between two and four."

"I'm afraid of being alone."

"You may stay here in the chapel, if you like. You're in good company. The saints will comfort you. It's late, and I've early morning rounds at the hospital." Father Gallagher rose, took Vincent's hand, and said, "God be with you." He smiled and left Vincent in good company. The saints provided eternal vigilance, solid and unflinching, bathed in the soft lights of Saint Vincent's Church, the largest Catholic Church in the San Fernando Valley. It was a scaled-down version of the Notre Dame, and though the church wasn't a cathedral, it had the feel of one. Vincent Salabrini chose it not for its size but its name. He felt instantly connected.

* * *

Father Gallagher's morning was full. He visited two hospitals to check in on three parishioners, one who had recently suffered a mild heart attack, and two elderly women suffering from pneumonia. He swung by the downtown cathedral, Our Lady of the Angels, and visited his best friend, fellow priest, and avid LA Lakers fan. Father Michael O'Neil and Father Gallagher had become inseparable since their freshman year at Thomas Aquinas College. They treasured their education, the intellectual freedom, the Great Books approach to learning—no lectures, no textbooks, just the original works, from Aristotle and Aquinas, to T. S. Eliot and Albert Einstein. "It is the truth that sets men free and nothing else," they said in unison, followed by a high-five and critique of last night's Lakers' win. It was their greeting and mantra all rolled up in one.

"I've a private matter," Father Gallagher said after their lighthearted greeting. "I need to pick your brain."

"Sure. Let's grab a quick lunch at Marie's and talk." The leisurely hoofed the three blocks, mostly talking sports.

In the name of health, they opted for salads, both men battling the bulge of post-middle-age spread. Last month, they both turned fifty-five—brothers for life.

"And what part of my brain interests you?" Father O'Neil said, lapsing into an Irish brogue. His eyes twinkled, and his gray beard danced about his chubby face as he laughed.

"The part that best deals with evil."

"That's a tall order. What's up?"

"I had a late-night visitor. After Mass, just before closing up, a man I've never seen before emerged from the shadows. I had just shut off the main chapel lights. He approached, nodded, and said he needed help. His dress was odd—a fedora, black patch covering one eye, and long dark coat. He was a bit hunched over and walked with a limp."

"What did he want?" Father O'Neil pushed his salad plate aside and stirred his coffee vigorously, splashing the saucer.

Father Gallagher relayed Vincent's story, being sure to include the graphic descriptions of demons, taunts, and Mephistophelean wagers.

"Be careful, my good friend, the line between demonic possession and mental disorders can be tricky. We both took that seminar at UCLA—gosh what was it, maybe ten years ago?"

"Yes, that's why I'm here. A second opinion, y' know."

"If you get involved, maybe you should seek a shrink. Better rule out brain disorders first."

"Yes, you're probably right. Epilepsy, Tourette's, schizophrenia, or dissociative identity disorder are all in play."

Father Gallagher felt better after touching base with his dear friend and sharing his concerns about Vincent. They left with an old joke about a drunken Irishman, a Catholic priest, and a rabbi.

The early afternoon traffic was light, considering it was Los Angeles, and Father Gallagher made it back to Saint Vincent's in time for his two o'clock with Mr. Salabrini. As his study clock struck two, a thud, followed by two quick knocks, alerted him of his visitor.

"Come in."

The door swung open, revealing Vincent Salabrini, decked out in his usual attire. He tipped his hat and said, "Top of the afternoon, Father."

"Please, close the door and have a seat. Did you stay the night?"

"I remained in the chapel till about five. I hit Denny's for an early breakfast. I needed to be around people."

Father Gallagher leaned back and stroked his gray beard, gazing at his mysterious acquaintance. He wished his dear friend, Father O'Neil, were here. He could use an extra pair of eyes and ears. "May I ask a favor?"

"Sure."

"Could we back up, have a look at your past?"

"What do you want to know?"

"Family background, education, profession, that sort of thing. By the way, are you Catholic?"

"I was brought up Catholic. My parents were devout followers; the Holy Book had all the answers to life's riddles. They ate fish on Fridays."

"And you?"

Vincent leaned forward, bracing himself with his cane, nodded his head, and said, "I've drunk deeply of the tradition."

"Are you a believer?"

"That's my problem," Vincent said, leaning back into his chair.

"How so?"

"If I believe in God, embrace Catholicism, I acknowledge the existence of the devil. If I deny God, turn my back on the spiritual, and accept only the natural world, then I'm crazy."

"That seems a bit black and white."

"But that's my bind. The demons haunt me, accusing me of faulting on a wager. If I believe, I lose my soul. If I don't, I'm soulless, crazy, out of my mind."

"Have you seen a mental health professional?"

"As I said last night, I'm not crazy."

"Vincent—may I call you Vincent?"

"Please."

"What do you do for a living?"

"I'm presently unemployed."

"What did you do?"

"I was a professor."

"Where?"

"Thomas Aquinas College. Great place—serene, good students, the Great Books, Socratic teaching, and small classes."

"That's where I went to college. Graduated in '78." Father Gallagher smiled, shoulders relaxed, tension thawing from his charged body, replaced by a tinge of enthusiasm. They shared a common love.

"I just missed you. I was there 1980 to 1999. Best years of my life."

"Where did you go to college?"

"Notre Dame, Ph.D. in philosophy, class of 1978."

"Why did you leave Thomas Aquinas?"

"I felt the need to see the world, traveled for three years. Saw a lot."

"Do you know Drs. Malcolm and Flanagan?"

"Yes. Fine scholars and good poker players. Fun to be around, liked to laugh, tell jokes, drink wine, and tell tall stories."

"Did you know a Professor Hooligan?" Father Gallagher threw in a fictitious name, checking to see if Vincent was telling the truth.

"No. The name doesn't ring a bell."

"My mistake. I meant to say Professor Monahan."

"Oh, yes. I knew him, but not well."

"So, did the demons appear after we talked last?"

"No, thank God. The chapel did wonders last night. I even nodded off, catching a few winks."

Father Gallagher and Vincent talked for over an hour, exploring the many faces of his demon-haunted world. Dr. Salabrini left, feeling better; he liked Father Gallagher, trusted his sincerity, and savored his kind words and keen insights. The parish priest was a great fit; he might be Vincent's ticket to the Truth. He had to admit to himself, it felt good being recognized as Dr. Salabrini again. The last couple of years had been hell, living in the shadows, dodging suspicious people, avoiding their accusatory glances. He was looking forward to his next appointment with Father Gallagher—two o'clock, the day after tomorrow.

* * *

Gypsy's Friday evenings were usually busy, catering mostly to the curious and the uninitiated. More often than not, it was the young and adventurous, flirting with the metaphysical, more for fun than serious counsel. Gypsy was about to have a light dinner when her doorbell sounded. She checked before opening, spying a tall man with a bushy moustache. His trench coat was open, and he was reaching for something in the inside pocket.

She opened the door and gazed up at the lanky man. "Yes?"

"Good evening. I'm Lieutenant Fred Thompson, LAPD." He presented his credentials, allowing her ample time to verify its authenticity. She remembered Doc's description. He matched it to a tee. "May I have a couple of minutes of your time?"

"Please, come in. I hoped you might drop by."

"How's that?"

"Doc told me about your visit."

"Doc?"

"Michael Mesmer, the hypnotist. He's known by his friends and clients as Doc."

The detective moved past Gypsy, gawking at the plush drapes and dark reds and pinks bathing the parlor. *Gaudy*, he thought. The wallpaper reminded him of his grandma's home, at least the way it looked when he was a kid. The parlor was old-world, nineteenth-century, definitely European.

"Is he a Ph.D.?"

"Not really. He's a hypnotist. We're committed to helping people."

"With magic?"

"No! We're good listeners, in touch with our clients' feelings."

"What's your feeling about Vincent Salabrini?"

"Please, Lieutenant, have a seat."

"Thanks." He removed his rumpled trench coat and retrieved a notepad and pen.

"He scares me."

"How so?"

"My tarot reading confirmed his worst fears." Gypsy stopped, her eyes wide and slightly glazed, staring off into space.

"Yes, go on."

"The demons," she squeaked. She cleared her throat and continued, "The demons demanding he pay up." Gypsy grimaced, thinking about her last encounter with Vincent.

"Pay up?'

"Yeah! He's a modern-day Mephistopheles. He entered a deal with the devil. Now it's payback time."

"His soul?"

"Yes."

"Doc said you offered him advice."

"Advice?"

"You said he should see a priest."

"Yes, Doc and I have little to offer. His troubles are best dealt with by a priest, one experienced with demonic possessions."

"That's a tall order. Besides, his troubles may lie elsewhere."

"Where?" Gypsy gazed at the lieutenant, genuinely puzzled.

"Psychiatric. He may be a nut case."

"You sound like Doc."

"How's that?"

"Doc refers to Vincent as Schizzy."

"That might just fit." Detective Thompson stood, thank Gypsy, put on his coat, and started for the door before pausing. "Say, do you have his phone number, address, anything to help me find him?"

"Sorry. He offered nothing more than his name."

"Why did he visit you?"

"An old friend referred him."

"Do you have a name?"

"Margaret Morley. But she's dead."

"I know."

"You know her?"

"Not personally. But she's possibly connected to Vincent Salabrini."

"How so?"

"I can't say. Please call me if anything comes up. I left my card on the table."

The lieutenant's visit comforted Gypsy; the authorities were now hot on Schizzy's trail.

Chapter Ten

Lieutenant Fred Thompson skidded the van to a stop and took a hard left into the alley.

"Jeez, Fred, why the rush? It's homicide," said Liz Rodriquez. "The guy's dead."

"I got carried away. This van reminds me of my hippie days."

"That's a hoot. I can picture it now, long haired, flowers, decked out in bell bottoms," Liz said as she opened the passenger door and jumped out.

"The girls loved me," he fired back. Fred hurried from the off-white van, on loan from the motor pool, and ducked under a tangle of yellow tape. Lights from the van and two LAPD cruisers lit up the alley. It was 3:00 AM, way too early for his taste. The victim was sprawled across the muddy alley, arms stretched wide, knees slightly bent. Blood pooled about his head.

"What do we have?" Lieutenant Thompson barked at a uniformed LAPD officer.

"Private investigator. We found his credentials in his coat pocket." The officer, Frank Williamson, flipped open his notepad and said, "He's with D-Day Investigations."

"Gunshot wound?"

"Definitely. Take a look. There's a small entrance wound at the right temple, massive trauma on the other side. The bullet blew out a big chunk of his prefrontal cortex."

"CSI here yet?" the detective yelled over the hum of activity. Paramedics, cops, and approaching sirens filled the air, causing Lieutenant Thompson to grimace. He hated chaos. Why he had become a cop was a mystery, more so to himself than anyone else. On the surface, he was a cool customer.

"They just arrived." Officer Williamson closed his notes.

"Let me see what you've got." Detective Thompson stood, looking about.

"Here, take a look. I'll be around for a while." Officer Williamson handed the detective his notes and rushed toward two approaching CSI techs.

Thompson, with the help of his Maglite, glanced first at the notes, then back at the victim. The position of the body reminded him of a crucifixion, the one he had stared at for four years at Saint Mary's. He loved high school. "Brooklyn's finest," his friend's would brag, but he hated the religious mural that greeted him first period. It ran the full length of the first floor, featuring church icons and the gruesome crucifixion scene. It gave him the creeps every time he went to class. The image had haunted him all these years, and was now played out right in front of him, in the middle of the muddy alley.

"Liz, what's your take?" Thompson's full-time partner, Dan White, was having some health issues. He'd been diagnosed with Leukemia two years ago. He had good and bad days, but lately, the bad had outnumbered the good.

Liz bent down, examining the wound. CSI techs were about ready to cart him off when she inquired about his personal belongings—wallet, keys, money, and receipts.

"It's all here in the officer's report—driver's license, investigative credentials, credit cards, and business cards. A hundred and twenty-one dollars, mostly twenties, were in his wallet. He was unarmed." Lieutenant Thompson handed the report to Liz and stepped aside, allowing the techs room to position the body on the gurney. The victim was packed up and carted off in less than five minutes.

Later that day, Detective Thompson dropped by D-Day Investigations. The secretary, a short, pudgy, middle-aged bleached blonde, was in shock. She'd worked for Leonard Eisenhower for five years. Detective Thompson left with more questions than answers, but did take with him several files containing active clients. Within in an hour, he had a list of five people to contact. Reverend Michael Mesmer was at the top of his list. The deceased private eye had recently questioned Doc. Ike, the fallen investigator, had also tailed him for several days.

* * *

Doc hit his office an hour early, allowing enough time to prepare for his nine o'clock. Brian Walker was a new client struggling with stage fright. He sounded anxious over the phone, worried about extensive speaking engagements required by his new position at AIG. Doc had an excellent track record with public speaking issues, so this should be a piece of cake. The buzzer sounded, startling Doc. He glanced at his clock. "It's only seven-thirty," he blurted. Much too early for his new client. *Maybe I should ignore it. No one knows I'm here.* The buzzer sounded again, irritating Doc and reluctantly sending him to the door.

"Lieutenant Thompson, what a surprise."

The detective smiled, towering over the hypnotist, making him feel insignificant. "May I have minute?"

"Sure, come in."

Lieutenant Thompson once again walked about the office, this time pausing in front of Doc's phony certificates. "Are you an accredited Ph.D.?"

"I was issued the title by London College."

"Is it real?"

Doc hesitated, slightly embarrassed, hating to face reality. He loved being called Doc. It sounded good and was great for business. He blushed and said, "The title's good for business. I'm a hypnotist. I don't do therapy, and I stay clear of emotional and mental disorders."

"Are you a reverend?"

"According to the State of California. I perform an occasional marriage."

"I've some disturbing news."

"Is it about Vincent?"

"Not directly." The lieutenant paused, smoothed out his bushy moustache, wrinkled his nose, and said, "Do you know Leonard Eisenhower?"

Doc blinked and cleared his throat before speaking. He felt trapped. "Yes."

"Was he a client?"

"No, a private investigator."

"Did you retain him?"

"No way." Doc took a deep breath. "He questioned me at my residence. Tailed me. I think he was interested in Vincent."

"Schizzy?" The detective grinned, knowing the Schizzy reference would throw him.

"What?"

"Gypsy told me that you refer to Vincent as Schizzy."

Doc cringed, sighed, and said, "Guilty as charged."

"Do you directly refer to him as Schizzy?"

"No way!" Doc was emphatic, irritated by the detective's suggestion.

"Well that's not why I'm here. When did you last see Leonard Eisenhower?"

"Well over a week."

"Can you be more specific?"

"It will be two weeks this Sunday."

"Have you had any communication with him—phone, e-mail, anything?"

"No."

"He's dead."

"What?"

"He was found in a pool of blood in an alley, not far from Saint Vincent's."

"Was it an accident?" Doc was visibly shaken, hands trembling, sweaty.

"Nope, bullet through the head. Say, Doc," the lieutenant stretched his neck, grimaced, and barked, "do you own a gun?"

"Shotgun. It was my dad's. I inherited it."

"Why would Leonard be interested in Vincent?"

"I don't know, but it seems half the world is."

"Vincent is popular." Lieutenant Thompson stood, stretched, and walked over to Doc's certificates. "They look real." He turned and headed for the door. Before leaving he said, "Don't leave town. We may need you."

Doc slumped down in his chair and buried his head in his hands. The buzzer sounded. His eight o'clock was on time.

* * *

Father O'Neil treated Father Gallagher to a leisurely lunch at Marie Callender's before dropping him at Saint Vincent's in time for his two o'clock with Dr. Salabrini. Earlier, Father Gallagher phoned Thomas Aquinas College in Santa Paula, and sure enough, Vincent Salabrini had taught there for nearly twenty years, was especially popular with the students, and was well liked by the faculty. A chatty secretary confided that she had received a postcard from Italy—about five years ago, she thought—signed *Vinny*. He liked being called Vinny.

At two sharp, a thump followed by two knocks brought a half smile to the priest's lips. *This should be interesting.*

"Come in."

The door opened slowly, only halfway, allowing Dr. Salabrini to dart through before slamming it behind him.

"Sorry. I think I'm being followed."

"What makes you think so? Are you sure?"

"I'm sure of little lately." Dr. Salabrini glanced back toward the closed door.

"You seem agitated," Father Gallagher said. "Could I offer you some coffee, tea, or perhaps a soft drink?"

"No thanks." Dr. Salabrini removed his coat but left on his fedora and the black patch covering his right eye. "I've had a run in with them." He settled into the chair opposite Father Gallagher, on the other side of the desk, and repeatedly gripped and released his cane.

"Perhaps you could put down the cane, free up your hands. Would you like to join me in my relaxation exercise? I do it every afternoon about this time." Father Gallagher folded his hands prayer-like and began counting backwards.

"Are you going to hypnotize me?" Dr. Salabrini released the cane and mimicked the priest, folding his hands, taking a deep breath.

"No, not really. Let's meditate. Prayer and meditation can do wonders for the soul."

"He's trying to take my soul."

"Who's *he*?" Father Gallagher looked into Dr. Salabrini's left eye, trying to get a feel for his state of mind. His exposed eye was severely bloodshot, watery, out of focus, gazing out the widow. He looked forlorn, as if his last friend had deserted him.

"The evil one, the Prince of Darkness, Mephistopheles. The devil demands my soul."

"Did he visit today?"

"Just now, before I entered the church."

"Is he here now?"

"I don't know. I don't feel his presence."

"Take a deep breath. Let the power and pure light of God's goodness flood your being." Father Gallagher stood, reached across his desk. "Hold my hands. Let us pray." Dr. Salabrini stood awkwardly, reaching down for his cane for support before holding the priest's hands.

"Your hands are cold," Father Gallagher said softly.

"He's here."

"Who?"

"Satan." Dr. Salabrini began to shiver. "I'm freezing."

The sun disappeared behind a dark cloud, instantly dimming the study. A raven slammed into the closed window with a hard thud. Steam billowed from Vincent's gaping mouth, more fitting for a cold East Coast winter's day than inside a California church.

Father Gallagher let go of Vincent's hands, grabbed a large crucifix from his desk, and waved it about, chanting, "God is with us; our hearts are pure." Father Gallagher suddenly stopped his chant; an eerie silence hung over the room for nearly half a minute, punctuated only by heavy breathing and the rhythmic ticking of an antique wall clock. Dr. Salabrini's left eye rolled upward, disappearing under his quivering eyelid. His body trembled, lips curled, and mouth foamed. A deep voice filled the room: "Leave him alone!" Father Gallagher looked about, bewildered, searching for the source of the voice. It didn't seem to come from Dr. Salabrini.

Suddenly Dr. Salabrini fell backwards, bounced off the high-back wooden chair, and crumpled to the floor, sending his fedora skidding across the study. Father Gallagher rushed around the desk and fell to the floor, first monitoring Dr. Salabrini's pulse, then checking his mouth and breathing, fearing he might have choked on the thick phlegm pooling around his lips. He raised the doctor's head, insuring his breathing was unobstructed. Within a minute, Vincent had regained consciousness, confused about what just happened.

Both men were shaken—Dr. Salabrini from yet another visitation, Father Gallagher from the intensity of the seizure. Whether it was medical or demonic, he did not know. He did know, however, that he would not rest until he knew the truth.

Chapter Eleven

Doc skipped lunch and went straight by Gypsy's, dreading her reaction to the latest on Vincent. Schizzy was at the center of their life, turning everything upside down. He was beginning to think of himself as Alice, falling down the rabbit hole. After a hug, a cup of tea, and friendly small talk about their respective clients, Doc told her about Lieutenant Thompson's morning visit.

"Doc, this is spiraling out of control."

"The detective told me to stick around, not leave town."

"He *suspects* you?" Gypsy vigorously stirred her tea, agitated with the latest turn of events.

"I hope not."

"I'm not staying alone anymore."

"I'll get you a key. You're welcome anytime."

"Thanks. I guess I got us into this." Gypsy sighed, stopped the incessant stirring, staring across the room at a figurine of a Grecian woman, head lowered, grieving over a babe in arms.

"Gypsy, this is no time for blame. We both willingly entered Vincent's world."

"Maybe, but entering his world was effortless. Leaving is nothing but a nightmare."

"Here, take my key. I've an extra at the office."

"You're an angel."

Doc hugged her reassuringly and kissed her on the cheek. "See you tonight. I'll be home around ten. I've a session with Alan Workman." Doc was actually looking forward to Gypsy's sleep over. Rationally he was cautious; emotionally he was receptive to her charms. Subconsciously, he was falling for her.

"The philosopher?"

"Yeah. Time with him is different; it's provocative and refreshing, but not abnormal. Schizzy is sick."

"Christ sake, Doc, he's evil." Gypsy frowned. Doc leaned down, this time planting a tender kiss on her full lips.

Her frown quickly morphed into a smile. "I'll see you tonight."

* * *

Alan Workman beat Doc to the punch. He was sitting with his eyes closed, waiting in the office reception area when Doc returned from dinner with Waldo.

"I'm early," Alan said with a broad grin.

"So I see. Let's do it." Doc was taken by surprise, wanting to collect his thoughts before the session. It was definitely new territory, far a field from the nagging concerns of smoking, weight loss, and stage fright. He was expected to help Alan do an end run around language, dumped labels, numbers, and concepts, and touch base with naked reality. It made Doc's head swim.

Alan tossed his leather jacket over the back of the sofa and rolled up his sleeves before sinking into the sofa. He was definitely Doc's most motivated client.

"Doc, before we get started, I must tell you about a dream."

"Will it help us with our mission?"

"It has to do with it. After you left my house, I was jacked, wanting to celebrate."

"Yeah."

"I popped a bottle of champagne, cranked up the stereo, and started dancing to Wagner."

"Jeez, that's weird."

"That's not the half of it. Before I knew it, I drained the bottle, collapsed on the floor, and entered another realm."

"What?"

"Doc, it was miraculous. Post-its flew about the study, books danced, and my beauties talked to me."

"Your beauties?"

"My fancy guppies and neon tetras besieged me to join them."

"What?"

"'Join the WIGGLY world,' they sang. I found a note on my desk. It read: WIGGLY (When In God's Glorious Land Yield). I was left alone, bookless, manuscript gone, nothing, not even a single Post-it."

"Hell of a dream." Doc leaned back, sending his chair rolling, slamming into the front of his desk. He felt at ease in his swivel chair, front and center, sandwiched between his client and desk, gliding about, never much, a few inches or feet, just enough to change his perspective. This time he nearly took flight.

"Prophetic," Alan said. "It was an omen."

"Alan, I want you to lean back, relax, clear your mind. Inhale slowly, a deep breath, exhaling slowly, very slowly." Doc's tone was somber, syncopated, as rhythmic as his metronome. Silence descended over the office, leaving only the ticking of the clock and the sounds of deep breathing.

"I'll count back from one hundred. Close your eyes and listen. Let my voice carry you away." By the time he reached eighty-five, Alan's head dropped slightly, tilting to his left. At seventy, his shoulders went slack.

"I want you to visualize your dream. The Post-its flying about, books dancing, and your little beauties calling to you. Step inside your dream. Drink of life as it is, without books and Post-its, free of words, symbols, and numbers. Leave the square world of thoughts and join the wiggly world of nature. Swim with your beauties, glide about your newfound world. Let go of your thoughts, just be." Doc paused briefly and continued his adventure into Alan's dream. He then planted the post-hypnotic suggestion. "Whenever in the study, working on the Weltanschauung, let go, stifle your thoughts, be at one with the world, and join the wiggly world."

Alan left the session with a smile, a spring in his step, and a new resolve. He wouldn't attack his problem, he would open up, let it take hold of him. He left Doc saying, "I'll not think it, I'll just be."

That evening, Gypsy and Doc talked of nothing but Vincent Salabrini. After exchanging their deepest fears, they once again fell asleep in each other's arms. At four, Doc covered her with a blanket and retreated to his study where he worked on his journal. Ever since Schizzy entered his life, he wrote about his concerns; it gave him comfort and helped release the tension. Because of Alan and Schizzy, he was finding his conventional world uninspiring. Perhaps they knew something he didn't. Doc lived vicariously, through his clients. He was a voyeur, observing, in the audience, not on stage. He wanted to feel what Alan and Schizzy felt. His world was too predictable, too conventional. He felt empty. He needed a fix. As he finished the journal entry, his eyes fixed on the unread paperback, *The Hypnotist: A Tale of Terror.* The title scared him; he was afraid to read it.

* * *

Father Gallagher prayed for a sign, but none came. He told Father O'Neil about his meeting with Dr. Salabrini, vividly describing every detail, from the cold hands, projectile spitting, and steamy vapors, to the raven striking the window and his violent seizure. Father O'Neil gave him the name of a Catholic psychiatrist, one experienced with differentiating demonic possessions from mental illness. Dr. Mario Salazar had a full schedule but agreed to stop by Saint Vincent's around eight o'clock. He had a dinner engagement at the Marriott in Woodland Hills.

At ten past eight, a dark haired man, graying at the temples, with a full moustache and bright smile, tapped on the open door. "Father Gallagher?"

"Yes. Please come in."

"I'm Dr. Mario Salazar."

"Dr. Salazar, so good of you to drop by. Please, have a seat." He looked patriotic, decked out in a navy blue suit, white dress shirt, and red and blue striped tie.

"I prefer Mario."

"Patrick here. I need your advice."

"Father O'Neil said you had a strange visitor."

"Very strange." Father Gallagher detailed his visit, overlooking nothing, providing the psychiatrist with a blow-by-blow account of what happened.

"Did he explain why he wagered his soul?"

"No. He talked about visitations, demands, and accusations."

"Has he sought medical help?"

"He said he isn't crazy."

"Is he a practicing Catholic?"

"I'm not sure. He taught at Thomas Aquinas College for twenty years."

"You verified that?" Dr. Salazar narrowed his eyes, sending Father Gallagher a skeptical look.

"I called the college and talked to a secretary. She remembered him well, gushed about receiving a postcard from Italy several years ago. It was signed Vinny. According to her, he was popular with both the students and faculty."

"Where did he get his education?"

"Ph.D. in philosophy. Notre Dame no less, 1978."

"He's evidently steeped in Catholicism."

"It appears so."

"It's widely believed among psychiatrists that mental illness exaggerates and amplifies the cultural, spiritual, and personal beliefs of the patient. Those who believe in demonic possession are the only ones who experience it. I've never encountered a case where a nonbeliever experienced demonic possession." Dr. Salazar leaned back, paused, and then said, "Is there any possibility of meeting Dr. Salabrini?"

"It would have to be here, in the church. He was defensive, even hostile when I questioned his mental health. He emphatically denied being crazy."

"Set it up, if you would. I'd like to have a crack at him."

"What's a good time?" Father Gallagher felt relieved. He definitely wanted a medical opinion.

"After five, preferably Monday."

"I'll try."

"Call me. Dr. Salabrini interests me."

On his way out of the priest's office, Dr. Mario Salazar glanced back and said, "I was baptized here."

"Before my time," Father Gallagher said. "Your parents had good taste. It's a great church."

The psychiatrist and priest parted, both irresistibly drawn to Vincent's story—a well-educated man, seemingly stable, whose aberrant behavior cried out for an explanation. Father Gallagher retired to his room, perversely rereading *The Exorcist*. Perhaps it contained the answer to Vincent. Before he fell asleep, he chewed on the dilemma: medical or diabolical? As a pursuer of the truth, he was excited. As a believer, he was fearful.

* * *

On the way out the door, Doc kissed Gypsy on the cheek. "Please help yourself to breakfast. There's fresh squeezed OJ in the fridge."

"Call me," she said as he closed the front door. She was curled up on the sofa, warm and content, feeling safe bundled up in Doc's comforter. It had the aroma of a California orange grove in full blossom.

Doc had only two clients before noon—his nine o'clock cancelled because of illness—so he decided to check in on Waldo. He found Waldo in the back room of his store, sitting and staring at his coffee as he stirred it.

Waldo pointed to the old newspaper on his desk and said, "Did you hear about the private eye gunned down in an alley a couple of blocks from Saint Vincent's? Eisenhower was his last name. Went by Ike. I knew his granddad."

"Before he was killed, he paid me a visit, even tailed me," Doc said.

"You knew him?"

"He was looking for Vincent Salabrini."

"Looney-tunes?" Waldo shook his head, grinning in disbelief.

"Yep."

"Did you go to the cops?"

"They came to me." Doc sat back, annoyed at Waldo's delight with Doc's plight.

"Same Lieutenant?"

"Yep. Fred Thompson wants me to stick around."

"You're a suspect?"

"Shit, I don't know."

"Small world, y'know. Detective Thompson visited me last night. Wanted to know if I'd seen looney-tunes." Waldo craned his neck, raising his eyebrows.

"Why'd he look you up?"

"That's what I wanted to know. Said he had his sources."

"Yeah, whad'ya tell him?"

"I've neither seen hide nor hair of him."

"That's a good thing, no?"

Waldo grinned and said, "I did tell him that you and I had talked. We think he's the crazy who escaped from Patton State."

"This is a fucking nightmare!" Doc shouted.

"It's more than that. It's homicide." Waldo returned to stirring his coffee.

"You think Schizzy and Ike are connected?"

"Doc, you told me they were."

"Don't bring up the matter around Gypsy. She's edgy. Stayed at my place last night."

"So you two *are* getting chummy." Waldo's eyebrows shot up.

"Just friends."

"We'll see," Waldo winked, irritating Doc.

"Later, it's getting hot in here."

Doc headed for Sammy's. It was time for a trim.

Chapter Twelve

ather Gallagher chalked up another day in God's service, tending
to the flock, visiting the sick, and counseling the troubled. To
others, he was a happy priest, joking and laughing his way through
the day. Behind this playful persona, coiled like a viper ready to strike,
were tangled memories, sights, and sounds of Dr. Salabrini—cold hands,
steamy vapors, convulsions, and echoes of that eerie voice that said, *"Leave
him alone."*

Evening Mass was over and the parishioners had gone, but images of
Dr. Salabrini sprawled across his floor lingered. He had finished *The Exorcist*
and looked forward to a more lighthearted read. He turned from the altar
and started toward his office when a deep voice filled the empty chapel.

"Father Gallagher. May I see you?"

The priest glanced back, and there emerging from the shadows was a
man in a navy pea coat and dark blue beret, waving his hand.

"Yes. But I'm about to retire for the evening."

"Don't you recognize me?"

As the man approached, Father Gallagher squinted. The man paused
several feet from the priest, bathed in the faint glow of the chapel's lights.
The overhead and altar lights had been turned off, leaving the two men
in semi-darkness. They were swallowed up in shadows, barely visible,
catching only residual light from the illuminated saints looking down
from the chapel walls.

"It's me, Dr. Salabrini."

Father Gallagher stared in disbelief. The man standing in front of him
stood erect, clean-shaven, no eye patch, and no cane. "You don't look like
him."

"Oh, I assure you, I'm *him*."

"What happened to the goatee, the limp?"

"All in good time. May I see you in your office?"

"It's late."

"Father, it's of the utmost importance."

"Just a few minutes."

Father Gallagher extinguished the exterior lights, leaving on the illuminated cross, beaming its message into the night, and led Vincent silently to his office. He turned on the lights and gestured toward the chair, the one where he had just days before witnessed Dr. Salabrini's violent seizure.

"What's happened to you?" Father Gallagher eyes widened.

"What?"

"Your appearance. I'd have passed you on the street, not giving you a second look."

"That's why I'm here." Vincent cleared his voice. "I've been given a reprieve."

"A reprieve?"

"I've been given a second chance. I've retained my soul."

"Let's start from the beginning. Just last week, in that very chair, you suffered a seizure." Father Gallagher leaned back and took a deep breath, trying to calm the uneasiness he was feeling.

"All I know is that they have consented to a compromise."

"Who?"

"The visitors, *his* minions."

"The devil?" Father Gallagher nearly choked on his own words.

"The one and only. They've given me a new lease on life."

Father Gallagher's mind raced, thinking of Father's O'Neil's warnings and Dr. Salazar's desire to observe Vincent. "You've entered into a new deal?"

"I've been bargaining for some time."

"You've entered into a bargain? Time? Time for what?"

"He's given me a second chance."

"I'm confused."

"Salvation."

"Salvation through the devil?" Father Gallagher was stunned, lost for words.

"Yes, but I do have a slight problem." Dr. Salabrini stood and walked about the priest's small office, stopping in front of the bookcase, perusing the titles. His posture was erect, and he walked with confidence, showing no sign of a limp. His presence was commanding, projecting style and poise. His words, however, were diabolical.

"I need your assistance."

"I'll have no dealings with the devil," Father Gallagher protested.

"He's sent me on a mission."

"And what might that be?"

"To spread the good news."

"God's gospel lives here!"

"Hear me out." Dr. Salabrini sat, beaming the priest a broad smile.

"I'm listening."

"He wants to convince you of his presence. He wants to put on a show."

"What?"

"Tomorrow night, during evening Mass, he'll make an appearance. Be sure to have your support team in order."

"My support team?"

"You know what I mean." Dr. Salabrini rose, standing tall, confident that his world was in order, challenging the priest. He opened his arms and said, "Join us. You'll not be disappointed." It didn't sound like Dr. Salabrini. It was the other voice, the one he had heard the afternoon of the seizure. It didn't look like him either. He seemed younger, energetic, born again. Vincent turned and vanished as mysteriously as he had appeared. His parting words haunted the priest. It was if he could read his mind. The priest immediately dialed Dr. Salazar and left a cryptic message on his voicemail: "Dr. Salabrini promises a show after tomorrow night's Mass. Please come." He followed up with a call to his friend Father O'Neil— same message.

* * *

Schizzy had vanished, failed to show for his sessions, missing in action for more than a week. In a way, Doc was relieved; but that was a lie. He was more than a high-paying client. Schizzy was an enigma. For Waldo, he was Looney-tunes; for Gypsy, someone to fear; for Lieutenant Fred Thompson, a person of interest; and for Doc, a mystery crying out to be solved. But down deep, Doc felt Schizzy was more than puzzling, more than a mystery. He sensed he was an omen.

Lieutenant Fred Thompson had dropped by earlier, checking in, looking for a lead, clue, or hint about Schizzy's whereabouts. Vincent Salabrini, or was it Vincent Valdez, had disappeared. The lieutenant left Doc's office disappointed but not dejected. Chasing fugitives was part of his job. "My leads have dried up. Call me if he shows." Evidently Doc was not the only one miffed, wanting but not getting answers.

The waiting room buzzer sounded, alerting Doc to his six o'clock. A glance at the clock indicated the inevitable. Alan Workman was ten minutes early. He stalled, not long, just a moment or two, enough time for suspense, letting Alan build steam. He sensed that tonight's session would be a doozie.

After their usual lighthearted greeting, Alan rolled up his sleeves, ready for action. Not only did he want the most bang for his buck, he was driven, obsessed, and hounded by his metaphysical challenge.

Doc counted backwards, setting the stage for another hypnotic trance. He revisited the dream, Post-its, acronyms, philosophy books, and talking tropical fish. He zeroed in on the mysterious note: WIGGLY (When In God's Glorious Land Yield).

"I want you to enter the WIGGLY world. Let go, allow it to take hold of you." Doc paused and added, "Don't think. Just be."

Alan, breathing slowly, shoulders slumped, head tilted and eyes closed, broke into a broad smile. Doc conjured up images of a free spirit mingling with "God's Glorious Land." He spoke of the eternal now, where reality is. He invoked Alan's little beauties, his guppies and tetras. Suddenly, at Doc's suggestion, the WIGGLY world enveloped Alan, stripping him of his ego, his will. "Suspend conceptions, ditch your ego, let go of past and future," sang his beauties. Alan giggled, then laughed. He was free, alive, whole again. He now understood. Language is linear, scrawny. He was here, in the moment, truly alive for the first time, leaving behind ghosts of the past and future. He felt at peace, freed from the stranglehold of his obsession. He no longer saw himself as a separate ego, dwelling in the body, inside the head, behind the eyes, seeking for answers. He was part of the whole, extended in space and time, and interrelated to everything else. He saw himself everywhere, interconnected, part of the web of life. There was no longer an inside and an outside, subjective and objective, right or wrong. Alan had been rescued from his island of consciousness, freed from his illusory ego. He felt in tune with the vibrating strings of reality. He didn't want to leave.

Doc brought him back, slowly, gently. Alan blinked, smiled, and said, "Doc, you look great."

"What?"

"Everything looks great. I can't explain it."

"Are we on for Friday?" Doc felt pleased, not sure why, just pleased.

"You bet."

Alan left, smiling, thanking Doc for a great session. "I don't know what just happened, but let's do it again. See you later."

* * *

Father Gallagher entered the chapel, and scanning his flock, he spotted Father O'Neil and Dr. Mario Salazar in the back row. The affable priest appeared calm to his worshipers, confidently moving through the service, eliciting reverence one moment, then laughter the next, providing the most hardened souls spiritual guidance and a fresh, revitalizing perspective on troubling times. At least 10 percent of his parishioners had lost their jobs during the recent economic downturn. It was all too easy to be down.

There was no sign of Dr. Salabrini. Father Gallagher was in two places, juggling two worlds. He served his faithful, conducting a spirited Mass. But unseen, lurking beneath the surface of Father Gallagher's easy manner and witty messages, were anticipation and fear, all connected to Dr. Vincent Salabrini. *Would there be a show? Would the devil appear?* It was a miracle that Saint Vincent's favorite priest kept it together.

The Mass ended, but not with fireworks. Several of his favorites chatted him up, praising him for his kind words of encouragement. As Father O'Neil and Dr. Salazar approached, he opened his arms, shrugged, and said, "A no show."

The three men stood stiffly in front of the altar, exchanging possible reasons for Salabrini's absence. On Father Gallagher's suggestion, they moved their talk to his office, behind closed doors, not wanting to be overheard. No sooner had the three gotten comfortable, kicking around another round of possible reasons for Salabrini's no show, that the office door flew open. Looming in front of the support team, standing tall, decked out in navy pea coat, beret, and a grin a Cheshire cat would envy, was Dr. Vincent Salabrini.

"Gentlemen, so glad you are all here."

"Dr. Salabrini, I had given up on you." Father Gallagher motioned to a chair in the corner. "Grab a chair and join us."

"I prefer standing." He moved to the packed bookcase, yanked a Bible from the bottom shelf, and clutched it to his heart. "Let's discuss the Good Book." He laughed, taking delight in his dramatic entrance, mesmerizing and stunning the surprised trio. An eerie silence hung over the gathering, setting the stage for Vincent's show.

"Listen well, for I'll not repeat myself." It wasn't Dr. Salabrini's voice. Whatever it was, it filled the room, bouncing off the walls, creating an echo chamber from hell. The tone was deep, resonating, creating a rolling rumble. The windows behind Father Gallagher's desk rattled, and a picture of the pope came crashing to the floor, the glass shattering. The room suddenly turned cold, causing the surprised trio to shiver in unison.

"I've been called many things—angel of the abyss, the devil, Satan, Lucifer, power of darkness, and that old serpent." His voice smothered the observers, loud, inhuman, commanding attention. "But my dear doubters, what's in a name? That which we call a rose by any other name would smell as sweet. Call me what you will, but I am *him*, power of darkness, inheritor of the universe." Dr. Salabrini opened his mouth wide, hissing, taunting, challenging his captive audience. "Priests and psychiatrist you may be, but you're ill equipped to deal with me. *Leave him alone!*"

Dr. Salabrini threw down the Bible, spun quickly, and dashed out, slamming the door. The support team sat in shocked silence. By the time they spoke, Dr. Salabrini had vanished into the night. Father Gallagher clutched his crucifix and said, "May God help us."

Father O'Neil crossed himself, turned to Dr. Salazar, and said, "Was that Vincent?"

"The voice seemed independent, originating from outside of him." The psychiatrist paused and added, "I've seen demonic possession, witnessed psychotic behavior, and treated troubled souls, but I've never witnessed *anything* like this."

"Is he sick or possessed?" demanded Father Gallagher.

Dr. Salazar folded his hands, steadying them, feeling the brunt of Salabrini's show. "Whether demonic or psychiatric, it was a powerful performance."

"What? You think it was a performance?" Father Gallagher stood, walked toward the bookshelf, and picked up the Bible from the floor, holding it to his chest.

"Whatever it was, it was powerful." Dr. Salazar stroked his chin, pensive.

"Does Dr. Salabrini have an acting background?" Father O'Neil asked, his voice weak, barely audible.

"We need to do some investigative work. I'll make an appointment to visit Thomas Aquinas College." Father Gallagher replaced the Bible on the bookshelf and opened his office door. The church was quiet, showing no sign of life until an outside door opened and the caretaker appeared. "Father Gallagher, I heard a loud voice. I saw a man running from the church. Are you okay?"

"Yes! We had an unexpected visitor. We're just finishing up."

It was late; the men were tired, and their nerves were frayed. They agreed to keep in contact. Father Gallagher would make arrangements to visit Thomas Aquinas College.

Chapter Thirteen

"Thanks, Doc. Another great session." Alan Workman had changed, now more relaxed and centered, feeling great about his work with Doc. He meditated, morning and night—twenty minutes each time. He had lifted the veil of language and symbols and glimpsed reality, uncorrupted by culture, preconceptions, and expectations. His worldview had shifted, his consciousness changed. Alan's world hummed, Zen-like.

Doc turned down Alan's invitation to socialize, have a beer and blow off steam. It was Friday night, time to let go. After Alan left, Doc cleared his desk, checked his calendar, and headed for the door when the buzzer sounded. *Who could that be? It's almost nine.* He waited, hoping the person would just go away, assuming Doc had left for the night. This time the visitor lay on the buzzer, demanding attention. *Damn it.*

Doc opened up. There, smiling and chuckling, was Vincent Salabrini.

"Doc, I must see you."

"I'm on my way out. Call and make an appointment."

"Don't you recognize me?"

Doc stepped back, gazing at the intruder. He wore a navy pea coat, dark blue beret, and stood erect, smiling, arms open, eyebrows raised. "Vincent Salabrini?" It was more guess than identification. Schizzy was on his mind.

"Bingo. I've missed you."

"Where've you been?"

"May I come in?" Schizzy's grin unnerved Doc.

"I'm beat. It's been a trying day."

"I'll make it worth your while."

"Just for a minute or so."

Doc acquiesced, allowed Schizzy in, motioning to the sofa. He dropped into his chair and nervously rolled, just a little, backward and forward, irritated, but also intrigued at Schizzy's sudden appearance.

"I have some news."

"Yeah, what's up?"

"Doc, you don't seem excited to see me."

"You've caught me at a bad time. But what's with the change?"

"What?"

"No goatee, eye patch missing, and walking without a cane."

"I've been born again." Schizzy flashed Doc a mischievous grin.

"Besides, I'm mad at you. You've stood me up for weeks."

"I've been busy."

"You made a commitment to work with me."

'I'm a new man.'

"How's that?" Doc frowned.

"I've worked out a deal with *him*."

"What?"

"Yeah, the devil has given me back my soul."

"What's happened?"

"I've joined forces with the dark side. It's working out."

"I thought you wanted my help. I thought you wanted to fight for your soul."

"I have my soul and more."

"I'm confused." Doc rolled back, sliding his chair next to his desk, looking for a fresh perspective.

"I misunderstood the bargain."

"Bargain?"

"Yeah, the deal I made with *him*."

"You were terrified before, begging for help. Now you're born again?"

"Doc, it's fantastic. I'm at peace and strong. I can walk without a cane, control my destiny, and bow to no one."

"Tell me about the bargain." Doc rolled back again, this time bumping into the desk. He felt he could glide about the room, slide in and out of every corner, and still lack a proper perspective.

"He emboldens me. I now have the strength to rebuff those who foolishly challenge me."

"Who's challenging you?"

"The others. They follow me, mock me, and accuse me of wrongdoing."

"Who's they?"

"They're everywhere, giving me suspicious looks, whispering behind my back, floating malicious rumors, trying their best to drive me mad."

"I thought it was the devil who was driving you mad."

"Oh, I falsely believed that, for a while. But now I know the truth. As they say, it will set me free." He chuckled, rolling his eyes.

"How can I help you?"

"I don't need your help, not anymore. I've come to thank you. You believed in me, gave me the tools to handle my problem. I just wanted to share the good news. Doc, I feel whole for the first time in my life."

"This is good news. Could you do me a favor?"

"Name it." Schizzy smiled, confident, no sign of self-doubt.

"I need your phone number, address, some way to reach you? I'd like to follow up on your progress, share your recovery with other clients."

"Perhaps in the future. I'm in transition, preparing for my next life."

"What?"

"When the time is right, I'll be back. I'll share my good fortune, turn you on to the truth."

"Where are you staying?"

"As I said, I'm in transition." Schizzy rose, approached Doc, and vigorously shook his hand. "Thanks again. I'll be in touch." He moved quickly to the office door, turned, and broke out in a full-throated laugh. "All in good time, Doc."

Schizzy vanished, leaving Doc more puzzled than ever.

* * *

Positioned at the head of the academic quadrangle, the new chapel, pristine white, red-domed, and with a three-tiered bell tower, stood majestically in the midmorning sun, sending shivers of delight through Father Gallagher. It had been nearly a decade since he had set foot on Thomas Aquinas College's campus. He paused briefly, admiring the chapel's architectural splendor, from the 135-foot bell tower to the Spanish Mission style façade. It was on this campus thirty years ago that he had bid farewell to his high school sweetheart, dedicating himself to lifelong learning and love of the Church. He would no longer experience infatuation; he was now married to the Church.

He'd check out the chapel's interior later. He glanced at his watch before hustling toward the faculty offices. He had a ten o'clock with Professor Hugh Livingston. He found his office door ajar and caught the white-haired, bearded professor chatting on the phone. The professor looked up, caught sight of the priest, and waved him in, pointing to a chair next to his desk. He quickly cut short the phone call and greeted Father Gallagher.

"Welcome to Thomas Aquinas." Professor Livingston stood and eagerly shook Father Gallagher's hand.

Feeling welcomed, Father Gallagher said, "Thanks, it's been awhile."

"When was your last visit?"

"Gosh, about ten years ago. Years earlier, I spent four glorious years here, graduating in 1978."

"I bet it doesn't look the same."

"Not by a long shot. I'd like to check out the new chapel."

"I'll give you a personal tour."

"Great! I know you have a busy schedule, so I'll get to the point. How well did you know Dr. Vincent Salabrini?"

"Why the interest in Vincent?"

"He's come to me for help." Father Gallagher looked about the office, recognizing several philosophers adorning the professor's walls.

"Personal or professional?"

"Personal."

"I see. Well, to your initial query, we had similar interests—modern philosophy, classical Greek philosophy, especially Aristotle and Plato."

"Did you socialize?"

"Quite often. Friday evenings, we played a friendly game of poker, shared a glass of wine, talked sports."

"How was his psychological health?" Father Gallagher leaned back, stretching his legs, looking down at his hands. *Might as well go for the jugular.*

"What do you mean?" The professor looked confused.

"Was he moody, irritable, or prone to depression?"

"Oh, goodness sake, he was jovial and sociable, a real jokester."

"What?"

"He liked to masquerade, come to our Friday poker parties in disguise. He'd go so far as to visit a local costume shop and then show up dressed like Socrates or Mark Twain. One night, he came looking like Nietzsche, big moustache, dressed in black, brooding."

"Nietzsche must have caused quite a stir."

"Indeed. He was heckled relentlessly. We all got a big laugh. Vincent was the consummate jokester."

"Did he joke under other circumstances?"

"Oh, yes. One afternoon he showed up for tennis, dressed in military fatigues and combat boots, with black paint under his eyes."

"Did he get any flack from the college?"

"Not really. His reputation as a trickster spread fast. His antics were not only accepted, but expected."

"Did you ever see Dr. Salabrini down?"

"Only once, when his father passed. He took a week off for the funeral, visited family, consoled his mom, but that's all. Otherwise, he was upbeat and fun-loving."

"Anything else unusual?"

"Well, not really. Oh, he did have a couple of weird hobbies. He was an expert on the devil."

"How so?"

"He prided himself as an expert on all things demonic. We would do a bit of research, try and trip him up. His knowledge of demonology was encyclopedic."

"Did he take it seriously?"

"No way. He'd play it for all it was worth, try to trick us, and then laugh. It was all a joke."

"And the other weird hobbies?"

"He was a consummate hypnotist. Loved to incorporate that with his interest in all things demonic. We would willingly play along. He had a knack, could take us under his spell and conjure provocative images. He would set the scene, prime us with hypnotic rituals, then drop the bomb."

"Yes, go on." Father Gallagher leaned forward, eyes riveted on the professor, mesmerized by his knowledge of Vincent.

"He'd project his voice, make us believe we were in the presence of evil."

"Give me an example." Father Gallagher scooted his chair closer, irresistibly drawn in, excited and alarmed.

"A couple of us would be relaxed, trance-like, and he'd make Satan appear. We'd hear this breathy voice that was forceful and unearthly, definitely eerie."

"A real performer." Father Gallagher got lucky.

"A cross between a thespian and a hypnotist. He was a real trickster. Let's check out the chapel." Professor Livingston stood, motioning to the door.

The professor and priest continued their chat as they walked about the campus, finishing their tour in the chapel. The interior of Our Lady of the Most Holy Trinity was awe inspiring, moving Father Gallagher to kneel and offer up praise of thanks. He gazed up at the high tabernacle of white marble, which provided an exquisite backdrop for the altar and an image of Our Lord suffering on the cross.

He bid farewell to Professor Livingston, checked in on an administrator, and visited a secretary he had talked to earlier by phone. They added nothing to contradict the professor's story. The secretary mentioned, however, that Dr. Salabrini appeared in several plays at a nearby community playhouse. She didn't attend any of his performances but said he played the lead actor in *Who's Afraid of Virginia Woolf.* Father Gallagher pressed her, wanting more on his acting career. All she remembered was something about him starring in a production at the Rubicon Theater in Ventura. Dr. Vincent Salabrini was not only an inveterate trickster, he was a thespian, a hypnotist, and an expert on the devil.

* * *

The support team met again, only five days after Dr. Salabrini's show. Father Gallagher ended Mass, talked briefly with two parishioners, and met Father O'Neil and Dr. Salazar in his office. Father Gallagher was eager to share the fruits of his investigation.

"The plot thickens. Not only is he a trickster, he's a walking encyclopedia on the devil." Father Gallagher smoothed his beard, leaned forward, and added, "And to beat all, he's a thespian and a hypnotist."

"I'm still shaken by his show. If it was merely theatrics, I'm impressed." Father O'Neil looked over at Father Gallagher and asked, "Did Professor Livingston say anything about Salabrini's acting?"

"I was on my way out when the secretary told me. Professor Livingston was in class and I was needed here."

"We need to follow up on his acting career," Dr. Salazar said, raising his brows in suspicion.

"Well, Doc, what do you think?" Father O'Neil rose, walked to the bookcase, and retrieved the Bible Salabrini had used as a prop.

"I need more, another look, more about his acting, and something about his past, especially his childhood. And what's this about being a hypnotist?" The psychiatrist stared at the Bible cradled by Father O'Neil.

"If it was an act, it was Academy Award quality," Father Gallagher added. "And what about the room turning cold? Were we in a trance, only thinking it was cold?"

"Perhaps we were in shock," the psychiatrist interjected.

"And what about the rumbling voice, rattling windows, and the pope's picture crashing to the floor?" Father O'Neil returned the Bible to the bookcase, shaking his head.

The support team called it a night, vowing to dig deeper into Salabrini's past, especially his acting career.

Chapter Fourteen

"I have a confession."

"You love me." Gypsy tilted her head, gazing into Doc's eyes, coy and playful, wanting him to fess up.

"Like family, but that's not my confession," Doc said. He leaned back on Gypsy's sofa, smiled and added, "Very close family.

"Like family! You sure know how to sweet-talk a girl." Gypsy joined Doc on the sofa, so close their thighs touched.

Doc cleared his voice, hesitated and said, "I've been sitting on this for days."

"What's new, you're always holding back." Gypsy hoped Doc would react, but he didn't.

"Schizzy paid me a visit last Friday night."

She lightly punched his shoulder and said, "Why didn't you tell me?"

"I didn't want to alarm you."

"What happened?" She reached over and gently turned his head toward her, gazing into his eyes.

Doc revisited Schizzy surprise appearance, describing his new look and born-again attitude. "He's hooked up with the devil."

"What?"

"He's joined forces with the dark side, found new strength, and is looking forward to the next life."

"Did you inform Lieutenant Thompson?" Gypsy frowned, feeling threatened once again by Salabrini.

"Not yet. I asked him for his address and phone number, but he rebuffed me."

"Doc, I'm calling the LAPD."

"Please, let's think this over. I'm afraid Detective Thompson will scare him off."

"That suits me just fine." Gypsy looked Doc in the eye, begging him to work with the authorities. "Please, what if he comes here."

"You can stay with me."

"What if he's behind the murder of the private eye?"

"Maybe, but I'll let the LAPD handle that." Doc hoped Gypsy would see his willingness not to get involved in Ike's murder as a concession.

"I wish you'd let the LAPD handle Schizzy."

"They'll have the last word." Doc smiled and headed for the front door.

"Don't I get a little sugar?"

Doc paused at the door, smiled, and blew her a kiss. "You have a key. The door's always open."

* * *

As waitresses scurried about, the joint hummed with energy, living up to its name. The Busy Bee Café on Main Street in Ventura was a blast from the past, a fifties café with a juke box at every table, and waitresses in bobby socks and cheerleader outfits, scampering over bright red-and-white checkered tiles. A young cheerleader flashed Father Gallagher a smile and said, "Ready to order?"

"Not just yet. I'm waiting for someone. When you get a chance, some coffee would be great." The perky waitress reminded him of Crystal, his high school sweetheart, with her bright eyes and brilliant smile, buzzing about the Busy Bee, bringing an abundance of good cheer to the hungry. Crystal had sent a Christmas card every year, without fail, beginning with his first year at St. Vincent's, keeping him up on her life. She lived in Kansas, had successfully raised four kids, all girls, and was happily married to a Baptist preacher. *She sure was consistent*, he thought, *attracted only to men of the cloth.*

Father Gallagher had the day off. He had a date with Mary Hemmingway, a long-time resident of Ventura. After numerous calls, several dead ends, and one woman hanging up, thinking the priest was a cop, he discovered Hemmingway, the director of several plays starring Dr. Salabrini. She had suggested the 1950s-style café after agreeing to meet for lunch.

"Father Gallagher?"

The priest looked up from the menu, smiled, and immediately stood. "Mrs. Hemmingway, please join me."

"Thanks. But it's Miss Hemmingway."

"Sorry."

"Oh, I'm not. Being single has been good for me."

"Likewise." They both laughed, instantly hitting it off.

She was a petite woman, slender with short auburn hair, surely dyed, for she was well past seventy. She radiated charm with her bright blue eyes, British accent, and quick wit. They ordered burgers and fries, talked politics, sports, and religion. When the theater came up, Father Gallagher zeroed in on Dr. Salabrini.

"How was Dr. Salabrini?"

"As an actor or a friend?" She flashed the priest a quick smile, raising her eyebrows quizzically.

"Both."

"I directed Vincent in three plays in the early nineties. Gosh, more than fifteen years ago." Miss Hemmingway glanced down at her wristwatch as if it were a calendar marking the progression of her life.

"Good actor?"

"Fantastic. He had great range but shined in heavy drama. He was as good a George as I've ever seen." Miss Hemmingway nodded her head, punctuating her enthusiasm for Vincent's talent. She would nod and bob her head rhythmically, a subtle dance revealing her inner life. If her head bobbing failed to communicate her feelings, her bright blue eyes said it all. She enjoyed her life, and loved acting.

"George?"

"He played the lead in *Who's Afraid of Virginia Woolf,* a brilliant portrayal. Edward Albee would have been proud." Her head bobbed firmly, conveying a definite yes.

"Any comedy?"

"No. Although, he was *funny.*"

"Told jokes?" Father Gallagher recalled his conversation with Professor Livingston, shaking his head as he pictured Dr. Salabrini masquerading as Nietzsche.

"Not really. He had a thing for costumes and practical jokes. He once came to a rehearsal dressed as Mark Twain—bushy white moustache, white suit, chomping on a cigar." She smiled, thinking back to the memories.

"Another time he came dressed in black with a top hat and tails. He put on a short magic show. Hypnotized two cast members!"

Father Gallagher's face lit up. "Tell me more about his magic, especially the hypnotism bit."

"He was a real trickster, performer. Hypnotism was just one of his many props."

"Was it just an act?" Father Gallagher leaned forward, eyes twinkling.

"The hypnotism?" She leaned back, her blue eyes as bright as a summer's day.

"Yeah."

"If it was, it was a damn good one." Miss Hemmingway's head bobbed a series of affirmatives.

"How was he to direct?"

"Quick study, eager to please."

"Was he ever irritable, depressed, down emotionally?"

"Never saw it. The only odd thing was his interest in all things demonic."

"What?" Again Father Gallagher leaned forward, the demonic theme haunting him.

"He could talk endlessly about Satan. I remember dining with him once, just up the street, the restaurant's gone now, but he went on and on, a real history lesson."

"On the devil."

"From a to z, he didn't miss a beat."

"Did you question him about his interest in the demonic?"

"I did."

"And?" Father Gallagher gazed into her clear blue eyes, searching for an answer, perhaps a key for unlocking the Salabrini mystery.

"It was just a hobby, a diversion from his academic work."

"Just a hobby?"

"That's what he said. His easygoing, affable manner only disappeared when talking about Satan. I only witnessed that one time. But obviously, it made an impression on me."

"How so?"

"I can still see his face—somber, heavy, as if carrying a great burden. Oh, dear, I almost forgot."

"What?"

"On several occasions, he was accompanied by a dark-haired woman who always dressed in black, usually a long skirt and boots."

"A girlfriend?" Father leaned closer, not wanting to miss a word.

"I don't think so. I asked about her several times. He was tight-lipped, saying only that she shared his passion for the demonic."

"That's all?"

"That's all I could get out of him. Say, why all the fuss about Vincent?" Miss Hemmingway tilted her head, momentarily halting the subtle bobbing.

Father Gallagher hesitated, not wanting to reveal too much. "He's come to me for some help."

"What kind of help?" She gazed at the priest, frowning slightly, waiting for Father Gallagher to answer.

"Religious."

"Oh, I see. Personal."

"Yes."

"Dealing with the demonic?" She tilted her head back, arching her brows.

"Possibly." Father Gallagher picked up the check, smiled, and said "My treat."

The two parted, the priest with a few more pieces of the puzzle, Miss Mary Hemmingway concerned, perhaps worried about Vincent, but delighted with her trip down memory lane. She enjoyed talking with the priest. She was brought up Catholic but had shied away from religion after graduating from college. Her spiritual side was nourished by the theater, both on stage and as a director. Acting was her life. It was her raison d'être.

* * *

Immediately after phoning Professor Livingston, Father Gallagher rang Father O'Neil. He picked up after the third ring.

"Mike, Salabrini's story is building."

"What's up?"

"Professor Livingston sweetened the pot. He saw and raised Miss Hemmingway's bet. Not only did Dr. Salabrini do legit theater, he starred in B horror movies after leaving Thomas Aquinas College."

"He told you that?"

"No, but he was aware of his interest in the theater. He never saw him act, but knew he performed at the Rubicon."

"What's this about B horror movies?"

"Professor Livingston remembered Salabrini talking about a director, a Phil Martini, worked for a time in Santa Barbara. I lucked out. He now runs a small playhouse, but several years ago he produced and directed three B movies. Dr. Salabrini starred in all three, playing a mad scientist, a renege psychiatrist, and—get this—a priest who performs exorcisms."

"You're pulling my leg."

"My hand's resting on the Bible, my friend."

"What was the name of the demonic possession flick?"

"Hold on to your hat. *Satan's Return: Souls For Sale.* Definitely creepy."

"Have you seen it?"

Father Gallagher cleared his voice and said, "It's available on the Internet."

"What?"

"I did some checking. I think the support team should convene an emergency meeting."

"Set it up."

"I'll contact Mario."

"I'm late for a meeting. Got to go. I'm available after seven."

"I'll touch base as soon as I set it up."

Father Gallagher gazed out his office window as his mind flooded with images of Salabrini. He feared that Dr. Salabrini was consuming far too much of his time, interfering with his already packed schedule, causing him to miss two morning rounds at Lincoln Memorial Hospital. Father Gallagher knew he was acting more like detective than a parish priest.

He picked up his mail from his desk and smiled as he recognized personal mail from a couple of old friends. He froze when he saw the last letter. No return address, just a name—Dr. Vincent Salabrini. He stared at the envelope:

Support Team
Father Gallagher
St. Vincent's Catholic Church

There was no postmark, street address, or city. It had been hand-delivered. He grabbed a letter opener, sliced it open, and found a formal invitation.

You are cordially invited to a Midnight Mass,
St. Vincent's Catholic Church
Wednesday, March 17, 2010
Hosted by yours truly,
Dr. Vincent Salabrini
RSVP by prayer.

He first called Father O'Neil, leaving only a message. Next he phoned Dr. Mario Salazar, catching him between clients. He gave him the lowdown, mentioning only the highlights of Dr. Salabrini's career as a thespian, his conversation with Mary Hemmingway at the Busy Bee, and the three horror flicks. He capped off the phone call with Dr. Salabrini's formal invitation to a Midnight Mass. The psychiatrist's reaction was succinct but emphatic. "Wow!" They agreed to an emergency meeting of the support team. "Tonight at nine, my office," Father Gallagher said.

He reached Father O'Neil on his cell and shocked him with the latest. He heard him gasp as he read Salabrini's formal invitation.

"Tonight at nine, my place."

"I'm in."

* * *

The support team huddled in front of Father Gallagher's desk, riveted to his laptop. *Satan's Return* delivered a punch, not because of its artistic value, but due to the performance of the lead actor. Robert Malloy, played by Vincent Salabrini, was summoned by a terrified Hispanic family to exorcise their sixteen-year-old daughter. The flick ran the genre gamut, from spooky scenes to sexual exploitation. Emile, the possessed teenager, entered into a Faustian bargain, selling her soul for diabolical favors. She bargained away her soul for physical beauty and the power to read others' minds. Dr. Salabrini's performance was eerie, drawing the viewer into the fierce struggle to save Emile's soul.

Father Gallagher had picked out five scenes for them to watch, all featuring Salabrini's theatrical skills. "Well, what's the verdict?"

"Not as scary as *The Exorcist*, but haunting." Father O'Neil looked over at his close friend and said, "Scarily realistic portrayal of a priest."

"He wasn't acting. He was being himself." Father Gallagher turned and faced the psychiatrist. "Dr. Salazar, what's your take?"

"Please, I prefer Mario. He was convincing. It was a compelling performance. But was it theatrically or psychologically inspired?"

"There's a third possibility," added Father Gallagher. "Was it demonically inspired?'

The support team advanced hypotheses, argued, debated, and by midnight called it a night. Father Gallagher agreed to check out the production company, especially the producer and director, Phil Martini. The three parted, making room on their calendars for Wednesday, March 17. They all commented on the "*RSVP* by prayer," but Father Gallagher was the only one to notice that March 17 was St. Patrick's Day.

Chapter Fifteen

Alan looked about his study, staring at the colorful Post-its, realizing they were artifacts and philosophical dead ends. Alan was born again. He had dismantled his Weltanschauung, cleared the rubble, and was starting afresh. Only moments ago, while deep in meditation, a new portal opened, allowing him to sense reality, naked, unspoiled by words and symbols. After silencing his overactive mind, it hit him. His ego had been in the way. That was it, simple, to the point. Welling up from his subconscious, a pearl of wisdom appeared, long forgotten, but finally recognized. It now made sense. "The mystery of life is not a problem to be solved, but a reality to be experienced." As a young man, Van Der Leeuw's quote rang hollow, cute but meaningless. He smiled and then burst out laughing, thinking of the old Buddhist proverb: "When the student is ready, the teacher will appear." The Dutch philosopher pointed the way, but it was Doc, his friend and hypnotist, who made it possible.

He gazed at his tropical beauties, swimming effortlessly, frolicking in the aquarium. Before today, WIGGLY was a cryptic message, part of a dream of flying Post-its and dancing books. Now it boldly expressed the Truth: "When In God's Glorious Land Yield." Under the spell of his Weltanschauung, he had only understood the meaning of the words, abstract and detached from reality. He was no longer a voyeur, looking in from the outside. He was connected. In twenty minutes, he'd share his revelation with Doc.

Sitting in Doc's waiting room, he was vibrantly alive yet calm. He was there to thank his teacher. Alan rang the buzzer, just once, knowing he was five minutes early for his six o'clock. Doc, like clockwork, would make him wait. But for the first time, it didn't matter.

The office door opened, but no Doc.

"Sorry, Alan. Doc had an emergency." Gypsy smiled politely, a little shy, only having met Alan once before. Doc had phoned her just a half hour earlier and asked if she would greet him. He knew Alan would be disappointed and thought Gypsy's presence would soften the blow.

"What?" His eyes widened with surprise.

"One of his clients needed help."

"Who?" He fidgeted and shuffled his feet.

"He didn't say. Besides, that's confidential."

"I need to see him." Alan looked down at his feet, dejected. He was sitting on big news—he needed Doc.

"He told me he'd call you in the morning."

"Tell him I've big news."

"Sure thing." Gypsy closed and locked the door behind her and walked Alan to the parking lot.

"Say, when you're in the mood, come by for a reading," Gypsy suggested lightheartedly.

"I just might."

Gypsy cut their chat short, hustling to her parlor, not wanting to miss her seven o'clock tarot reading. Alan headed for a friend's house, needing to share his epiphany. Since his friend was not home, Alan drove up Topanga Canyon, pulling over at a roadside park overlooking the glittering lights of the San Fernando Valley. A full moon lit up the night sky, revealing an owl perched on a nearby pine. He locked his car, hiked five minutes down a deserted trail, and found a bench beneath an old oak tree. Inscribed on a brass plate on the back of the bench was, "This is for you, Tommy Little," followed by a quote from John Muir: "When one tugs at a single thing in nature, he finds it attached to the rest." He didn't know Tommy Little, but John Muir's insight was right on.

The bench provided a panoramic view of the valley, divided and subdivided by a grid of streets and boulevards, colorful lights outlining the human ingenuity. The patterns, geometrical, precise, and ruled by sharp edges, signified boundaries, blocks, districts, towns, and cities carved up for human convenience. Alan gazed down on Calabasas, Woodland Hills, and Tarzana, his hometown. He pinpointed his neighborhood amid the grid of lights, approximated the location of his home, knowing that his study, festooned with Post-its and crammed with volumes of philosophy books was just another box with sharp edges. The landscape was overrun with compartmentalized thinking.

The owl spotted earlier swooped down, landing on the upper branch of the sprawling oak. Its wide eyes, reflecting the light of the ascending moon, bore down on Alan, staring, probing, demanding his attention. Suddenly, it dropped from the branch, landing on a boulder a few feet above his head. Its stare intensified, eyes widened, hooting and animated, yet composed.

Alan counted backwards, breathing deeply. His mind was silent, at one with the here and now. The owl gracefully dropped down from the boulder, landing on the far corner of the bench. Alan gazed into its luminous eyes, losing himself, transfixed by their knowing power. He became one with the owl, seeing what it saw, freed from human concepts and language. He saw the WIGGLY world, direct, unfettered by human consciousness. He flew through the night, freed at last, caught up in the eternal now. He was home, immersed in the web of life, sensing reality.

When he awoke from his trance, the owl was gone, and the moon had crossed the heavens and was about to set. He glanced at his watch, shocked that it was midnight. He'd been there since eight, communing with nature, connecting with the real.

* * *

Doc was impressed. It was a first. He was not Catholic, not even religious, but passing through the massive cast-bronze doors sent chills down his spine. Towering three stories and weighing twenty-three metric tons, they welcomed the faithful. Tonight, Doc was on shaky grounds; he had an emergency meeting with Schizzy.

He thought it odd that visitors entered, not at the cathedral's center, but off to its side, proceeding down a long corridor on a kind of spiritual journey. After entering the nave of Our Lady of the Angels, he moved down the sloping marble floor, gazing up at the towering walls, adorned not with stained glass windows, but giant tapestries of saints looking east, toward the altar. The towering walls and sloping floors pushed him forward, as if propelled by some unseen force. A dozen or so worshippers had congregated toward the front of the cathedral, leaving the central area vacant, except for a man in a navy pea coat, waving and motioning Doc over.

"Thanks for coming. Is this your first time?"

"Yes. The cathedral's certainly not traditional, but impressive." Doc looked about, recognizing only a few of the 135 saints.

"It's a great monument, fitting for the powers to be." Schizzy opened his arms, gazing up at the saints.

"God?" Doc arched his eyebrows, checking out Schizzy, looking for any sign of distress.

"Doc, let's sit."

"What's up? Why the emergency?" Doc sat, still not yet used to Schizzy's transformation.

"I need your help."

"You got me here. Lay it on me." Doc leaned back, crossing his legs, trying to get a read on Salabrini.

"I need you to join me." Schizzy flashed Doc a dazzling smile.

"What?"

"I have an important performance on St. Patrick's Day."

"Performance?"

"I'm introducing a couple of priests and a psychiatrist to my new associates."

"Vincent, what are you talking about?" Schizzy's new demeanor was unsettling.

"I'm carrying out my commitment to *him*."

"Him?"

"I've regained my soul and a lot more."

"I'm lost." Doc shook his head. "Listen, Vincent, talk straight with me."

"I want you to hypnotize me before the performance. I need to concentrate my powers. Work with me, Doc."

"We've been through this. Besides, you stood me up. I can't rely on you."

Schizzy reached into his pocket and retrieved an invitation to the performance. "Be there a half hour early. You'll not be disappointed."

Doc watched in amazement as Vincent Salabrini hustled down the aisle, turning toward the back of the nave, moving quickly past the saints, laughing loudly, causing worshippers at the front of the cathedral to turn and stare. Schizzy's mocking laughter echoed off the walls, softened only by the absorbent material of the saint-dominated tapestry. He had to get to the bottom of this. He had a date on St. Patty's Day.

* * *

Doc phoned Alan early Saturday morning as he had promised, his emergency meeting with Schizzy still weighing heavily on his mind. Alan answered after the first ring, eager to share the news.

"Doc, we've got to talk."

"I've a couple of appointments this morning. How about noon?"

"Great. Can we meet at my place?"

"Sure, Alan. I'll see you at noon."

The morning sessions went well. He talked to Juan by phone and was delighted to hear about his winning streak—he was now eight and two as a starting pitcher. He'd only seen him pitch one game, but he looked impressive. Doc would love another crack at the big leagues, but that was impossible. He was also excited about a new client wanting to polish his salesmanship skills. After his last appointment, he drove over to Alan's, thinking about last night's dream. Perhaps nightmare was more accurate. It featured Schizzy standing at the front of a chapel, smiling, arms wide open, welcoming the faithful to his performance. Behind him appeared two angels bowing to a howling Satan. Loud shrieks erupted in the church, awakening Doc from his demon-haunted world. It was bad enough that Schizzy had taken over his waking life; now he had invaded his dreams.

"Good morning, Alan."

"Doc, it's 12:15. The morning is long gone."

"Sorry about last night. I had an emergency."

"Come on in. Let's use the study." Alan led the way, his walk and demeanor calmer than usual.

Doc looked about the study, amazed at its transformation. "Where are all the Post-its?"

"Gone, buried along with my Weltanschauung."

"The books have taken on a new look." Doc craned his neck, turning from side to side, surveying the wall-to-wall books."

"They've been rearranged. I had to make room for the latest edition."

"Oh? What's new?"

"In the middle row, across from my tropical beauties, a section on meditation, Buddhism, and self-hypnosis."

"You've found the truth?"

"Thanks to you, Doc. Our sessions have paved the way."

"How so?"

Alan launched into a blow-by-blow description of his radical transformation. He had a fresh perspective, a new way of being in the world. But his methodical habits, honed by many years working as an engineer, had not died. He was methodical, even with his new philosophy. He finished up, sharing with Doc last night's encounter with the owl.

"Doc, I found my bliss, wisdom, and freedom all rolled up in one." Alan smiled and added, "And many thanks to you."

"What was the key that opened the door?"

"It was me! I was the problem."

"The truth was in you?"

"The self was the problem. My ego was getting in the way."

"How so?" Doc glanced about the study. The only anchor still in place was the aquarium housing his guppies and neon tetras.

"I was haunted by ghosts from the past. Descartes' mind/body dualism is a mistake; the proverbial ghost in the machine is dead. We are not separate souls inhabiting material bodies. The idea of an ego inside a bag of skin is an illusion."

"You sound like Alan Watts." Doc was not philosophical, but he had been turned on to Alan Watts years ago while attending his first hypnotherapy conference.

"Yes, and Buddhism. I've shed the spotlight, and now use the floodlight."

"You discovered a bird's eye view of the world?"

"I am the world. My superficial self acted like a spotlight, paying attention only to this and that, discrete units, separated and distinct from all the rest. My Post-its spotlighted things. But there is another self, an ego that is more us than I. It works as a floodlight, illuminating the ground of being. The floodlight lit up the world, revealing an inner connectedness with being. Now I realize that the I, me, and self are illusions, and we are all tethered to everything else." Alan smiled and added, "I've returned home, perhaps only briefly, but I got a glimpse. I felt a oneness with being."

"You sound more like Gypsy than Alan Workman."

"Maybe I should get a reading from Gypsy."

"She's a good woman—honest, forthright, and loyal."

"Sounds like you approve of her."

"That and a lot more."

"Well, Doc, I just wanted to thank you. How about lunch? It's on me."

"You're on."

PART TWO:
Evil Comes in Pairs

Chapter Sixteen

Lieutenant Fred Thompson gazed at the bold lettering on the front window of a small shop on Reseda, four blocks north of Ventura Boulevard: Spiritual Advisor. In smaller script, Medium and Clairvoyant identified the kind of spiritual advice offered. He saw the storefront operation as a scam, preying on the superstitious and ignorant. But duty called; he needed facts, not mumbo jumbo. Murder was his game. He was there because of Leonard Eisenhower. He entered the small waiting room and rang the bell. While waiting, he checked out photos lining the walls, a collection of pictures showcasing Margaret Morley's satisfied customers.

"Lieutenant Thompson?"

The detective turned and smiled. "Yes. Miss Morley?"

"I prefer Mildred. Please, join me in the parlor."

"Thanks. Your mother's photos?"

"Yes. She had a thriving clientele."

"It looks like you're following in her footsteps."

"She was my mentor."

Mildred Morley had inherited the business after her mother's death. She had planned on becoming a psychologist but wanted to keep her mother's mission alive. Her tragic death had been devastating, both to her and her mother's clients. Taking over the practice had eased the pain, kept her mother's memory alive, and fulfilled her need to be close, even in death. Subconsciously Mildred felt responsible for her mother's death. Consciously she was conflicted, tormented by her emotions, not ready to face the truth. Guilt haunted her.

Detective Thompson blinked a couple of times, adjusting to the subdued lighting. The parlor was a mosaic of scarlet and gray, with red tones dominating the walls and tabletop. Pictures, individually lit, lined the walls, a tribute to legendary spiritualists from the past. The only person Lieutenant Thompson recognized was a black and white photo of Edgar Casey. His mother dabbled in the clairvoyant and was especially fond of the famous spiritualist. He was suddenly whisked back to his childhood, Friday evenings, huddled around the dining room table where he and his sister played with the Ouija board.

"Please, Lieutenant, have a seat."

"I recognize only Edgar Casey," the lieutenant said, gesturing to the illuminated pictures."

"A virtual who's who of the occult. Aleister Crowley, Dion Fortune, and Gerald Gardner were some of Mom's favorites."

"Has your mother's death adversely affected your practice?" Lieutenant Thompson didn't know how to refer to the services offered. Did she have clients, customers, or followers? To him they were suckers. He kept that to himself.

"I knew many of her clients. I would drop by after school, help Mom out, keep up the place."

"I see." Mildred reminded him of a younger Gypsy, reddish brown hair, full lips, and large green eyes. Her breathy voice and elegant manner conveyed a theatrical quality, certainly a plus for her business. She was definitely attractive, probably in her late twenties.

"You said on the phone you had a few questions about D-Day Investigations."

Lieutenant Thompson pulled some notes from his coat pocket, flipped a couple of pages, and said, "Do you know Leonard Eisenhower?"

Mildred looked down, lightly tapping her fingers on the cloth-covered table. "Yes."

"Did you hire him?"

"Yeah. Ike gave me peace of mind."

"Are you aware that he's been murdered?"

"I was shocked. It's made for some sleepless nights." She looked up, her eyes moist, on the verge of tears."

"Why were you in need of a private eye?"

"I'm scared. He's on the lam?"

"Who?"

"Vincent Valdez. He's escaped from Patton State." A tear trickled down her rosy cheeks. "Please excuse me." She dabbed her eyes with a tissue and said, "He ran down my mother. He's a coldblooded killer."

"You think he might come after you?"

"He's crazy. He blamed my mother for his problems."

"So you hired Leonard Eisenhower to track him?"

"Yes. Have you found him?"

"No, not yet."

Mildred looked the lieutenant in the eye and asked, "Did he murder Ike?"

"He's a suspect. How well did you know Vincent Valdez?"

"I met him several times. He saw my mother off and on for a year."

"Was he satisfied with your mother's spiritual advice?" Lieutenant Thomas flipped a page in his notebook and glanced up at Mildred.

"Yes, until their last two meetings. He lashed out at her, accused her of cavorting with the devil."

"What happened?"

"After two altercations, he stopped coming. Then he ran her down."

"Had your mother had any other confrontations with clients?"

"Not many. She was well liked."

The lieutenant flipped a page in his notes. "Wasn't she sued by a disgruntled client?"

"That was a scam." Mildred narrowed her eyes and glared at the lieutenant.

"She was sued by David Settle for blackmail, voodoo curses, and emotional threats."

"That was settled out of court. This is a tricky business. Some of our clients live on the edge."

"How did your mother meet Vincent Valdez?"

"He was referred by an old friend."

"A client?"

"No. A friend she met while attending church."

"Your mother was religious?"

"She was brought up Catholic. She occasionally attended Mass."

"Were you?"

"Not really. But I did attend Mass with Mom."

"Do you know the name of the person who referred Vincent Valdez to your mother?"

Mildred thought about it, then shook her head and said, "I don't recall."

"Where did you go to Mass?"

"Saint Vincent's on Ventura, near De Soto."

"If you see or hear from Vincent Valdez, call me."

"If I do, I'll dial 911."

Lieutenant Thompson stood and handed Mildred his card. "I'll be in touch."

He let himself out, sensing he had not gotten the full story. He'd see Mildred again; of that he was sure.

* * *

Father Gallagher welcomed the support team, eager to share the latest on Dr. Vincent Salabrini. Father Gallagher had spent yesterday afternoon in Santa Barbara interviewing Phil Martini, the producer and director of *Satan's Return*. Mass was over; it was almost ten, and the church was quiet, only a couple of faithful praying in the chapel. The trio, now christened Ghostbusters by Father Gallagher, huddled around his desk, finishing up another round of outtakes from Salabrini's three horror flicks. His dear friend and the shrink balked at the name Ghostbusters, thinking it too comical. Father O'Neil made references to the movie and Dr. Salazar showed a rare moment of humor by leaping to his feet, imitating Bill Murray chasing ghosts. But Father Gallagher lobbied hard, thinking a bit of levity wouldn't hurt. After a spirited debate punctuated with laughter and goofy charades, he got his way, leaving Dr. Salazar and Father O'Neil shaking their heads. Father Gallagher made some coffee and they finally got down to business.

"The more I learn about Dr. Salabrini, the creepier his flicks become." Father O'Neil looked at Father Gallagher. "Well, what did you find out?"

"Phil Martini discovered Dr. Salabrini at the Rubicon Theater in Ventura, caught his performance in *Who's Afraid of Virginia Woolf*, and was hooked. Vincent was perfect for a horror flick Martini had in the works."

"What did Salabrini bring to the table?" Dr. Mario Salazar stood, stretched, and moved about the priest's office, pausing in front of the bookcase and picking up the Bible handled just last week by Dr. Salabrini.

"Martini took in another couple of performances, befriended Dr. Salabrini and an *enigmatic friend*." Father Gallagher raised his eyebrows. "What?" Dr. Salazar closed the Bible and put it back on the shelf.

"Salabrini had a girlfriend. She shadowed him, was at every stage performance and movie take, decked out from head to toe in black."

"What's with the broad?" Dr. Salazar said bluntly.

"When asked about her, Dr. Salabrini said little, just that they had a passion for the dark side. When pressed, he'd shrug, and say 'We love demonology,' then quickly change the subject."

"Did Martini talk to the woman?" Father O'Neil pushed back his chair and joined Dr. Salazar, moving about the office, slowly shaking his head.

"Very little. When she spoke, which was not often, she was cordial, answering only direct questions, never initiating conversation. Her voice was so soft it was almost inaudible. But there's more. Martini said she was young, perhaps half his age." Father Gallagher looked up at the two Ghostbusters pacing about his cramped office. "The two of you pacing about is making me nervous."

"What's her name?" Dr. Salazar stopped, suddenly self-conscious about his nervous pacing.

"Morley."

"Is that her last name?" Father O'Neil asked.

"That's all he had. He didn't know if it was her first or last name." Father Gallagher was running out of answers.

"Doesn't ring a bell," Dr. Salazar said, taking his seat.

"What was Martini's take on Dr. Salabrini's movie career?" Father O'Neil said, pausing in front of the bookcase.

"A true find. He begged him to sign a contract for three more flicks. Salabrini turned him down. He had other commitments and was leaving for Italy in the fall."

"What about his teaching assignment?" Father O'Neil took his seat, still shaking his head in disbelief.

"He had terminated his tenure at Thomas Aquinas College and was on a quest." Father Gallagher grinned, and said, "He was doing research at the Vatican."

"What sort of research?" Dr. Salazar stroked his chin, gazing at the priests.

"He was researching the history of demonology." Father Gallagher opened his arms and said, "What else!"

"Just as I suspected," Dr. Salazar blurted. "His obsession is in charge."

Father O'Neil stood again, pacing about the office. "Does Martini have any personal information for Salabrini—addresses, phone numbers, social security number?"

"Here comes the strange part. He sent his checks to a P.O. box. He offered nothing personal, no address or phone number."

"What about a social security number?" Dr. Salazar said.

"That's all he had." Father Gallagher shook his head.

"We could track him with that. Maybe we should hire a private eye," Father O'Neil suggested.

"Perhaps." Father Gallagher stood and said, "I'm bushed."

"Yeah, let's call it a night. But one more thing," added Dr. Salazar, "what about the enigmatic chick? What's her name, Morley?"

"She's the missing link."

The Ghostbusters called it a night, looking forward to Saint Patrick's Day.

Chapter Seventeen

Lieutenant Thompson rang the bell, hoping to catch Gypsy. It was noon, so he had a chance; she was busiest in the late afternoon and early evening.

Gypsy answered, surprised at the detective's unannounced visit.

"Lieutenant Thompson, I wasn't expecting you."

"Sorry, I should have called. Could I have a moment?"

"Sure, please come in."

He took a seat at the center table, feeling more comfortable there than at Mildred Morley's parlor. He sensed that Margaret's daughter was holding back, not being upfront with him, perhaps protecting her deceased mother. Maybe Gypsy held the answer; she was, after all, Margaret Morley's friend and fellow traveler.

"What's up?" Gypsy said.

"Yesterday, I looked in on Mildred Morley."

"How is she? I've not seen her in months."

"She seems well. You two have a lot in common—same profession, even look alike."

"Oh, thanks for the compliment, but she's much younger." Gypsy looked down, blushed, suddenly feeling self-conscious.

"Not by much. But listen, I'm trying to tie together a few loose ends."

"How can I help?"

"Were you aware that she hired a private eye?" Lieutenant Thompson reached into his coat pocket and pulled out a notebook.

"No! What's happened?" Gypsy frowned.

"She's worried about Vincent Valdez."

"Have you found him?" Gypsy fidgeted in her seat, instantly upset at hearing his name.

"Not yet. How well did Margaret know Vincent Valdez?"

"What do you mean?" Gypsy was taken aback by his question.

"Was he more than a client?"

"He was a client for nearly a year. He'd come once a week for a month, disappear for weeks, and then reappear." Gypsy looked down, wringing her hands, visibly shaken.

"Was he a friend?"

"What?"

"Did Margaret and Vincent have a friendship, independent of her role as a spiritual advisor?"

"What are you getting at?"

"Did they see each other socially?"

"They weren't lovers!"

"Did they see each other, away from her parlor?"

"She enjoyed the theater, occasionally taking in a play."

"Margaret went to the theater with Vincent Valdez?"

"On several occasions. She mentioned that at one time he did a little acting, community playhouse, small theaters. They shared an interest in intimate theater."

"Intimate theater?"

"Y'know, small, maybe a couple of hundred seats."

"Did she say anything about his acting career?"

"No, just that it was fun getting out and having a good time."

"How long did this go on?"

"Not long."

"A year?"

"Maybe, I didn't keep track."

"More than a year?"

"I don't know." Gypsy's hand-wringing became more pronounced.

"Was she open about her personal life?"

"We talked. We were close."

"What did she tell you about Vincent Valdez?"

"At first, just girl talk. She loved going to the theater with him."

"Anything more personal?"

"Only later, when he accused her of siding with Satan."

"Go on." Lieutenant Thompson scribbled something in his notebook.

"During the weeks leading up to her death, she said he was acting weird, accusing her of playing along with the devil."

"That's all?"

"That's all! Isn't that enough?"

The lieutenant closed his notebook, stood, and said, "Thanks, you've been helpful. So, it's safe to say they knew each other for at least a year, maybe more."

"Yes." Gypsy stood, a bit wobbly on her feet, and slowly walked the lieutenant to the door.

"Thanks, I may need to see you again. You have my number. Call me if anything comes up."

Lieutenant Thompson left, knowing he'd call on Mildred Morley. She was definitely holding back.

* * *

Lieutenant Thompson hoped for better results the second time around. He knew it would be more confrontational. Once again, he gazed at the bold lettering on the window: Spiritual Advisor. He wasn't seeking spiritual advice; he needed answers. The waiting room was deserted, so he rang the bell.

Moments later, Mildred appeared, frowning at the detective, obviously not thrilled with his return visit. *Jeez, he was just here yesterday*, she thought as she tried to wipe the frown from her face.

"Lieutenant, what brings you back so soon?"

"Good morning. Could I have a few minutes?"

"Sure, but I thought we covered everything yesterday."

"You've been helpful, but something's come up. Can we talk in private?"

"I assure you we're quite alone, but sure, let's use the parlor."

Lieutenant Thompson followed her, noticing her provocative style; she was decked out from head to toe in black, wearing a sweater, long skirt, and boots. Large gold hoop earrings bobbled as she walked. He thought her gait was more strut than walk.

"Please, have a seat."

"Thanks." As he lowered his lanky frame, he flipped through his notebook, finding what he wanted.

"So, what's up?"

"Do you know Gypsy?"

"Maria Dumitrescu?" Mildred smiled as she used Gypsy's real name.

"Yes. We talked yesterday. She mentioned a couple of things I'd like to verify."

"How is Gypsy?"

"She's fine."

"My mother and her go way back."

"That's why I'm here."

"Please detective, let's get to the point." Mildred resented the detective poking around in her business. She wanted the cops to find Vincent Valdez, not invade her privacy.

"Gypsy told me that Vincent and your mother saw each other socially, that they were theater lovers."

"They weren't lovers," Mildred snapped defensively.

"I said theater lovers. Gypsy said they especially loved intimate theater."

"They took in a couple of plays. What's the big deal?"

"It sounded like that they took in more than a couple of plays. According to Gypsy, they saw each other for more than a year." The lieutenant threw down his notes and looked directly at Mildred, challenging her.

"He was a client, not a boyfriend."

"Perhaps, but they saw a lot of each other."

"Not so! They went to the theater. So what?" She glared at the detective, upset with his insinuations.

"How well did you know Vincent Valdez?"

"What?"

"Did you see much of him?"

"Only a couple of times."

"Did he come to the house to pick up your mother?"

"No! They met here. Mostly for sessions."

"Why did Vincent seek out your mother's services?"

"That's confidential. Mother didn't share what took place during her sessions."

"Didn't you say you learned the profession from her?"

"Yes, but we didn't abuse confidentiality."

"Were you ever alone with Vincent Valdez?"

"Never! I only saw him here, at the parlor."

Lieutenant Thompson sensed he'd hit a sensitive nerve. He was pushing her buttons and she was becoming increasingly hostile. "Did you ever see him act?"

"What?" Mildred's eyes widened, threatening to pop their sockets.

"He was an actor, didn't you know?"

"He was my mother's friend."

"It turned sour."

"What?"

"He ran her over, killing her with his Lincoln Town Car."

"Lieutenant, I've had enough."

"That's it for now. Don't leave town, I'll be back."

Lieutenant Thompson chuckled to himself as he left, leaving Mildred Morley stewing in her anger. She was beginning to crack, but he knew he had barely skimmed the surface. *Shit, she's not only protecting her mother, she's covering her own ass.*

* * *

Father Gallagher retrieved a large volume from the bookshelf and lugged it to his desk. It was an apropos find, one he had picked up at Wally's Emporium, his favorite bookstore. The cover said it all: *The History of Demonology: From A to Z.* He knew the Bible never referred to people as being literally possessed by demons; it did, however, make elliptical references, like "being demonized," the most frequent expression, and "having a Demon," where the person possessed the demon. His faith was rock solid, his commitment to the Church never regretted; his skeptical side surfaced, however, for all things demonic. Many of his friends believed that Satan was originally a good angel, made by God, but became evil through bad choices. Father Gallagher was not convinced, sensing that folklore had corrupted sound theology. *Evil exists, but it will never triumph. God is omnipotent, omniscient, and omni-benevolent, the foundation and reason for all that exists.* He would never let Satan win.

He pushed aside the volume on demonology and picked up a smaller book, *Malleus Maleficarum. Great title*, he thought. His Latin was good: "The Hammer of Witches." Before continuing where he left off, he flashed on a quote from C. S. Lewis: "The greatest trick the devil ever pulled was in convincing the world he didn't exist." He flipped open the smaller book and finished the second section, the one he plowed through last night. At the core of *Malleus Maleficarum* were three elements necessary for witchcraft: an evil-intentioned witch, the complicity of the devil, and the permission of God.

Most of the work was dreadfully dull, but flared with meanness when discussing the fairer sex. Misogyny ran rampant throughout the work, claiming women were weaker in faith, more carnal than men, and often disobedient, arousing the anger of the establishment. Since witches were accused of infanticide, cannibalism, and casting spells, many met a fiery death. For Father Gallagher, *Malleus Maleficarum* was insidious propaganda, providing a scapegoat for those who wanted to control women and the Church. He threw the book on his desk, wondering if Satan was working through Dr. Vincent Salabrini. He was also puzzled about Martini's recollection of the enigmatic woman, the missing link known only as Morley. Since St. Patrick's Day was just a week away, he had more detective work to do.

Chapter Eighteen

The towering cross shone brightly, dwarfing the parishioners as they entered Saint Vincent's Parish. It was St. Patrick's Day, the evening of "The Performance." Father Gallagher's loyal followers graced the front half of the church, dutifully exercising their faith, comforted by his lyrical tone as he carried out the Penitential Rite. *"Mea culpa, mea culpa, mea maxima culpa"* echoed off the tapestry-draped walls. The saints appeared to come alive as they looked down from either side of the chapel, sanctioning the Mass, providing historical context for the devout.

Toward the back of the sanctuary, a small but diverse group of observers had gathered, nervous and uncertain about tonight's service. They were motivated by curiosity, formally invited by the enigmatic Dr. Vincent Salabrini. The worshipers, however, were unaware of "The Performance," there only for the Eucharist. They sought comfort; they were there to celebrate the consecration, the moment Father Gallagher transformed the bread and wine into the body and blood of Christ.

Tension built as the Ghostbusters looked on, hoping for a show, while Doc and Gypsy sat several rows back. Doc was curious, Gypsy fearful, both unaware of the Ghostbusters.

Father O'Neil leaned over and whispered to Dr. Mario Salazar, "Five dollars says he won't show."

"He might pull the same stunt, wait till after the Mass," Dr. Salazar whispered.

"He wants an audience." Father O'Neil smiled as he watched his good friend at the altar. It had been a long time since he had seen him in action.

The Liturgy of the Word and the Liturgy of the Eucharist filled the chapel, ending with the parishioners kneeling in readiness, patiently waiting the moment when Jesus appeared, spiritually present on the altar.

Before Father Gallagher uttered the closing words, "The Mass has ended! Go in peace to love and serve the Lord!" a man dressed in a navy pea coat and dark blue beret dashed toward the priest, stopping abruptly before the altar. He turned and faced the worshippers. Dr. Vincent Salabrini opened his arms and spoke in a deep, rumbling voice, "I have good news. You will be saved. It is I, Satan, who will deliver you from sin. I'm the one, the only one. Blessed are those who follow me."

The lights in the chapel flickered, and then went out. Thunder rumbled, and the ceiling lit up, temporarily blinding the worshippers. The stained glass windows glowed eerily while the smaller windows, high above the tapestry, showered the faithful with flashes of light.

Moments later, the interior lights came back on, showing shocked parishioners staring in disbelief. Father Gallagher stood before the faithful, eyes glazed over, stunned. Dr. Vincent Salabrini had vanished, leaving chaos in his wake.

"Father Gallagher, what happened? Who was that?" a middle-aged man in the first pew cried out.

The faithful erupted, shouting questions as the high-pitched cries of women and children rippled through the sanctuary. Dr. Mario Salazar rushed toward Father Gallagher, put an arm around his shoulders, and addressed the congregation.

"Please be calm. It was a power outage. The lightning struck close by. Our visitor was evidently frightened. I'm a psychiatrist. I think he's in need of medical help. Please go in peace. All is well with the church."

Doc and Gypsy sat in stunned silence, mesmerized by the theatrics. Gypsy suddenly threw her arms around Doc, whimpering. "Dear God, what happened?"

Doc hugged her, whispering, "He's gone."

"Please, Doc, let's go."

"Vincent showed."

"Haven't you had enough of him?"

"For tonight, yes!"

"He's possessed," Gypsy said as she pulled Doc to his feet and led the way out of Saint Vincent's.

After answering a barrage of questions, the Ghostbusters retired to Father Gallagher's office.

"Father Gallagher, you held up well. The parishioners were freaking out," Dr. Salazar said, collapsing into the nearest chair.

"Thanks for the support. Without the two of you, I'd have lost it." Father Gallagher stepped behind his desk and slowly took a seat.

Father O'Neil closed his cell phone and said, "I couldn't get through to Edison, so I touched base with Barry at the *Daily News*. Edison reps confirmed power failures in the area due to lightning strikes."

"The timing couldn't have been better for Salabrini," Dr. Salazar commented as he checked for messages on his cell.

"The lightning strike, was it natural or supernatural?" Father Gallagher's voice was strained, his face ashen.

"Wow, old friend, the evening's events have gotten to you." Father O'Neil rounded the desk and patted his friend on the shoulder.

"Salabrini's voice gave me the creeps," Dr. Salazar said.

"It was theatrical." Father O'Neil walked to the bookcase and picked up a Bible.

"It was demonic," Father Gallagher said. "Let's pray."

The Ghostbusters ended the evening with a prayer. They also agreed to hire a private eye.

* * *

Doc spent a sleepless night, doing his best to console Gypsy. She fell asleep at three, but Doc tossed and turned until six. He left a note promising to check in on her after lunch. After his third client, just before noon, his phone rang.

"How'd you like the show?"

"Who is this?"

"Come on, Doc, who else." The caller's voice suddenly deepened and amplified, echoing in Doc's ears. It was the same voice that had traumatized the worshipers at St. Vincent's.

Doc hesitated and then said, "What do you want?"

"I have a proposition."

Doc cleared his throat, paralyzed by the haunting tone. "What is it?"

"Meet me at Our Lady of the Angels tonight, nine sharp. Come alone." Vincent Salabrini hung up before Doc could reply. He sat in stunned silence, frightened but knowing he would show.

He looked in on Gypsy but said nothing about the morning call and Salabrini's proposed meeting. Curiosity got the best of him; he wanted another look at Vincent; he wanted to hear his proposition. It was all terribly, horribly irresistible. He wasn't a private eye, surely not a cop, not even an amateur sleuth. But Vincent Salabrini had pushed his button.

Chapter Nineteen

A solitary figure sat stoically in the midst of lit candles and burning incense, meditating, mesmerized by the flickering shadows playing hide and seek on the barren walls. Clouds of smoke hung in the air, softened by the pleasant aroma of jasmine. His head swayed rhythmically, responding to the structured sounds of his favorite Gregorian chant. He sat patiently, trance-like, waiting for a sign. He needed help.

"Vincent." A rumbling voice filled the spacious room in the second-story loft above an abandoned hardware store, only blocks from St. Vincent Parish. "I have come."

Vincent smiled and said, "I knew you would not forsake me."

"I need your help." The voice resonated in the barren room, rumbling, nearly silencing the Gregorian chant.

"Yes, Master, I'm here to serve you." Vincent slid from the overstuffed chair, kneeling in supplication.

"I need a field general." The disembodied voice echoed off the walls, eerie, otherworldly.

"Master, I'm not a military man."

"No, my son, I need you to lead a group of disciples."

"Disciples?"

"I want you to recruit an inner circle, loyal to the dark side. Doc's a good start. Spread the good news."

"The good news?"

"I have returned. I will prevail. I will win over mankind."

"Your wish is my command." Vincent closed his eyes, kneeling, committed to his mission.

"Begin immediately. I'll be with you every step."

The voice was gone. Vincent stood slowly, wobbling on unsteady legs, and then collapsed back on the sofa. He blinked, searching through the smoked-filled room for the source of the voice, aware only of the incense and flickering candlelight. The recorded chant had ended, leaving him to his thoughts.

He was not alone. He had not been forsaken. Yes, it was true, friends had deserted him, strangers stared, and the man, the establishment, misunderstood him, thinking him crazy. Little did they know he had the upper hand. Vincent smiled, feeling a surge of strength. *He has my back. He will have the last word.*

Vincent fumbled about the end table, seeking his favorite past time. He found the hand-rolled joint, lit it, and inhaled deeply. Mary Jane wasn't a saint, but she delivered the goods. He'd secretly leaned on her for support, especially during trying times. Publicly, he opted for red wine, preferably cabernet sauvignon, but privately, he savored the euphoria of weed.

He was invisible, so he thought, tucked away in the sparsely furnished, deserted loft. The downstairs hardware store had been put out of business by the big warehouse chains and the sagging economy. He broke in last month and found the electricity still on, necessary for security and the downstairs lights. The previous owner was kind enough to leave behind some creature comforts—a smattering of furniture, a fridge, and an old mattress. He lived like a monk, and that suited him just fine.

No one had come to check on the place, leaving him to come and go as he pleased, all free of charge. His oasis was strategically placed, close to Saint Vincent's Parish, Doc and Gypsy, and his P.O. box, his lifesaver—a repository of paper power, driver's licenses, social security numbers, and an ample supply of cash. Vincent was one alias; he had more. Now backed by Satan, he was eager to take on his new mission.

The dope had kicked in, sending him into a warm and fuzzy place. He flashed on his childhood, his superstitious mother and alcoholic father. His mother was old school; she liked her theology black and white, and divided the world into two warring camps, the good guys and the bad guys. Every room in his childhood home had a saint standing guard, warding off evil spirits. For her, the supernatural world was real, everything else a mere shadow. Later, while in college, he discovered Plato. One day, he called his mom a Platonist; she thought it a curse and forbade him from mentioning the word ever again.

His father had always been unavailable; even when he was at home, he was a functional drunk, staving off the slings and arrows of misfortune with Neil Diamond's "Cracklin' Rosie." Vincent broke into song now, singing aloud the lyrics he so clearly remembered: "You're a store-bought woman, but you make me sing like a guitar hummin'." That was his dad in a nutshell. He loved his booze more than the family.

Vincent fired up his boom box, once again savoring the sounds of his favorite Gregorian chant, "Crux Fidelis." He felt empowered, excited about putting together the inner circle. Satan would return, and *he* would have his disciples. He popped an upper, needing a burst of energy for his date with Doc. *These are times that try men's souls*, he thought as he prepared for tonight's encounter. But I'm not alone. I have two brothers, one supernatural, and one family.

* * *

It was a dicey proposition, best suited for an adrenalin junkie. Doc wrestled with it, turning it over in his mind, obsessing for hours, at one point deciding that the best option was to run like hell. But he couldn't; he was hooked. He gazed up at the massive bronze doors at the cathedral's entrance, covered with traditional Catholic symbols. He recognized a Japanese character for heaven and a Chinese symbol of harmony. He hoped it was a good omen.

Doc walked the long corridor, passing traditional and modern art and narrow chapels. Emerging into the nave, he instantly spotted Vincent, same pea coat and beret, bowing in supplication near the front of the cathedral. He was to one side, separated from a couple of dozen worshipers. As Doc inched his way to the front of the cathedral, his mind raced, questioning the wisdom of his decision to meet with Vincent. *This is crazy*, he thought, rounding the pew where Vincent sat, head down, mumbling something in Latin.

"Good evening." Doc peered down at his former client, still unsure of why he was there.

Vincent looked up, eyes still closed, finishing his soliloquy. After a moment of silence, he slowly opened his eyes and said, *"Carpe noctem."*

"What?" Doc blurted.

"Seize the night."

Doc hesitated and then asked, "What's your proposition?"

"In good time. Please, join me in prayer."

"This might be the place, but it's not the time." Doc frowned, not wanting to play games.

"Please, kneel with me. I have good news."

He didn't want to make a scene or have an argument, so he joined Vincent, kneeling, holding his arms prayer-like.

"I've been instructed to enlist you in *The Cause*."

"*The cause!* What cause?"

"Satan has singled you out to head up the apostles."

"What apostles?"

"That's the proposition. *He* needs twelve loyal minions to join The Cause, spread the good word, herald the coming of Satan."

"What's that got to do with me?" Doc's voice wavered.

"You've been chosen. It's your destiny." Vincent's voice became darker and breathy.

"My destiny?" Doc panicked, falling prey to Vincent's theatrics. He was scared, sensing they were not alone.

"Start with Gypsy and then spread out, enlisting only those dedicated to the *Truth*."

"Gypsy? She'll run to the cops."

"She loves you; she'll do anything for you. Go, gather the disciples, for we shall inherit everlasting life."

Vincent stood, smoothed his pea coat, straightened his beret, smiled, and said, "Meet me Friday night, your office. Bring a new recruit." He turned, moving quickly down the aisle and then out the back of the cathedral. Doc got to his feet, dazed and unable to shake the feeling that someone was watching him. He dashed out of Our Lady, stunned, scared, and confused. He was being absorbed into Schizzy's world. He was terrified.

* * *

Doc desperately needed someone to talk to, someone perceptive and open to the unusual. Gypsy would freak, Waldo would blow him off, and Gwen would think he had lost his mind, but Alan Workman owed him. On his way back to the Valley, Doc phoned Alan and found him receptive to the late-hour visit. He was in his study by ten, gazing at the tropical beauties frolicking in the aquarium. He was hyper, rattled by Vincent's proposition.

"Here, I think you need this." Alan handed him a Bud Light and joined him, savoring his first beer in a month.

"Can you keep a secret?"

"Sure, Doc. What's up?"

"I don't quite know where to start."

"Take a deep breath. It's my turn to listen." Alan leaned back, tugging on his beer, enjoying the role reversal.

"Remember me talking about Vincent Salabrini?"

"Yeah, your seven o'clock. Isn't he the one who freaked out Gypsy?"

"Yeah, he's the one. I refer to him as Schizzy."

"Why?"

Doc gulped some beer and launched into a half-hour account of his dealings with Vincent. He was not used to talking fast, but the words literally flew out of his mouth, erupting into a dizzying depiction of either the devil incarnate or insanity.

"Jeez, Doc, I thought I was eccentric. But this beats all." Alan had finished his beer and fetched two more. "You call him Schizzy; so you think he's crazy?"

"At first, yes. But now, I don't know."

"You think he's for real?"

"He not only wants me to be a disciple, he wants me to recruit others."

"Don't tell me he wants twelve." Alan laughed, then quickly stifled it.

"Bingo. He said Satan is making a comeback."

"Are you falling for this?"

"No! But I could use your help."

"How's that?"

"I'll set up a meeting so you can meet him.'

"What?"

"Yeah, I need your take on him."

"Doc, he sounds crazy."

"Yeah, when I describe him. But I want you to experience him. Remember your transformation and the bit about the mystery of life is not a problem to be solved."

"Yeah, yeah. It's a reality to be experienced." Alan smiled and said, "I'm in. Besides, I owe you."

"Thanks. Meet me Friday at seven, my office."

"Is Vincent coming?" Alan's eyes widened, surprised how quickly he got sucked into Doc's problem.

"He wants to see my first recruit."

"Doc, this is crazy."

"We'll know more Friday night."

Chapter Twenty

Father Gallagher stared at a headline in the California section of the *LA Times*, not believing his own eyes—St. Vincent's Parish: "The Devil's in the Detail."

The more he read, the angrier he got. The short article featured a photo of the church, and a witty but sober account of Dr. Salabrini's show. The author of the piece, a member of the parish church, attended Mass the night of Vincent's theatrics. His take was satirical, describing the lightning strike, power outage, and demonic show as alarming, perhaps spooky, but in reality, just another example of our inability to take care of the homeless and disabled. The newspaper account came down on the side of insanity; the devil had been reduced to mental illness. The closing paragraph pleaded for more funds and facilities for the mentally ill.

After touching base with Father O'Neil and Dr. Salazar, he made a noon appointment with Shamrock Investigations. It was time for professional assistance. The office was on Topanga Canyon, a mere ten minutes from the church.

The waiting room was empty, and no one was at the front desk, so he rang the bell.

A voice boomed from a backroom, "I'll be right there."

Father Gallagher glanced about the small reception area, checking out a collection of photos showing the San Fernando Valley, now and then. The oldest and dearest structure, of course, was the San Fernando Mission. It was his favorite, founded in 1797, and still magnificent after enduring a half dozen restorations.

"Father Gallagher, sorry for the delay. The secretary is at lunch. I'm William Preston; we talked on the phone earlier."

"Thanks for meeting me at such short notice." As they shook hands, Father Gallagher glanced at the photos lining the walls. "I love your collection."

"Thanks, my father's a professional photographer. Please, come on back." William was youthful, mid-thirties, and wore his sandy hair long, just above his shoulders. With piercing blue eyes, he looked like one of the quintessential hunks adorning the front cover of flashy romance novels. He was definitely a lady-killer.

His office hummed with energy, two computers, TV, fax machine, photocopier, two cell phones, and a land phone. He was definitely plugged in. "Coffee?" William pointed to a deluxe coffee brewer, probably a Starbucks clone.

"No thanks. I've had my limit."

"Please, have a seat."

The priest sat, not exactly comfortable about hiring a private eye. He was a man of the cloth, not used to cloak and dagger. Since meeting Vincent, his life had been consumed by detective work.

"Tell me more about your problem." William leaned back, his blue eyes sparkling, eager for a new challenge.

"My parish has been targeted."

"How so?"

Father Gallagher took a deep breath and began from the beginning. He told of his first encounter with Vincent, and then his office visits, seizure, and transformation in appearance. He talked about his trip to Thomas Aquinas College, Vincent's stage and movie background, his penchant for costumes, his reputation as a trickster and hypnotist, and "The Performance." He admitted that the case was becoming too big for the Ghostbusters.

"Your buddies refer to themselves as Ghostbusters?" The private eye grinned, desperately trying not to laugh.

"It was my idea. I thought a touch of levity might be helpful. Now I don't know." Father Gallagher arched his brows and shrugged.

"Humor can be a virtue. So, you want me to find him?"

"Yes. Where he lives, his true identification, family background, early schooling, fingerprints, the whole works. We especially want to know his mental health history."

"We have several investigators, but this is intriguing. I'll take up your case right away."

"Oh, I have his social security number."

"Excellent."

Father Gallagher ended the meeting with a thousand-dollar retainer, courtesy of Dr. Salazar, a handshake, and a blessing. The blessing was appreciated. William was Catholic.

* * *

"Father Gallagher, while you were out you got a phone call from the archdiocese. It's important. Got to run." His secretary handed him a name, phone number, and was gone before he could say anything.

Alice Whitmore was always in a hurry. She volunteered her time ten hours a week, Monday, Wednesday, and Friday, rain or shine. She was efficient, walked fast, talked fast, and frowned on laziness. She'd more than once bailed him out of an administrative snag. Her only flaw was that she never laughed.

He dialed, puzzled. The name and number didn't register.

"Richard Spencer, how may I help you?"

"Father Gallagher. My secretary just handed me the message."

"Thanks for being so prompt. Cardinal McMahon would like to see you."

"Oh, I hope I'm not in trouble."

"It's regarding an article in the *LA Times*. Are you free at four?"

"Today?"

"Yes. A meeting has been canceled. He's anxious to see you."

"Okay. I'll be there at four, but where?"

"In his office. Thanks again for your punctuality." Richard had hung up before Father Gallagher could respond.

Father Gallagher finished up some paperwork and was at Our Lady of the Angels twenty minutes early. He tried to reach Father O'Neil by phone but had no luck. So he dropped by his office and found the door open, his best friend's feet propped up on his desk, reading the sports section of the paper.

"Lakers lost," Father Gallagher said, shaking his head. "That's two in a row."

His friend looked up, grinned, and said, "What brings you here?"

"I got a call from Richard Spencer. Know him?"

"Yeah, he works in Cardinal McMahon's office."

"He wants to see me."

"Richard?"

"No. Cardinal McMahon."

"What?" Father O'Neil took his feet off his desk, put the paper down, and sat up straight.

"It has something to do with the *LA Times* article."

"The cardinal saw it?"

"How could he miss it?" Father Gallagher took a seat and added, "The plot thickens."

"Yeah, the devil's in the details. Now we'll have the cardinal looking over our shoulder."

"Have you heard any rumors?" Father Gallagher glanced at a photo on the corner of his friend's desk. It was the two of them hamming it up on a retreat years ago. They were both slimmer and had no gray hair.

"Nada."

"Well, wish me well."

Father O'Neil could see that his friend was nervous, so he changed the subject to sports until it was time for him to leave. At 3:50, Father Gallagher headed for Cardinal McMahon's office, hoping he wouldn't have to spill the beans.

"Father Gallagher here to see Cardinal McMahon."

A young priest, with short hair and a trimmed beard, looked up and smiled. "The cardinal will be here any moment. Please have a seat."

The reception area was three times the size of Father Gallagher's office at Saint Vincent's. Exquisite photos of all twenty-one California missions were artfully framed and arranged on three walls, from San Diego de Alcata, to San Francisco Solano. The San Fernando Mission was still his favorite.

"Cardinal McMahon will see you now." Father Spencer, knocked, waited a moment, and then opened the door to the cardinal's inner office.

Father Gallagher took a deep breath, entered the spacious office, confidently greeting His Eminence with a hearty handshake. "It's a pleasure to see you again."

"Please, Father, have a seat. Would you like something to drink?"

"No thanks. I love the photos in the outer office."

"It's a grand collection. I remember reading about the missions as a kid in grade school. They're one of the reasons I'm here. I wrote a paper on the Santa Barbara Mission, fourth grade." The cardinal smiled, eyes twinkling as he thought about his youth.

"What a coincidence. I did a book report on the Santa Barbara Mission." Father Gallagher appreciated the small talk, knowing it would soon end.

"Father Gallagher, the *LA Times* article about Saint Vincent's caught my attention. A rather sensationalistic headline, don't you think?"

"The devil's in the detail?"

"Yes. The article sloughed off the theatrical intrusion, saying it reflected badly on how society treats the mentally ill. What was your take on the intruder?"

"In what way?"

"Was it a case of an unbalanced man frightened by a thunderstorm?" Cardinal McMahon leaned forward, his eyes narrowed, intensely gazing at Father Gallagher. "Or is there more to the story?"

Father Gallagher hesitated, visualizing Vincent, the seizure, and "The Performance," before answering. "I must qualify my answer, for the incident upset me. I might be too close to the case to be objective."

"Father, all I want is the truth, of course, as you see it." He leaned forward, about as far as he could without coming out of his chair.

"It was not my first encounter with Dr. Vincent Salabrini."

"Dr. Salabrini? I've heard nothing about him being a doctor."

"He first approached me three weeks ago, after a weekday Mass. He claimed he was being visited by demons, had sold his soul to Satan."

"Why didn't you report this?" The fifty-eight-year-old Cardinal frowned, sending waves of wrinkles upward across his forehead.

"It was late, and I was tired, not thinking clearly. I met with him next afternoon."

"And?" Cardinal McMahon sat back again, eyes boring into Father Gallagher, making him feel as if he were being cross-examined.

"At first he appeared calm. We chatted for a while. Then it happened."

"What happened?"

"A cloud momentarily obscured the sunlight, darkening my office. A raven slammed into the window, and the room chilled. I could see Vincent's breath. Then he blurted, '*He's* here.'"

"Who?"

"The devil! But that's not all. His eyes lost focus, and his body started twitching, escalating into a full-blown attack."

"An epileptic attack?"

"Maybe, I don't know. I revived him, and as soon as he regained his strength, he disappeared."

"Have you followed up on him?"

"Yes. I later found out he taught at Thomas Aquinas College."

"I know the college well."

"Well, he's no longer there."

By this time, Father Gallagher was in too deep to back out. For the next thirty minutes, the cardinal was held spellbound by the demonic tale.

Before leaving, Cardinal McMahon sat up a meeting for seven, Friday night. He wanted to talk to the Ghostbusters. The way he said it, it was more a command than a request. Father Gallagher felt the worst was about to come. He dropped by Father O'Neil's office, but he was out, so he called and left a message on his mobile phone.

On the drive back to St. Vincent's, he wondered why the cardinal wanted to get involved. His plate was full, fending off the explosive sexual abuse crisis, overseeing a $660 million payout to victims, and waging a legal campaign to keep sensitive documents secret. He was tenacious. He had chosen to fight the release of priests' files all the way to the U.S. Supreme Court. Father Gallagher didn't want to get on the wrong side of Cardinal McMahon.

Chapter Twenty-One

Alan arrived at Doc's office ten minutes early, happy to help him out, curious but skeptical.

"Will he show?" Alan asked as he flipped through a book on hypnosis, recognizing a technique he now employed. Self-hypnosis had opened new worlds, allowing him to mellow and appreciate his senses. He was no longer boxed in by rigid categories and fixed formulas.

"He was insistent. He'll show." Doc glanced at his antique clock. It was seven sharp.

The buzzer sounded, causing Alan to flinch. "Jeez, Doc, that's loud."

"He's here." Doc walked slowly toward his office door. "Keep your cool and let him run the show."

The show began immediately, Vincent taking center stage, showing off his latest attire. Gone were the pea coat and beret, replaced by gray slacks, a navy blue blazer, a white shirt, and a bold red tie. A gray fedora and dark glasses shadowed his face. The cane was back, but he had no discernable limp.

"Good evening, gentleman. Doc, join your friend on the sofa. I'll try out your chair."

Doc moved to the sofa, gazing at Vincent, searching for an appropriate greeting. "I like your attire. Very business-like."

"Indeed, we've important business tonight. Doc, introduce me to your friend."

"Vincent, it's my pleasure to introduce you to Alan Workman. Alan, Vincent Salabrini."

Alan stood and extended his hand.

"We'll shake later, after we agree on the terms of the deal." Vincent smiled, waved his hand for Alan to sit, and commandeered Doc's favorite chair. It was Vincent who would roll about, looking for the best perspective. Important decisions had to be made.

"Doc, I'm surprised. I was expecting Gypsy."

"She'd run to the cops."

"Maybe I'll pay her a visit." Vincent flashed Doc a wicked grin. "But now back to business. We've a deal in the works."

"What deal?" Doc blurted.

"All in good time. Please, Alan, tell me about yourself. What's your line of work?" Vincent rolled forward, just a few inches, leaning on his dark black cane.

"I'm an engineer by profession."

"Good. We need clear-thinking men, rational, logical, to the point. Any hobbies?"

"I'm an amateur philosopher of sorts."

"A philosopher, excellent. We also need men of vision. I've come bearing good news. *He* wants twelve disciples by the new year." Vincent moved back and played with the brim of his fedora. "*He* has a message for us."

"He, who's *he?*" Alan said, arching his brows.

Vincent stood, moved to Doc's bookcase, and performed a quick half turn, raising his arms overhead and clutching the black cane. "I have good news." A deep rumbling voice filled Doc's office, loud and terrifying. Suddenly it changed, morphing into that breathy, Darth Vader tone. "*I'm* here to offer you everlasting life. Join me and reap the benefits. *I* now grant you the power to change the world. Give me your soul, and you will inherit the world."

Alan and Doc were speechless, transfixed by Vincent's theatrics. The breathy voice, deep and resonating, echoed off the walls. Doc's certificates jumped and slid, and his clock stopped at twelve past seven.

Doc struggled to find an appropriate response, and finally said, "Who's making the offer?"

The booming voice answered, coming from everywhere, "It is *I*, Lucifer, king of kings. Alan, Doc, shall we shake on it?"

Alan cleared his throat and asked, "What are the terms of the deal?" His question lacked force, his voice weak and cracking.

"Your allegiance and your soul. No more and no less." The volume lowered, but the tone was still otherworldly.

"What's in it for me?" Alan squirmed on the sofa, rattled by the eerie voice and Vincent's stare.

"You'll gain everything, mental and physical power, the inside track to the *Truth*, and *eternity*." Vincent approached the two men, still seated, mesmerized and unsure. "Is it a deal?"

Silence descended on the trio as Vincent stared at Alan. Time seemed to stand still. The new recruit was paralyzed, not by fear or infirmity, but by the solemnity of the moment. Alan impulsively stood, offering his hand, driven by an internal force. Vincent's hand was ice cold, his stare diabolical. They shook on the deal before Alan realized what had happened. Time had stopped, leaving Alan suspended in a netherworld, alien, spooky, yet irresistible. He felt like something had invaded him.

Doc followed suit, shocked at the icy feel of Vincent's handshake. He was conflicted, feeling foolish yet curious.

"I'll be back, next Friday, same time. Bring a new recruit."

Vincent moved quickly to the door and glanced back before leaving. "You've been granted new powers. I'll be watching."

Doc and Alan stared at one another after the door closed.

"What do you think?" Doc said, collapsing on the sofa.

"Rationally, I've no answer. His presence sucked me in from the start. I felt controlled, powerless to question," Alan answered, joining Doc, feeling wobbly.

"Rationally speaking, it's crazy. But there's nothing rational about Vincent. What's your take on the voice?" Doc said.

Alan took a deep breath and said, "Haunting and compelling. It seemed to come from everywhere, bouncing off the walls. If that was Vincent, alone, with no assistance, hell, he deserves a *fucking* Oscar."

Doc stood, shaking his head, and said, "As far as I know, he's no ventriloquist."

"Yeah," Alan said, standing, pacing back and forth. "Whatever the source, something powerful is at work here."

"Well, what's the verdict—insane or evil?" Doc slid into his favorite chair and rolled back, slamming into his desk.

Alan grinned, stroked his chin, and said, "My rational side says he's crazy. My emotional side says otherwise."

"Evil?" Doc frowned.

"Diabolical!" Alan shouted. Vincent had struck a sensitive nerve. Alan was born again, trusting his senses.

"You up for next Friday?" Doc said.

"I'll be here. But, Doc, I feel like I've been hypnotized."

* * *

Across town, just over the Santa Monica Mountains, another meeting was in full swing. Cardinal Roger McMahon's curiosity about the *LA Times* article and the subsequent discussion with Father Gallagher, brought the Ghostbusters to his office. The two priests and the psychiatrist had just arrived and were checking out the photos of the California Missions when the cardinal opened his office door.

"Gentlemen, thanks for being on time. Please, come in."

"Good evening," the three men said in unison, causing the cardinal to chuckle.

The chairs were arranged in a tight semicircle, with Father Gallagher in the middle, flanked by Father O'Neil and Dr. Salazar. It was not only a first for the Ghostbusters, it was a first for Cardinal McMahon. The most influential priest west of the Mississippi was not accustomed to chasing ghosts. His soft-spoken demeanor didn't accurately reveal the man. Under the calm exterior, near to the surface, was a cool, calculating politician accustomed to controversy and obsessed with power. He relished presiding over four million Catholics, making his archdiocese the largest in the United States. Nothing happened on his turf without his blessing.

"I know Fathers Gallagher and O'Neil, but I haven't had the pleasure of meeting you, Dr. Salazar." The cardinal smiled, extended his hand, and warmly greeted the psychiatrist. "Although, I've read a couple of your articles on demonic possession."

"Pleased to meet you. I hope my articles were helpful." Dr. Salazar smiled, appreciating the cardinal's firm handshake; vice-like grips and limp handshakes were a turn off.

"Gentlemen, my curiosity has morphed into concern by recent events at St. Vincent's. Father Gallagher has briefed me, but I need more facts. Dr. Salazar, what's your medical opinion about Dr. Vincent Salabrini's behavior?"

"My direct observations are limited—one in Father Gallagher's office and the one reported in the *Times*."

"Based on the two, what's your take?" The cardinal picked up a ballpoint pen, toying with it, eyes narrowed, quickly adopting the role of an inquisitor.

Dr. Salazar launched into a detailed account of Dr. Salabrini's behavior, the haunting, breathy voice and polished theatrics. His description was thorough, reflecting his medical training.

"Excellent description. Fathers Gallagher and O'Neil, did he leave anything out?"

The two priests shook their heads, answering in unison, "No, sir."

The cardinal laughed and said, "Much more of this and we'll have a choir."

The room erupted in laughter, slicing through the tension, before Dr. Salazar answered, "I've insufficient evidence. What I can say is this: whether it was a performance, an affliction, or a possession, it was powerful."

"Dr. Salazar, could you expand on that?" The cardinal continued playing with the pen, nervously rolling it between his fingers.

"First, if it's a performance, it's Oscar quality. The voice, stage presence, and poise were first-rate. But this would require a strong motive. Second, if he suffers from an affliction, such as schizophrenia or dissociative identity disorder, he needs treatment and supervision. And third, if he's possessed, God help us, it would require an exorcism."

"Are you leaning one way or the other?" The cardinal put down the pen and leaned back.

"Too early to tell. But any way it goes, I see a problem for the Church." Dr. Salazar paused and then added, "We need to find him."

"Have you enlisted the help of anyone else?" Cardinal McMahon looked first at Father O'Neil, then at Father Gallagher.

Father Gallagher looked at his fellow Ghostbusters before answering, "Yes, we've retained a private investigator. Dr. Salazar was kind enough to cough up a thousand-dollar retainer."

"Excellent. I want Vincent Salabrini found. We need to nip this in the bud. Keep me updated. His apprehension is of the utmost importance. Dr. Salazar, I'll arrange for a reimbursement. This is Church business."

The meeting ended precipitously, as the cardinal had another meeting. Several high-profile lawyers were waiting in the outer office. The cardinal's plate was full.

On the way to the parking structure, the Ghostbusters shared their relief at the cardinal's support. "We've a green light. The search is on," Father Gallagher said as he bid good-bye to Dr. Salazar. Father O'Neil and Father Gallagher opted to swing by their favorite Irish pub for a nightcap.

Chapter Twenty-Two

Sounds of Spanish guitar rekindled fond memories of Madrid. Vincent had been happy then, celebrating his newly acquired Ph.D. It was a summer of love, passion, and youthful indiscretion, newfound friendships, late-night parties, and lazy, spontaneous days. Maria, a sensual thirty-five-year-old, had taught him about love; she had also rekindled his interest in drugs.

Candlelight and incense once again filled his senses; only this time, he wasn't alone. Vincent handed the half-smoked joint to his guest and said, "Just like old times."

The slender hands of the woman steadied Vincent's hand, carefully sliding the joint from his grip, placing it between her full red lips. She inhaled deeply, holding it for as long as possible, absorbing the magic, until she nearly coughed, exhaling forcefully. The wispy smoke enveloped her, shrouding her dark outfit, reminding Vincent of a scene from his first horror movie. She was there at the beginning, shadowing his acting career, so young, so beautiful. That was five years ago; she was still young, beautiful, and inexplicably drawn to the enigmatic professor turned actor.

They had polished off the cabernet, finished the joint, and shared their dreams for tomorrow. Twenty-five years separated them, yet they were soul mates, dedicated to their shared obsession. Their commitment had been solidified, in blood, among throngs of people celebrating Christmas Eve in St. Peter's Square. Vincent had skillfully pricked the ring finger of his left hand and quickly repeated the process on her, mingling their fluids, making them one, committed in blood and oath. That cold night, they had embraced, kissing and hugging, glancing up at the illuminated façade of St. Peter's Basilica. The evening was special, certainly in a way that would have alarmed and repulsed the Christians around them. Those who had gathered to celebrate the birth of Christ were indeed strangers, adversaries, worshiping the wrong person for the wrong reason.

Vincent turned and whispered softly in her ear, "Remember Christmas Eve in Rome, St. Peter's?"

"I will never forget. Pure magic."

"It was Pope Benedict's first Christmas eve midnight Mass. The cold air showed off my steamy breath. I can see him now, at his study window, gazing out at the massive gathering, pilgrims enthusiastically singing Christmas carols." Vincent smiled. It was a night for the ages.

"Bells filled the night air, celebrating our oath." Vincent's guest chuckled, her marijuana high adding levity to her remembrance of that special night.

"You were so beautiful then and more so now. Our love has grown, our passion for the truth matured. That was only the beginning. We're in our second phase."

The woman turned, looking into Vincent's eyes, searching for the truth. "Are you sure?"

"Yes, *he* has spoken." He gently lifted her left hand, caressing her fingertips, reenacting their blood oath. "The disciples must be in place by the New Year."

"You have me."

"That makes three." Vincent smiled, knowing that Doc and Alan had already committed.

"I might be able to help." His guest leaned closer and whispered in Vincent's ear, "Let's celebrate."

"I'm counting on you. And yes, it's time." Vincent was blessed, knowing he would savor her sensual beauty. Her breathy voice, silky smooth skin, and youthful passion rejuvenated him. Vincent was convinced she was a gift from *him*. Her passion consumed him, charging his libido, giving him the energy and staying power of his youth. His guest stood and seductively shed her long skirt and sweater. Candlelight played across her flawless skin, bathing her full breasts and thighs. He did not disappoint her, writhing and pounding into the early morning. He hoped their cries and screams had gone unnoticed. Before the night was over, they had once again shared bodily fluids.

* * *

William Preston was a hit at Thomas Aquinas College, at least with Mary Martin, the senior administrative secretary. He was also a hit at a diner on Main Street, creating quite a stir among the female patrons. He had sweet-talked Mary into lunch in downtown Santa Paula. Two teenagers gawked, giggling as the ruggedly handsome P.I. slid into a front booth. The twenty-something waitress was extra attentive; a good tip took second to a good look at the new hunk.

Over burgers and fries, he learned not only of Vincent's acting career, he discovered that Dr. Salabrini had a secret lover. Well, it had been secret until Mary did a little snooping of her own. She confessed that at one time she had a crush on the professor. But before long, her crush had morphed into an obsession. She tailed him, kept a diary detailing his every move, and snapped hundreds of photos. William kissed her on the cheek, rewarding her for sharing a half-dozen close-range shots of the woman in black.

Before leaving the gushing older secretary, he confirmed Dr. Salabrini's social security number, got a copy of his work history at the college, and his curriculum vitae. The paperwork was routine, easily available, but the photos were straight from God. If he believed in miracles, this was one. But it was only the first. "There's one more thing," Mary confided. "I think Vincent has a twin brother."

"What?"

"My amateur detective work yielded a double. I was tailing Vincent on a Saturday after morning Mass when he pulled over at a county park. He jumped from the car, hustling across the grass, meeting his mirrored image in front of a small amphitheater. The two look-a-likes chatted for a half hour and then parted with a handshake and hug. I nosed around, but found little. I think Vincent has a twin."

"Did you confront him with this?"

"No way. I didn't want him to know I was tailing him."

The second miracle blew the case wide open. If Dr. Salabrini had a twin, it was a game changer.

Later that evening, William phoned Father Gallagher and told him about the photos. He held back on the twin thing. He was keeping *that* close to the vest. He promised to drop by in the morning, share them, circulate copies, and come up with their version of the "Most Wanted" list. He studied the paperwork, but nothing jumped out. Mary did say he spent time in Rome, at the Vatican, researching the history of Satanism. He decided to comb local libraries and bookstores, looking for anyone with an interest in Satan. She also remembered him giving her a book on the Gnostic gospels. He was especially interested in the gospels of Thomas, Judas, and Mary Magdalene. But since *The Da Vinci Code*, who wasn't.

He contacted Martini, the movie director, but got little on the woman in black. He confessed that Vincent didn't have groupies; he had a solitary fan who was quiet and mysterious but easy on the eyes. The photos were still the hottest lead.

* * *

At Wally's Emporium, he got his first bite. William befriended the proprietor, entertaining him with Polish jokes. Wally's cynical side delighted in the jaded pastime of put-downs. Hell, dumb blond jokes would do. Wally invited the strapping P.I. to the back room for some Texas crude. He politely refused but stayed long enough to talk books, especially demonic ones. During the discussion, Vincent came up. They talked about Vincent Valdez, the escapee from Patton State Hospital. Wally also mentioned Vincent Salabrini, Doc, and his habit of referring to his client as Schizzy. That piqued the investigator's curiosity, so he pulled out a notebook and jotted down the hypnotist's name. Doc, Michael Mesmer, had joined the growing list of leads.

Chapter Twenty-Three

It was early morning, hours before dawn. The cathedral was quiet, as the worshippers and visitors had not yet arrived. In secluded quarters overlooking the plaza, Cardinal McMahon bolted upright, staring at a dark figure at the foot of his bed. He blinked and rubbed his eyes, straining to make out who or what it was.

"Who are you?" The sharpness of his own voice startled him.

"We've not met," said the hooded figure, dressed in black. "But soon we'll be partners."

"What?"

"You'll see."

"How did you get in?" The cardinal's eyes began to focus, seeing only the outline of the hooded figure.

"I have my ways. I've been given a message from *him*."

"What?" The cardinal jumped, unnerved, clutching a pillow.

"I've been instructed to find twelve loyal followers, disciples for the new order." The hooded stranger's voice was theatrical, breathy, conjuring images from the dark side.

"Please, move closer so I can see you," the cardinal said.

The intruder stepped to the side of the bed, emerging from the shadows. A gust of wind sent the branches of an outside tree in motion, exposing a full moon, briefly illuminating the stranger's face. The cardinal got only a glimpse, but it was memorable. He had a long pointed nose and dark eyes, almost black. His baggy clothes and hooded sweater revealed little else.

"You have been chosen."

"What?" The cardinal felt trapped, thrown into an echo chamber, held captive by an image. Or was it? His senses reeled as images spun wildly, making him dizzy.

"My superior knows you, your soul, and your doubts. He knows you're ready."

"Ready?"

"It is the second coming, but not what you expect. Our Lord will appear, and the chosen will recognize his glory. I will be back, but next time, I'll put on a show."

The hooded stranger disappeared into the shadows, leaving the cardinal stunned. He collapsed, losing consciousness the moment his head hit the pillow. While asleep, his mind had become a theater of the absurd, images of saints and demons battling for his soul, shrieking their message, taunting, interrogating, finally sealing his fate. He was abandoned at the gates of hell, cowering before a snarling winged demon exhaling fire from its contorted mouth.

Hours later, reflected sunlight lit up a crucifix dangling from a nearby chair. The cardinal slid from bed, stretching, trying to rid the stiffness from his aching body. He felt as if he'd been at war. He limped slowly to the bathroom, his arthritic knees stiff, relieving himself before staring at his bloodshot eyes in the brightly lit mirror. He looked down at his trembling hands, recalling the nightmare. *It was only a dream, wasn't it?* His conscious mind was skeptical, dismissing the event, attributing the nightmare to overindulgence—a late-night meal, spicy food, and that extra glass of wine. At the core of his being, he knew better. The cardinal's subconscious mind was full of dread.

He popped two diet pills and downed three cups of coffee before breakfast. The cardinal had experimented with energy drinks and green teas, but nothing rivaled this. At first a habit, but now a tradition, it was the best way to kick start the morning.

The day was long, packed with a litany of headaches, including meeting with his defense team, talking strategy, and looking for leverage. But the dam had breached; wayward priests and sexual misconduct cases were economically and emotionally draining. Newspaper headlines cried foul, accusing cardinals, archbishops, and bishops of cover-ups. Internet blogs were more vicious, labeling offending priests as pedophiles, degenerate clergy, donning the Catholic cloak to diddle the private parts of young girls and boys. He felt like he had been thrown into hell.

His late-night meeting on immigration reform stalled, going nowhere, trying what patience he had left. Earlier, he had made good on a promise, doing a photo shoot for a local Catholic charity—cassock and all. It wasn't until eleven that he found the solitude of his apartment. As soon as he closed the door, he immediately shed his ceremonial garb, an ankle-length, close-fitting robe, red with black buttons and sash. He tossed his red hat on a lamp, casting a red hue on the liquor cabinet, his destination. He viewed his options, opted for his favorite, and poured a fine cabernet. *Damn good for the heart.* But tonight, it didn't pack a punch. He was consumed by images of the hooded stranger, that eerie voice, and talk of disciples and a new order. He was haunted by the words, "My superior knows you, your soul, and your doubts."

He had been exposed, but by what and by whom? The cardinal was adept at compartmentalization, separating the world, cleaving it into manageable boxes—political, economical, moral, and theological. But underneath this tidy arrangement, down deep, was an eternal doubter. The controlling self, his real self, was a pragmatic puppeteer. Breaking through in moments of clarity, he saw the truth. He tried to deny it, but he couldn't. He was a political animal, addicted to power and control. His theology was a charade. The Catholic Church was merely a stage, a highly visible venue, a great place to show off.

He curled up in his overstuffed chair, crying, moaning, confessing his sins. He shuddered and trembled, feeling like an emotional and spiritual wreck. He believed in God. That was bedrock. So he thought. In reality Jesus was not who the Catholic Church made him out to be. He prayed for strength. "Please, God, I've not forsaken you!" he bellowed. "Please, forgive me!"

As a child, the future cardinal collected butterflies and delighted in anesthetizing, killing, and preparing them for show. A massive glass showcase dominated an entire wall of his bedroom and was the talk and envy of his boyhood friends. His collection of animals ran the gamut from amphibians to zebra fish. His quest for power started with dominating lower animals, but soon spread to controlling his friends at school. He was a natural leader, in charge, the decider. He was now top dog, the most powerful Catholic on the West Coast, shepherding his loyal flock.

The cardinal harbored a secret. He was an admirer of the Jesus Seminar. He had read the controversial *The Five Gospels: The Search for the Authentic Words of Jesus.* Initially he felt guilty staying up late at night and enthusiastically devouring the iconoclastic work. It set off a five-year struggle that shook his theological beliefs to the core. At first he thought he was being tempted, challenged by the devil. But he finally gave in, accepting the findings.

The book was a media sensation, the product of liberal religious scholars who skillfully applied the methodologies of social anthropology and history. It was entertaining, a real literary romp, a forbidden fruit slowly savored. He secretly admired the group's scholarship as they doggedly searched for the historical Jesus, separating fact from fiction. The scholars addressed two questions: "What did Jesus really say? And what did Jesus really do?" Their conclusion, after argument, discussion, and democratic vote, was alarming to the faithful but not to the cardinal. Only 18 percent of what Jesus reportedly said was true. In the end, after a five-year battle for the cardinal's soul, his pragmatic nature won out. For the first time in his life, he had faced and accepted the truth. He secretly agreed, believing that much of theology was a product of politics. He knew because he was an insider, part of the game. But the truth had been boxed up, sealed off, never tackled head-on. Now the cardinal knew. But he was not alone. The stranger and the stranger's superior also knew. That familiar voice cried out from his subconscious, "My superior knows you, your soul, and your doubts."

He avoided sleep, fearing the stranger would return. He sat up the entire night, occasionally napping, praying for strength. But who was in charge? Who really ruled the world? He was gripped by a crisis of faith. He longed for God to speak. Now he heard only the voice of Satan.

* * *

Doc glanced at his clock, feeling good about the morning sessions. It was high noon, two hours before his next client. He was about to leave for Waldo's when the buzzer sounded. *Damn, probably another salesman*, he thought as he reluctantly opened up.

"Michael Mesmer?"

"Yes, I'm Doc Mesmer."

"William Preston, private investigator. May I come in?" He flashed his credentials.

"What's this about?" Doc looked up at the towering figure. His movie-star good looks and disarming smile were intimidating. It made Doc feel small and insignificant.

"I'm trying to locate Dr. Vincent Salabrini."

"Dr. Salabrini? I know a Vincent Salabrini." Doc looked puzzled.

"That's the one. Please, just a few minutes."

"I'm on my way out. Five minutes." Doc reluctantly let him in and pointed to the sofa. "Have a seat."

"When was the last time you saw Dr. Salabrini?" William placed a manila envelope beside him, then retrieved a small notebook from his blue blazer and jotted something down.

"Last Friday. But what's with the *Dr. Salabrini?*" Doc frowned, thrown by Vincent's new title.

"I've been retained to locate Dr. Salabrini. Wally told me you call him Schizzy."

"It's just a running joke. I don't talk about my clients." Doc was instantly defensive.

"Well, Wally mentioned that you believe Vincent Valdez and Vincent Salabrini are the same man."

"That's his opinion. But what's with the doctor bit?"

"He's a former college professor."

"The Vincent I know wasn't, so maybe we're talking about two different guys." Doc's confusion built, causing him to roll about in his chair.

"That's possible, but I have something more pressing." William opened up a manila folder and handed Doc several photos. "Do you recognize this woman?"

Doc flipped through them, shaking his head. "No, I've never seen her."

"You sure?" William studied Doc's reaction.

"Positive. But back to Vincent, who are you working for?" Doc was irritated, not comfortable talking about Salabrini.

"I've been commissioned to locate him. My employer is anxious to speak with him."

"Who you working for?" Doc rolled forward, trying to turn the tables, ask the questions.

"That's confidential."

"It's a two-way street; I'll play ball if you do." Doc stood, letting the investigator know his time was up.

"When's your next appointment with Vincent?"

"He hasn't made one yet." Doc lied, but it was a white lie. Vincent was due Friday night, but it wasn't technically an appointment. He was returning on a recruiting mission, and damn if he was going to tell the private eye that.

William stood, smiled, and handed Doc his business card. He walked over to the proudly displayed certificates. "Are these real?"

"What?" Doc glared, then walked to the office door and opened it.

"The diplomas."

"I'm a minister. I do marriages."

"What about the Ph.D.?"

"It enhances my credibility."

"Do you treat mental or emotional disorders?"

"Never!"

William Preston passed by Doc slowly, looking down, grinning, and said, "I feel you know more about Vincent than you're letting on."

Doc slammed the door, resenting the investigator's demeanor. He paced his office and paused before his prized certificates, his face reddened with anger. "Bastard!" he yelled. He grabbed his keys and headed for Waldo's. He was pissed at him too.

Chapter Twenty-Four

Gypsy was tense, tired, and downright angry. Doc had begged, sweet talked, and charmed her into playing along with Vincent. It took a night out, French cuisine, a bottle of chardonnay, and a few hugs to win her over. It was not what he said that swayed her; it was how he said it. She sensed he loved her. Her growing feelings for Doc quieted her anger and fear. He was now a missionary, doing Vincent Salabrini's bidding, taking part in his delusion. Curiosity killed the cat, but Doc plowed ahead, oblivious, ignoring Saint Augustine's admonition: "God fashioned hell for the inquisitive." Alan Workman, Gypsy, and Doc stared at the antique clock, silently counting the chimes. Not more than a heartbeat after the last chime, the buzzer sounded.

"He's here." Doc looked at Gypsy. "Be strong."

Doc walked slowly to the door, paused, glanced back at his comrades, and smiled. "It's show time." He opened the door, but no one was there. He glanced about the small waiting room, but it was empty. Suddenly, the outer door flew open, and a dark figure brushed past Doc, nearly knocking him over. It was Salabrini in black Nike sweats, sneakers, and a Yankee baseball cap.

"Top of the evening, Doc. You look surprised. Sorry about the delay. I stepped out for a second." Vincent grinned, curtsied, and said, "Let the meeting begin."

Vincent motioned to the sofa, directing the three to sit. He perched himself on the edge of Doc's desk, looking fit, a middle-aged athlete ready to workout. But this was not a gym, and Vincent wasn't interested in their bodies. He wanted their souls.

"I've good news. We're about to be joined by Roman Catholic royalty. We are growing in number." Vincent Salabrini smiled and then added, "Gypsy, so good to see you."

Gypsy frowned, sighed, and hesitantly spoke in a quiet voice, "I don't want to be here. It's a favor for Doc."

"In the end, it will be a favor for us all," Vincent answered softly, not wanting to upset Gypsy.

"Vincent, before we get started, I've a question," Doc said.

"What's up?" Vincent stretched out his legs, leaning back on Doc's desk, relaxed, professorial.

"I was visited by a private investigator."

"Oh, what did you do? Mistreat a client?" Vincent delighted in putting Doc on the defensive.

"No such thing. He was looking for you."

"Really?" Vincent leaned forward.

"He was looking for a Dr. Vincent Salabrini, a former college professor."

"Very interesting. Dr. Vincent Salabrini sounds impressive. But we're not here to talk about me. We're here to welcome a new disciple." Vincent looked at Gypsy, smiled, and said, "We need you, we need the feminine. There are worlds best understood by the fairer sex."

Gypsy nervously looked down, furious with Doc and appalled by Vincent's demeanor. He was condescending, arrogant, and demented. To her, he was Schizzy.

"I'm not here by choice."

"Please, Gypsy, give me a chance and hear me out." Vincent's voice deepened, taking on the distinctive breathy tone. "Join us; we'll inherit the world, become masters of the universe."

"This is madness!" Gypsy shouted, surprising Doc and Alan with her burst of anger.

"Gypsy, come here, I've something that's right down your alley."

Gypsy stonewalled him, not budging. "No way!"

Vincent Salabrini quickly arranged two chairs on either side of Doc's desk, reached into his sweat pants, and produced a deck of cards. "Please, join me. This time, *I'll* do the reading."

Doc gently nudged her, whispering, "Play along."

Gypsy reluctantly joined Schizzy at the desk, sitting across from him as he spread out a Celtic cross. As he worked the cards, he coaxed her, getting her to raise specific questions that played into his hand. Early on, he played a Four of Swords, a card depicting a man lying on a bier, accompanied by a horizontal sword. "Let's bury the hatchet," said Schizzy. "So say the cards." A little later, the Eight of wands was played. Wands were air elements, standing for inspiration and communication. "The cards say it all. *He* is communicating, offering you the world."

Vincent worked his magic, skillfully plying Gypsy's trade. His stage presence was undeniable. At first, Vincent's theatrics were bold and irritating, but they soon became mesmerizing. Schizzy was at home in Gypsy's world, connecting with the supernatural. Between his voice and the Tarot cards, she was under his spell. Doc and Alan were equally captivated by Vincent's show.

Salabrini shouted, "We are one! We will do *his* will." With that, he departed as mysteriously as he had appeared.

There was a long silence before Doc spoke. "Gypsy, are you all right?"

"I saw something."

"What?" Doc and Alan sang in unison.

"All I could make out was a hand reaching through the clouds, beckoning, encouraging me to follow."

"I think we've been had," Alan said, looking at Doc.

"We have." Doc stood, shaking his head. "The last time I felt like this, I'd been hypnotized at a conference."

Gypsy looked at Doc and said, "Doc, walk me home. I'm not feeling well."

The three disciples left in a daze and headed to Gypsy's place, not sure what had just happened. Vincent Salabrini would celebrate, knowing he had one more disciple. Tonight, he had a date with an angel.

* * *

Vincent gazed into his angel's eyes, smiling, hoisting the champagne glass for a toast. "We are now five, growing, spreading the good word. We'll be six at the month's end."

Vincent's lover clinked his glass and linked arms with him, savoring the arrival of their newest disciple. Tonight she was dressed in an all white, floor-length gown, slit to mid thigh, giving Vincent glimpses of her flawless flesh. Her green eyes glowed in the candlelight encircling the loft. Vincent had carefully arranged a semicircle of candles, three deep, height staggered, softly illuminating a pentagram dominating the improvised altar.

"I need your advice," Vincent said, leaning back on the sofa, peering at his angel and savoring the champagne.

"I'm flattered."

"I paid a visit to the cardinal."

"Roger McMahon?"

"The one and only."

"At the cathedral?"

"In his apartment. I promised him a show." Vincent sipped the champagne, smacking his lips. "Perhaps a debut at the cathedral."

"Impossible," his angel exclaimed, for the first time shocked by his boldness.

"Nothing's impossible. We have *him* on our side. Come, let us pray." Vincent stood, offering a hand to his angel. Together they knelt, solemn, loyal, pleading for advice. Vincent's loft glowed with candlelight as a Gregorian chant bathed them with haunting sounds from the past, transforming the abandoned loft into a sanctuary for *him*.

A deep, masculine voice sliced through the reverent moment, at first loud and intrusive, but then soft, breathy, answering their prayer. "I will be with you in spirit. Go to the cathedral, spread the good news, and tell them of the second coming."

"Vincent, *he's* here. *He* answered our prayer." His angel turned and embraced him. "Let's celebrate." She trusted Vincent. They were of one mind.

"We've all night to pay homage to the master." The two lovers finished the first bottle of champagne and celebrated by reenacting the blood oath first taken at St. Peter's. After the exchange of blood, they smoked, danced, and drank themselves into a sexual frenzy. Vincent had been born again, in body and spirit.

Chapter Twenty-Five

L ieutenant Fred Thompson studied the police report, awkwardly juggling a sixteen-ounce Starbucks' dark roast and a jelly donut from his favorite bakery. He normally hated being called in on his day off, but today was an exception. Vincent Valdez was in custody, shackled, surly, showing his contempt for the system. Groggy from a late-night emergency, lack of sleep, and one too many beers, he peered through the one-way glass, sizing Vincent up.

He looked down and resumed reading the report, learning that Vincent had been apprehended Saturday morning near the corner of Reseda and Ventura Boulevard. A convenience store clerk spotted him arguing with an MTA bus driver. When the argument turned nasty, gathering a crowd, the store clerk called 911. A police cruiser on patrol arrived within minutes, just in the nick of time. According to arresting officers, the suspect was threatening the bus driver, pumping his fists, screaming obscenities. The trouble started when Vincent insisted on boarding the bus even though he was penniless.

Bringing his coffee with him, the lieutenant entered the interrogation room. Vincent looked forlorn; his head was lowered, and he was mumbling something under his breath. The lieutenant cleared his voice and said good morning, but got no response. The lone prisoner continued mumbling, self-absorbed. Lieutenant Thompson eased into a straight-back chair, savoring his coffee.

"Vincent, you've been giving us the runaround."

"I hate that place." Vincent looked up at the lieutenant, snarled, and said, "It's a loony bin."

"Are you referring to Patton State?"

"I'm not crazy. I need a lawyer."

"You'll have a public defender." The lieutenant grimaced, hating every moment in Vincent's presence.

"Big fucking deal!" Vincent glared at the lieutenant.

"You're an escapee, twice over. You got a big hill to climb." Lieutenant Thompson flipped closed the police report. "We're sending you back to Patton for further psychiatric testing."

"Don't waste the tax payers' money. I'm as sane as you." Vincent shrugged his shoulders, his hands cuffed. "I want to go back to my cell."

"All in good time, but first, why the change in appearance?"

"What?" Vincent frowned.

"Gone are the goatee, cane, and limp. The arresting officer said you were physically fit, even light on your feet."

"I feel just fine. I shaved, trying to throw you guys off. The arthritis comes and goes. Besides, if I had a cane, I would've used it on the officers."

"Well, Vincent, you gave us a run for our money. This time, we'll nail the door shut."

"You'll never keep me under lock and key. I'll be out in less than a month."

"Big talk for a guy in shackles." The lieutenant stood. "That will be all for now."

"We'll see." Vincent sneered, again mumbling something.

The lieutenant called for an officer who whisked Vincent back to his cell. He later called Patton and talked with an old friend, giving him the heads up on Vincent's promise to escape. *Not this time,* they both vowed.

* * *

Since I'm here, wide awake, I'll kill two birds with one stone, Lieutenant Thompson thought as he left the Parker Center. The Saturday morning traffic was light, his headache nearly gone, thanks to two Tylenol and another cup of Starbucks. Twenty minutes later, he pulled up in front of Mildred's shop in the Valley. It was just before ten, but the neon was lit. He took a deep breath, entered, and rang the chrome bell shaped like a Buddha. *This should be fun.*

Mildred emerged from the back, her eyes wide with surprise. "Lieutenant, what gives? Isn't Saturday your day off?"

"As a rule, but I've good news."

"Oh, that would be a first." She folded her arms defiantly.

"Vincent Valdez is in custody."

"What?" Her eyes widened. She dropped her arms and leaned on the front counter for support. "When?"

"This morning. He's back at Patton where he belongs. You can relax now."

"When can I see him?"

"*What?*" That was the last response he expected to hear. "Why would you want to see him? I thought you hated him. Last time we talked, you feared for your safety."

"I want to be sure you have the right guy."

"It's the right guy. He's been printed and mugged."

"I've got to be sure," she insisted.

"He won't be available for visitation for some time." The lieutenant was intrigued by her urgent need to see him.

"How long?" Mildred was flustered, her eyes welling up with tears.

"I don't know. You'll have to arrange visitation through the hospital."

"Thank you for coming, lieutenant. But I must excuse myself. I have a client at ten."

"Oh, one more thing." The lieutenant pulled a notebook from his coat. "We've recently uncovered some startling facts."

"What?"

"He's used several aliases. We've confirmed that he's used the name Vincent Bartolli. He also studied acting in Hollywood under the stage name of Vincent Alvarez."

"This is all news to me." A tear trickled down her right cheek.

"I'll be in touch. If anything comes up, please call." He pulled a card from his wallet and left it on the counter. He smiled and said, "Rest easy; he's under lock and key now."

* * *

As soon as the lieutenant left her parlor, Mildred phoned Vincent. He picked up on the first ring. "Vincent, I need to see you."

"My angel, what a surprise. What's up?"

"Detective Fred Thompson was here. He said Vincent is in custody."

"Where?"

"He's back at Patton State."

"I'll take care of it."

"What will you do?"

"My angel, I have my ways."

"Please, Vincent, be careful. We can't jeopardize our mission."

"Nothing will interfere with *that*."

"When will I see you?"

"Soon."

Vincent Salabrini abruptly signed off, anxious and fearing the worst. He inhaled deeply, clearing his mind. He would not let his brother waste away in Bedlam. He smiled, flashing on their childhood. The twins were Catholics through and through. When Dad hit the sauce, they'd escape to the safety of the basement, crank up the stereo, and belt out a few verses of "Cracklin' Rosie." Strains of "you're a store-bought woman, but you make me sing like a guitar hummin'," echoed off the walls, followed by cathartic bouts of laughter. They couldn't confront their frustration, so they sublimated, throwing themselves into song. By the time they were high school seniors, the music was accompanied by the soothing high of marijuana.

The two went separate ways after graduating from college; his brother joined the seminary, eventually becoming an ordained priest, and Vincent entered graduate school, becoming a professor of philosophy. They were both named Vincent, only differing in their middle name. Their old man was a big-time boxing fan, adopting George Foreman as his favorite. He followed Big George's lead, who named all of his sons by the same first name, George. For the senior Salabrini, the twins were named Vincent, after the old man. Gorge Foreman had George III, George IV, and George V. Vincent had Vincent Amadeus, and Vincent Van Gogh. His brother lived up to the Van Gogh moniker—although, so far, he hadn't cut off his ear.

PART THREE:
The Cardinal's True Colors

Chapter Twenty-Six

Cardinal Roger McMahon looked out at his kneeling flock, reverential before God, dedicated, compliant, secure in their faith. It warmed his heart to see such a turnout, the biggest Mass of the year; worshipers crowded the front half of the nave, eagerly embracing their commitment to Christ. As the faithful held hands, the cardinal recited the Lord's Prayer. A spiritual calm gripped the congregation, sanctifying the moment.

Today the cardinal was on autopilot, effortlessly gliding through the Sunday morning ritual, habitually mouthing the words. For the observer, he was the consummate ambassador for the Catholic Church. But carefully hidden from others, deep within, the cardinal was troubled, lost in a fog of doubt. As the words flowed effortlessly, his mind cried out in existential despair: *why am I here?*

He knew he put on a good show, appearing devout, committed in body and soul. But today, a lingering skepticism haunted him, rearing its ugly head like an ancient sea monster, breaching the water's surface, spewing fire, snarling, threatening his spiritual life. In his inner most being, he knew the truth—he was addicted. It wasn't faith that motivated him, not really. He lusted for political power. When candid, which was not often, he understood that he was a political animal, pragmatic to the core. The pomp and circumstance of the morning Mass was a classic misdirection, the work of a magician. He couldn't deny it; he was a master of deception.

Suddenly a deep voice sliced through the church, wrenching the worshippers from their devotion. "Welcome, my brethren. I've good news!" the disembodied voice boomed, filling the bowels of the spacious sanctuary and causing instant confusion. The worshipers' heads bobbed and swiveled as they searched for the source of the voice.

"Listen carefully. This is your moment, your chance at everlasting life. *He* will soon come for your soul. Lucifer is the one, the only one, the original giver of life. Open your ears, open your hearts, listen, and make way for the *truth*." The eerie voice, amplified and self-assured, sent shock waves through the congregation, setting off shrieks and groans. The cardinal glanced about, terror-stricken, seeking the source of the familiar voice. "He's back," he mumbled, grabbing the altar, rendered speechless by the intrusion. *There's no protocol for dealing with this.*

Cardinal McMahon stepped back from the altar table, nodding to a nearby priest, vigorously pointing to the eighty-five-foot-high pipe organ dominating the front wall. Within seconds, the intruder's voice was drowned out by the sheer power of the forty-two-ton organ, over six hundred pipes erupting with "Jesus, the Lord of Life." The cathedral vibrated, the parishioners temporarily soothed by the wraparound sound. They not only heard the organ, they felt it. The walls and floors rumbled and shook, much like an old wooden basketball court, trembling from the frantic jumping of excited fans. The cardinal motioned for the congregation to rise, at first with arms wide open, then prayer-like, bowing to the almighty.

The congregation responded in kind, folding their hands in prayer. The cardinal motioned to the priest to quiet the organ before he spoke. "Please forgive us, but we've been the target of a practical joke. I don't take this lightly, but consider it an abomination, sacrilegious, an attack on the *Church*. Please join me in prayer." The cardinal's voice rang out with the Lord's Prayer, quieting the pockets of chatter, bringing civility back to the Mass. His eminence took quick action, assuring the congregation that it was only an ill-tempered prank, but one that would be dealt with swiftly and severely.

After Mass, before consoling several hysterical longtime members of the Los Angeles Diocese, Cardinal McMahon directed Father Williamson to alert the LAPD. "I want a complete investigation." After calming the parishioners, he retired to his office and called Father Gallagher. He reached him on the second ring.

"Father Gallagher, we've an emergency."

"What's happened?"

"*He* has returned. Just moments ago, he put on a show, causing chaos at morning Mass. Alert the Ghostbusters and bring along the private eye. We'll meet at my office, tonight, nine sharp."

"Yes, sir. Can you give me a heads up on what happened?" Father Gallagher was stunned. He had never witnessed the cardinal so upset and rattled.

"I'll let you know tonight. Be prompt." The cardinal signed off and went back to the nave, looking for answers.

A priest approached, nodding his head. "We've uncovered the source. The speaker system has been compromised. The mystery visitor spliced into the sound system. The rear panel was ajar, several wires and clips dangling from the amplifier."

"Have the police arrived?" The cardinal grimaced.

"They're on their way." Father Williamson again shook his head in disbelief.

"Thanks. Alert me when they arrive. I'll be in my office." On his way to his office, it occurred to him—*Lucifer knows; he's after my soul.*

* * *

After a gentle knock at his office door, the cardinal's secretary entered and softly said, "Lieutenant Fred Thompson is here to see you."

"Thanks. Send him in." The cardinal stood and rounded his desk, greeting the lieutenant with a firm handshake. He was eager to hear his report.

"Good morning, Your Eminence." This was awkward, a first. The lieutenant had never spoken with a cardinal—he was definitely clueless about Catholic protocol.

"Not so good for our congregation. Please, have a seat. I'm eager for anything positive." The cardinal motioned to a chair and settled in behind his massive mahogany desk. An orderly pile of unopened files were stacked to his left, a crucifix and an hourglass were off to the right. The cardinal enjoyed controlling the length of meetings— the old fashion way.

"LAPD techs dusted for prints, collected hair and fiber samples, and thoroughly checked out the sound system. There's clear evidence of tampering with the amplifier. Several clips and wires were discovered."

"Any specific leads?" The cardinal eased back in his chair, trying to get a read on the lieutenant. *His bushy moustache must be a nuisance*, he thought. He hoped he was more like Sherlock Holmes than Dr. Watson.

"Too early for that. We interviewed several priests, two upset parishioners, and a custodian. One thing did stand out."

"Go on." The cardinal slid forward, leaning his elbows on the desk.

"The custodian." The lieutenant paused and consulted a small notebook. "Jose Gonzales noticed an unfamiliar priest walking about early this morning. He said that he carried a black bag and was checking out the sound system."

"Did he approach the priest, talk with him?" The cardinal's eyes narrowed, keenly interested in the mystery priest.

"No, but after his break, he returned to the cabinet containing the sound system. All was normal, so he went back to work."

"Did he give description of the priest?"

"Yes, but rather vague. A middle-age man, clean-shaven, wore a collar, dark suit, and black sneakers. He thought the black sneakers were odd. That's why he checked back on the sound system."

"Please, for the safety and sanity of Our Lady of the Angels, find the person who did this horrible thing to us. It's more than a prank. It's an abomination."

"Yes, sir, I fully understand. We'll be all over it."

"I'm in your hands," the cardinal sighed.

"Maybe we should be in his hands." The lieutenant pointed to the crucifix, stood, and excused himself.

"God be with you." Cardinal McMahon smiled and then walked the detective to the door.

"Thanks. I welcome *his* help on this one."

* * *

Ghostbusters had grown, now four in number. William Preston of Shamrock Investigations, the newest member, made it one short of a basketball team. The two priests, psychiatrist, and private eye sat patiently in the cardinal's outer office, anxiously waiting to get started. The door suddenly swung open, and the cardinal, dressed in ceremonial red, welcomed the foursome with a loud good evening. "Please, gentlemen, come in. I'm not accustomed to wearing such formal attire for private meetings, but I had an important prior engagement."

Four chairs were arranged in a semicircle in front of the cardinal's massive desk where the hourglass and crucifix stood like sentinels, guarding the special meeting. "Please, gentlemen, be seated."

Father Gallagher spoke first, introducing William Preston.

The cardinal smiled and said, "We're in dire need of a super sleuth. I hope you can fill the bill."

"I'll do my very best."

"I'm embarrassed—and angry. He's struck again, this time shocking a thousand, ruining morning Mass. He must be stopped." The cardinal paused, checking out the newest member of the Ghostbusters. "What's the latest on the investigative front?"

William took a deep breath. "I've just learned that Dr. Vincent Salabrini has a brother, perhaps a twin."

"What?" the two priests exclaimed! They turned, staring at each other, bewildered.

"My trip to Thomas Aquinas College turned out to be a gold mine. Over lunch, the administrative secretary, former admirer of Dr. Salabrini, confided that she once had a crush on the professor. Blushing with embarrassment, she admitted to following him, obsessed with his every move. One day, she spotted Dr. Salabrini and a man at a local park. They were indistinguishable from each other. She studied the duo for nearly fifteen minutes. She was sure they were twins."

"This really complicates things. Have you identified the mystery man?" Dr. Mario Salazar's eyes widened, intrigued by the possibility of a twin.

"Yes. I've accessed Dr. Salabrini's high school records. There were two Salabrinis in his graduating class; both were named Vincent. They differed only in their middle name."

"Have you contacted anyone who knew the twins?" the cardinal asked, troubled by the news.

"I'm working on it."

The phone rang, causing the cardinal to frown. He picked up. "We're not to be disturbed."

The secretary apologized but informed the cardinal that Vincent Salabrini was on the phone. "It's an emergency. The man's insistent," the secretary said, once again apologizing for the intrusion.

The cardinal froze, starring into space, eyes glazed over. After a moment he blurted, "Put him through. I'll put him on speakerphone." The cardinal was terrified. But he needed witnesses, another take on what was going down.

"Yes, sir."

The speakerphone filled the room with Vincent's breathy voice, giving the private eye his first taste of the enigmatic professor.

"Gentlemen, thank you for your cooperation. Time is precious. *He* has given his word. On New Year's Day, *his* minions will unite, revealing the Truth."

"Dr. Salabrini, I resent your intrusion. Your attack on the Church is unacceptable. You will pay dearly for this." The cardinal's tone was defiant, oozing with disgust.

"Please, gentlemen, move to the office window. Gaze down at the plaza." Dr. Salabrini's voice was hypnotic, mesmerizing.

"I'm not playing your silly game." The cardinal was emphatic, nearly shouting at the speakerphone.

"Please, it's the second installment. It's *show time.*"

The Ghostbusters rose in unison, joining the cardinal at the window. His curiosity overruled his fear and anger. Three stories below, in a private garden off the main plaza, stood Dr. Salabrini, wearing a dark gray trench coat, fedora, cane, and black gym shoes, waving a cell phone. The five men stared in disbelief as Vincent shed the coat and hat, revealing the costume of a horned monster, red tights, black tail, waving his cane. Vincent loved being on stage. He especially delighted in mocking the Catholic Church, a cardinal in the audience no less. He did a jig, took a bow, and hurriedly put back on his coat and hat, then disappeared from the garden.

The cardinal summoned his secretary, directing him to alert security. "Damn, the Church has been put upon twice on the same day."

The Ghostbusters had once again witnessed Vincent's insanity. The cardinal was livid. *Was this insanity or an omen?* Conflicting emotions surged through him. He didn't know if he was angry or frightened.

Chapter Twenty-Seven

Doc shook his head, not believing what he had just read. But there it was in black and white, on the front page of the *LA Times*. The headline grabbed him like a crazed wrestler: "Cardinal McMahon Angered by Intruder."

It was an instant replay of St. Vincent's, "The Devil's in the Details." On the third time around, he read bits of the article aloud. Alarmed by the news, he dialed Gypsy, reaching her on the third ring.

"Gypsy, it's Doc. Have you seen the morning paper?"

"No, why?"

"It's Vincent. Can we talk?"

"Sure."

"I'll be right over."

A short time later, Doc collapsed into a straight-back chair, out of breath. He threw the newspaper on the parlor table. "Check out the front page."

After devouring the article, Gypsy read aloud the opening paragraph. "During Sunday morning Mass, an eerie voice interrupted the Eucharist with an announcement from the dark side: 'Welcome, my brethren, I've good news.'"

"The guy's got balls. Got to give him that." Doc grinned.

"Or maybe he's got a loose screw. Schizzy—right, Doc?"

"Maybe, but I'm not sure it's all his doing."

"What do you mean?"

"Gypsy, it's too big for one man."

"Meaning?"

"It's a big production. He needs back up." Doc stood and started pacing about Gypsy's parlor.

"You think he has an accomplice?" Gypsy furrowed her brow, puzzled.

"Perhaps."

"Who?"

"I don't know. Maybe he's getting special help." Doc stopped his nervous pacing, looking directly at Gypsy.

"How's that?"

"Maybe he's getting help from the dark side."

Gypsy gasped. "Doc, you're scaring me."

"Sorry, but I have a funny feeling."

"What?"

"Just a funny feeling. I've an appointment in ten minutes. I'll come by tonight. We'll talk."

"Oh, Doc. I'm not staying alone."

"You can stay at my place. Just come over. See you tonight."

* * *

Patton State was locked down. No one had entered or left during the past hour. Vincent Valdez had vanished, plunging the psychiatric hospital into a state of emergency. Sally Overstreet, the head nurse, was livid.

"He challenged me, wagering that he'd be gone in two weeks. I was foolish enough to take him up on the bet." Sally paused, catching her breath. "He's embarrassed me, made a fool of my entire staff."

"May I check out his room?" Lieutenant Thompson had been to Patton several times but never during lock down. It was a ghost town, the day room and hallways silent, not a soul in sight.

"Sure, Lieutenant, but let me get my notes. I've jotted down a few things that may be of help."

Sally ducked in her office, retrieved some notes, and led the lieutenant down connecting hallways to Vincent's room. "I hate returning to the scene of the crime. He was my nemesis."

"You're taking this personally." The lieutenant stepped aside as she opened Vincent's room.

"He taunted me, challenged my authority, always oppositional. He laughed at the staff, boldly predicting his escape. He placed bets with other inmates."

"He made good on his word."

"That's what galls me. Here are my notes. I'll be in my office if you need me."

"Thanks." Lieutenant Thompson looked about the sparse room: a single metal bed and a metal nightstand, both bolted to the floor. The only movable items were a foam rubber mattress and two paperback novels, both by Dan Brown. He wasn't into fictional evil; he confronted it every day.

He studied Sally's notes, but nothing caught his eye on the first page. The last paragraph of the second page was explosive. Vincent Valdez was off his meds; a week's supply was found hidden behind an air vent, wrapped in a napkin. A note was found with the meds: "I'm drug free. Catch me if you can." Sally was right about the taunting. The report finished with a zinger. "Bob Wingate was found nude, bound and gagged. His uniform, wallet, and staff badge were missing." *Damn*, thought the lieutenant, *he walked right out the front door*.

After taking a few notes, he returned to Sally's office. The door was ajar, so he peeked in. "Do you have a minute?"

"Please, have a seat."

"Your notes were helpful. Can you fill me in on the meds and the psych tech?" The lieutenant pulled out his notes, still standing.

"He was on Seroquel, a new antipsychotic. He was on a trial program. Are you familiar with it?"

"A little. It's effective with those suffering from hallucinations and delusions."

"Yes."

"Now that he's off his meds, what can we expect?"

"The same bizarre shit that got him here."

"What about the tech, the missing uniform and staff credentials?"

"Bob was new to the unit. Vincent befriended him, studied and probed him, pushed his buttons. I warned Bob about Vincent, his craftiness. Told him to keep his distance."

"So, Vincent walked right out."

"He easily cleared security. Bob wore a baseball cap to and from work. We checked the security camera's tape. Sure enough, at a few minutes after midnight, a tech with a Dodger's cap strolled out the front door, waving at the security camera."

"Brazen!" The lieutenant scribbled something in his notes, shaking his head.

"I told you he was oppositional. He even taunted me on his way out!" Sally looked down, obviously furious with Vincent's antics. The office went silent, the nurse livid, and the detective puzzled. She raised her head and said, "It's hard to swallow. I hope you nail the bastard." She was near tears.

"I'll do my best. But one more thing—I thought nurses monitored the taking of meds."

"We do."

"How'd he skip his meds?"

"Under his tongue, regurgitated them … hell, if there's a will, there's a way."

"Got ya. I'll be in touch."

Chapter Twenty-Eight

"Vincent Van Gogh, it's party time."

"I'll second that." The reunited twins clinked glasses, downing the champagne with gusto. "Those clowns at Patton were a joke. The deluded bastards, thinking they could contain me." Vincent Van Gogh raised his glass, offering a toast. "Here's to our mission."

"To the mission." Vincent Amadeus took a sip, then lit and handed a joint to his twin. "We have the cardinal on the run. He's full of fear and doubt."

"I told you. Our first year at seminary, Roger McMahon let his guard down, confiding in me, revealing his doubts. At first, I thought it was merely growing pains, early jitters, nervous about committing his life to the Church. But he trusted me, opening up after a wee too much wine." Vincent Van Gogh took a heavy hit on the joint, exhaling slowly.

"He hasn't changed. The cardinal fooled everyone but us. He's ours."

"What's our next move?" Vincent Van Gogh's speech slurred, surrendering to the pot.

"We'll talk later. But tonight, we party. I have a surprise."

"What's up, bro?" Vincent Van Gogh loved surprises.

"The guest of honor is due any minute."

"Give me a hint, Amadeus."

"It's a she."

"Mildred?"

"I think that's her now." Vincent Amadeus peered through the peephole. "It's party time!" he yelled out, pulling her through the door, hugging the life out of her.

"Where's Van Gogh?" She looked across the spacious loft, not seeing him.

"Bro, you've got a female caller." Amadeus motioned toward his twin.

"Mildred, you are truly a sight for sore eyes." He emerged from the kitchen, arms wide. The two embraced, rocking back and forth with delight. "The old gang's back together."

"We're gathering steam. Next, it's the cardinal. There's nothing like an inside job." Mildred laughed with delight.

The three disciples of Satan danced in a circle, laughing, delighted Vincent Van Gogh was free. They whirled about the loft until Amadeus lost his balance, falling to the sofa. Van Gogh collapsed beside his twin, followed by Mildred. She was giddy, sandwiched between the twins, feeling protected, loved, and needed. After catching her breath, she asked, "When do we strike again?"

"Soon!" Vincent Amadeus exclaimed. "But tonight we celebrate."

The trio smoked and drank until early morning.

"Tomorrow is a new day," Dr. Vincent Amadeus shouted before passing out.

"It's the beginning of the end," Vincent Van Gogh slurred, curled up in a ball, hugging an empty bottle of champagne.

Mildred was already asleep, nestled on a giant beanbag pillow, smiling, dreaming of a better world.

* * *

"Tell me about the seminary, more juicy tidbits on how you got close to the cardinal." Vincent Amadeus handed his twin a mug of freshly brewed coffee. Mildred had just left for a late-morning spiritual reading, leaving the brothers alone to plan their next move.

"Roger was studious and an astute observer. He could size up a person in minutes. But he had a fatal flaw." Vincent Van Gogh sipped his coffee and thought back to his time at the seminary.

"He liked sex and rock and roll?" Vincent Amadeus quipped.

"Hardly! I thought he was the real deal, committed to the Church, devout to the core. But by our last year, after many late-night bull sessions, I experienced his dark side."

"He was attracted to men?" Amadeus laughed, knowing that was a stretch.

"No, but he was ambitious. Political power was his thing. One night, after a bottle of merlot, he opened up, confiding in me. He made me swear on the Bible that I would never repeat it."

"And you obliged him?"

"Of course, I was also in the bag. We had each polished off a bottle of wine."

"Well, what was the secret?"

"He said that he had an encounter with the devil."

"What?" Amadeus's eyes widened as he smiled.

"Satan had come to him in a vision, offering him unfettered powers in exchange for his soul. He sweetened the pot with promises of political powers. He ensured Roger that he would be the pope before his seventy-fifth birthday."

"He told you this when he was drunk?" Amadeus's eyes lit up.

"Yes, but not just once. We were very close during our last year. He said he had this vision three separate times."

"Did he sell his soul?" Amadeus leaned forward, searching his brother's dark brown eyes. It was like looking in a mirror, their facial features and expressions identical.

"He never said. I inquired about his secret at bull sessions, only when we were alone and drunk."

"How did he see the devil?" Amadeus was searching for a weakness or some clue to his mental makeup.

"He saw him as a real power, a force to be dealt with."

"But he harbored doubts about his faith?"

"He believed in God, thought the Church the best way to get close to the truth. That's what he said when he was sober. But when drunk, he hummed a different tune, seeing the Church as a theater to play out his political ambitions. To him, God was the great politician and master puppeteer, part magician and part raconteur. Only a great storyteller could weave such a plot, tales of turning water to wine, parting the Red Sea, and building an ark big enough to accommodate the entire animal kingdom. He wanted to be close to the seat of power. He said to me, his speech slurred, just before passing out, 'As God is in heaven, I'll be on earth.' He didn't laugh or smile. He was dead serious."

"Do you think we can control him, make him think we're Satan?" Amadeus leaned back, finishing off his coffee.

"He's ambitious and addicted to power. We all have our obsessions. For some, it's money, sex, booze, or gambling. For the cardinal, it's political power. He had to be in control."

"We'll approach him with an offer too good to refuse." Amadeus stood, stretching out his arms, visualizing the next performance. But this time, he would not be alone.

* * *

Cardinal McMahon was halfway through his mail when he spotted a lavender envelope, addressed to him in flowing script. Curious, he tore into it. A few seconds later, he was stunned by its content:

You are cordially invited to take a walk on the dark side. I've come to finalize the contract. The terms and conditions remain the same; your soul in exchange for being head of the Church. Say yes and you will be the next pope. I'll be back.

The cardinal's hand trembled as he stared at the letter. There was no postmark or return address, nothing to indicate the source of the missive. He flashed back on the mysterious visitor. Was it *him*? Was it Vincent Salabrini? Were they one and the same?

Suddenly he recalled a drunken confession. He was young, having fun, sharing inner secrets and indiscretions with a fellow seminarian. Vincent Van Gogh Salabrini was ancient history. Or was he? He also had a twin— Vincent Amadeus Salabrini. Visions of Dr. Vincent Salabrini dancing in the courtyard hit him in the solar plexus. "The devil's a trickster!" he yelled. He was alone in his office, utterly alone.

Chapter Twenty-Nine

William Preston got a jump-start on the day, arriving at Shamrock Investigations before six-thirty. By eight, he had learned that Cardinal Roger McMahon attended St. John Seminary in Camarillo and was a roommate of Vincent Van Gogh Salabrini. Both received Master of Divinity degrees. After graduation, Roger McMahon headed east for Catholic University in Washington D.C., while Vincent was ordained and became a parish priest at Our Lady of Mount Carmel in nearby Santa Barbara.

The P.I. put down his notes, digesting the info. With their close ties severed, they drifted apart, pursuing their separate dreams. *This is one hell of a case. The cardinal needs to be filled in.*

He placed a call to St. John's Seminary and got an appointment with Father O'Malley who had a hand in educating Cardinal McMahon and Vincent Van Gogh. By two, he was sitting in his office, gazing at the wall-to-wall pictures of former seminarians.

"You must be proud," the private eye commented, motioning toward the expansive photo gallery.

"We've had some prominent Catholics walk the hallways. Cardinal McMahon was a student of mine."

"How was he as a student?" William was impressed. Father Michael O'Malley was at least seventy-five, with snow-white hair and a ruddy complexion, but he had the energy of a much younger man.

"Excellent linguist and a Bible scholar second to none, with a nose for politics." The father chuckled, flashing back on his famous student.

"Politics?"

"Roger was a leader and good at organizing people; he knew what he wanted and went after it. But please, before I ramble on, why all this interest in the cardinal?"

"I'm actually working for the cardinal."

"Oh?"

"I'm here to find a good friend of the cardinal's." William flipped his longish hair, trying to appear casual. "You mentioned on the phone that Cardinal McMahon and Vincent Van Gogh Salabrini were close."

"Yes, it's hard to forget such a middle name." The priest once again chuckled, remembering the two young seminarians. "They were roommates, on the same committees, and class officers. But there was one noticeable difference. Roger was serious and cautious; he always played his cards close to the vest. But Vincent, that's another story."

"That's the story I want to hear. Please." William flashed the inveterate priest a disarming smile.

"He was a trickster, fond of imitating others; he loved to play practical jokes."

"What sort of jokes?"

"He liked to show up at a meeting or social function, disguised, causing much laughter. He came dressed as a medieval monk one time and the next as Nietzsche, big moustache and all. That bit got him in hot water."

"How is it that you recall such specifics after all these years?"

"If you'd have been there, you'd recall them too. Two memorable characters, without a doubt, but why all the interest in Vincent?"

"The cardinal would like to reconnect with him. Do you have any idea how I might get in touch with him?"

"No, all I have are fond memories. I've seen the cardinal a few times but lost touch with Vincent. He was at a Santa Barbara parish for several years after graduation. But he moved on."

"Is there anything else about Vincent that might be helpful?'

"No, not really. Although, and this is confidential, he did have a mental breakdown during his last year. He was hospitalized, lost a month of school."

"Do you have records of this?"

"Yes. I looked them up before you came. You said you were interested in locating Vincent, so I did a little digging. The research brought back a lot of memories."

"Good ones, I hope." William stood and thanked Father O'Malley. "You've been very helpful. Oh, by the way, could I have a copy of his medical records, especially the mental breakdown? Cardinal McMahon would greatly appreciate your cooperation in the matter."

"Not for just anybody, but for the cardinal, sure thing."

William left with a smile and an explosive medical document. When Vincent was prescribed lithium, his mental problems stopped, and he reverted to his playful, jokester ways. He immediately wondered if Vincent Amadeus was taking meds. They were, after all, identical twins. Since he was close to Santa Barbara, he visited Vincent Van Gogh's old parish. He found out that after a five-year stay, he was transferred to Saint Mary's in New York. There the trail went cold. After two tumultuous years at his new post, he went AWOL. The Church lost track of him; he was missing in action. William phoned a priest who knew him at Saint Mary's. He said one day Vincent failed to show at dinner, never returning. He had inexplicably vanished into thin air.

* * *

As the cardinal put down his second glass of wine, a knock at the front door invaded his thoughts. He glanced at the wall clock: 10:30. He suddenly remembered that his secretary was dropping off some legal briefs.

"Coming, Richard." He moved across his living room, feeling the effects of the cabernet. He swung open the door and nearly fainted. Two priests pushed him inside, quickly closing the door.

"Cardinal McMahon, I hope you're ready to party. I have a surprise," Vincent Amadeus said with an expression of delight.

Vincent Van Gogh curtsied, smiling from ear to ear. "Remember me?"

The cardinal's eyes ballooned, revealing both shock and indignation. "I resent the intrusion. I'm calling security."

"Roger, is that any way to treat an old friend?"

"I don't know you!"

The twins, flanked on either side of the livid cardinal, escorted him to the sofa, firmly leaning on his shoulders, causing him to plop back, dislodging his reading glasses.

"Please, Roger, take a good look at my twin brother," Amadeus said, throwing his arms wide, laughing with gusto.

The cardinal studied the man. He was a mirror image of Dr. Vincent Salabrini. He leaned closer, still puzzled. "Who are you?"

"Roger, for goodness sake, it's your old roomy. Remember the seminary, good old St. John's, our late night bull sessions, your confession?" Vincent Van Gogh grinned, feeling elated with the reunion. "It's a special occasion. Amadeus, break open a new bottle of cabernet. The night is young."

"Capital idea. Come cardinal, it's time we get to know each other." Vincent spotted the liquor cabinet, found a cabernet, Winston Hill, 1999, and with the grace of a seasoned sommelier poured three glasses and proposed a toast. "Here's to a budding friendship with promise for a better tomorrow."

"I'm not playing your game." The cardinal glared at the twins. The mention of St. John's and the late night bull sessions sliced through his inebriated consciousness, unleashing a torrent of conflicting emotions.

"Game? This is no game. This is the beginning of the end." Vincent Amadeus said, pushing a glass toward the cardinal.

"Roger, let's take a walk down memory lane." Vincent Van Gogh said. "We'll start at St. John's, our bull sessions, the spontaneity of youth."

"It *is* you!" The cardinal's eyes widened; he couldn't deny it.

"Of course, who else?" Vincent Van Gogh placed the wineglass in the cardinal's hands, lightly brushing his fingers.

"That was a long time ago," the cardinal said, hesitantly accepting the wine. "We were finding our way, only on the first steps of our spiritual journey."

"But now we've come full circle, ready for the truth." Vincent Van Gogh lifted his glass. "Cheers."

The twins sampled the cabernet and shouted in unison, "Great taste, Cardinal! The cabernet is superb."

"The wine, yes, but not … this. Not you just showing up here. Vincent Van Gogh, you could have made an appointment, a civilized gesture."

"Yes, but this is much more dramatic."

"Vincent, let's talk about Roger's confession." Amadeus slid down beside the cardinal, skillfully juggling his wine.

Van Gogh joined his twin, slowly sipping the cabernet. "Remember our last year at St. John's—drinking, dreaming, baring our souls, and the visions of Satan promising extraordinary powers? Well, the future is now. The world is ours. *He* has our back."

"Our talks were nothing but drunken bull sessions, products of youthful imagination."

"I'd rather think of them as omens and prophesies, previews of today. Today is here. We've come for you. *He* is keeping *his* promise; today a cardinal, tomorrow the pope."

"This is madness!" shouted the cardinal.

""No, this is the *truth*," countered Amadeus.

"Drink up, for tomorrow you will rule the Catholic Church, and *he* will rule the world," said Van Gogh.

The twins coaxed the cardinal to drink up, the third cabernet of the evening. They also arranged for a meeting. Next Sunday, at nine sharp, the twins, the cardinal, and special guests would resurrect a Steve Allen classic: *Meeting of Minds.*

Chapter Thirty

Cardinal McMahon kept it under wraps, telling Richard, his secretary, that it was a charity event. The cardinal had been handed a guest list with instructions to arrange a roundtable discussion, a clandestine affair open only to the cardinal and future disciples. The handpicked guests were punctual, the last arriving at the conference room next to the cardinal's office at exactly nine o'clock.

Richard stood guard outside, ensuring total privacy. Nameplates had been arranged for each guest seated at the oblong conference table. The cardinal sat at the head of the table flanked by the Salabrini twins, while Doc, Gypsy, and Alan Workman completed the inner circle. Mildred was seated at the far end, directly across from the cardinal. Mildred's presence shocked Gypsy but only mildly puzzled Doc.

"Good evening," said the cardinal. "We gather tonight at the request of the Salabrini twins. I, like yourselves, have been summoned to attend tonight's event. I must reveal that the twins are wholly responsible for tonight's agenda. Without further comment, I hand the meeting over to Vincent Amadeus Salabrini." The cardinal leaned back, arms folded, rigid and defensive. Nothing angered him more than losing control of a situation; he felt bullied, blackmailed by the twins.

Vincent stood, flashing the group a wide grin. "Welcome, my friends. Tonight we honor *him,* the anointed one, the giver of life and the source of truth. Please, look at the back of your nameplate. There you will find your assigned role. Tonight we will engage in Socratic dialogue in search of the truth."

The guests flipped over the nameplates, each discovering their fate. The cardinal smiled when he saw he was assigned Christ; Gypsy and Doc were to be themselves, speaking for contemporary spiritualists and hypnotists; Alan Workman was Buddha; Amadeus chose Nietzsche; Van Gogh felt comfortable being Freud. The twins dressed for the occasion, Amadeus sporting an enormous dark moustache, and Van Gogh a gray beard and unlit cigar. Tonight they would draw on their thespian background. Mildred Morley was designated chief secretary, observer, and keeper of the truth.

"The rules are few, but the importance of the dialogue life-altering," Amadeus announced, opening his arms in a gesture of cooperation. "All we ask is that you speak from your heart. Your role has been carefully selected, based on your knowledge and sensitivities."

Amadeus sat down, giving the floor to his brother. "Here is the one rule: *you must speak the truth.* No pretending, posturing, or playacting allowed. Tonight we enter *his* presence. We will be judged by word and deed. *He* knows us," Van Gogh said, nodding to his brother.

Amadeus stood again and proposed the topic. "Why God? Short, sweet, to the point. I'll defer to my twin, speaking as Freud, to kick start the first Meeting of Minds."

"Thank you, Amadeus. But from now on, I'll be Freud, and you Nietzsche. Now, to answer the question, I know why the majority of mankind clings to God. It's quite simple. We all need a big daddy, someone to help us out of a tight spot. When the going gets tough, the tough get going. The trouble is, most of us are weak, powerless to take care of ourselves. We're children in need of a protector. Belief in an all-powerful God is our ticket out every time."

"Excellent," said Nietzsche. "But belief in God is outdated, a bad hangover from more superstitious times. God is dead, and we have killed him with science and philosophy. We no longer need to bow to God's wisdom. We have replaced the omnipotence of God with the awesome power of science and technology. We no longer need to look to the heavens for the answer to life's riddles. The real answer lies in our own hands. We are naïve to believe in the existence of God."

Alan Workman, speaking as Buddha, had been reluctant to attend tonight's affair, but was now hooked. He took the floor from Nietzsche and said, "But why God? A personal being, a father figure, an omniscient parent—however you look at it—is merely an illusion, a concept interfering with our ability to see clearly. We are self-centered, projecting onto reality distorted concepts, fantasies, emotions, and painful memories. Instead of seeing each moment, pristine and clear, we react to experiences and events from our past pains and frustrations. We hide behind pet ideas and explanations, trapped in a bag of skin, separated from nature, real experience, and one another. God is just another idea clogging our minds and warping consciousness."

"Well done, Buddha," Nietzsche said, "but I would go further. The universe lacks meaning and purpose; there are no universal standards to judge and guide our behavior. Without God, we are alone to fend for ourselves. Morality is merely an invented game. All values—moral, political, and social—are merely creative interpretations."

"But, Nietzsche," interjected Buddha, "we need to get beneath this veil of words and concepts and experience reality directly. If we live within creative interpretation of phenomena, we are condemned to suffering."

Nietzsche looked over at Gypsy, smiling, extending his arms. "Gentleman, please. We need to defer to our feminine side. If there's a yin, there's a yang. Please tell us, Gypsy, how a practicing spiritualist sees reality."

Gypsy cleared her throat, not at all comfortable about entering the fray, still stunned that Vincent had a twin. "I'm a practical person, seeking to help my clients find answers to their troubles. I sometimes use Tarot cards to connect to the unseen. My intuition tells me that there lies behind the everyday world a vast reservoir of wisdom and energy readily available to those with an open mind." She paused, and then continued, her European accent charming, mystical. "If the mind is open, the heart will follow. There are indeed unseen powers affecting our lives. I sense that not all of these forces are benevolent. The Salabrini twins frighten me. They are playing with fire."

The cardinal stepped in. It didn't look good, just standing by idly, allowing God to be put through the ringer. After all, he was an officer of the Church. "In Matthew 5:43, Jesus said, 'You have heard it said, you shall love your neighbor and hate your enemy. But I say to you, love your enemies, bless those who curse you, do good to those who hate you.' Jesus has spoken, and I follow his words. I will not return hate for hate."

"You put on a good show, Cardinal McMahon. And Gypsy, we're so sorry. It is not our intention to frighten you. We are seekers of the truth." Nietzsche looked over at Freud who nodded in agreement.

Doc jumped in, feeling a need to support Gypsy. "Gentlemen, I think this is a game within a game, a production of sorts. I make my living as a hypnotist. I have been quite successful solving my clients' practical problems, such as weight loss, addictions, confidence building. But of late I've witnessed the perversion of my trade. I think the Salabrini twins are conducting a program of group hypnosis. They want us to believe in Satan."

"Jeez, Doc, I'm shocked at your skepticism. Perhaps it is time to elevate our *game,* as you put it." Nietzsche looked over at Freud for a sign of agreement. He nodded. Nietzsche stood and called out *his* name, summoning Satan's approval.

Suddenly, a deep voice rumbled, "You will soon know the truth. I'm resurrected and empowered, ready to launch the new order. There's no stopping us now. There's a crack in the cosmos, and the foundation is giving way. If you value your souls, you'll follow the twins, for they know the truth."

Vincent Amadeus retrieved an envelope from his coat pocket and placed it before the cardinal. "Please, Your Excellence, open the envelope. It's quite important."

Cardinal McMahon hesitated, frowning before he spoke. "What's this?"

"It's from *him*. All he needs is a signature," said Amadeus.

The cardinal opened the envelope, revealing a legal size document. "This is gibberish!"

"No, it's a contract," Van Gogh said.

The cardinal's face turned bright red. "This is heresy!"

"Please read it carefully. *He* needs an answer by next week. We'll be in touch," Vincent said, delighting in the cardinal's predicament. He'd been caught with his pants down. His biggest fear was being found out.

The Salabrini twins stood, bowed, and made a hasty exit, followed closely by Miss Morley. They left Alan and Doc bewildered, Gypsy frightened, and the cardinal trembling.

"We've been scammed by two lunatics. I'll notify the authorities," the cardinal said, looking at his puzzled and fearful guests. "I'm sorry you had to suffer through this insanity."

The cardinal's secretary burst into the room. "Your Eminence, are you okay?"

"Three of our guests were upset. Richard, please leave us alone for a bit. I would like to talk with the remaining guests."

"Yes, sir." Richard closed the door, leaving Alan, Doc, and Gypsy alone with the cardinal. He consoled them, ensuring them that he would get to the bottom of this. He said he would go to the authorities, but what he was really thinking about was how he was going to get out of the preliminary deal with Satan he had made years ago. He stared at the document. The last line read: "Your consent guarantees your greatest dream. Today Roger McMahon, tomorrow Pope John Paul III."

Chapter Thirty-One

T he cardinal savored the first sip of cabernet as he contemplated the one question on his mind; becoming the pope had no equal—but was it worth his soul?

By the end of the second glass of cabernet, his ritual of self-medication had kicked in and melted his internal tension. Ruling from the Vatican, presiding over the wealthiest church in the world and the religion of kings and queens, would set his world right. Cathedrals, universities, hospitals, and the Vatican in Rome represented only a fraction of his beloved church's wealth. There were also priceless art treasures and staggering investments; it was surely one of the wealthiest institutions in the history of mankind. But these things were nothing compared to the power of the pope. *I want to be him.*

He flashed on his early years at St. John's, secretly flirting with the dark side and making a deal with the devil. He had thought it was only an adolescent fantasy, but now he knew otherwise. The flirtation had morphed, presenting him with a game changer. He was at a crossroads.

A knock at the door ripped him from his quandary. He stayed still, hoping whoever it was would go away. To his dismay, the knocking grew louder and more insistent.

"Who's there?" he bellowed.

The knocks escalated into a pounding, reluctantly forcing him to the door. As he opened up, the twins rushed by.

"We're back!" they proclaimed.

He closed the door, stunned, but summoned the strength to yell, "I've notified the authorities!"

"Impossible," Van Gogh said, smirking, knowing it was a lie. The deal was too good to turn down. "*He* says you're ready."

"You're insane!" The cardinal poured another glass of cabernet.

"You're an alcoholic!" shouted Amadeus.

"What?" The cardinal had never been accused of such a thing.

"You're drinking alone." Amadeus approached the small bar.

The twins popped open a new bottle and proposed a toast. "To the next pope." They clinked glasses, both downing half a glass at the first gulp.

"Who said, *I'm ready?*" The cardinal's speech was slightly slurred; his lips tingled.

"*Him!* He's informed us you are ready to sign on the dotted line."

"It's time. Where's the contract?' Amadeus glanced about the apartment, looking for the linchpin of their scheme.

"In my desk, top drawer."

Amadeus retrieved the document, snatched up a pen, and handed it to the cardinal. "It's a once in a life time chance," he said, smiling.

"How do I know you represent *him?*"

"Trust me." Amadeus folded his arms, self-assured.

"Trust you? I need proof." The cardinal suddenly felt empowered. He loved the feeling.

"Join us," Van Gogh said, opening his arms, welcoming the cardinal to join hands.

The cardinal stood, slightly uneasy on his feet, meeting the twins at the center of the room. They joined hands, Amadeus beseeching *him* to appear. Within seconds, the compelling voice filled the room. "Sign and the world is yours. Today a cardinal, tomorrow the pope."

The cardinal's eyes were closed, hands trembling. The twins stared at each other, smiling, knowing the cardinal was on board. Before the twins departed, the cardinal signed on the dotted line.

* * *

Doc was about to close shop and call it a day after seeing five clients and suffering a heated discussion with Gypsy at noon. She insisted they go to the authorities, using the cardinal to authenticate their bazaar encounter at the cathedral. Doc wanted more time, a chance to expose the twins. He was convinced they were using mass hypnosis.

He returned Gwen's call and reached her voice mail. He thanked her for the invitation to visit an art show in Santa Monica, saying only that he had other plans. He asked if he could take a rain check, and left it at that. Down deep he knew he had feelings only for Gypsy. The thought of dating Gwen sent guilt feelings rippling through him. That was a first.

As the wall clock chimed, the buzzer sounded. He grabbed his keys and headed for the door. Whoever it was, he was through for the day. As he emerged from his office, William Preston greeted him, smiling and asking for a moment of his time.

"I'm on my way home. I have an important appointment." It was true he had plans, but only to check in on Waldo. He hadn't seen him in a week.

"This will take only a few. Please, may I come in?"

Doc took in a deep breath and frowned. "Okay, but make it quick. I'm in a hurry."

Doc sat on the edge of his desk, while William stood in front of Doc's certificates, stroking his chin. "I've late breaking news."

"Oh?" Doc opened his arms, receptive. "Let's hear it."

William turned toward Doc, looking him in the eye. "Vincent has a twin."

"What?"

"Come on, Doc, play ball."

"What do you want from me?"

"The truth!"

"I'm no liar."

"You're holding back!"

"What?"

"You've seen them yourself—two Vincents."

Doc dropped his head, nervously rubbing his hands together before responding, "I just found out."

"Go on." William eased down on the sofa, eager to hear Doc's story.

Doc shook his head. "William, you won't believe what I'm about to say."

"Try me."

Doc took a deep breath and then detailed the Meeting of Minds and the response the twins had demanded be made by next week. He suddenly felt calm and relieved, glad someone else would expose the twins.

William smiled, charged by the news. "Thanks for coming clean." He moved quickly for the door, flashing Doc thumbs up. Now he needed answers; first he'd talk with the Ghostbusters, then the cardinal. Something wasn't right.

* * *

Lieutenant Fred Thompson wiped his moustache clean, smacking his lips, enjoying the last morsel of his jelly donut. He had a hunch that good things were about to happen. Last night's fortune cookie predicted a rare find. Early this morning, Doc Mesmer phoned, urging the detective to look up William Preston. He said the private eye had inside information about Vincent Salabrini.

At nine o'clock, he entered Shamrock Investigations and was confronted by a middle-aged secretary, back to the door, hunched over a computer, hammering the keyboard.

"Excuse me, I've a nine o'clock with William Preston."

The secretary turned, smiled, and said, "Detective Fred Thompson?"

"Yes."

"He'll be right with you."

At that moment, the private investigator rounded the counter and greeted the lieutenant. "Lieutenant Thompson, I'm William Preston. Come on back."

William motioned to a chair across from his desk, stacked high with reports. "How can I help you?"

"Doc Mesmer called me early this morning. He said you had inside info on Vincent Salabrini." Detective Thompson gazed about, amazed at the humming array of electronics, televisions, cell phones, copying machines, and computers, all fired up, giving off frenetic energy. It made him edgy.

"I've been hired to dig up anything I can on him."

"Who's interested?"

"That's confidential."

"I can force your hand, so we can make this easy or hard." Lieutenant Thompson grinned, knowing he had the upper hand.

"Why the interest in Vincent Salabrini?" William smiled, maintaining civility, not wanting any trouble with the LAPD.

"He might be a fugitive from justice."

"In that case, I'll be candid. I'm working for Cardinal McMahon. He's trying to locate an old friend, a former seminarian. Cardinal McMahon and Vincent Van Gogh Salabrini studied at St. John Seminary in Camarillo."

"Vincent Van Gogh?" Lieutenant Thompson flipped open his notepad, rapidly working his stubby pencil.

"Vincent, it seems, has a twin. The two have the same first name; only the middle name's different."

"What?" The lieutenant raised his brows, feverishly scribbling in his notes.

"One is named Amadeus, the other Van Gogh."

"Didn't Van Gogh slice off his ear?" Detective Thompson looked up, halting his note taking.

"That's what I hear."

"Have you seen the Vincent twins?"

"One of them."

"Which one?"

"Not sure."

The lieutenant resumed his note taking. By the time he had finished the interview, he'd taken four pages of notes. When he reached his car, he phoned the cardinal's office and made an appointment for five o'clock. Richard, the cardinal's secretary, tried to put him off, but the detective was insistent.

Chapter Thirty-Two

The Ghostbusters had cornered the cardinal, demanding an emergency meeting. The LAPD was closing in, aware of the twins, suspecting that Vincent Van Gogh was Vincent Valdez. Attorneys representing abused boys besieged him with embarrassing lawsuits. The cardinal was an emotional wreck; but he vowed not to show it.

Cardinal McMahon flung open the inner office door, greeting the ragtag collection of gumshoes with aplomb. He didn't want to appear rattled. "Greetings! Please, come in."

The two priests entered first, bowing slightly as they skirted past the cardinal, who was dressed down tonight, wearing black offset by the traditional white collar. The psychiatrist smiled at the cardinal as he stood before his chair, but William Preston grimaced; he looked nervous. He was the one who spilled the beans to the LAPD. The Ghostbusters remained standing, waiting for the cardinal to settle in behind his massive desk.

"Gentlemen, we could cut the tension with a knife. Let's be frank. Why the urgency? William, why don't you start the meeting."

The private investigator was dressed in a dark suit, his hair pulled tight in a ponytail. "Sir, it is imperative that we sever any connection with the twins. Lieutenant Fred Thompson is breathing down our necks. He's on to the twins. He suspects that Vincent Van Gogh is Vincent Valdez. We have no choice but to cooperate."

The cardinal wanted to appear relieved; after all, it was the Salabrini twins who had humiliated and blackmailed him. He *had* to appear relieved; help was on the way, and he had a lot at stake in the contract he signed. "I'm with you. They've been a thorn in my side for far too long."

Dr. Mario Salazar looked puzzled, squirmed in his seat, and then said, "Cardinal McMahon, I've been sitting on this far too long."

"Yes, what is it?" The cardinal leaned back, trying to appear relaxed, as if his mind wasn't racing and his emotions weren't threatening to erupt.

"Are the twins psychotic, or are they demonic? We've all experienced their performances. It's surely madness. But what's the source?"

The psychiatrist's question hung over the meeting, demanding an answer. The cardinal folded his hands prayer-like as every member of the Ghostbusters sat in silence, waiting for a response. They all knew the question was directed at the cardinal.

The cardinal unfolded his hands, gesturing to the psychiatrist, and said, "Dr. Salazar, you asked the question, but surely you have an option. I'd love to hear from you."

"Well, there is clear evidence of psychosis. The twins are being moved by a strong force. In my opinion, their bizarre behavior is the product of faulty brains and twisted minds. A more scientific diagnosis would require more observation and analysis."

"You think they're crazy," the cardinal commented, looking first at the psychiatrist before turning to the priests. "Father Gallagher, it started with you. What's your take?"

Father Gallagher sighed and shook his head. "I respect Dr. Salazar's opinion and wish it were true. But down deep, far below my rational mind, when I'm anywhere near Vincent, either one, I'm frightened. They're connected with something very dark."

"Evil," said Father O'Neil. "The twins are evil."

The cardinal turned to William Preston. "Can you add anything here?"

"Sir, from my research and limited observations, I think the twins are tricksters, obsessed with practical jokes and pulling off a big hoax. Are they crazy? Well, both had suffered mental breakdowns, been treated and heavily medicated, especially Vincent Van Gogh. I think Van Gogh is Vincent Valdez. So does Lieutenant Thompson. I'm sure he's about to make his move."

The cardinal leaned back again, weighing his options. "I'm calling the lieutenant right after our meeting. The twins must be put away."

Cardinal McMahon quickly closed down the meeting, ensuring the Ghostbusters he'd place the call. But the first call was not to the LAPD. The cardinal had been given the twins' cell number. As soon as he was alone, he made the call. He warned them of their impending arrest. They thanked him, saying only that they were moving on for now. They'd be back. Their last words were, "Remember the contract. Your soul belongs to him."

PART FOUR:
The Pope

Chapter Thirty-Three

It took a full year before Pope John Paul III understood the miracle that was his life. He was the first American pope, a cardinal from California, and a product of the San Fernando Valley. The American dream had been realized. The United States had its first black president; the Catholic Church had its first pope from the new world. The popular press loved the new pontiff; his gracious smile, quick wit, and political acumen combined with his charisma to create an international superstar. What lay hidden, beneath the public persona, was about to explode on the world scene.

Pope John Paul III was finally alone, tucked away in his study, far from the prying eyes and ears of the Vatican. His formidable political will and sharp instincts had kept him one step ahead of the watchful eyes of his enemies. They were everywhere—jealous cardinals, paranoid Catholics, priests from both the left and right, conservatives fearing he was too pragmatic, liberals thinking he was stuck in the status quo. Catholic insiders sensed he lacked a deep appreciation for the sacred. He was, it was rumored, too glib, too conciliatory, and way too hip.

The new pope, only in his second year, poured another glass of cabernet and smiled. The stress of the day dissolved, allowing for a rare moment of reflection. It all happened so fast. Immediately after signing the *contract* and the disappearance of the twins, his career had blossomed; he'd been propelled straight up the Church hierarchy, soaring over every obstacle in his path. It was as if he were acting out a role, his character and destiny orchestrated by some unseen force. Ten years before, he was a young cardinal, fighting legal battles, protecting wayward priests, and overseeing the successful construction of Our Lady of the Angels Cathedral. Today, he was arguably the most powerful, and surely the wealthiest, holy man alive.

Pope John Paul III flinched, glimpsing a pair of shadows on the study wall, moving slowly, growing larger. He turned quickly, nearly fainting when his eyes settled on two priests standing side by side, smiling and reverently bowing.

"Congratulations. Sorry it's taken us so long, but we've been doing *his* work."

Pope John responded, instinctively challenging their intrusion. "Who are you?"

"Have you forgotten us already?"

A flood of disturbing memories washed over him. "How did you get in?"

"We enjoy the extraordinary help of our support team." Amadeus glanced about the study. "Just love the décor."

"What support team?" the pontiff asked.

"*Him!*" exclaimed the Salabrini twins, their voices harmonizing.

The nightmare was back, exploding in his face, jarring him back to the truth. He was pope, true enough, but not by his hands alone. "What do you want?"

"We've come to collect on the bargain." Vincent Van Gogh smiled.

"What?"

"The bargain, the *contract*. But let's be merry. You know, Roger—may I call you Roger?" Van Gogh's smile broadened.

"No! I'm calling security. This is the Vatican!"

"Calm down, Your Holiness. Let's have a drink and discuss our business like the gentlemen we are." Amadeus moved to the liquor cabinet, checked the selection of cabernets, and settled on a Dalla Valle Maya, 1994. "Nice, a California wine."

"I haven't forgotten my roots," the former cardinal from Los Angeles muttered, sinking back in his chair, fully aware that the twins were in charge, at least for now.

The unlikely trio settled into some serious drinking, reviewing Cardinal Roger McMahon's meteoric rise to the papacy. After singing his praises and celebrating the mission accomplished, the twins addressed the real subject at hand. "We have orders from *him*." Amadeus grinned, feeling tipsy, more from the power he had over the pope than from the fine California wine.

"What?" The pontiff's eyes glazed over, slightly anesthetized from the fourth glass of cabernet. He had definitely exceeded his limit.

"He wants you to write an encyclical." Amadeus paused, smiling. "One addressing the role of women in the church. *He* insists on the ordination of women."

"Blasphemy. That's ridiculous!"

"*He* was there. Mary Magdalene was a disciple, perhaps his closest," Van Gogh said, slowly sipping his wine.

"This is a revisionist's lie, fodder for popular culture." The pope flipped his right hand, visibly dismissing such an idea. He looked around, making sure they were alone. He was embarrassed by such nonsense. If the hallowed ancient walls could talk, they'd vehemently protest.

"*He* was quite clear. Mary was Christ's closest disciple. Any revisionism came from political infighting in the early church. The other disciples embraced the idea that women were imperfect men."

"That was a common belief during that period of history." The pope squirmed in his chair, not liking the direction of the conversation.

"Look," Amadeus said, "people today think of male and female as two characteristics of the same thing. There are human beings and they come in two types. But during Christ's time, there were not two types of human beings; there were merely degrees of human beings. Hence, women were thought of as imperfect humans."

"The church is rooted in tradition," the pope snapped.

"But we know the truth. Men pushed aside the feminine, blinded by their prejudice. *He* wants to set the record straight." Amadeus walked to the window, peering out at the glowing night sky illuminated by the lights below. "Even your study has a view of St. Peter's Square."

"You need to begin writing the new encyclical. Let's call it 'Hail Mary,'" Van Gogh said, beaming the pope a Cheshire grin.

The pope shook his head, scowling.

"*He* wants the encyclical started immediately," the twins said in unison.

"Who says?" Pope John Paul III stood, a bit shaky, more from the conversation than the wine.

"*He* said you owe him." Amadeus approached His Holiness, looking him straight in the eye.

"Owe *him?*" the pope said sarcastically. "Owe *him* what?"

"Your soul!" Amadeus shouted, causing the pontiff to flinch.

"I need proof. I need tangible evidence to convince the cardinals." The pope opened his hands and added, "Show me something tangible."

"*He* anticipated your reluctance." Amadeus retrieved a thick envelope from his coat pocket and handed it to the pontiff. "Inside you will find instructions. Faithfully follow them and you will have your proof. You are instructed to start an archeological dig immediately. We'll return in a week to check on your progress. Keep our meeting secret. Any funny business and there'll be dire consequences."

The twins made a quick exit, leaving the head of the Roman Catholic Church reeling, struggling to digest what had just happened. *It was the wine,* he rationalized. But he knew better. Down deep he understood how he had become the new pope, bishop of Rome. He owed *him*.

* * *

The pontiff passed out just after the twins departed his study. The wine and invasion by the Vincent twins had traumatized him, knocking him unconscious. At three in the morning, he bolted upright, eyes wide, staring at the thick envelope on his desk. He had hoped it was a bad dream and the envelope would just disappear. But there it was, beckoning him, a siren from the dark side.

He reached for a letter opener and slowly sliced the envelope open. For the next ten minutes, he studied the contents of the mysterious missive. The third page contained the directive:

It is imperative that an archeological dig commence immediately. Begin the excavation five feet directly behind the altar of the Basilica San Giovanni of Laterano. Approximately twelve feet beneath the recent layers of concrete, covering the original sections of stone, there is an opening to an ancient vault, the resting place of manuscripts that will rock the world.

Saint John Lateran, the mother of all churches, contains a lost gospel beneath the original church circa AD 314, buried by a secret society two centuries before Constantine the Great. Here, beneath the basilica, over top the Castra Nova equitum singularium, the New Fort of the Imperial Cavalry, established by Septimlus Severus in AD 193, you will discover the original Gospel of Mary Magdalene, the forbidden document, suppressed by the early church.

The pope read and reread the document, frightened but clearly understanding his role. The facts rang true. The twins knew their history. That morning, he convened a committee and began plans for the dig. Several cardinals owed him a political debt, and he cashed in. The commission sanctioned the dig, giving in to the pope's request; the cardinals understood it was an order. Archeologist broke ground within seventy-two hours of the twins' visit.

Chapter Thirty-Four

The ringing phone caught Father Gallagher just as he was about to head out for lunch. He hesitated, his hunger pushing him out the door. But guilt overruled; it could be someone in need.

"Father Gallagher here."

"Patrick, have you seen the morning headlines?" Father Michael O'Neil's voice crackled with excitement.

"I was about to crack the *Times.* I was doing rounds at the hospital all morning."

"Have you had lunch?"

"No! I'm famished."

"I'll meet you at Gerry's on Ventura, the one closest to the 405 in thirty minutes," his best friend said. "We got a lot to talk about."

"You buying?" Father Gallagher chuckled, testing his generosity.

"Be there! I'm leaving the cathedral this very second."

Father Gallagher's stomach growled and rumbled all the way to Gerry's. He'd already decided, pastrami on rye.

Father Gallagher spotted his friend in a corner booth making small talk with a waitress. He hustled over and caught only the last few remarks. "Were you flirting with that cute young thing?"

"Flirting is as far as it goes. What took you so long?" His longtime friend beamed a wide smile.

"I started with the *LA Times,* then read the *New York Times* and *Washington Post* online." Patrick opened the menu, then immediately slammed it shut. Pastrami on rye, he hadn't changed his mind.

"The rumors have proven true." Father O'Neil drummed his fingers on the table.

"You think this is the real deal?" Patrick stroked his snow-white beard, oblivious to his friend's nervous habit.

"The pope's completely behind it." Father O'Neil retrieved an envelope from his coat pocket. "Check it out."

Father Gallagher put on his reading glasses, at first frowning, then groaning as he skimmed the document. When he finished, he dropped the letter, immediately distancing himself from its message. "I sense something sinister here."

"You're not alone. The cathedral halls have buzzed with rumors about an urgent archeological dig all week. Pope John Paul III is making history; the sudden discovery of two manuscripts, one in Latin, the other in Greek, is about to transform the Church. The Gospel of Mary Magdalene is no longer a fairytale." Father O'Neil folded his hands prayer-like, brows arched, his eyes baring his soul. He was skeptical. "The pope has commissioned biblical scholars and linguists to conduct further study. So far, 80 percent of the linguists are convinced. The documents are authentic, paper and ink date to the first century CE."

"Are you thinking what I'm thinking?" Father Gallagher searched his friend's eyes.

"The Salabrini twins?" Father O'Neil said.

"Bingo! They've been gone for years, but not far from my thoughts," Father Gallagher admitted, slowly nodding his head.

"Five to be exact. Patrick, you think they're in touch with the pope?"

"I'd bet my last dollar on it."

"My good friend, it's time to resurrect the Ghostbusters." Father O'Neil smiled.

"I'll call Dr. Mario Salazar. You think he's still game?" Father Gallagher leaned back, giving the waitress room to position his pastrami on rye directly beneath his snow-white beard.

"Got to be. The soul of the Church is at stake." Father O'Neil opted for a salad. He was on a diet.

* * *

"It seems like old times. How long has it been?" Dr. Salazar eased into a chair across from Father Gallagher, glancing at the bookshelves. "Over there, Vincent flaunted the Bible. Quite a show."

"Five years! Time flies when you're having fun," quipped Father O'Neil, as he got comfortable beside the psychiatrist. "But when we last saw him, fun wasn't the operative word."

"Now there are twins, doubling up on the pope." Father Gallagher paused, then added, "And Father O'Neil and I think they've an inside track to His Holiness."

"What's your proof?" Dr. Salazar's eyes narrowed, interested but skeptical at such a possibility.

"Nothing concrete, just a hunch," Father Gallagher confessed.

"We need more than that."

"But it's a hunch I'd put money on." Father Gallagher leaned back and explained, "At our last meeting with then Cardinal McMahon, Father O'Neil and I both sensed that the former cardinal was rattled by the twins. They knew something, had something on him. Now since he has become pope, they've come back, ready to collect on a debt."

"What's all this talk about gambling and debt? How could the pope owe the twins anything?"

"Because of their connection with Satan," Father O'Neil said.

"What?"

"We both believe the Salabrini twins have mesmerized the pope," Father Gallagher said, his voice tinged with dread.

"You're reading too much into this." The shrink frowned, his skepticism having the upper hand.

"What about the archeological find?" Father O'Neil turned, staring at Dr. Salazar.

"Scientifically interesting, theologically explosive." Dr. Salazar smiled and added, "There's bound to be a change in how the Church views the role of women."

"How do you explain the pope directing the dig, hitting pay dirt, discovering the Gospel of Mary?" Father Gallagher stood, looking out his office window as if searching for the answer to the riddle.

"There have been rumors about such a gospel for centuries. And remember the gospels found in Egypt?" Dr. Salazar paused. "The pope just got lucky."

"It's more than luck," the two priests responded in unison, looking at each other, laughing.

"We're making a trip to the Vatican." Father Gallagher turned from the window, looking down at the shrink. "We need your help—both your psychiatric expertise and financial assistance. We're looking toward the first of next month. Are you with us?"

Dr. Salazar stood, sighed, and then said softly, "I'm in."

* * *

"Amadeus, check out the latest." Van Gogh dropped the morning edition of the *L'Osservatore Romano* on the kitchen table.

"Bro, I don't read Italian." Amadeus looked up at his brother, frowning.

"It's the English edition." Van Gogh walked to the corner window of the third-floor flat, glimpsing the entrance to St. Peter's Square. The one-bedroom apartment had been convenient, only a fifteen-minute walk from the pope's residence.

Amadeus chuckled as he read the featured article. "The holy father's cautious but excited about the Gospel of Mary. I think it's time for another visit."

Van Gogh turned from the window and said, "Read the third paragraph aloud. It lights my fire."

Amadeus cleared his throat, stood, and motioned for his twin to take a seat on the sofa. He adjusted his reading glasses and then began. "According to Vatican historians, the existence of this gospel was unknown until the turn of the last century when several fragments were discovered in Egypt. Until now we have been limited to an assortment of disjointed fragments, all Coptic translation, the original Greek text lost to antiquity. But now archeologists, under the supervision of Pope John Paul III, have unearthed what appears to be the original Greek version of the Gospel of Mary Magdalene."

Amadeus smiled at his brother. "Shall I read on?"

"Please, the best is to come."

"Linguists and historians have dated the Greek text to the first century CE, and biblical scholars are now engaged in an intense analysis of the text, looking at style, references, and consistency with the Gospels of Matthew, Mark, Luke, and John. The Greek text, if authentic, will indeed rock the Christian world, revealing Mary Magdalene as a strong leader, charismatic, most favored disciple of Christ, and closest spiritual confidant. The text details several conflicts with Peter; especially telling was her fear that Peter was envious of her special role and disciple insider. Peter, the document asserts, was forceful, using political leverage, fiercely protecting his position as overall leader of the disciples. Scholars are examining Mary's account of several arguments with Peter and his brother Andrew over revelations Jesus had shared with her. As political infighting grew, Mary became increasingly disenchanted; she was disheartened that the Lord's message was edited, de-emphasizing the role of the feminine. The corruption of truth, the gospel declared, caused her to leave the intimate circle of disciples."

"Magnificent! Tomorrow we make a late-night visit to the pope." Amadeus sprang from the sofa and hurried to the window, gazing down at pedestrians clogging the streets below.

"He will be pleased," Van Gogh said, joining his brother at the window.

"The pope?" Amadeus asked, grinning.

"No! Satan." Van Gogh laughed. "Tonight will be a hoot."

Chapter Thirty-Five

Father Gallagher gazed up at the papal apartments, sweaty palms revealing his angst. "It took some arm twisting, but we made it," he said, grimacing. "It's time for some answers." The Ghostbusters had a date with destiny; they had a nine o'clock appointment with Pope John Paul III. He was, however, still Cardinal Roger McMahon to them.

Fathers Gallagher and O'Neil turned to Dr. Salazar, both motioning up to the corner windows of the Apostolic Palace.

"I'm ready. Let's hope His Holiness is candid. I've some pointed questions," the shrink said, having rehearsed many questions on their flight to Rome. The trio was a long way from Los Angeles. They hoped the pope had not forgotten his roots.

The papal apartment wrapped around two sides of the palace, featuring a vestibule, and His Holiness's beloved library boasting 20,000 volumes, many rare and out-of-print first editions. Next to the library was a small room for the papal secretary, and Pope John Paul III's private studio from which he blessed the crowd every Sunday. But his favorite room was the library; he coveted books, his least offensive vice. At the doorway, opening onto historic loggia decorated with frescoes, the pope's private secretary, Father Antonio Manghetti, greeted the Ghostbusters.

"Welcome. His Holiness will receive you in his private studio," the elderly priest said in a thick Italian accent. "He's been looking forward to the reunion."

Father Manghetti ushered the trio into the quaint apartment, motioning to the twin sofas facing each other. "Please get comfortable. Pope John Paul III will be right with you. His Holiness prefers the Windsor chair facing the fireplace."

As the trio heard the familiar voice, Father Gallagher nervously blurted, "He's here!"

His Holiness entered, smiled warmly, hoping his old friends from Los Angeles would bring good news. "Welcome to the Vatican."

The Ghostbusters stood, bowed, and waited for the pontiff to take the Windsor chair. The two priests sat to his left while the psychiatrist sat to his right.

"It's a blessing to see you. We've all followed your meteoric rise with great fascination," Father Gallagher said. "And now, we're at a crossroads, a period of great change."

"The discovery of the Gospel of Mary is a blessing." The pope smiled.

"What made you begin the excavation?" Dr. Salazar asked, itching to probe the real reason for the dramatic move.

"It's a topic near to my heart, one I've devoted considerable time and energy to. A recent article on the lost gospels motivated me to act on a long-held intuition." The pontiff motioned to the wall-to-wall books at the far end of the room. "I've quite a few books on the subject. It all came together."

"May we be candid?" Father O'Neil asked, nervously rubbing his hands together.

"By all means," the pope said, gently smiling at his former friends. He sensed their friendship was about to take a serious turn, remembering a tense meeting when he was cardinal in Los Angeles.

"Have you seen the Salabrini twins?"

"Who?" The pontiff flashed his former friends a puzzled look. He needed a moment to consolidate his thoughts.

"You surely have not forgotten the twins, Amadeus and Van Gogh?" Dr. Salazar looked directly at the pontiff, studying his reactions with the eye of a trained physician.

"Oh, those two. It's been so long. What an embarrassment." The pope shifted forward in his chair, pausing before he spoke. "We've much better things to discuss than those two."

"We need some answers," Father Gallagher said, not wanting to drop the subject. "We all feel that the Vincent twins are involved in your success."

"Excuse me?"

"Please, hear us out." Father Gallagher took a deep breath and said, "We know about your school days with Vincent Van Gogh, that you were roommates at St, John's, as well as fellow class officers, close friends, and drinking buddies."

"What are you saying?" the pontiff said, his eyes narrowing.

Suddenly, the inner door of the studio burst open, and in walked two priests.

"It's homecoming," Van Gogh announced.

"Revelation time," Amadeus added. "It's time to face the truth."

"How did you get in?" The pope turned bright red.

"We have connections," Amadeus said. "Well look who it is, Fathers Gallagher and O'Neil, along with Dr. Salazar. Say, we're only three short of a baseball team."

"I resent this. I'll call security!" The pope stood, awkwardly pumping his fist.

"Please, Your Holiness, sit down and relax. We've a lot to discuss." Van Gogh approached the pontiff, smiling, gently pushing him back. "We've some old business to take care of."

Amadeus moved to the fireplace, spun around like a bullfighter, and proclaimed, "I take great pleasure in introducing my twin brother to Fathers Gallagher and O'Neil. And we must not forget Dr. Salazar. I don't think you've met Vincent Van Gogh."

Van Gogh bowed and said, "It's indeed a pleasure. Well, time is of the essence, so let the meeting begin."

"The first order of business," Amadeus said, nodding to everyone individually, "is past business. Pope John Paul III is under contract. It's time to honor that contract."

"That's it. I'm calling security!" The pope attempted to stand up.

Amadeus sprang forward, this time shoving him back, the Windsor chair tipping precariously before righting itself on the antique carpet. "Stay seated. We're in charge now. Your time will come."

All three Ghostbusters were speechless.

Van Gogh retrieved an envelope from his coat pocket, opened it, and read aloud. It was the contract signed years ago by then Cardinal Roger McMahon. As Van Gogh read the contract, the pope slumped in his chair, eyes rolling upward. The Ghostbusters gasped in unison when they heard the final line of the contract. "I hereby exchange my immortal soul for the power and destiny promised me. When I'm pope, I'll pledge total allegiance to *him*."

"This is an insane charade," the pope protested.

"It's the truth. Embrace the truth, and it will set you free!" Van Gogh shouted. "I heard those words at St. John's, and I witnessed the signing of the contract at the Cathedral of Our Lady of the Angels."

"This requires a toast!" Amadeus strutted to the liquor cabinet, then turned to the stunned group. "A California cabernet sounds perfect, don't you think, seeing that we're all from the Golden State?"

Father Gallagher rose to protest the cruel charade, but was pushed back by Amadeus. Dr. Salazar stood, attempting to subdue Amadeus when Van Gogh shouted, "Cease and desist!" He brandished a dagger, waving it at the unruly group, adding, "I'll use this if I must."

"How'd you get that through security?" the pope shouted. His sanguine complexion and clinched fists revealed his anger.

"You should know that by now," Van Gogh barked.

"Now for that toast," Amadeus said.

"No way!" Father Gallagher snarled.

"Suit yourself. My brother and I will celebrate for you." Amadeus prepared two glasses of cabernet and proposed a toast; the twins clinked glasses and drank up. The stunned group watched in silence as the insanity played out.

"The prince of darkness has issued a proclamation," Van Gogh said. "Pope John Paul III is hereby ordered to direct the Roman Catholic Church to acknowledge the authenticity of the Gospel of Mary Magdalene and permit females into the priesthood."

Amadeus yelled, "The truth will set us free!"

Suddenly, a deep rumbling voice filled the private studio, echoing off the walls. "I hereby authorize the pope to carry out *My Will*. The Church is now *mine*." The familiar voice sent chills through His Holiness. It was ominous, causing the trio of Ghostbusters to wince simultaneously.

Amadeus and Van Gogh swiftly exited the macabre scene, leaving the pope and the Ghostbusters stunned.

Chapter Thirty-Six

After excusing the Ghostbusters with a hasty apology, the pope called security. He ordered an immediate doubling of surveillance and scheduled an early morning meeting with top security officials. "The Vatican is under attack!" he yelled into the phone. Rumors quickly circulated, fueling the already highly charged papal state. It had been only three weeks since the Vatican announced the discovery of the Gospel of Mary Magdalene. Excitement and tension gripped the Holy City.

The Ghostbusters, shocked and disoriented, needed to clear their minds, so they descended on Taverna Angelica, a modest restaurant a short walk from the Vatican. They were more in need of a stiff drink than rich Italian cuisine. The amateur sleuths settled for two bottles of a 1997 La Palazza Magnificat, a local cabernet.

Father Gallagher was the first to voice his frustration. "I'm more confused than when we arrived."

Father O'Neil wrinkled his nose, frowning, and added, "The pope is up against the wall. As the authenticity of the Gospel of Mary is proven, the political opposition to the ordination of women will mount. Conservative cardinals will wage a political war. It's going to get nasty."

"Yes, and toss the Salabrini twins into the mix," Dr. Salazar said, pausing, savoring his wine, "and all hell will break out."

"You think the pope will bow to the twins?" Father O'Neil asked.

"He looked rattled. I don't think he's in his right mind." Father Gallagher sighed.

"Bingo! He's not in his right mind. He's succumbed to the machinations of those two charlatans. The twins are conducting a campaign of mass hypnosis. Their flare for the theatrical combined with their amateur psychology has mesmerized ole Roger." Dr. Salazar leaned back, sipping his cabernet.

"Ole Roger?" Father Gallagher grinned.

"Yes, the pope is still Cardinal Roger McMahon to me."

"And what's that mean?" Father O'Neil said.

Dr. Salazar chuckled and said, "He's more politician than theologian. Add his shaky mental state and we've got a recipe for disaster."

"This is no laughing matter," Father Gallagher said.

"It's nervous laughter. We're in for a real ride."

"Let's polish off the wine and get a fresh start in the morning. The midnight hour is upon us." Father Gallagher raised his glass for a toast. "Here's to the Ghostbusters."

* * *

After his meeting with the head of security, Pope John Paul III met with linguists, archeologists, biblical scholars, Cardinal Paul Cameron, head of the traditional wing of the Church, a battle-tested politician who fiercely opposed female ordination, and Cardinals Williamson and Johnson, members of the pope's inner circle. It was a spirited meeting; the linguists and archeologists were cautious, not yet thoroughly convinced of the authenticity of the Gospel of Mary, but every day more impressed with the document. As the scientific evidence gained ground, so did the political infighting.

Cardinal Paul Cameron, the pope's nemesis, called the archeological discovery a fraud and a hoax perpetrated by the liberal wing of the Church. "It's a conspiracy aimed at undermining the authority of the Church." He didn't name the pope as a conspirator; he didn't need to. His longtime feud with Pope John Paul III was well known, finalized when the College of Cardinals chose Cardinal Roger McMahon to be the next pope. The gossip spread, whispered among political allies, naming the cardinal from Berlin as second in the final vote count. It was only gossip, but it was the talk of the town. No one knew for sure except the College of Cardinals, and they weren't talking. Everyone knew that the election of the pope was deliberated and voted in secrecy; they also knew that the penalty for disclosing any secrets was automatic excommunication. But the gossip had Cardinal Cameron in a close race, supported by an informal but credible survey of Vatican priests. Behind closed doors, it was known as the day "John trumped Paul."

Immediately after the meeting, Pope John Paul III convened his inner circle; it was time to talk strategy with Cardinals Mark Johnson and Mathieu Williamson. The challenge was clear: two thousand years of conservative theology managed by men. The gospel of Mary and female ordination were synonymous with heresy—so believed the establishment.

"We've our work cut out for us." The pope grinned at his closest allies. He was ready to roll up his sleeves and get started.

"Cardinal Cameron was livid. His face turned darker and darker red as the meeting proceeded," Cardinal Johnson said, taking a seat across from John Paul III, sequestered in the pope's private chambers, away from prying ears. The liberal cardinal disliked Cameron's politics and demeanor. They kept their distance, suspicious of each other, sometimes cold in their interaction, often openly hostile.

"He's an obstacle," the pope said, "but it's time the Church joins the twenty-first century. The conservative wing has buried its head far too long. It's time for reason and science to prevail. The best biblical scholars in the Church are impressed with the Gospel of Mary, and linguists and archeologist are now 90 percent certain of its authenticity. The skeptics have only Church tradition on their side. The evidence is overwhelming."

"I agree," Cardinal Williamson said, "but the Church moves slowly, lurching its way through history. It took centuries to apologize to Galileo. Copernicus and Galileo were both right. The heliocentric system is more coherent, simpler, and more elegant than the earth-centered hypothesis. The same is true here. The Gospel of Mary will open up history and shed light on the truth. Mary was a close disciple of Christ."

"Will the truth set us free?" the pope asked, leaning forward, searching for an honest answer.

"It will indeed, and we must make it happen." Cardinal Johnson smiled, exuding confidence. He, the most liberal of the cardinals, was the youngest, brightest, and most trusted ally of Pope John Paul III. His Holiness needed his support.

"We agree philosophically," the pope said, "but that's only half the battle. The arm twisting and political skirmishes will demand the best from us."

"Do you have a plan?" Cardinal Johnson asked.

"I have an ace in the hole. You two work on the arm-twisting. Target the usual suspects. I'll take on Cardinal Cameron." The pope stood. "The battle begins."

Only the pope's inner circle was privy to his liberal leanings, his belief in the findings of the Jesus Seminar, and his commitment to bring the Church into the twenty-first century. His liberal beliefs took second only to his quest for power. Now it was time to use his ace in the hole. The Salabrini twins were the perfect solution for the Cardinal Cameron problem. They were near; he could feel it.

* * *

The pope didn't have to wait long for the twins to reappear. That night, only hours after meeting with his inner circle, Van Gogh and Amadeus slipped through security dressed as priests. They breezed by Father Antonio Manghetti, he had been secretly given the okay earlier by the pope, allowing them access to the pope's private quarters an hour before bedtime.

"Top of the evening to you." Van Gogh said, grinning at the pope before turning and thanking the secretary for alerting His Holiness.

"We sensed you needed our services." Amadeus headed for the pope's bar and selected a merlot. "A little heavenly nectar before bedtime. It has marvelous soporific qualities."

The pope pretended to be put off but was secretly delighted with their visit. He had a request of his own. His feigned irritation eventually thawed, and by the second glass of merlot, he sprang his request.

"I have a favor to ask," the pope said, cracking a smile.

"A favor? This is a first." Van Gogh peered suspiciously over the rim of his wine glass.

"It's intimately linked to your plan," the pope said.

"Our plan?" Amadeus sprang to his feet. "The Gospel of Mary and female ordination?"

"Yes. I've reluctantly come around," he said. "But I'll need assistance." The pope leaned back in his favorite chair, sipping his wine, for the first time controlling the conversation.

"Your request is our command." Van Gogh tipped his wine glass toward the pope. "Name it!"

The pope cleared his voice and said, "I need your flare for the dramatic to convince Cardinal Paul Cameron to join forces."

"Isn't Cardinal Cameron your adversary?" Amadeus cocked his head. "The word on the street is that he's your nemesis. As I recall, the buzz around the Vatican had Cardinal Cameron as runner-up for Pope."

"I'm not privy to such talk. But it's true, he's my political nemesis." The pope cringed internally, fighting to carry on with the twins. He was not accustomed to such vulgar dialogue, especially of the street thug quality. But, he needed them.

"Do you want us to scare him or convince him?" Van Gogh asked.

"Whatever it takes. I'm on board with the plan." The pope felt mischievous. It was a scene out of *The Godfather*, a sit-down with assassins. But destiny called; un-equaled political power, fame, and historic proclamations were within his grasp. Pope John Paul III, the pope that reconciled science with theology, authenticated the Gospel of Mary, and restored the feminine to its proper place in Church history. *How sweet*, he thought. The twins left with a smile. The pope was elated.

Chapter Thirty-Seven

Pope John Paul III peered down at St. Peter's Square, savoring a rare moment of privacy. "When the moment's right," he said aloud, "I'll return home, visit California, say hello to Our Lady of the Angels." He moved slowly away from the window, lost in thought. It would be a PR coup; what better place to appeal to the people and gather popular support for the acceptance of the Gospel of Mary, and then push for female ordination. California was the seat of progressive politics; and best of all, Los Angeles was a hot bed of innovative thinkers with deep pockets. It was time for the Catholic Church to lead the way, he mused. The only American pope, born in the San Fernando Valley, reared and educated in Southern California. *I'm the perfect choice to lead a theological revolution.*

The pope finished his second glass of cabernet. *I'll become a saint*, he thought as he prepared for bed.

As soon as his head hit the pillow, he was fast asleep, dreaming, relishing images of the faithful singing his praises, heralding Pope John Paul III as a savior of the modern Church. Heads of state praised him, women adored him, and even his most ardent political foes held their tongues. The pope was a theological superstar.

Slicing into this dreamy collage of adulation and praise came the howling laughter of the twins. Vivid images of Van Gogh and Amadeus's raucous laughter shattered the pope's dream, twisting it into a nightmare. Suddenly a familiar breathy voice awakened the pope in the dead of night. "You have gained the world only to have lost your soul." The pope blinked, still in the grip of his nightmare. The voice was gone, leaving him in a deep sense of dread. He stared at the bedroom ceiling, alone, haunted by medieval images of purgatory. He was the leader of the Church, but not captain of his own soul.

* * *

Van Gogh gazed at his twin with great fondness. Amadeus's raucous laughter was infectious, moving Van Gogh to leap to his feet, joining his brother as they hugged and danced with Mildred, celebrating her arrival in Rome. Their comrade from the dark side was the final but indispensable member of the team.

"It's time," Mildred said, laughing with pure delight.

"Is the magical hour upon us?" Amadeus said, smiling broadly.

"Indeed it is," Van Gogh chimed in. "It's time we speak of intrigue."

"Lay it on me." Mildred purred, sandwiched between the twins on the sofa, excited to be back in action. She didn't mind taking a break from her practice as a spiritual adviser; duty called. Her superstitious clients believed she was on a two-week vacation in Rome; the twins knew she had a date with destiny.

"You'll play the femme fatale." Van Gogh stood and pulled around a chair so he could look his comrades in the eye.

"What do you mean?" Mildred said with a chuckle.

"Cardinal Cameron is our target, and you, my dear, will deliver the fatal blow."

"I'm not an assassin!" Mildred's eyes widened in alarm.

"Not so fast," cautioned Van Gogh. "It's not his death we intend. We need you to shock him, cripple his fierce opposition to the pope—the acceptance of the Gospel of Mary and female ordination."

"How could I possibly oppose such a powerful cardinal?" She turned and looked closely at Amadeus, searching his eyes for the truth.

"The classic way, just as Homer described in *The Odyssey*." Amadeus smiled, reaching for her delicate hand, caressing it lightly. "Odysseus was challenged at every turn. His survival depended as much on wit as brawn," he explained. "His goal was to return home battling both physical challenges and moral temptations. He thought temptations were to be embraced, not avoided. When he and his men passed the island of Sirens, lured by their song, Odysseus tempted fate by covering the ears of his men but leaving his unprotected. He forced himself to endure the alluring music by tying himself to a pole on the ship. He believed that a man must overcome temptation in order to reach moral virtue and enlightenment."

"But what's this have to do with me?" Mildred asked.

"You, my dear, are to play the role of the Siren, seductive and alluring, challenging Cardinal Cameron's moral virtue."

"You want a fortune teller to seduce an elderly cardinal?"

"Exactly!" Amadeus said smiling.

"That's crazy," Mildred said.

"And his outdated views are not?" Van Gogh broke in. "He's nothing but a prejudiced holdover from medieval times. It's time to bring the Catholic Church in line with the truth. With the Gospel of Mary, truth is on our side."

"But how can I be a Siren?" Mildred asked.

"Van Gogh and I are thespians. We'll coach you. We have a plan. We'll either lure him or shock him," Amadeus said, "but tonight we party. Tomorrow we'll work out the details."

"Here's to a new Church," Van Gogh said, raising a glass for a toast.

"And here's to a new world order," Amadeus said, joining his brother, "an order controlled by a new prince."

"Here's to the prince of darkness," Mildred added, clinking her glass.

* * *

Cardinal Cameron made a sign of the cross uttering, *"In nomine patris, et filli, et spiritus sancti,"* before getting up from his kneeling position at the side of his bed. It was a prayer for the ages, calling on his Father in heaven to give him the strength and guidance to do battle with the demons knocking at the door of his beloved Church. The former bishop of Munich was deeply troubled by the revolution brewing in the Vatican. The Gospel of Mary had gained near universal acceptance by linguists, archeologists, biblical scholars, and mainline theologians. His greatest fears were being realized; his fellow cardinals were caught up in the excitement of the moment. "Please God," he prayed aloud, "stop this madness and right the holy ship of the Roman Catholic Church."

He turned off the bedside lamp and propped himself up on several overstuffed pillows, attempting to ward off the ravages of acid reflux. The recent stress had made peaceful sleep nearly impossible. He had always been a committed defender of the conservative values of the Church. His beliefs were categorical and unwavering, allowing for no exceptions. He was an admirer of the German philosopher Immanuel Kant, impressed with the rigor of the categorical imperative. But Nietzsche, a philosopher he generally despised, aptly summarized his feelings about women: "Man shall be educated for war, woman for the recreation of the warrior, and all else is folly." It was possibly the only thing written by Nietzsche he agreed with.

His cherished beliefs were straightforward and easily recognized: he believed, without the slightest doubt, that the teaching of the Roman Catholic Church was God's word, without exception; he encouraged Catholics to attend Mass and receive communion daily; he considered a priest's vow of chastity sacred; he openly opposed the ordination of homosexuals; he never wavered in his opposition to abortion, believing it should be illegal everywhere; and he championed the subordination of women. "Men lead, women follow," he said aloud. This was God's plan. The Gospel of Mary contradicted God's word. It was the work of Satan. "It is an abomination," he mumbled again and again before drifting off to a restless sleep.

Chapter Thirty-Eight

The neatly trimmed beard was in place, brows darkened, and hair slicked back. Mildred had morphed into a handsome priest, thanks to the artistry of the twins—after all, they were incorrigible impersonators. "We've not lost our touch." Van Gogh said, admiring their handiwork.

"Acting is in our blood, perpetrating pranks a passion. Have a look." Amadeus handed a mirror to Mildred.

She gazed at her reflection, eyes wide with surprise. "Incredible! I make a handsome priest."

"But beauty is not the goal. Tonight we spring our trap," Van Gogh said, putting away the makeup.

Amadeus pulled a priest's coat and trousers from the closet, handing them to Mildred. "Please, try them on."

While Mildred excused herself to try on the clothes, the twins reviewed their plan, looking for any possible glitch. Tonight they'd do a dry run, tomorrow the real thing.

Mildred strutted to the center of the living room, made a half turn, and said, "Gentlemen, let the games begin."

"Indeed," the twins said in unison, "let the games begin."

* * *

It was a first for the pope, a personal invitation to Cardinal Cameron to visit in private, share their feelings, connect over a glass of wine. It was a grand overture, two bitter rivals baring their souls far from the prying eyes and ears of the Church's inner circle. It was a bold move, orchestrated not by the pope, but the twins.

"Your Holiness, Cardinal Cameron is here," Father Antonio Manghetti announced.

"Please, show him in." The pope stood, smoothing out his robe, smiling, a bit nervous about meeting in his private quarters.

"Please, Cardinal Cameron, get comfortable. I'm so glad you accepted my humble invitation."

"I'm at you service, Your Holiness." The cardinal looked about, noticing the wine glasses and his favorite cabernet. He sank slowly into sofa across from the pope, smiling. "This is a first."

"And I hope not the last. I've taken the liberty to choose a wine." The pope retrieved two wine glasses and poured a small portion for the cardinal's approval. It was a five-year-old Casanova Di Neri from nearby Tuscany.

"Wonderful. My favorite."

The two agreed to converse in English, Cardinal Cameron being fluent in four languages, having learned English as a youngster. "We've all been laboring under such tension," said the pope, "the discovery of the Gospel of Mary, linguists, biblical scholars, archeologists, and concerned Catholics throughout the world dissecting every morsel of information. It's been hectic."

"I'm a conservative man, as you well know, cautious and respectful of tradition. The pressure to accept the Gospel of Mary has challenged my core beliefs. The evidence is impressive, so new—and surely intriguing—but under-evaluated. We need time to assess the significance of the document." Cardinal Cameron leaned back, savoring the cabernet. "But this wine is not new. It's aged to my liking."

"We do agree on our wines. Hopefully we'll extend that to our theology." The pope smiled, adding, "We are both devout Catholics, committed to the Church, firmly rooted in God's teaching."

"But did God sanctify the Gospel of Mary?"

The cardinal's question was cut short when two priests burst through the private chamber doors, laughing and dancing, like clowns at a circus. Following on the heels of the cavorting priests was a third priest, shorter, walking slowly, smiling broadly. The pope and the cardinal were stunned. Their intimate talk and wine tasting was over; the twins had a surprise.

"Your Holiness, please excuse the interruption, but we come bearing gifts from *him*," they sang. Amadeus and Van Gogh spun around, light on their feet, then stopped abruptly and bowed. The priests grinned in unison, gesturing to the shortest of their party.

"We take great pleasure in introducing Mary Magdalene."

The mystery guest curtsied, took off her coat, fluffed her hair, shed the fake beard, and smiled. "I'm Mary, and I've been sent by *him*."

Cardinal Paul Cameron and Pope John Paul III stared at the spectacle, speechless.

"The cat got your tongue? Well, we do understand," Amadeus said, "but history cannot wait. We've got the real deal. *He* insisted that you hear the truth from Mary."

The pope stood, shook his fist, wanting a good show for the cardinal, and threatened to alert his secretary to notify security. He looked at Cardinal Cameron, shook his head in disgust, and turned abruptly, pointing at the twins. "You must remove yourself from my chambers. Immediately! The cardinal and I were engaged in a very private matter."

"Oh, but that can wait. Tonight we make history. Tonight we hear the Gospel of Mary, *from Mary.*"

The cardinal stood and demanded that the threesome vacate the pope's apartment.

The pope shook his fist, his face red with anger—a bit of theatrics, orchestrated by the twins with his eager approval.

The next thirty minutes were the best of intimate theater, Mary quoting her gospel, Amadeus and Van Gogh supplying theological commentary. At the end of the performance, the twins summoned Satan, his breathy voice and stern commands echoing, causing the cardinal to slump, gasping, holding his chest. The twins and Mildred then vanished, leaving the pope momentarily paralyzed, watching his political nemesis writhing on the floor, moaning.

"Cardinal Cameron, are you okay?"

The cardinal's body contracted into a fetal position, and saliva pooled about his mouth. "Please help me," he chanted in a strained tone, his face twisted in agony.

The pope summoned his secretary, who alerted Vatican medics. The cardinal was rushed to Rome's Gemelli Hospital where he was treated and sedated. He had suffered a major heart attack.

Hours later, the pope finished the bottle of cabernet, assessing the twins' performance. He secretly admired the theatrics, relishing the impact it made on the cardinal. His coronary would surely slow his opposition to the Gospel of Mary. But the pope couldn't shake Satan's voice. The quoting and analysis of scripture was moving, certainly within the range of competent actors. But the voice overwhelmed the pope. It must be *him,* he thought. No human unaided by sophisticated sound equipment was capable of this.

Chapter Thirty-Nine

Father Antonio Manghetti gently shook the pontiff's shoulders, whispering in his ear, trying desperately to awaken him. "Your Holiness, please wake up. Please! There's an emergency," he said in his heavily accented English. It was three in the morning.

The pope stirred, then blinked several times. "What is it?"

"Your Holiness, you're needed at the hospital."

"What?"

"Cardinal Cameron is dying!"

"Are you sure?" he slurred, wiping the sleep from his eyes.

"Yes, Your Holiness. Please, we must hurry."

Within twenty minutes, security had hustled the pope to the cardinal's bedside where two doctors were tending to an array of monitors showing irregular heart rhythms and plunging blood pressure. Nurses and emergency personnel clogged the hallway leading to the cardinal's private room; the tension was palpable. The pope leaned over the fading cardinal and peered into his cloudy eyes.

"Cardinal Cameron, can you hear me?"

The cardinal blinked slowly, moaning softly. "Please help me." His response was barely audible, nearly silenced by the whirring of machines monitoring his lagging heart and respiration.

The pope, sensing the urgency, began the holy sacrament, knowing it was necessary for his salvation. While administering the Eucharist to the dying cardinal, he was seized by a prophetic vision. A smile briefly graced his face, visible only to the nearly unconscious cardinal, as he savored the image of standing at his apartment window addressing a crowded St. Peter's Square, adorned in ceremonial robe and miter, celebrating the official recognition of the Gospel of Mary. *The roadblock to immortality has crumbled*, he thought as Cardinal Cameron exhaled for the last time.

* * *

Cardinal Paul Cameron's unexpected death at Rome's Gemelli Hospital left the Vatican in turmoil and the Ghostbusters stymied. The medical staff exhausted their options, Herculean in their efforts to save the cardinal, but the second heart attack proved fatal. The three amateur sleuths from Los Angeles made several requests to visit the pope, but were denied. Dr. Salazar and Fathers Gallagher and O'Neil reluctantly returned home, still in the dark about the pope. The inner workings of the Vatican were impenetrable. But the political buzz surrounding the Gospel of Mary and Cardinal Cameron's sudden death created an opportunity for Pope John Paul III. And he would not be denied.

The pope convened his inner circle, laying out the details of his plan to Cardinals Mark Johnson and Mathieu Williamson. They were on board, believing the time was right. His Holiness would visit the United States, culminating in a special homecoming ceremony at his beloved City of the Angels Cathedral.

Chapter Forty

Doc devoured the front-page article, instantly propelled to another time. It was a blast from the past. The headline said it all: "Pope John Paul III Returns Home."

Visions of Vincent Salabrini flooded his mind, releasing a torrent of emotions. Vivid images of Vincent morphing from a stooped, hooded man with a cane and eye patch to the dashing philosophy professor, the performance at Saint Vincent's the night of the electrical storm and blackout, and the Meeting of Minds in Cardinal Roger McMahon's office consumed him. It was at the cardinal's office that he, along with Gypsy and Alan Workman, discovered that Vincent had a twin. He remembered nearly every word uttered by the twins, Amadeus playing the part of Nietzsche, and Van Gogh becoming Freud. The following years failed to mitigate the impact that Schizzy and his enigmatic brother had on him. Doc couldn't wait to break the news to Gypsy, but he thought it better do it in person. She had successfully repressed her memories of the twins, not even mentioning their names in years.

He rang Gypsy and made a date for seven-thirty. Doc had a break, so he'd discuss the latest with Waldo, a warm-up before laying it on Gypsy. After making a few notes on a client's chart, he ducked out of his office, eager to hear Waldo's response.

A new clerk was at the front desk, a middle-aged woman recently divorced. Doc sensed Waldo had a crush on her. She was a bit overweight and deeply wrinkled, a perfect match for the aging proprietor. But Doc knew Waldo was all talk and no go. He said hello to the new clerk and asked about Waldo.

"He's in the back room," she smiled. Mary was flirtatious but definitely not Doc's type.

Doc went into the back room and greeted his friend. "Wally, what's crackin'?"

"Your boy Juan Perez made his pitching debut with the Boston Red Sox. He's now hurling fast balls in the big leagues." Waldo grinned and added, "Remember when we saw him pitch at Pierce College."

"I've followed him for years. He called me two weeks ago and told me he was breaking into the starting rotation. My guided imagery sessions must have worked."

"Why didn't you tell me?' Waldo frowned. Shaking his head, mumbling something into the morning newspaper spread open on his lap.

"It slipped my mind." Doc remained standing, lost in thought. Juan was definitely one of his favorite clients.

"Big news for Catholics," Waldo grunted, not looking up from the newspaper.

"What's the latest?" Doc said absentmindedly. He shook his head, dislodging thoughts about Juan, and sat down.

"The pope's coming to town."

"That's why I'm here."

"To talk about the pope?" Waldo looked up, grinning, showing off his stained teeth.

"You bet. It's great news, local boy returns home. He's the biggest thing to come out of the San Fernando Valley."

"I thought that was Judy Garland." Waldo folded the paper and leaned back.

"No way! Judy was born in Grand Rapids, Minnesota. She moved west as a kid and lived up in Lancaster for a while."

"I liked her in the Andy Rooney flicks."

"I'm not here to talk about Judy Garland. Remember Vincent?" Doc said.

"The Salabrini dude. Schizzy?"

"I have a feeling that when the pope hits LA, the Salabrini twins will surface." Doc shook his head once again, recalling their antics.

"I thought Schizzy and his twin were a pain in the ass for both you and Gypsy. If she gets wind of your interest in stirring up that stuff again, you're in for some heavy trouble." Waldo stood and said, "Enough of the idle chit chat. I got to check on the hired help."

Waldo's disinterest did little to prepare Doc for Gypsy's reaction to the pope's homecoming. Doc left by the back door, not wanting to lay eyes on Waldo. He was in a bad mood.

* * *

Doc was apprehensive about his date with Gypsy. They hadn't mentioned the Salabrini twins in years, so when the door opened, he gasped. "Holy shit!" There, dressed as a priest, was Schizzy, laughing with manic energy.

"Van Gogh, we've company," Amadeus shouted over his shoulder. "Please Doc, join us." He stood aside, bowing, motioning toward Van Gogh and Gypsy. She and Schizzy's twin were seated at her consulting table, looking up from the Tarot cards spread out in the classic Celtic cross.

"Gypsy, are you okay?" Doc asked as he quickly made his way over to her.

She looked up, her eyes full of fear. "Our date is on hold."

"We have important matters to attend to," Amadeus explained. "It's time to reconvene *his* disciples."

"What are you talking about?" Doc said.

"Have you forgotten? We called Alan Workman, and he's on his way."

Speechless, Doc pulled up a chair and slid close to Gypsy. Her trembling hands, flushed face, and unfocused eyes conveyed more than fear. She had confronted evil before; she had challenged it, fought it, and resisted it. Now it threatened to possess her.

"The pope is scheduled to visit Our Lady of the Angels in two weeks," Amadeus said. "We're planning a hell of a homecoming."

"Gypsy, let's begin," Van Gogh said. "I need an edge on our future."

"I can't!" Gypsy leaned back and folded her arms, staring blankly ahead.

"I'll pay to play," Van Gogh offered.

"She's upset," Doc said, coming to her rescue.

"All hell is going to break out if you don't cooperate." Amadeus took a chair next to his brother. "Curses and witches are nothing compared to our arsenal of weapons. *He* has our back! So, let the reading begin."

Three quick knocks sent Amadeus scurrying to the front door. He swung it open and quickly ushered in Alan Workman. "Alan, please come in. We're about to do a Tarot reading." Amadeus pulled up another chair, and the reading began. Gypsy's trembling hands dangled a swinging crystal from a chain, cleansing the cards.

Doc and Alan flashed each other a suspicious look, then simultaneously blurted, "The plot thickens." Over the last few years Doc and Alan had become very close; they could read each other's mind.

She looked up at Van Gogh, eyes glazed over by an unholy blend of rage and fear, and sighed. "What's your question?" Gypsy's tone was tentative, voice cracking. She cleared her voice and gazed at Van Gogh. His dark brooding eyes caused her to shiver—her soul ached.

"Will *he* show at Our Lady of the Angels?" Van Gogh smiled, his eyes locking on hers, sending another round of shivers through her tension-racked body. She was able to continue only by disassociating from her body, disengaging from the physical. She floated above her emotion-racked body, insulated from her feelings. She'd become a disembodied apparition.

"*He?*" Gypsy uttered, not really wanting a response.

"Our savior, the *True Prince*." Van Gogh grinned.

"True prince?" Gypsy feared the dark side, especially the twins' obsession with evil. Doc often said they were psycho; she felt they were demonic.

"Will our true father show, sanctifying the Gospel of Mary?" Amadeus broke in, irritated at Gypsy's stalling tactics.

Gypsy rolled over the challenge card, revealing an eight of Wands. She cleared her throat again, pressing her hands firmly into the cloth-covered table, momentarily halting her incessant trembling. "I see contact with someone important, an inspirational moment."

"It's *him*!" Van Gogh shouted, causing the others to flinch.

"That's it." Amadeus pulled his brother from the table and whirled him around, dancing, laughing, bellowing, "*He's* with us!"

Doc, Gypsy, and Alan silently observed the madness, afraid to interrupt the twins' antics. Doc and Alan were convinced of their madness; Gypsy feared for her soul.

Amadeus suddenly stopped in his tracks, bowed to his brother, and said, "*He will* show at Our Lady of the Angels. And you, *his* trusted disciples will witness the truth."

Van Gogh yelled out, "Praise the true prince!"

"But before we leave," Amadeus said, "we've orders from *him*." He slid into a chair next to his brother and said, "*He* wants his disciples at the cathedral, front and center, ready to carry out *his* will."

"What?" Doc and Alan blurted in unison, turning toward each other.

"We have been instructed to pack the cathedral with all those sympathetic to the pope's goal of sanctifying the Gospel of Mary. *He* wants political support for the pope's plan; the pope's plan is *his* plan."

"We don't have the political connections," Doc said. "Besides, why should we help the pope?"

"Exactly!" Alan shouted. "What's the pope done for me lately?"

"Join us and embrace the truth, for the truth will set you free. Besides, you don't want to be on *his* bad side. Right, Gypsy? " Amadeus and Van Gogh glared at Gypsy, then turned to Doc and added, "Doc, you don't want to expose Gypsy to unnecessary harm, do you? They grimaced at Doc, held their stare, then stood and bowed to the others. "We'll return with more orders. *His* will be done," the twins shouted and slammed the door.

Chapter Forty-One

Doc and Alan consoled Gypsy for the better part of two hours, sipping green tea and sharing their feelings about the twins' theatrics. After that, they switched from green tea to merlot, a Christmas gift stashed away in Gypsy's pantry. The heavenly nectar finally took effect, dulling the angst raging within her. Doc carried her to bed, covered her with a blanket, and decided to go to Alan's place for a nightcap.

Alan had years ago turned his humble abode into a Buddhist shrine. In addition to the new mediation garden, he had converted an extra bedroom into a second library containing various works on Buddhism and meditation. He wanted to keep the spiritual part of his life separate from his love of philosophy and science. He was still an engineer, methodical and organized, his life compulsively compartmentalized.

They didn't want to mix their booze, so they uncorked another bottle of merlot, an inexpensive jug wine. Doc leaned back in a wingback chair, sipping his merlot, admiring Alan's little beauties. He'd added a second aquarium, larger and more exotic than the first, featuring discus fish, a flattened freshwater fish native to the Amazon River basin. Gone were the Post-its, but Alan still tinkered with his philosophy, settling for a blend of East and West. Buddhism, he confided to Doc years earlier, gave him peace of mind. Western philosophy, he complained, cramped his style. "Too many conundrums," he'd say, shaking his head. Enlightenment was to be had with meditation and Buddhism, the exclusive domain of his second study.

"I still favor the neon tetras," Doc said, watching them swim about. "But we're not here to talk about fish."

"Jeez, Doc, I thought we'd seen the last of the Salabrini boys," Alan said. "They need to be locked up, the key thrown away."

"They sure did a number on poor Gypsy. She thinks they're possessed." Doc took another drink of the merlot, needing to dull his senses.

"They're crazy, pure and simple." Alan drained his glass and poured another.

"Tell me, Alan, what's real? What's going on? Amadeus, Van Gogh, the first American pope, from the San Fernando Valley no less—it all makes a guy's head swim."

"It's theater of the absurd," Alan sighed.

"You think they're play acting?" Doc said as he replenished his drink.

"That and more! But I think they're kicking about an existential theme, playing with it, theatrically mad." Alan frowned, flashing on his prior philosophical struggles.

"I need some help here," Doc said. "I don't have your philosophical grounding. What's with the theater of the absurd?"

"Theater of the absurd was coined by the Hungarian critic Martin Esslin in the early sixties. A few European playwrights in the fifties and sixties grappled with themes advanced by the French philosopher Albert Camus." Alan paused and added, "In the *Myth of Sisyphus*, Camus depicted the human condition as basically meaningless."

"Well, my experience with the Salabrini twins, if not meaningless, is surely absurd," Doc said, thinking of the pain they just caused Gypsy.

"I think Camus was saying that a fully satisfying explanation of life was beyond our reach. I think he meant that, for us, the universe must be seen as absurd." Alan stood and walked over to his beauties. "But the dignity and grace of my little beauties is not absurd. They're real."

"Alan, do you think there's a devil?" Doc chugged the last of his wine. His head was spinning.

"I don't think there's a Christian Satan hanging out in hell. But I do believe that ignorance, prejudice, and blind emotions can wreak havoc."

"Do you think that Amadeus and Van Gogh are mad?" Doc slurred his words for the first time, slumping in his chair.

"They're mad, but maybe not in the classical sense."

"What do you mean?" Doc leaned his head against the back of the chair.

"They're not mad in a modern psychological sense."

"Is there a Satan giving them orders?" Doc closed his eyes, overwhelmed by stress.

"The twins believe there is, but I don't." Alan found a blanket, covered a sleeping Doc, and went out back to check on his koi. He needed some space.

The small waterfall feeding the koi pond eased Alan's tension, providing a respite from the evening's madness. The Western side of his mind yearned for an objective explanation of Schizzy and his brother. His intuitive mind, nurtured by the stoicism of Buddhism, brought him back to his favorite quote: "The mystery of life is not a problem to be solved but a reality to be experienced."

* * *

Father Gallagher turned off the main lights in the chapel and retired to his study, waiting for Father O'Neil and Dr. Salazar. It was the first meeting of the Ghostbusters since they'd returned from the Vatican. The news of the pope's upcoming visit had them anxious; they sensed the twins were not far away.

As Father Gallagher glanced at the clock, Father O'Neil walked in, followed by Dr. Salazar.

"Right on time," Father Gallagher smiled.

"The traffic at this late hour is light—what a treat," Dr. Salazar said, sliding into a chair across from Father Gallagher.

"From my office at Our Lady to here in twenty-five minutes." Father O'Neil pounded his chest, proud of his time.

"Lead foot," Father Gallagher teased, knowing his friend's penchant for pushing the speed limit.

"The pope's arrival is near, so there's no time to waste." Father O'Neil took a chair next Dr. Salazar, stretching his legs. "Just two weeks."

"It's imperative we get a few minutes alone with him. We need answers," Dr. Salazar said.

"We've got answers!"

Father Gallagher looked up, and Father O'Neil and Mario spun around. They were shocked but not disappointed.

"We're back," the twins bellowed in unison. They wore black tuxedos, top hats, white ties, and each twirled a cane.

"It's a glorious moment in history; local boy makes good—dedicated priest, ambitious bishop, and cunning cardinal. And to beat all, the first American pope," Amadeus announced.

"We're thinking of a real gala, Hollywood style." Van Gogh flanked his twin in front of Father Gallagher's bookshelf, leaning slightly on an oversized open Bible.

Dr. Salazar stood, shook his fist, and shouted, "Look here, this is madness! I'm a doctor of psychiatry! I think delusional thoughts fuel your eccentric behavior. I'm concerned for your mental well-being and the safety of the pope."

"Bravo! Wonderful speech, full of Shakespearian excesses, but woefully off the mark." Amadeus glared at Dr. Salazar. "This is not a psychological issue."

"You shrinks reduce reality to psychobabble. We have our eyes on the truth. The record must be set straight." The veins on Van Gogh's neck bulged, flushed with anger.

"What record?" Dr. Salazar barked.

"The Gospel of Mary, the role of women in the Church," Amadeus said, pointing his cane at Dr. Salazar.

"*He* is in charge now. The pope has signed on the dotted line. *His* will must be done," Van Gogh said authoritatively.

Dr. Salazar shook his head. "I'm calling 911."

Amadeus laughed, pulling a derringer from his coat pocket. "I'll use this if I must. Now sit down and listen."

Dr. Salazar collapsed in his chair, muttering, "This is insanity."

Van Gogh retrieved an envelope from inside his coat and threw it on the desk in front of Father Gallagher. "You will find enclosed your instructions. Follow them to a tee. Any deviation will cause you great harm."

"Farewell for now!" Amadeus shouted as they left.

Father Gallagher rushed to the door and checked the hallway. Nothing. He moved quickly to the back door. The twins were nowhere in sight. John, the new custodian, emerged from the rear corner of the cathedral, carrying a waste can full of paper.

"Did you see two men, formally dressed, tuxedos?" asked Father Gallagher.

"No, sir. I was cleaning the storage area."

"Thanks."

Father Gallagher rejoined the Ghostbusters and said, "Out of sight and out of their minds."

Father O'Neil and Dr. Salazar were standing, leaning over the desk, reading the instructions. Father O'Neil sat down, shaking his head. "You better take a look, my friend."

Father Gallagher picked up the two-page letter, scanning it quickly. He threw it down in disgust. "They're simply mad."

The letter, written in elegant script, midnight black on pale blue stationary, glowed eerily under the desk lamp, mesmerizing the Ghostbusters. Its message was simple but disturbing:

The pope's visit must be well supported by political activists, especially those opposed to sexism, misogyny, and the Catholic Church's patriarchal hierarchy. The Ghostbusters shall rally vigorous religious and political support. Fathers Gallagher and O'Neil must spread the word. Our Lady of the Angels must be packed by faithful followers of the pope, those dedicated to bringing the Catholic Church into the twentieth century.

Fathers Gallagher and O'Neil shall arrange for supporters of the pope to engage in political rallies supporting acceptance of the Gospel of Mary and female ordination. They must exploit the news media's eagerness to cover the pope's visit.

The pope is to be praised for his foresight and commitment to the truth. All those opposing the pope's message shall be demonized and exposed as prejudiced medieval bigots.

His Holiness shall henceforth be looked upon as a saint, a true savior of the faith, a loyal Christian, and an advocate of the truth.

And last, but most urgent, the pope's visit will culminate with a shot heard around the world. It is written; martyrdom is the pope's fate. The Ghostbusters are hereby charged with enshrining this event in the annals of the Church's illustrious history.

He is the way, the word, and encompasses all that is true and sacred.

In his name,

Vincent Amadeus and Vincent Van Gogh

Chapter Forty-Two

Detective Fred Thompson had hit the archives early in the morning, dusting off an old case. It wasn't just another cold case; it was the twins, Amadeus and Van Gogh. The dormant case had not been forgotten. Detective Thompson loathed unfinished business and desperately wanted another crack at the crazies before he retired. A flood of memories washed over the LAPD veteran: Doc, Gypsy, a murdered private eye, and the elusive Mildred Morley. He relished having another go at *that one*. In twenty minutes, he had an eight o'clock with two priests and a psychiatrist at Saint Vincent's. Father Gallagher's morning phone call was emphatic; the twins were back, this time threatening the pope.

Motoring out of the city after rush hour was a pleasure; he was allergic to gridlock. As he passed Our Lady of the Angels Cathedral, he thought of the pope; he wasn't Catholic, but the buzz over his upcoming visit was palpable.

As Detective Thompson pulled into the parking lot at Saint Vincent's, worshippers were leaving after the early evening Mass. He stopped an elderly white-haired lady walking with the aid of a cane and asked for directions to Father Gallagher's office. She spoke slowly, offering too many details, gushing over how nice the priest was. "I've known him for nearly twenty years. Gosh, what can I say, he's a real peach of a guy," she said, peering up at the lanky detective, her pale blue eyes cloudy, tired with age. "He's the rock of this parish," she added in a gravelly voice. She turned away, grinning as if she knew a secret, and walked slowly toward the parking lot.

The door to the priest's office was open, but the detective knocked gently, alerting the three men gathered around a book-cluttered desk. Two were wearing the cloth.

"Father Gallagher?"

"Detective Thompson, I presume." Father Gallagher stood and introduced the LAPD detective to the Ghostbusters. "Please pull up a chair. But before we get started, take a look at this." Father Gallagher retrieved a letter from the top drawer of his desk.

Detective Thompson put on reading glasses and read. When finished, he asked, "Where did you get this?"

"From the twins, Amadeus and Van Gogh," Father Gallagher said. "They were here last night."

Detective Thompson adjusted his glasses and read aloud, "The pope's visit will culminate with a shot heard around the world. It is written; martyrdom is the pope's fate." The detective peered over the rim of his glasses, brows arched. "Is this a prophecy or a threat?"

"That's why you're here. We think the pope's in danger," Father O'Neil said. "Crazy or not, we believe they're capable of violence."

"Maybe we need to go back to square one. Tell me of your involvement with the twins," the detective said.

Father Gallagher again reached into his desk and retrieved a large manila envelope, then handed it to the detective, saying, "I took the trouble of chronicling our relationship with the twins, from the moment I met Vincent Amadeus in the chapel until now. Please, have a look while I get refreshments. Coffee all around?"

"Please, black for me," said the detective as he began to read the detailed notes.

After ten minutes of puzzled looks, sighs, and "I don't believe it," Detective Thompson put down the ten-page document, shook his head, and said, "Damn. Why didn't you contact the LAPD?"

"We were conflicted." Father Gallagher sighed.

"It's been a living hell for us," Father O'Neil added, finishing the last of his coffee.

"Any contact information—an address or phone number?" Detective Thompson asked.

"Nothing! We hadn't seen them since the incident with the pope at the Vatican." Father Gallagher looked over at Father O'Neil and Dr. Salazar and said, "Our last contact with the twins was traumatic."

"The pope was livid, our meeting aborted. We were quickly shown the door. Further attempts to meet with the pope were repeatedly denied," Dr. Salazar said.

"You think they'll return?" The detective opened a notepad and began scribbling.

"Maybe," Father Gallagher said. "They've made a habit of visiting Saint Vincent's."

"Father O'Neil and Dr. Salazar, I need some contact info. He handed his notepad over to the psychiatrist. "Cell number too. I've a feeling I'll need your help. I'll give you my card. On the back you'll find my private cell number. Don't hesitate to call."

"What's your next move?" Father Gallagher asked, walking the detective to the door.

"All points bulletin to start. I'll have the church staked out. I'll be in touch."

After the detective left, the Ghostbusters hatched a plan of their own. They would join the search for the twins. The amateur sleuths agreed to activate Shamrock Investigations. "I'll call William Preston the first thing in the morning," Father Gallagher said as he walked his friends to their cars.

* * *

The sun had dipped below the hills of the west valley, rush hour was in full swing, and the small shops on Reseda were closing up. Detective Thompson was on his third cup of coffee when Mildred emerged from her parlor with a young woman, paused by her car, chatted for a moment, and then waved good-bye, disappearing down the alley. He immediately fired up the Ford Taurus, knowing there was only one exit. Moments later, she pulled out on Reseda. He was on her side of the street positioned to make a move, expecting her to travel south toward Ventura Boulevard. She didn't disappoint, heading south in a late-model Honda Accord. He pulled out, tailing her two cars back, protecting his cover.

At Ventura, she hung a left, heading east, traveling in the right lane. The traffic was thick, trying his patience. Ten long minutes later, she pulled into a lot down the street from Wally's Emporium. He found a spot on Ventura a half block away. Mildred hesitated outside the bookstore, checking out the window display before moving on; she crossed the street and walked toward a liquor store. She passed the store's entrance and went into a side door directly below a neon sign that said Spiritual Advisor. "Gypsy!" he muttered. *Maybe I'll get lucky, kill two birds with one stone.*

He waited a few minutes, allowing the spiritualists to get comfortable. Timing was everything; he needed answers. When the timing felt right, he sprang up the stairs and rapped hard on the door. "Police!" he shouted. The door cracked, then swung open. Gypsy's pale complexion reddened as she stared up at the towering detective.

"Top of the evening. May I come in?"

"Detective Thompson?" Gypsy's eyes widened.

"Yes. It's been awhile, but I've urgent business. Can we talk?"

"I have company."

"I know. That's why I'm here."

Flustered, Gypsy stepped aside, allowing him in. He smiled wryly as his eyes met Mildred. "Well, well, it's been awhile."

"Detective Thompson, so good to see you. Are you seeking spiritual advice?"

"Not tonight. But I do have a few questions."

"Please, pull up a chair and join us." Mildred said.

Detective Thompson pulled a notepad from his coat pocket, smoothed out his moustache, and sank into a chair, flanked by the two spiritualists. "I hope I'm not interrupting anything important."

"We were catching up on old times," Gypsy said, trying to keep it together. Her heart was in her throat. The detective's surprise visit meant trouble.

"Well I've some catching up of my own. I'll get directly to the point. Have either of you seen the twins?"

"What twins?" Mildred frowned, looking away, averting the detective's eyes.

"I've reliable information that Amadeus and Van Gogh are in town."

"Where are they?" Mildred asked, "I need to see them."

"That's why I'm here. I thought you could be of assistance." The detective looked up from his notes, staring at Mildred. He didn't trust her or believe anything she said.

"Well, are we going to play games or be truthful?" The detective looked first at Mildred, then Gypsy. "We could talk about this downtown."

"I fear for their safety," Mildred blurted.

"You should! If things go our way, we'll soon have them under lock and key. I've ordered an all points bulletin. Their mugs will be plastered all over town."

"What have they done?" Gypsy asked.

"Plenty. Escaped custody, harassed officials of the Catholic Church, and threatened innocent citizens." The detective turned to Mildred and said, "You've been in contact with them, haven't you? The twins are like family, aren't they?"

"No way!" she lied. She knew the detective didn't believe her.

"If you two are lying and something bad happens, you'll be held accountable."

"What bad thing is going to happen?" Gypsy's fear was apparent in her voice.

"The twins have threatened the pope." Detective Thompson leaned back, glancing first at Mildred, then at Gypsy, enjoying the effect his zinger had on the two spiritualists.

"That's ridiculous!" Mildred insisted.

"They were here," Gypsy blurted.

"What?" Mildred frowned, staring at Gypsy.

"I did a Tarot reading on Van Gogh," she said softly, her hands trembling as a tear trickled down her right cheek.

Detective Thompson reopened his notepad, jotted down a few words, smiled, and said, "Please, Gypsy, go on."

"They were both here, barged in, insisted I do a reading."

"Were you alone?" the detective asked.

"At first. But then Doc showed."

"He saw the twins?"

"Yes. Van Gogh forced me to do a Tarot reading."

"What did he want to know?"

"He was interested in the pope. Van Gogh wanted to know if *he* would show."

"He?"

"Satan—he wanted to know if Satan would show at Our Lady."

"He wanted to know whether the devil would show at Our Lady of the Angels Cathedral?"

"Yes!" Gypsy clasped her hands, wringing them.

"This is crazy!" shouted Mildred.

"It is indeed." Detective Thompson asked several more questions and then thanked Gypsy for her cooperation. He looked over at Mildred and said, "Don't leave town. I've some unanswered questions."

He stood, walked slowly to the door, then glanced over his shoulder and asked, "Was anyone else here?"

"A friend of Doc's," Gypsy admitted.

"Who?"

"Alan Workman."

"Thanks again. I'll be in touch."

Back at the car, he phoned downtown and arranged for surveillance. "I want Mildred Morley tailed, around the clock."

Chapter Forty-Three

Amadeus's movie career had been short, but it still had its perks. Danny Villanova, a horror film director, now producer, had made it big. He was on location in Mexico and would be out of the country for three months. The twins made him a rental offer he couldn't refuse. The Hollywood Hills, three-bedroom stucco was now home to the twins. From the deck, they could see Hollywood, the Miracle Mile, and on a clear day, downtown LA. With a bit of imagination, they could make out Our Lady of the Angels.

Van Gogh stood next to his brother on the deck, looking out at the panoramic view, and said, "Soon we revolutionize the Catholic Church."

"We need to celebrate. What's a party without Mildred?" Amadeus reached for his cell phone, then waited out several rings before she answered. "Mildred, it's party time."

"Oh, thank God you called. I'm being tailed."

"What happened?"

"I called on Gypsy. I was at her place no longer than five minutes when Detective Thompson showed up. He knows about Van Gogh's Tarot reading. He's on to us."

"Why didn't you alert us?"

"I was afraid my phone was bugged. I was going to use a pay phone, but I'm being shadowed. I'm scared."

"Hold tight tonight. Van Gogh and I will come up with a plan. Don't call us; we'll call you."

"Please, I need to see you. They're all over me."

"Keep the faith. We'll be in touch." Amadeus flipped the phone closed and took a deep breath.

"Trouble?" Van Gogh said.

"She's being tailed. That LAPD dick is tightening the noose. We've got to play it safe."

"What does he know?"

"He knows that Gypsy did a Tarot reading on you."

"He knows about the pope?"

Amadeus grimaced and said, "Possibly."

The evening was upon them, and the twins had their work cut out for them.

"It's crunch time," Amadeus said.

* * *

Doc was filing some paperwork when the buzzer sounded. He glanced at the clock. It was after eight. After the buzzer sounded again, this time more insistently, he reluctantly answered the door.

"Little slow opening up," the detective said, pushing his way into Doc's office. He walked directed over to the phony certificates, then chuckled and turned to face Doc. "We need to talk."

"What's up?" Doc sank into his swivel chair, expecting the worst.

"Why didn't you tell me about the twins being back?"

Doc just shook his head and rolled his eyes.

"Come on. I dropped in on Gypsy. She spilled the beans." Detective Thompson eased down on the sofa and looked about. "Nothing's changed over the years. Same decor, same phony certificates."

"What do you want from me?" Doc slid back a bit.

"Cooperation. You're holding back—which makes you an accessory."

"What?" Doc was genuinely puzzled.

Detective Thompson pulled out a notepad and scribbled something. Looking up, he said, "An accessory to a crime is any individual who knowingly and voluntarily participates in the commission of a crime."

"I've done *nothing* wrong," Doc insisted.

"You are concealing information. You were a witness to Van Gogh's Tarot reading, the twins' plea for support of the pope and the Gospel of Mary. Gypsy said the twins were ordered by *him*," the detective paused, "to gather the disciples and aid the pope, politically, theologically, in every way."

"She said that?"

"Was she lying?"

Doc stalled, sliding back and forth, rolling in his favorite chair, looking for a fresh perspective. He inhaled deeply and then exhaled slowly. "No."

"Do you want to come downtown?"

"No! I've done nothing!" Doc stood and walked around his desk, distancing himself from the detective.

"That's the problem. You've done nothing! You need to cooperate."

"What do you want?"

"Work with me. Do you have a recording device? Something you use with your clients?"

"Yeah, sure."

"When the twins return, a certainty in *my book*, I want them recorded. Can you handle *that*?"

"Yeah."

"Then do it. And inform me if they contact you. We'll be watching."

The detective stood. "You've got a nice business here," he said, pointing to the certificates adorning the back wall. "Cooperate, and you and your business will be fine."

* * *

Doc dropped by Gypsy's and tried to console her, but his words fell on deaf ears. "I promise to cooperate with the detective," he said as he left. "I'll see you in the morning."

He phoned Alan and said he'd drop by after grabbing a bite to eat. He thought about checking in with Waldo, but hesitated. *I'm still pissed at him.*

A little after nine, he was sipping a beer, gazing at Alan's little beauties. The gliding and darting of the neon tetras was entertaining, the lazy meanderings of the discus fish hypnotic. The beer was a gift.

"I had a surprise visit tonight." Doc gazed at the tropical beauties, waiting for Alan to get comfortable. He was fussing with the aquariums.

"Oh? Something good?"

"The LAPD. Detective Thompson made a social call."

"The twins?"

"Yes. He knows."

"Knows what?"

"Gypsy's Tarot reading, the disciples, the pope—ah shit, he's on to the whole sordid mess."

"That's a good thing, no?"

"Detective Thompson was rude and pushy, threatening me."

"What?"

"He demanded cooperation, made derogatory remarks about my certificates. He wants me to record the twins."

"They're crazy. They need to be stopped." Alan popped a second beer and handed it to Doc. "Drink up. You're making me nervous."

"Do you think the pope's in danger?" Doc downed a third of his Bud, smacked his lips and gushed, "That went down easy."

"The twins are demented. I wouldn't put anything past them."

"I think Gypsy's losing it." Doc finished his second Bud and asked for another.

"What can we do?" Alan was uneasy with feely touchy things. His passion was for knowledge, Buddhism, and his little beauties.

"Be there for her." Doc's shoulders eased, tension lessening. He felt lightheaded.

"Doc, you're in the bag."

"Can I stay the night? I'm going to tie one on."

"Be my guest. I've a convertible sofa in the Buddha room."

"I can handle that."

Chapter Forty-Four

Detective Thompson glanced at his notes before addressing the special task force. Fifty officers had been assigned to Vatican One, a melding of LAPD, the LA County Sheriff Department, and the FBI. Their mission was to protect the pope and apprehend the twins. He approached the mike, adjusted it, and smiled. He spotted several longtime colleagues, nodded, cleared his voice, and broke the ice with an old joke. "After the Christmas Mass, the pope was interviewed by a foreign correspondent. 'Your Holiness,' he asked, 'how do you get holy water?' The pontiff paused, smiled, and said, 'You boil the hell out of it.'"

"Boooo!" Mike Garcia yelled from the back of the room. "I heard that in the fifth grade."

"Sorry, guys, I'm not good at telling jokes. And the task facing us is no joke. Please open the envelope you picked up at the door. Look at page three. There you will find the salient facts of the case. *First*, we're faced with a monumental security challenge. The pope is making his first trip to Los Angeles, and we're in charge of his safety. *Second*, we have strong evidence that Vincent Amadeus Salabrini and Vincent Van Gogh Salabrini pose a threat to the pope. We have solid testimony; they mean him grave harm. *Third*, the Salabrini twins are fanatics, either delusional or evil. Take your pick; if the motivation is unclear, their goal is not. They want to capitalize on the pope's support for the Gospel of Mary, turn him into a martyr. His life is in our hands."

Detective Thompson explained the plan, strategy, and priorities before breaking up the task force into three groups. "You'll meet with your group leader, get briefed, and receive your assignments. We'll not convene again unless necessary. Good luck, and be vigilant. The twins are resourceful, cunning, talented, and dangerous. They're masters of disguise."

After dropping by each group, greeting old friends and sharing what he learned so far, he returned to his office. He had a hunch. He was the task force commander but itched to check out a loose end. Mildred was at the top of his list. They had unfinished business.

He placed a call to the spiritualist. She answered, but he didn't. *She's in.*

He headed for the valley, just ahead of rush-hour traffic, primed for the shakedown. In less than thirty minutes, he stood outside Mildred's parlor. He took a deep breath, entered, and rang the counter bell.

"I'll be right with you," she said from the next room.

She entered the waiting room and stopped abruptly; her mouth dropped open. She cleared her voice. "Detective, what brings you here?"

"You!" He stared, dwarfing her.

"What's up?" She swallowed hard, brows furrowed.

"That's for me to ask. Can we speak in private?"

"We're alone."

"Not here. Perhaps we could talk in your parlor."

"Sure, come back."

He followed his prey, more sure than ever she was hiding something.

"I have a reading in fifteen minutes, so can you just get to the point?" she blurted, more from desperation than courage.

"That depends on you. I don't play games."

"What?" she snapped.

"Let's cut to the chase. We have strong evidence that you're in contact with the twins."

"Who?"

"Come on, shoot straight. We know that Vincent Amadeus and Vincent Van Gogh are in town. We know they visited the pope, verified by two priests and a psychiatrist."

"Where did you hear that?"

"Directly from the horse's mouth. Are you going to play ball or not? If not, I'm taking you in."

"What do you want from me?"

"Where are they?"

"I don't know."

"You're lying!"

"I don't know."

"When did you last speak with them?"

"I haven't."

"That's it." The detective stood, retrieved his cell, and dialed.

"What are you doing?"

"Requesting a warrant for you arrest," he bluffed.

"Please, no!"

"Then answer my question."

Mildred's land phone rang, causing her to flinch.

"Are you expecting a call?"

"No."

"Pick up."

She rose, walked to the waiting room, and picked up the phone. "Yes?" She stood, leaning on the front desk, hands shaking. "I can't talk now," she blurted and hung up.

"That's it, we're going downtown. Get your purse."

"Give me a second." She disappeared through a curtain toward the rear of the shop. Seconds later, the detective heard a door slam. He dashed to the back of the shop, struggled with the door, reared back, and thrust it open with his shoulder. A white Honda lurched forward, tires squealing, and sped out of the lot, nearly hitting a postal truck. He sprinted to his car, but by the time he fired it up, she had disappeared, moving south on Reseda toward Ventura Boulevard.

He phoned headquarters with the necessary info. "She's driving a late-model Honda," he reported. "California license, SPIRIT, vanity plate." He had done his homework.

* * *

"Mildred's in trouble. When I called, she barely spoke. She said, 'I can't talk now,' and abruptly hung up." Amadeus grabbed his wallet, keys, and a thirty-eight special. "You up for a trip to the valley?"

"Mildred's place?"

"None other."

Van Gogh frowned. "Isn't that risky?"

"She's worth it. Put on the work clothes. We're repairmen tonight."

Within thirty minutes, the twins pulled over on Reseda in front of Mildred's. Their wheels, an old Ford 150, work clothes, and tools were convincing. AV Plumbing was stitched across the back and over the front pocket of the blue work shirts. Van Gogh wore a tool belt. They entered and rang the counter bell. Nothing. They checked out the parlor and backroom. The place was deserted. Amadeus checked the back door, found it ajar. "Someone made a hasty exit."

"You think she's on the run?" Van Gogh walked outside, scanning the parking lot.

"She was being tailed. I think the authorities made their move." Amadeus motioned his brother inside. "Let's hang here. She might return."

"We better lock up. The cops might return too." Van Gogh hustled to the front door, locked it, and hung the closed sign.

The twins kicked back, amusing themselves with Tarot cards. "It's your turn, Amadeus. Gypsy did me, now I'll do you."

"Why not. Let's see what the future brings."

Chapter Forty-Five

Father Gallagher sipped his morning coffee and stared at the front-page headline: "Pope John Paul III, a Homecoming."

The *LA Times* article chronicled the pope's roots in the San Fernando Valley and outlined his service as a priest, bishop, cardinal, and now pope. *It's a superficial romp*, Father Gallagher thought. The article did little but whitewash Roger McMahon's career, glorifying his successes and ignoring his shortcomings. Father Gallagher was a loyal Catholic, every fiber of his being devoted to God and the Church, yet he couldn't deny that the pope's former archdiocese was tarnished by egregious moral transgressions and economic setbacks. The most embarrassing were the sexual abuse cases. But the article skirted these blights on the Church and focused on the Gospel of Mary. The article implied that if the long lost gospel were accepted as equal to Matthew, Mark, Luke, and John, the Church would join the modern world, the pope immortalized.

Father Gallagher tossed the paper on his desk and shook his head. There was only one short paragraph on street closures and beefed-up security, and of course nothing on the twins. Preparations were in full swing, gearing up for the pontiff's arrival, one week from tomorrow. The priest felt antsy, unsettled by both the *Times* article and Detective Thompson's insistence that the Ghostbusters meet with him tonight at the church. The detective hinted that he wanted to set a trap, had a hunch the twins would surface again, probably at Saint Vincent's.

The day flew by, Father Gallagher making hospital rounds, lunching with Father O'Neil, touching base with Shamrock Investigations, the private eye complaining about the lack of leads, and performing early evening Mass. He was physically exhausted but psychologically up for another round of playing the amateur detective. His fellow Ghostbusters had arrived, anxiously awaiting Detective Thompson.

The two priests and shrink were sipping coffee, discussing the *LA Times* article when Detective Thompson lumbered in, trench coat dripping, clutching a large Starbucks coffee. "I hope I'm not late." He pulled up a chair, shed the wet coat, and said, "I have a plan."

"I hope we're not the bait," Dr. Salazar said.

"Hear me out. You three were ordered by the twins to whip up support for the Gospel of Mary. So, we'll oblige them, throw a big rally, right here—speakers, the press, and especially young Catholics, progressive, fully behind Mary and female ordination."

"No way! The pope will be here in a week. There's not enough time," Father Gallagher said, looking at Father O'Neil for support.

"Look, we have the manpower and resources. We'll advertise in the newspapers, on the radio, and on the Internet. How about Wednesday?" Detective Thompson sipped his coffee, now lukewarm.

"Who will the speakers be?" Father O'Neil asked.

"Two priests and a renowned psychiatrist. Great stuff!" The detective stroked his chin, pleased with his idea.

"Jeez, a real blockbuster," Father Gallagher said, shaking his head.

"Come on, guys, it'll work. No one's thinking about anything else. The Gospel of Mary and the pope, it's the talk of the town."

"I'm overwhelmed," Dr. Salazar sighed.

"I'll handle everything. The wheels are already in motion." Detective Thompson leaned back, smiling. "I've already kick started the mission. You guys are on in three days."

* * *

"Hey, Doc, there's a rally for the pope at Saint Vincent's. Didn't you say the twins put on a show there, electrical storm and all?" Waldo said.

"Yeah, quite a night. I didn't think you were interested in the pope," Doc answered, his eyebrows raised.

"Yeah, well, big doings Wednesday night. Two priests and a psychiatrist are talking up the Gospel of Mary. What's the world coming to—the Catholic Church recognizing and honoring the role of women? Never thought I'd see the day."

"Who are the speakers?"

Waldo folded the paper and tossed it to Doc. "Here, take a look. I'm needed out front. Oh, did you see the latest. Our boy Juan Perez is six and two as a starter for the Red Sox."

'He's a winner.' Doc unfolded the paper and read the article twice, intrigued by the topic. *Maybe I'll take Gypsy, or better, Alan Workman.* He read between the lines, sensing something sinister. It was at Saint Vincent's that Dr. Salabrini had put on a show; it had even gotten the attention of the press, "Saint Vincent's Parish: The Devil's in the Details."

* * *

Doc, Gypsy, and Alan arrived early, snatching the last available seats at the rear of the chapel. Saint Vincent's was packed, the audience spilling out into the foyer and front steps. Temporary speakers flanked the massive front doors, providing audio for the overflowing crowd. Outside, the folding chairs arranged in a semi circle were already starting to fill up. The press, radio, and a local TV station were on hand, adding to the building drama. Two groups were picketing the event.

It's a media circus, thought Detective Thompson, grinning broadly, delighted. The trap was set. All that was left was the waiting game, something the seasoned detective knew well. He waded through the crowd to the back of the church where Father Gallagher's office was. As expected, both priests and the psychiatrist were there.

"The turnout is amazing," Detective Thompson beamed, proud of what he had pulled together so quickly.

"I hope we don't disappoint," Father Gallagher said, rolling his eyes.

"Have you no faith?" Detective Thompson smiled, and added, "I expect a real show."

"Well, if the twins take the bait, a show there will be." Dr. Salazar shuffled some note cards, stood, and said, "Let the games begin."

"The message is real, the venue holy, but our strategy questionable." Father O'Neil said.

"Give it your best, fellas." Detective Thompson returned to the sanctuary, finding a saved seat in the back, next to his new partner, Max Holiday. He was hyped and edgy; drama hung heavily in the packed church.

Father Gallagher addressed the congregation, pleased at the hearty turnout. "We are blessed to be Christians, fortunate to discover a long lost document, to witness the truth, and finally resurrect The Gospel of

Mary. She had been quieted, but not silenced. She had been ignored, but not forgotten. Her abandoned message and the Lord's guidance shall set us free."

Fathers Gallagher and O'Neil spent the next forty-five minutes publicly parsing the document, highlighting Mary's account of Jesus, revealing a fresh, vibrant, and personal account of her relationship with Jesus. The feminine voice rang pure and clear, soaring high, providing a balanced counterpoint to the masculine tone of Matthew, Mark, Luke, and John. Dr. Salazar closed the formal part of the presentation, adding both a historical and psychological analysis of Gospel of Mary and the Church's reluctance to female ordination.

After a short break, the Ghostbusters entertained questions from the audience. Detective Thompson stepped out front and checked on his surveillance team. The only excitement was a shouting match between two picketers. The combatants were separated before the fight became physical.

The event at Saint Vincent's was a wild religious success, the audience energized by the wit and analysis of the guest speakers. Detective Thompson was disappointed but not defeated. He had a backup plan.

Doc convinced Alan and Gypsy to hang for a while, hoping for a chance to question Fathers Gallagher and O'Neil. He got his chance, engaging the receptive priests with questions about the Gospel of Mary, receiving some refreshingly honest answers. When Doc brought up the Salabrini twins, they clammed up. The priests politely excused themselves, shaking Doc's hand before turning to answer more questions. Many parishioners stayed late, peppering the three men with endless questions, their enthusiasm contagious.

A short block west, unnoticed by authorities, two men were waiting at a bus stop with sombreros, guitars, and a shared pair of binoculars. The colorfully attired men watched from a distance, chuckling, strumming their guitars, adding their sound track to the event. After a twenty-minute serenade, they boarded the bus, laughing, singing "Vaya con Dios."

"It was a hoot!" shouted Amadeus.

"I just loved the turn out. Detective Thompson looked so disappointed." Van Gogh strummed his guitar singing, "Our lady, here we come."

"And who is our lady?" Amadeus grinned, leaning close to his brother, brows arched.

"Mildred, of course," Van Gogh whispered. "The night's young."

Chapter Forty-Six

Mildred swerved her Honda to the curb, making an abrupt stop at the corner of Reseda and Ventura Boulevard. Bystanders gawked as two caballeros jumped in the back of the car, singing, tossing their broad-brimmed hats over the front seat.

"Thanks for being on time," Amadeus said.

"Thanks for finding me. I'm a fucking fugitive." Mildred glanced to the backseat, smiling.

"And a beautiful fugitive you make." Van Gogh reached forward, lightly patting her on the shoulder.

"Take us home. We're in a partying mood."

She turned south on Coldwater Canyon, crested the hill, and meandered through a series of cross streets, ending in the hills above Hollywood. She had no GPS, so Amadeus gave her directions from the backseat.

The twins pushed through the front door, tossed their hats, cranked up the stereo, and poured wine, all the while giving Mildred a play-by-play of the evening's events.

"Detective Thompson appeared dejected. I'm sure he expected us." Van Gogh handed Mildred a glass of cabernet, then gave one to his twin, and started to propose a toast.

"Please, allow me one of my own." Mildred frowned.

"The floor is yours." Van Gogh bowed, deferring to the fairer sex.

"Here's to the son-of-a-bitch that made me a fugitive."

"I'll drink to that," the twins harmonized.

"May Detective Thompson burn in hell." Mildred raised her glass. "He makes my skin crawl."

"I know what will help your mood!" Amadeus exclaimed. "Let us pay our respects to *him*."

Van Gogh lit the candles, put on a Gregorian chant, turned off the light, and offered a prayer. "To the light, the word, and the be all and end all of existence. We bow in reverence, eternally faithful."

"Amen," Amadeus said loudly, forever in *his* debt.

"Amen," Mildred added softly, still shaken. She'd never been a fugitive.

* * *

Doc drove Alan home after dropping Gypsy off. She was tired, grateful the twins didn't show, but in no mood for drama. Doc was restless, needing to talk.

Alan popped a couple of Buds, handed one to Doc, and said, "Bottoms up."

"Here's to the Gospel of Mary," Doc bellowed, taking a tug on the cold brew.

"What was your take on the rally?" Alan sipped his beer, leaning back, knees bent, new Nikes planted on top of his desk, leveraged for a leg press.

Doc gazed at Alan's little beauties, lazily gliding about. The softly illuminated aquariums were mesmerizing. He shook himself and said, "The priests stonewalled me."

"How so?"

"When I mentioned the Salabrini twins, they stopped talking."

"They were being mobbed. Questions were coming from all directions. The faithful were excited."

"I saw something more. When I mentioned Salabrini, Father Gallagher's eyes widened, then he quickly looked away."

"You think they know about the twins?" Alan finished his beer and retrieved two more.

Doc stared at the neon tetras, transfixed. He took a gulp, belched, and said, "They've met, I'm sure of it."

"What makes you think so?"

"Just a hunch. I'm going to nose around. Do some checking. I'll start with the two priests, the shrink. I smell something rotten in Denmark."

"Doc, Denmark's a hell of a long ways from here."

"But the stench is strong. And that's not all."

"What else?"

"Detective Thompson."

"What about him?"

"He was on the hunt. His head was on a swivel, restless, moving about Saint Vincent's like a bloodhound. After talking to the priests, he paid his respects. I could see it in his eyes. He was expecting someone."

"Who?"

"He was expecting the twins to show."

"Well, if you're right, his instincts failed him."

"Maybe," Doc said. "Or maybe they were there and none of us saw them."

* * *

Father Gallagher had alerted Shamrock Investigations of the rally, and so William Preston had arrived early and opted for a bird's eye view from the stairwell of a second-floor office building, a bit west of Saint Vincent's. He had patiently watched, entertained by the media, police, and protesters. He had laughed aloud when the protesters got nasty, hoping a fight might break out.

Scanning Ventura Boulevard, he caught sight of two men in sombreros with guitars, sharing binoculars and pointing toward Saint Vincent's. *That's odd*, he thought. After rapidly descended the stairs, he emerged from the building on the north side of Ventura, walking west for a closer look. As he neared, the two men caught a bus traveling east, and by the time he started his car, the bus had disappeared.

He gave chase and spotted the bus again at Tampa Avenue. He tailed them to Reseda where the two men emerged from the bus. In less than five minutes, a Honda pulled over, and the two jumped in the back seat. William followed in hot pursuit, catching the Honda as it turned south onto Coldwater Canyon. He maintained his surveillance, three cars back. A red Porsche sped by on the left, pulling quickly in front, causing the private eye to slam on his brakes. Up ahead, an old Ford pickup had swerved to miss a coyote, skidding to the side of the road. Traffic piled up; the Honda had disappeared. All he had for his hard work was a license: vanity plate, SPIRIT.

Chapter Forty-Seven

etective Fred Thompson stood at the corner of Grand and Temple, admiring the pope mobile, a custom-built two-door Mercedes ML 430. He was surprised by the lack of markings—only the Mercedes logo on the front grille, the Vatican coat of arms on each door, and a specialized license plate, SCV1, an acronym for the Vatican in Italian and the number of the Holy Father's place in church hierarchy. The Southern California sun cast soft shadows on Our Lady of the Angels as Pope John Paul III waved to the crowd through the car window as the pope mobile slowly disappeared into the cathedral parking structure. The detective breathed a sigh of relief. It was just the front end of a three-day visit, but so far no glitches.

Back at headquarters, he reread the task force's priorities for the umpteenth time. He ticked off an exhaustive list, finishing with a final check of the pope's entourage. Traveling with the pontiff were Roman Curia officials, liturgical advisers, doctors, media experts, and security personnel. They all had their jobs to do. So did the detective. And it was daunting. The "portable Vatican" had accompanied popes since Pope Paul VI first hopped a plane in 1964.

He flipped open a notepad and was confronted with a lengthy to-do list. His cell chirped. *Damn, not a minute's peace.*

"Detective Thompson."

"This is William Preston, the private eye with Shamrock Investigations."

"Yes, William. What's up?"

"I was at Saint Vincent's the night of the rally."

"Great turn out."

"Well I've been sitting on something for a couple of days."

"Go on."

"I observed two men at a bus stop a block west of Saint Vincent's. They were wildly dressed, with sombreros and guitars, and shared a pair of binoculars. After they left, I tailed them to Coldwater Canyon, but then lost them."

"How's does that concern the LAPD?"

"I think it was the twins."

"What?"

"I got the plates. Vanity plates: SPIRIT."

"Oh shit!" Detective Thompson said.

"Was my gut feeling right?"

The detective paused and said, "It was right on. Why the hold up in telling me?"

"I wasn't sure. But it's been nagging me."

"He who hesitates … but anyway, thanks for the lead. Next time, be more prompt."

Detective Thompson hung up and immediately checked with the main dispatcher for anything on the vanity plate. Nothing.

* * *

Cardinal Emanuel Martinez invited Pope John Paul III to his office for a private late-night chat. The pope was tired, emotionally drained from endless interviews. Though he was delighted with the press's coverage, he needed some down time.

Cardinal Martinez met the pope at the outer door of his office, bowed, and kissed his hand. "Welcome home."

Vivid memories, mostly good, seized him, bringing a faint smile to his lips. "Thanks for the invitation. I see that my beloved missions are still in place." The pope walked the perimeter of his former office, pausing in front of each featured mission, commenting on his love of early California history. "It's hard to single out a favorite, but the Santa Barbara Mission tops my list. I wrote an essay about the mission in elementary school, fourth grade."

"Being surrounded by images of the missions is comforting. Their spirit lives on. Your Holiness, would I be out of line?" The cardinal walked to a side table, raised an unopened bottle of Merlot, and said, "Shall we?"

"By all means. I need to unwind." The pope was delighted with the cardinal's selection, a 2002 Lewis Cellars.

"It's advertised as having rich aromas of juicy cherry with hints of chocolate," the cardinal beamed, proud of his choice. The cardinal deftly opened the merlot and poured two glasses, waiting for the pope's approval before fully filling his glass.

"You've good taste." The pope stood, raising his glass. "Here's to the Gospel of Mary."

"To the Gospel of Mary," Cardinal Martinez echoed.

The pope eased himself into the wingback chair, savoring the gentle aroma. *I'll need more than one*, he thought, his shoulders tight with tension. *I hope my quarters are well stocked.*

"All's in place for tomorrow's evening Mass. Two scholars will present brief papers touting the authenticity of the gospel. A traditional Mass will follow. Your Holiness, with your permission, will conclude the evening's worship."

"I will have some special words. May God be with us." The pope again raised his glass, leaned forward, and clinked the cardinal's glass.

"Vaya con Dios." The cardinal smiled broadly, thrilled about the pope's visit. It would put his archdiocese on the map. He, like the pope, was politically ambitious.

* * *

An aging Mercedes left behind a dark vapor trail as it pulled out and merged with traffic on Hollywood Boulevard. Amadeus swooped into the vacated parking spot in front of Adele's of Hollywood. It was famous for renting and selling costumes since 1945.

"It's an old diesel," Amadeus complained.

"Dirty little bastard," Van Gogh said. The twins broke out in laughter as they descended on the costume shop.

Van Gogh made a B-line to the movie star section and picked up a Darth Vader mask. "I'm here for you, on the dark side," he said, giving his best James Earl Jones impersonation.

Amadeus eclipsed him, mimicking the famed actor to a tee. The twins moved up and down the aisles, entertaining anyone in hearing distance, impersonating their favorite stars. For Amadeus, it was second nature. Van Gogh's efforts needed some polish.

They scored everything they needed, two gray beards, a couple of dark suits, and the requisite white collars. The shop even had contact lenses, perfect for transforming their dark brown eyes to blue. They made a second stop to pick up a makeup kit, before ending their spending spree with a case of cabernet from their favorite wine shop on Santa Monica Boulevard.

"We're home!" Amadeus yelled, alerting Mildred.

"We've got the goods." Van Gogh opened the case of wine, selecting a bottle to begin the evening.

Mildred emerged from the bedroom wearing a long black skirt and black sweater, face drawn. "I'm bummed out. Being a fugitive is the pits," she pouted.

"We've just the medicine. Guaranteed to kick the funk out of you," Amadeus laughed. "It's time for the dress rehearsal."

Van Gogh popped the cork on a bottle of Beringer Cabernet Sauvignon 2005, a California cabernet, while Amadeus cranked up the stereo, filling the hillside home with the haunting sounds of a Gregorian chant.

"Time for some cinematic magic," Amadeus said, shouting over the medieval chant.

"Indeed!" Van Gogh pulled two beards from a large plastic bag.

For the next thirty minutes, the twins entertained themselves, morphing into two highly visible priests. With beards, contacts, and appropriate makeup in place, they bowed to one another.

"It's my pleasure to introduce Fathers Gallagher and O'Neil." Amadeus beamed, proud of his handiwork. His many years as a thespian had paid off. He was not only a seasoned actor but also a fine makeup artist. The twins had miraculously become priests, but not just any priests. They had become two well-known priests with easy access to the inner workings of Our Lady of the Angels. They could come and go as they pleased. Their sinister plan was taking shape.

"I don't believe it," Mildred laughed, feeling better, the wine and dress rehearsal lifting her spirits. "Their own mother couldn't tell the difference."

Chapter Forty-Eight

The pope was at home; his former apartment had been made available for his three-day stay. Cardinal Martinez apartment was down the hall, his apartment redecorated to suit his taste. He was part Native American, preferring a blend of early American and Indian culture. His ancestry was a blend of Mexican and Chumash, with a pinch of Navajo.

Pope John Paul III smiled, uttering, "God bless," as he surveyed the well-stocked bar. Two California cabernets caught his attention. He opted for another Lewis Cellars. The wine, privacy, and a cool gentle breeze from the opened french doors calmed him. He went to bed a short time later, drifting into dreamland before midnight. A full moon lit up his spacious apartment, shinning brilliantly on his slumbering figure. At 2:30, he flailed about the bed, shouting, "No! Not again!"

He sat upright, shaking uncontrollably. His mind reeled, juggling a collage of horrifying images. He shuddered, recalling two priests laughing manically, accusing the pope of heresy. The hooded priests snarled, chanting, "Hypocrite, political pragmatist, king of duplicity ... You're nothing but a political whore ..."

He propped himself up on two pillows. It was in this room, not long ago, the twins visited him. He forced himself out of bed, walking slowly, mumbling. He switched on the bedroom lights. He was alone.

Sensing they were close, he dropped to his knees at the foot of the bed, asking for strength and guidance.

* * *

A client cancelled, giving Doc a two-hour break in his hectic schedule. He phoned Saint Vincent's and got lucky. Father Gallagher was free at two. On his drive west on Ventura Boulevard, he rehearsed his questions. He had many.

It was only his second visit to the parish church, so he stopped a custodian and asked for Father Gallagher's office. He was directed to the back of the church, so he headed down the middle of the chapel. Doc recognized two saints adorning the towering walls, Saint Augustine and Saint Thomas Aquinas. He had read a bit about Aquinas and knew some scuttlebutt: he was overweight, spoke slowly, and was referred to as the "Dumb Ox." The official line on the Catholic philosopher was more noteworthy. He resurrected Aristotle's philosophy to support and strengthen Christian doctrine.

Doc found the priest's office door ajar, knocked lightly, and entered.

"You must me Michael Mesmer."

"Yes, but my clients call me Doc."

"Please come in. Didn't we meet at the rally?" Father extended his hand and shook Doc's.

"Briefly. That's why I'm here."

"We were pleased with the turnout. I was overwhelmed by questions." Father Gallagher leaned back, smiled, and added, "How may I be of service?"

"I think we share a mutual acquaintance." Doc paused, cleared his throat, and said, "Do you know a Vincent Salabrini?"

Father Gallagher looked down before raising his head and answering, "Yes, I have met him." The priest couldn't lie. It wasn't in his nature.

"I think he means trouble for your faith."

"How so?"

"Allow me to start from the beginning. Gypsy, a spiritual advisor and good friend referred Vincent to me. He wanted to learn self-hypnosis. He thought it might help him combat his demons." Doc paused, searching the priest's eyes.

"Please, go on."

"We had several sessions, then he disappeared. Much later, he reappeared, but not alone. Were you aware he has a twin?"

Father Gallagher took a deep breath, exhaling slowly. *I must be guarded, but not lie.* "Yes."

"There's more. Vincent's appearance changed radically. At first he looked old, hunched over, walking with a cane, wearing an eye patch, but later he morphed into a dancer, athletic, light on his feet." Doc leaned back, assessing the priest.

"But what's this got to do with my faith?"

"Plenty. He tried to recruit Gypsy, Alan Workman, a close friend, and me. He wanted us as disciples for *him*."

"For him?"

"We were recruited to be Satan's disciples."

"What?"

"That's just for starters. The three of us met with Cardinal McMahon before he became pope. We played a game."

"What kind of game?"

"Meeting of Minds. Have you heard of it?"

"No." Father Gallagher squirmed in his chair, visibly agitated, periodically glancing at the opened office door. He rose, making a B-line for the door, and closed it quietly. "We must be careful."

"Well, we convened in the cardinal's office, had assigned nameplates, and playacted."

"Playacted?"

"Yes. Vincent's twin, Van Gogh, was Freud, Vincent Amadeus was Nietzsche, and the cardinal was Christ. We all played a role. The theatrics were explosive. The twins put on quite a show." Doc went on for ten minutes, barely taking a break, breathless when he finished.

"I'm flabbergasted. What do you want from me?"

"We need to cooperate. I sense that they will return. The pope is in grave danger. The twins are working for Satan."

Doc and the priest continued their talk. He learned that Father O'Neil and Dr. Salazar were in the know. Father promised to keep in touch, and both vowed to share any breaking news. They were both on high alert.

* * *

That evening, after Mass, the Ghostbusters met at Saint Vincent's. Father Gallagher informed his buddies of Doc Mesmer's surprise visit. "The hypnotist shared some eerie encounters with the twins," he reported. "Doc also gave a riveting account of the Meeting of Minds."

"That's an old TV show. Steve Allen was the host," Dr. Salazar said, smiling. "The twins may be evil, but they're erudite."

"Doc is convinced the twins are after the pope."

"What's his take?" Father O'Neil stroked his light gray beard, his sanguine cheeks aflame.

"He calls him Schizzy. Thinks he's nuts." Father Gallagher grinned.

"Bingo. It takes a hypnotist to call a spade a spade," the shrink observed. "And his last name is Mesmer. What a hoot!"

They all laughed. Before the laughter died out, Detective Fred Thompson appeared at the door. "Gentlemen, I'd like a moment."

The Ghostbusters just stared. Father Gallagher was the first to respond. "What's up?"

"Your P.I. sat on some news." The detective leaned against the bookcase, his right hand resting next to an open Bible.

"He said he spoke to you last night." Father Gallagher glanced at his fellow Ghostbusters.

"A bit late. He tailed a Honda over Coldwater Canyon. An auto accident blocked his pursuit. The car is owned by Margaret Morley."

"What's the connection?" Dr. Salazar frowned, not liking Detective Thompson's unannounced visit.

"She's intimately involved with the twins. She's definitely an accomplice."

"Is she with the twins?" Father O'Neil asked.

"Perhaps. They're here. We need to spread the word. There's an all points bulletin for a Honda with vanity plates: SPIRIT. The owner is a fortuneteller" Detective Thompson stretched his neck and added, "We're all too familiar with their resourcefulness. Honestly, I'm worried. They're masters of disguise, capable of playing many parts."

"It's only theater to them. They live for drama. They flirt with the blurred edges of appearance and reality," Dr. Salazar said, staring off. He longed to put them on his couch.

"Perhaps. But this is not a play. The pope's life is at stake. I need you to be at the cathedral starting early tomorrow. We need to keep our eye on the prize." The detective moved toward the door.

"Is extra security being employed?" Father Gallagher asked.

"Our Lady of the Angels will be crawling with security, uniformed and undercover."

The detective departed, leaving the Ghostbusters concerned. Father Gallagher yelled, "Spirit! Certainly not the holy spirit."

"It's not spirit as we know it." Father O'Neil shook his head, more out of disgust than frustration.

"Saturday's good for me." Father O'Neil looked over at Dr. Salazar. "Mario, can you make it?"

"I've an early morning appointment. I'll be there by ten."

"Good. The Ghostbusters will be front row and center." Father O'Neil escorted his fellow amateur sleuths to the church parking lot.

After a glass of merlot, Father Gallagher turned in. *Tomorrow's a big day.*

Chapter Forty-Nine

The twins awoke early Saturday morning, primed for "Act One: Diversionary Saturday." They had secured the necessary props, made a trip to the desert for a test run, and were now ready for their demolition debut. The eyes of Angelinos were on Our Lady of the Angels, the pope, and his much-anticipated message supporting the Gospel of Mary. The twins had their eyes on something smaller—Saint Vincent's.

At three in the afternoon, the church was nearly deserted. The faithful were downtown hoping for a glimpse of the pope. The twins were in full dress, beards in place, stepping onto the stage for a raucous first act.

"Good afternoon, Father Gallagher," said a part-time custodian. "I thought you were downtown."

"We were. Just stopped by to pick up something. Are you leaving?" Amadeus loved acting. He was definitely in his element.

"Yes. The church is deserted. Everyone's at Our Lady."

"That's where we're off to in a minute." Amadeus smiled, not out of politeness, but good fortune.

The two priests entered the chapel and hustled to the front of the nave, clutching two briefcases tightly. Amadeus opened his first, placing the plastic explosive on the linen covered altar. He removed a chalice and communion plates, and set them aside.

"We don't want to be sacrilegious." He glanced at his brother. They both laughed.

Van Gogh set up the timer and detonator, meticulously carrying out their plan, barking out the completion of each step.

"Timer and wiring in place," Van Gogh exclaimed.

"Detonator armed!" Amadeus shouted, hands sweaty, but steady.

"C-4 ready!" Van Gogh announced, trembling slightly. He was on fire, but jittery. Amadeus was more comfortable working with the highly malleable material.

Amadeus meticulously shaped the plastic explosive, positioning it for maximum vertical thrust. The twins retreated, leaving by the side door. They walked down Ventura Boulevard, crossed the street at De Soto, got in their Ford F-150 and drove to the Target department store down the street from Saint Vincent's.

"Are you ready for a little drama?" Amadeus's grin was mischievous.

"Act One, Scene One. It's a take," Van Gogh answered.

Shock waves rocked their truck, the deafening sound stunning everyone in sight. Two ladies pushing shopping carts hit the asphalt, and a girl in a nearby car screamed. Flames shot through the roof, and smoke drifted down Ventura Boulevard, partially obscuring the collapsing church.

Traffic came to a screeching halt, and an MTD bus stalled, blocking a cross street. The twins slowly exited the Target parking lot, admiring their handiwork.

"I think we found a new calling." Amadeus said.

"Ain't we got fun?" Van Gogh exclaimed, now more excited than nervous.

"Better than sex?" Amadeus asked as they headed east on Ventura.

"Haven't had much of that."

The twins motored back to the Hollywood Hills; they couldn't wait to tell Mildred.

* * *

Doc caught Waldo in the back room watching his favorite soap when the program was interrupted by a news flash. They huddled around an aging thirteen-inch Magnavox, glued to the small screen. "Oh my God!" he uttered, as he and Waldo stared in disbelief. Camera crews, news reporters, and curious pedestrians jammed the sidewalk. Ventura was blocked off; fire trucks and police cruisers filled the once busy boulevard. The remains of Saint Vincent's smoldered, smoke bellowing from the ruins, firemen darting about. Fire hoses snaked about the charred remains, inundating the fiery scene with voluminous streams of water.

A news reporter for ABC cornered a fire chief, wanting answers.

"It's too early to establish a cause. We're concerned with putting out the fire and securing public safety."

The chief started to move away, but the reporter persisted. "What's your best guess as to what happened?"

"We don't like to guess." He moved quickly away, calling out to two fire fighters positioning a fire hose.

Doc turned to Waldo. "I was just there, less than two days ago."

"Arson?" Waldo frowned, suspicious.

"More sinister! I think the twins are involved."

"Really?"

"I've got to go." Doc left by the back door of Wally's Emporium, dashing back to his office in record time. As soon as he unlocked the door, he phoned Detective Fred Thompson. He was unavailable, so he left a terse message. "It's the twins! Saint Vincent's gone. Call Doc, ASAP."

* * *

Detective Fred Thompson was at Parker Center, LAPD headquarters, when he got the bad news. He watched several news reports and checked with an officer at the scene; he smelled a rat. It had the twins written all over it. He sent two members of the task force over to Saint Vincent's, hoping to get a few leads. As the tension mounted, his laser beam focus intensified. *Tonight the pope performs Mass at Our Lady. Hell, it's the fucking twins. The demise of Saint Vincent's is nothing but a diversionary tactic.*

He checked with Tim Hardy, the LAPD detective in charge at Our Lady, and Sam Ogden, with the FBI. They reported that all was well at the cathedral but shared his concern about Saint Vincent's. They both said the same thing: "Something's up."

Detective Thompson rang Father O'Neil's cell, catching him in his car.

"Detective Thompson, checking in. Have you heard the news?"

"Yes. We're devastated. Father Gallagher and I are on our way to Saint Vincent's."

"How's he holding up?"

"Not well. We're almost there. Oh, jeez." The priests got their first glimpse of what was Saint Vincent's. Peeking through the smoke were the skeletal remains of Father Gallagher's beloved church. A tear trickled down his cheek, disappearing into his snow-white beard. He made a sign of the cross, uttering, "Oh my dear God."

"Let me know what you need." Detective Thompson felt their sorrow. He was both depressed and angry. The attack on their church was mean, senseless. *I'm going to nail those bastards!*

"Before I sign off, is Dr. Salazar at the cathedral?"

"No. He had an urgent call. He's meeting us later at Our Lady."

"Good. Catch you tonight."

* * *

Mildred and the twins stared at the TV, watching the pope perform Mass. It was only six-thirty, but they were on their second glass of cabernet, early for party time. Their celebration couldn't wait. The twins delighted in recounting their afternoon's handiwork. Mildred was elated, proud of her pyrotechnic neophytes.

"Mission accomplished." Amadeus raised his glass.

"Now for 'Act Two: Diversionary Sunday,' my friends." Van Gogh raised his glass.

"I'm in," Mildred said, feeling giddy, more from the excitement than the wine.

Chapter Fifty

The pope mobile entered Chavez Ravine and headed for Dodger Stadium. Throngs of people lined the streets, hoping for a glimpse of the pope. Cheers erupted inside the stadium when his approach was announced over the PA system. As the pope mobile emerged from the bullpen, the decibel levels peaked, making ordinary conversation impossible.

Detective Thompson looked down from the press box, scanning the ballpark. On the temporary stage, directly behind the pitcher's mound, dignitaries awaited. Cardinal Martinez was the first to greet him, climbing several stairs to the platform where the mayor, three supervisors, and the governor of California were seated. Bulletproof glass shielded His Holiness as he stood, waving energetically at the crowd.

It was well known by Angelinos that the pope was an avid baseball fan and a loyal Dodger. He had enjoyed many games here, watching the likes of Sandy Koufax, Don Drysdale, and Fernando Valenzuela. But Vin Scully was his favorite. Next to his favorite cabernet, Scully's mellifluous play-by-play was unequalled, the ultimate evening tonic for his troubled soul.

Father O'Neil reached over and tapped Detective Thompson on the shoulder. "Thanks for the invite. Father Gallagher and I need to get our mind off of Saint Vincent's."

"It's my pleasure. Plus, I'll need your services this evening at Our Lady. We're not out of the woods yet." Detective Thompson leaned forward, flashing thumbs up to Father Gallagher. He appeared forlorn, his face drawn, his eyes bloodshot. "Father, hang in there." *Christ, nothing I say will help.* The seasoned detective felt helpless.

After introductions by the mayor and governor, the pope spoke, thanking the audience for their enthusiasm and support. "My roots are here. I was born and raised in the San Fernando Valley." He paused, opened his arms wide, and reached out to the crowd. His gray hair shone pure white in the brilliant afternoon sun. "It was here that I served as priest, bishop, and cardinal, most of it within a twenty-minute drive from the stadium. I feel at home near the pitching mound, remembering fondly the baseball lore of Dodger blue."

After walking down memory lane, citing some of his favorite players, he addressed the issue of the Gospel of Mary. He spoke enthusiastically of the archeological find for the ages, a discovery that would transform the Catholic Church. "We've finally heard her voice, and she speaks to us eloquently, elevating the feminine to its proper place. May God bless you, and please give Mary her due." Thunderous applause gripped the stadium, surely setting an all-time decibel reading.

Detective Thompson bid good-bye to the two priests. "I'll see you two at Our Lady. I need your assistance." The detective descended from the press box, hurrying to the infield. He wanted to be close to the pope. His senses were on high alert. Security was in high gear, but so were his instincts. The twins were close by.

$$* * *$$

"Good afternoon, Fathers. I thought you were at Dodger Stadium." The longtime security guard of Our Lady opened the locked side door, allowing the two priests admittance.

"We saw the pope and left early to avoid traffic." Father O'Neil smiled.

The two priests nodded to a fellow priest and said hello to an LAPD officer, confidently walking the hallways to the pope's temporary apartment, each carrying a briefcase. The twins had sensitive cargo. They jimmied the lock and slipped in without being detected. Security cameras were no problem; their mugs were well known. They'd done their homework.

"Easy as pie." Amadeus walked to the window, gazing out over the courtyard.

"I'm pumped." Van Gogh checked out the bar. "Excellent taste. I love the pope's choice of cabernet."

"We must act quickly. We know the drill." Amadeus pulled opened his briefcase and removed the plastic explosive.

"Let's hit it." Van Gogh emptied his briefcase, organizing the wiring, timer, remote control, and detonator. If the timer failed, the remote was backup.

Within ten minutes, the bomb was armed and positioned beneath the bathroom sink. The twins made a quick exit, easily walking out the front entrance of Our Lady of the Angels, saying hello to several priests, two security guards, and a custodian. The twins' performance was impeccable, the disguise pure art. For them, it was great theater. For the Catholic Church, they were diabolical, fiends from hell.

As the twins headed east, threading their way through the crowded sidewalk, Doc Mesmer jumped from a Prius, waving good-bye to Gypsy. He smoothed out his coat as she motored east, searching for parking. Across the street, two priests stopped and chatted with several teenagers, then turned and walked east on Temple. Doc and Gypsy had planned on catching the pope's evening Mass; Father Gallagher had promised tickets. This was no ordinary Mass; it was revolutionary for some, heresy for others. Security was tight.

Doc squinted and stared, not sure. The two familiar looking priests were on the north side of the street, he on the south. He whirled around, tailing them. *What's Father Gallagher doing walking away from the cathedral? It had to be him, the white beard and rosy chicks. He promised tickets.*

Doc had dressed up for the occasion, wearing a dark blue suit, white shirt, and striped red tie. He was wearing a navy blue fedora, a recent gift from Gypsy. The hat had its advantages, shading his face from the afternoon sun as well as providing effective cover. *Something's not right.* He was about to call out to them when they disappeared into a public parking lot. He ducked into an alleyway, waiting, but not for long. In less than five minutes, the two priests exited the parking structure heading east on Temple. They were in an old Ford F-150. He got the license plate: California 5NPR666.

He cursed, thinking he had lost them when Gypsy rounded the corner, signaling to Doc. He ran over to her new Prius hybrid, throwing open the door. "Follow that old Ford pick-up," he yelled, causing Gypsy to flinch.

"Why the panic?"

"Something's weird. Father Gallagher's in the old Ford truck. He promised to meet us."

Gypsy inched forward, tailing the battered pick-up, three cars back. "Everyone and his aunt's looking for parking."

Doc took off his fedora, wiping his brow. "I've a hunch."

"This is crazy. The area's a mad house. Police, closed streets, and no parking." Gypsy sighed, frowning.

"Don't lose sight of them." Doc was sure he had it right. Father Gallagher had just lost his church. The pope was due to deliver evening Mass. *Why would they be retreating from the action? It doesn't add up.*

"Doc, level with me. What's up?"

"I think we're tailing the twins," Doc said softly, trying to minimize the impact on Gypsy.

"No!" Gypsy shrieked.

* * *

Fathers Gallagher and O'Neil returned from Dodger Stadium, pleased with the pope's message, eager for evening Mass. They approached the side entrance, waiting for security to open up.

"Back again," the security officer said. "Busy bees."

"The pope's message went over big." Father O'Neil patted the security guard on the shoulder. "We need something from my office."

"Weren't you just there?" The security guard flashed the priest a funny look.

"What did he say?" Father Gallagher looked perplexed.

"He thought we were just here." Father O'Neil grinned, looking confused.

"Oh well, so much for security." Father Gallagher laughed nervously.

As soon as they reached Father O'Neil's office, Father Gallagher's cell chirped.

"Hello."

"Detective Thompson. Where are you?"

"We just arrived at Our Lady. We're in Father O'Neil's office."

"I just received a call from the hypnotist. He swears he saw the two of you in an old Ford pick-up, heading east on Temple."

"We don't have a pick-up. Haven't been in one in years."

"He's sure he saw you guys leaving the cathedral, heading for the freeway. He said you promised him tickets."

"We're at the cathedral. And yes, I promised him and his friends tickets to the evening Mass."

"According to Doc Mesmer, you two left the Cathedral on foot, got into an old Ford truck heading east on Temple."

"No … We were with you at Dodger Stadium, just got back to Our Lady."

"Keep your phone handy. I'll be in touch."

Chapter Fifty-One

The twins garaged the Ford F-150, went inside their home, uncorked a bottle of Beringer Cabernet Sauvignon, and tuned into TV coverage at Our Lady. CNN had nonstop coverage, liberal Catholic theologians calling it a miracle, conservative clergy cautious, at best seeing the pope's enthusiastic backing of the new gospel as premature, at worst, a dog and pony show. The entire country was riveted to the TV. His Holiness was media savvy; he insisted on live TV coverage. The word must get out.

"Midnight can't come too soon." Van Gogh sipped his wine, feet propped up on an oversized ottoman.

"Fireworks free of charge." Amadeus reached over, clinking his brother's glass.

"What if it fails to detonate?" Van Gogh cocked his head, brows arched.

"Easy. We make a house call. We drive near the cathedral and use the remote." Amadeus flashed a wicked grin.

"How close to the target?"

"Specs say a half mile. We could do it from the freeway." Amadeus was clinical, emotionless.

"You want to watch it on TV or be there, up close?" Van Gogh was edgy and restless, his mind racing.

"Maybe we can use the binoculars, watch it from the deck."

"Let's test it." Van Gogh leaped to his feet, retrieving the Bushnell's from the kitchen counter.

The twins leaned over the deck's railing, glimpsing the downtown skyline. Their Hollywood Hill's vantage point proved ideal. There were a few scattered trees, but the view was breathtaking.

"The downtown skyline is visible. We should be able to see the fireworks from here." Amadeus smiled, satisfied.

Mildred came out to see what was happening. She'd been napping in the back bedroom. "What's up?"

"All's in place. Join us for some wine. At midnight, the celebration begins."

* * *

Fred Thompson posted himself on the north side of the nave, fifty feet from the pope. His eyes were everywhere, looking for anything suspicious. *Doc spotting Fathers Gallagher and O'Neil leaving the cathedral didn't make sense. Plus, security seeing the priests at Our Lady was impossible. They were with me at Dodger Stadium!*

The pope completed the Mass, bowing and blowing kisses as he descended from the altar, walking slowly down center aisle, smiling, gracious, taking full advantage of the media coverage. His warm smile lit up the cathedral, intensified by blazing TV cameras. Escorted by his private entourage, His Holiness slowly made his way to Cardinal Martinez's office where they celebrated more intimately. It was nine-thirty; the pope was elated but hungry and weary. The cardinal did not disappoint, providing the pope with his favorite wine and an assortment of snacks and desserts.

The pope and cardinal shared a bottle of cabernet, bathing in the glow of a historic day.

"Your address at Dodger Stadium and tonight's Mass crowned a glorious day. We've turned the corner. The Gospel of Mary has been accepted by the faithful."

"I share your enthusiasm. But we cannot rest until Mary is enshrined along with Mathew, Mark, Luke, and John."

The pope thanked the cardinal for his hospitality and retired to his temporary apartment, escorted by security. He bid goodnight, thanking both his private security and the LAPD. He was nearly alone, aided only by his private secretary. He turned to Antonio Manghetti and said, "I need rest. Wake me at seven."

Antonio bowed, said a quick prayer, and then quietly closed the outer door.

Alone at last! The pope opened a cabernet, sitting peacefully, savoring it, thrilled more by the high than the taste. A smile morphed to a chuckle. He was tipsy. After preparing for bed, he gazed out over the interior plaza, bathed in the glow of a full moon. Before turning in, he knelt in prayer. Within ten minutes, he was fast asleep. It was 11:45.

* * *

The twins had limited their wine consumption to one glass, and that was hours earlier. Sobriety was of the essence. If the timer failed, they'd move to plan B, drive to Our Lady and employ the remote.

Amadeus glanced at his watch. "It's 11:55. We'll soon know."

The next five minutes slowed to a crawl. At first, Amadeus peeked at his watch, and then stared. Van Gogh paced the deck, hunched, compulsively walking the perimeter.

"Midnight!" Amadeus barked.

Nothing. The lights from downtown twinkled in the distance. The city slumbered.

"12:01! What the fuck!" Amadeus refocused the binoculars.

Van Gogh stopped, staring east. "Something's wrong."

"We'll give it another five. If nothing happens, we fire up the truck."

Mildred appeared at the sliding doors. "Well?"

"Nothing!" Amadeus passed by her in a huff. He picked up the keys to the truck and shouted to his twin. "Plan B. Let's hit it."

Fifteen minutes later, the twins were nearing the cathedral, traveling east on the Hollywood Freeway. They were less than a mile from Our Lady. The traffic was light, the old Ford hugging the middle lane, cruising at the speed limit. The cathedral loomed ahead, bordering the freeway.

"Push the button!" Amadeus kept a tight grip on the steering wheel.

"Here goes." Van Gogh squeezed, eyes closed, hands trembling.

"Nothing! What the hell." Amadeus glanced to his right, the cathedral quickly receding behind them.

"We're at ground zero." Van Gogh opened his eyes, looking back, the cathedral now out of sight. "What were those specs again?"

"Half a mile. Shit, we were less than a block from the pope's quarters." Amadeus drummed the steering wheel hard.

"What's plan C?" Van Gogh slammed the remote down.

"Careful. We'll get off the freeway and hoof it." They were still disguised, two bearded priests on the prowl.

"That's too risky." Van Gogh said. "Let's head home, mellow out."

"Are you bailing on me?" Amadeus exited the freeway, pulling to the curb in front of a liquor store. Two bums staggered by, a third tapped on the passenger side window.

"No way. We need time. Our Lady's crawling with security. C'mon, bro, tomorrow's another day. These guys are creepy."

Amadeus pounded the steering wheel, made a U-turn, nearly hitting an inebriated youth, and headed home. They drove the freeway in utter silence. At home, they found Mildred asleep. Van Gogh soon crashed, but Amadeus sat on the deck, staring east. He didn't move from the spot for two hours. His mind raced, going over every detail of the failed mission. After dozens of reviews, he had an epiphany. "Eureka! I've a plan."

* * *

While the pope was at breakfast, a maid ran screaming from the guest apartment. "A bomb. A bomb!" Security descended on the bathroom, quickly disarming the plastic explosive. The LAPD bomb squad conferred with the FBI. There was no doubt: C-4 putty explosive.

Detective Thompson convened the special task force. At the top of the detective's list were the two priests allowed access to Our Lady during the pope's visit to Dodger Stadium. An all points bulletin was issued; two recent photos of Fathers Gallagher and O'Neil were circulated. Under orders from Detective Thompson, the LAPD withheld the discovery from the press. He feared tipping off the twins.

Chapter Fifty-Two

Cardinal Martinez arranged for Fathers Gallagher and O'Neil to spend a week at Thomas Aquinas College in Santa Paula. It was in part a gesture of compassion. Father Gallagher had lost his church. It was also a tactical move. If the two priests were spotted in LA, it would be the twins.

Pope John Paul III was scheduled to return to the Vatican the next day, so security was thick. The bomb scare was hushed up, although rumors circulated on the Internet. When the pope heard of the planted bomb, he laughed, "Probably a practical joke." But he knew better. It was the twins. He requested a change of accommodations. Cardinal Martinez relinquished his apartment, security was doubled, and the pope was not allowed privacy. Guards were posted inside and outside his room. He was never alone.

The twins scoured the Internet, looking for news about the pope. The only mention of a bomb scare was on Scuttlebutt, a conspiracy blog. The Gospel of Mary dominated the news. The tide was turning.

"I was up half the night." Amadeus took his first sip of coffee. He'd removed his disguise, his eyes were bloodshot, and his hair was still damp from a shower.

"What's up?" Van Gogh had also shed his gray beard. He'd been up an hour, refreshed from a good night's sleep, but down.

"I've a new plan."

"The last one bombed."

"That's a hoot." They both laughed as Mildred entered the living room.

"What's so funny?" She asked, irritated with their antics.

"Our plan bombed." Amadeus blurted, laughing.

"I'm glad you're so giddy. I'm scared."

"Hear me out." Amadeus abruptly stopped laughing, eyes focused, face drawn.

"We're all ears." Van Gogh refreshed his coffee. "Mildred?" She nodded. He filled her cup and waited for Plan C.

"Are you up for a European holiday?" Amadeus grinned. "We'll get more bang for our buck at the Vatican."

"That's crazy! The place will be locked down," Mildred said.

"But *he* has our back."

"What?" Van Gogh and Mildred exclaimed in unison.

"The plan came in a vision. *He* spoke to me." Amadeus stood, opened his arms wide. "The world is ours."

"*He* didn't speak to me," Van Gogh said, tilting his head, suspicious.

"Are you in?" Amadeus clapped his hands, excited.

"Haven't heard the plan yet." Van Gogh stood his ground.

Amadeus retrieved a notepad from the coffee table. "It's all in here."

"Let's see it." Van Gogh reached toward his brother, taking the notepad.

For the next five minutes, he sat reading, occasionally smiling, finally uttering, "Amen. Brilliant but dicey."

Mildred took her turn, reading in silence. She put it down. Her response was terse. "Insane."

"And we're not?" Amadeus rested his case. "Tomorrow we make travel plans. We should be in Rome in less than a week."

"Do the plans include me?" Mildred asked hesitantly.

"Sorry. The mission's far too dangerous. Besides, why risk the consequences?" Amadeus said firmly.

"What will I do? Where will I go?"

"Stay put. We have the house for another month. I checked my voicemail yesterday. The owner's tied up in Mexico doing a shoot," Amadeus said.

"Shit! I'm on the lam, alone, with few options." Mildred was forlorn.

"When we return, the three of us will take a vacation." Amadeus stood and walked over to her with open arms. "A hug."

"What about my practice?"

"It'll spring back. You've got the magic touch." Amadeus gently pulled her from the sofa, folding her into his arms. "You're safe here. *He's* watching our back."

* * *

The line lurched forward, jammed with tourists, a few students, and a sprinkling of business types. That was Van Gogh's take. Amadeus agreed. With baggage checked and tickets in order, they cleared security. Their papers were impeccable. Two religious scholars headed for the Vatican. Amadeus had a safety deposit box full of passports and identifications. He had been masquerading for years. He felt invincible.

The twins headed for the nearest lounge for one last drink before the long flight. The United Airlines boarding gate was just around the corner. They had shed the priest disguise and opted for the professorial look—jeans, sweater vests, and sport jackets. Amadeus wore tweed, his brother corduroy. Amadeus had resurrected the eye patch and cane; it felt right. Before they finished the merlot, a short balding man with a large red badge approached. Amadeus squinted, checking out the badge: Airport Security. "Sir, this fell out of your coat pocket during the security check."

Amadeus smiled. "Thanks so much." He handed the man a five-dollar bill. "You're a life saver."

The security officer grinned and hesitated, then took the tip and rushed off.

"What was that all about?" Van Gogh sipped his wine, lost in thought.

"Oh, nothing. Just the notebook with Plan C."

"Jeez you're nonchalant."

"Just a thespian doing his thing."

Across from the bar, unnoticed by the twins, Doc nursed his coffee. Gypsy had five minutes before boarding a United Flight to Bucharest, and Doc had come to see her off. Aunt Bella, her mother's oldest sister, had lost a yearlong battle to lung cancer. Repeated pleas from her grieving mom to return home could not be denied.

Doc had been supportive of Gypsy, encouraged the visit, sensing her need to see the family and touch base with her friends and loved ones. It had been ten years since she'd been home. She especially missed her mother.

"Doc, they called my flight."

Doc stared at the two men at the bar, not responding to Gypsy. "Doc, it's time."

Doc squinted for a better look, then turned and said, "I'll miss you."

"I'll be home in two weeks. Check on my place. Promise?"

"Sure thing." Doc walked her to the boarding gate, gave her a big hug, and kissed her tenderly on the lips. He felt paternalistic. After all these years, they still had not consummated the relationship, much to Gypsy's dismay.

She'd been more like a sister to Doc. But recently his feelings had changed. She was a soul mate. *I love her.*

He waved and retreated to the bar area, grabbed the sport section of the *LA Times*, and pretended to catch up on the latest scores. He peered over the top of the paper, getting a closer look at the two men at the bar. The mannerisms of the two were hauntingly familiar. The eye patch and cane set off a flood of memories. *It's him!*

Doc stood ready to approach the twins when Schizzy flamboyantly tipped the bartender, acknowledging his service with a bow, nod, and quick gesture with his cane. Now he was more certain than ever. The walk, dress, and theatrics sealed it.

The twins disappeared around the corner. Doc hesitated and then moved quickly down the main corridor toward the boarding gates. They were nearing the ticket agent when a familiar voice rang out. "Hey, Doc!"

He turned to his right, instantly recognizing an old friend. "Gwen, so good to see you." His response was automatic but his brain needed to catch up.

"What brings you to LAX?" She stepped closer, arms spread, offering a hug.

Doc smiled and closed the distance, responding with a warm hug. "I brought a friend to the airport. You remember Gypsy?"

"Of course. The spiritualist."

Doc gazed forlornly at the United Airlines boarding gate. The twins were gone. "What brings you here?" He was conflicted. He was elated to see Gwen. It had been awhile. But the timing couldn't be worse. He was on to Schizzy, but fate seemed to have other plans.

"I was helping out my boss. He has a conference in Atlanta."

"Same chiropractor?"

"Yeah. He's been great. How about lunch?"

"Jeez, Gwen, I'd love to, but I've a full calendar."

"You got time for a coffee?"

"I'm so sorry, but I really have to go … I'll call you soon. Promise."

Doc gave her a quick hug good-bye, apologized once more, and then ran to his car and phoned Detective Fred Thompson. He picked up on the second ring. "Detective Thompson."

"Doc Mesmer. I need to see you. I spotted the twins."

"Where?"

"I'm at Lax. I saw Amadeus and Van Gogh at an airport bar. They boarded a flight for Rome a short time ago."

"Can't be."

"Why?"

"We've had all point bulletins, extra security, and the support of the FBI working around the clock. We had LAX covered. Nada. We've got nothing."

"I'm sure of it. They're on a United Airlines flight to Rome as we speak."

"Doc, thanks for the tip. Don't call us, we'll call you."

"You don't believe me."

"We'll check it out. Keep in touch."

He signed off without a good-bye. Doc was miffed. He'd been dismissed, ignored, and patronized in one short phone call. He berated himself for blowing off Gwen in order to make the pointless phone call.

Doc's mind raced. Kaleidoscopic images of Schizzy and his crazy twin consumed him on the ride over the Sepulveda pass. He descended into the San Fernando Valley and headed for his office. He had a one o'clock with a client.

His afternoon was full, leaving little time to think of the twins. At five, he dropped by the emporium, needing to unload on Waldo.

He greeted the checker with a smile and a quick hello. "Is Wally in the back?"

"Yep. On break."

Doc slid into a chair, grimacing at Waldo's stained mug. "What's up?"

"Same old song. Young kids listening to noise and old ladies trying to cheat me."

"Listening to music?"

"Doesn't sound anything like music to me. I'd rather listen to a jackhammer."

"Hey, Wally, I need some advice."

"You're in the wrong place for that."

"I took Gypsy to LAX this morning."

"Bucharest, right?"

"Yeah, she decided to see her mother. Listen, I need your help."

"Need a loan?"

"No! It's Schizzy."

"You're obsessed with him. Get another hobby."

"I saw Schizzy and his twin at the airport."

"You sure?"

"Bet my life on it."

"Call that detective friend of yours."

"I did."

"Well?"

"He blew me off."

"That's two of us. Read the tealeaves."

"You're a big help."

"That's what my dead wife used to say, God bless her soul."

"No compassion here."

"Fresh out. Besides, you need to move on. Take care of Gypsy. She's the best part of you." Waldo rolled up a section of the front page and beat the table. "If I knew better, I'd rap you over the head, knock some sense into you."

"Thanks for being a friend." Doc got up, even more dejected than before, and left by the back door.

He had no clients this evening, so he phoned Alan Workman. He got him on the second ring. "Alan, how about dinner? It's on me."

"That works."

"Gerry's on Ventura okay?"

"My favorite."

"How's seven sound?" Doc suddenly felt better.

"See you then."

Doc decided he had one more call to make. *Yeah, William Preston might have an angle.* He searched the top drawer of his desk and found his card.

He phoned the agency and got a secretary. "He's on another line. Can he call you back?"

"Sure. Tell him it's an emergency."

Five minutes later, Doc's phone rang. He picked up after the first ring. "Doc here."

"William Preston. What's up?"

"I need your advice."

"Shoot."

"I saw the twins at Lax. They were at a bar, waiting for a United Airlines flight to Rome."

"You positive?"

"Schizzy brought back the eye patch and cane. The mannerisms and theatrics were a dead giveaway."

"You call the police?"

"Yeah, sure. They didn't believe it."

"How can I help?"

"I'm going to tail them."

"What?"

"I'm headed for Rome. Any advice on locating them?"

"Risky business."

"I know."

"Follow the pope," the P.I. suggested.

"That's it?"

"That's it."

Doc thanked William and headed for the restaurant. He found Alan at a front table near the street-side window.

"Thanks for coming. How's work?"

"Same drill. Too much work and too little appreciation." Alan opened the menu, flipping through it, looking for something new.

"I took Gypsy to LAX this morning, and guess who I saw?"

"Elvis."

"I'm not that nutty. No, I saw the twins."

"You sure?"

"Yeah, they were waiting for a flight to Rome. The two were sipping wine, carrying on with the same theatrics. Schizzy's brought back the eye patch and cane."

"Call the LAPD."

"I did. Detective Thompson would have none of it."

"It's out of our hands. We're powerless. Hell, the LAPD and FBI have done little." Alan ordered a vegetarian pizza. Buddhism and his doctor had gotten him off meat.

"I'm booking a flight to Rome." Doc leaned back, satisfied. He'd decided.

"I'm going after Schizzy. His twin too."

"That's crazy."

"And they're not!"

Doc and Alan got caught up on the latest. Alan thanked Doc for the meal and gave him a vigorous handshake. "Be safe. I believe you. I just don't have your resolve. I'm content with my little beauties, my philosophy, and peace of mind. I'm not enlightened, haven't discovered nirvana, but have found the middle way. Chasing two crazies halfway around the world is out of my pay grade."

Doc went back to his office, searched the Internet for the best deal on a flight to Rome, then called his clients and cancelled for the next week. He was on the hunt.

Chapter Fifty-Three

Father Gallagher lunched with Father O'Neil, happy to be back at the cathedral, rejuvenated from their short stay at Thomas Aquinas College. His heart was heavy, the embers of his beloved church smoldering in his soul. The pope was gone; Our Lady was back to normal, and Father Gallagher found an agreeable temporary assignment alongside his longtime friend. Ten minutes ago, Cardinal Martinez named him committee chairman to rebuild Saint Vincent's. *That's next month. For now, I'm just hanging with my bud.*

The evening of their first day back, Father Gallagher received a call from William Preston. The private eye ran down his phone call with Doc. He cautiously confessed that the hypnotist was on to something. This alarmed the priest, so he called for an emergency meeting of the Ghostbusters. It was a momentous meeting. After three hours of intense discussion, they voted. It was unanimous. The Ghostbusters were making a second trip to the Vatican. Cardinal Martinez was at first vehemently opposed to the idea, but after some arm twisting, he reluctantly granted the two priests a week's leave. Dr. Salazar, again, footed the bill.

* * *

Doc sipped his coffee, studying the faces around him, hoping to run into the twins. The café, the closest one to the Vatican, was packed, people ducking in from the rain. It hadn't stopped since he arrived. It was already his third day in Rome, but nothing. He was about to leave when he spotted familiar faces. He waved excitedly, approaching their table. "Fathers Gallagher and O'Neil."

"Doc! We heard you were here."

"Really? Who told you?"

"William Preston. Please, join us." Father Gallagher stood, sliding over a chair to make room. "You know everyone."

"Yes. Greetings, Dr. Salazar." Doc smiled, the first break since he'd arrived.

"We heard you spotted the twins at LAX. For you to make the trip, you must have been convinced." Father O'Neil leaned back, allowing the waiter to serve the coffee. "Please, bring another cup for our friend," the priest said in Italian, gesturing to make things clearer. His Italian wasn't the greatest.

"I am as sure as I am sitting here with you. It was them!" Doc was animated.

Dr. Salazar cleared his throat and asked, "Why were you at the airport?"

"A favor for a dear friend. She needed a ride and moral support."

"Moral support?" The shrink studied Doc's demeanor, suspicious. Many a client had tested him.

"She was on her way home to visit her mother. Her aunt had recently died from cancer." Doc paused and added, "But what brings you three to Rome?"

"Same thing that brought you." Father O'Neil warmed his hands over the steamy brew. His hands were cold and clammy from the incessant rain.

"You must trust me." Doc smiled as the waiter brought him coffee. It was his fourth, a sure formula for the jitters.

"William Preston got a good read on your sighting. Listen, tomorrow the pope is addressing biblical scholars at one of the Vatican Museums. We have an extra ticket. You game?" Dr. Salazar grinned, brows arched.

"Do you think the twins will show?" Doc didn't want to waste time. He could only afford a week in Rome.

"The pope is a veritable magnet. Plus, he's agreed to meet with us after tomorrow's meeting." Father Gallagher took a sip of coffee and added, "He's still shook up over the bomb scare at Our Lady."

"I'd like to tag along when you meet with the pope." Doc was antsy, the coffee kicking into high gear.

"That's a tall order. We'd have to clear it with Vatican security." Father Gallagher frowned, shaking his head.

"I'd appreciate it. Remember Gypsy and I participated in the Meeting of Minds at Our Lady."

"That helps. But clearance takes time. We made arrangements before we left the States." Father Gallagher looked over at Father O'Neil. "What do you think?"

"We'll give it a go."

Doc and the Ghostbusters drank and talked for more than an hour before leaving the café. Doc said, "See ya tomorrow. Make the pope thing happen."

* * *

As Doc turned in, a sudden downpour pelted the hotel window. The far wall came alive, lit up by the crackling lightning. The thunder unnerved him; it was midnight. Between the coffee and the storm, he was wired; he didn't fall asleep until two. At five, he stirred, awakened by visions of the twins. The breathy voice spewed demonic threats, punctuated by thunder and lightning. He peered out the window at the street below. Deserted. His only companions were visions, disturbing images of Schizzy and his demented twin. He sank into the soft mattress, forlorn.

Sleep was intermittent, leaving Doc's face drawn and his eyes bloodshot. "Thank God I'm not here for a beauty contest," he said aloud, applying shaving cream to his haggard mug. He shaved, showered, and dressed. The rain had stopped. *A good omen*, he mused as he rode the elevator to the lobby.

After breakfast and a brisk walk, he headed for the Museums, threading his way through the crowded, rain-slick streets. He had a date with the Ghostbusters, biblical scholars, and—hopefully—the pope. *They better have gotten me security clearance.*

Doc spotted the Ghostbusters at the entrance of the Vatican Museums. Dr. Salazar gesticulated wildly, pointing heavenward. The trio broke out in laughter, enjoying themselves immensely.

"You three are in a gay mood," Doc greeted them, feeling their energy.

"Doc, we've pulled it off. You're invited to our private two o'clock with the pope."

"Excellent!"

"But first the biblical scholars. There's a formal presentation by three hotshot theologians, then a message from His Holiness." Father Gallagher was eager to hear what they had to say, but he was more pumped for their private meeting with the pope.

The foursome entered the vast complex of thirteen museums and hoofed it to the Ethnological Missionary Museum, a large complex featuring religious objects from four geographical areas: Asia, Oceania, Africa, and America. They headed for the second floor, laughing but nervous. Doc was delighted that he was included. The lack of sleep and the afternoon schedule had him reeling; his senses were on steroids.

The lower floor was jammed with museum goers. Serious looking scholars with long faces dominated the second floor. It was here they would listen to biblical scholars and the pope. The Ghostbusters plus one stood out, lively, alert, but fidgety. They sensed the twins were near, but none would admit it.

After clearing security, the Ghostbusters and Doc found seats in the back corner of the hall. It served as a multipurpose room designed for discussion groups and lectures. At the front of the room were several long tables for the speakers, and on the stage three oversized, high-back chairs for the pope and two cardinals.

As the biblical scholars took their seats, the pope entered the room and ascended the stage. Everyone stood as the pope bowed and eased into the elevated chair, smiling, eager for the presentation. He knew what they would say. He had parsed their reports earlier, demanding a few key revisions. Any hints of doubt about the authenticity of the Gospel of Mary were censored. The acceptance of the gospel was his legacy. *I'm at the crossroads of my career. It's my destiny. I'll be canonized.*

The three international scholars delivered their findings, skillfully summarizing the technical data and analysis for the press. It was brilliant PR orchestrated by a politically savvy pope. At the close of the session, a bearded man with an eye patch rose, waved his cane, and bellowed, "I've a question."

The moderator, Cardinal Jose Chavez, acknowledged the man by saying, "One last question."

"I'm a philosopher, once taught at Thomas Aquinas College in California." The man paused, cleared his voice, and continued. "I'm puzzled, amazed, and delighted with the discovery of the Gospel of Mary. But please indulge me. How did the archeologists know where to begin their excavation? It appears to be a miracle. If I'm not out of order, I'd like to hear an answer from His Holiness."

Cardinal Jose Chavez immediately intervened. "I think that question is best reserved for a later time."

"Please indulge me. The information is in your hands. The world has a right to know."

Father Gallagher nudged Father O'Neil. "Are you thinking what I'm thinking?"

"Bingo! It's Vincent." Father O'Neil turned to Doc. "Does the philosopher look familiar?"

"It's Schizzy." Doc tried to stand but was immediately restrained by Father O'Neil. "Let this play out."

The pope stood and opened his arms wide, smiling. "I have the answer. For years, I've dusted off many a book, digging through the literature, compiling a mass of information. It's been a hobby, a passion, and a calling all wrapped in one. The facts were there. The dots needed to be connected. With much work and more prayer, it came to me. I've had God's help. Now go and spread the word. The feminine voice will now be heard."

The pope waved as two cardinals escorted him from the room. The audience stood, applauding enthusiastically. A tall man in the front row yelled out, "Long live the pope!"

Doc sprang to his feet and slipped through the packed room looking for Schizzy. He leapt on a chair looking out over the large conference room. He caught glimpse of the bearded man with the eye patch leaving the door, brushing past security. By the time he reached the main corridor, he was gone.

Doc and the Ghostbusters reconnected outside the museum. Doc's face was bright red. As he approached the Ghostbusters, he said, "That was Schizzy. I'm sure of it."

Father O'Neil agreed. "Brazen move. I'm a philosopher. Taught at Thomas Aquinas. Dead giveaway."

Dr. Salazar raised his hand. "I think it was a ploy."

"Really?" Doc said.

"I think he was sending a message to the pope." Dr. Salazar stroked his bearded chin.

"What if the pope cancels his meeting with us?" Father Gallagher frowned.

"He won't. Let's have lunch. The best is yet to come," Doc said.

Chapter Fifty-Four

"Your Holiness, the Los Angeles friends are here."

Pope John Paul III glanced at his secretary, smiled, and said, "Give me five minutes."

Antonio Manghetti quietly closed the library door, leaving the pope in deep thought. His plan was unfolding perfectly. Vincent Amadeus asked the million-dollar question, stoking the fires, raising the final unanswered question. "How did the pope know where to look for the Gospel of Mary?" *It's phase two and I'm ready.*

The pope walked to the library door, cracked it, and said quietly, "I'm ready to receive my guests." *Round two,* he thought as he found his favorite chair across from the fireplace.

The Ghostbusters and Doc greeted His Holiness, bowing with respect. It was Doc's first visit to the pope's private quarters, and it showed. He was bug-eyed, head on a swivel, simply overwhelmed.

"It's so good to see you. I occasionally get homesick, so your visit is appreciated." The pope paused, smiled, and added, "Would you care for refreshments?"

Father Gallagher answered politely, "No thanks. We've just had lunch."

"I want to thank you, Your Holiness, for allowing me to tag along." Doc smiled, and added quickly, "I love the books."

"They're my friends. I couldn't live without them. Buried within several of the volumes lay the clues to the recent discovery." The pope leaned back, looking closely at his guests, searching, hoping to get a read on the Ghostbusters.

"We're on a mission," Dr. Salazar said firmly. "We have good reason to believe your life is in danger."

"What?" the pope said, fidgeting in his chair.

"The bombing of Saint Vincent's and the aborted bombing of Our Lady is the work of the twins." Dr. Salazar leaned forward. "I'm sure of it."

"You have hard evidence?" The pope sensed he was playing with fire, the twins, and now the Ghostbusters.

The shrink nodded and said flatly, "The LAPD, FBI, and yours truly have no other suspects. It's them."

"And you say you fear for my life?"

At that moment, the outer door burst open, and two bearded men appeared, one with an eye patch and cane, the other carrying a briefcase. "Greetings. Your secretary will be fine. We had to anesthetize him. Please give him our best." Amadeus turned to his brother and added, "We've a surprise."

Dr. Salazar stood, pumping his fist. "Not this again!"

"Please, my dear Dr. Salazar. We're in charge of the theatrics." Van Gogh turned abruptly, knocking the shrink to his seat. He struggled to get up but was held back by Amadeus, his cane lodged snuggly in the middle of his chest, causing him to cough.

The pope tried to stand but was deterred by Amadeus. He didn't use the cane on him but just waved it menacingly, nearly clipping his nose.

"Please, let's be civil." Father Gallagher opened his hands in a gesture of cooperation.

Three uniformed men barged through the door, weapons drawn. A fourth and fifth quickly cuffed the twins, whisking them away. Van Gogh's shouts of protest echoed down the hall, bringing the twins' performance to a dramatic halt.

The Ghostbusters and Doc sat paralyzed. The pope stood, brushed his hands, ridding himself of them for good. They'd serve their purpose. He thanked and excused the head of Vatican security.

"Gentlemen, I both thank you for your visit and apologize for the commotion. I've planned the trap for some time. The twins were on my radar."

After a long pause, Dr. Salazar spoke. "We are elated with their capture. But they raised an important question. How *did* you know the location of the Gospel of Mary?"

"It was there all the time," he said, smiling, gesturing toward the wall-to-wall books, "lying quietly among my friends."

"But what of all the theatrics—Satan, the eerie voice, and the Faustian bargain?"

The pope smiled, arms open, issuing his final statement on the matter. "It was merely a lot of empty drama, a tale told by idiots. As you well know, Dr. Salazar, they're insane."

The pope ushered his American friends out, putting on a phony show, thanking them for their support and cooperation. As soon as they left, he phoned security, checked on the health of his secretary, and looked in on the twins. They had been interrogated, jailed, granted access to lawyers, and were in the custody of American authorities. They had a date with the U.S. courts.

* * *

It had been two weeks since the twins were arrested. They were back in California waiting to stand trial. The pope's popularity, driven by the media frenzy surrounding the Gospel of Mary, had soared. He had the majority of cardinals on his side, and his political adversaries were either powerless or dead.

He had finished his third cabernet, prayed, and was snuggly tucked in bed waiting for sleep. He flashed back on the early years, relishing the good times, thinking of the Faustian bargain. It was only fantasy, playacting, the product of an overactive imagination. Before drifting off, he thought of the twins, laughing, frolicking, jesters at best, mad at worse. *They're gone, thank God.*

Hours later, in the dead of night, a full moon lit up the pope's face. He stirred, bolted upright, screaming. The bloodcurdling screams echoed off the walls, amplified, reaching the sensitive ears of his secretary. Images of the twins taunting, pointing, shrieking, and yelling sent the pope reeling. The voice, breathy and loud, filled his senses. Out of the chaotic fog of vitriolic visions came the repeated phrase, "You made a deal. Now I'm here to collect. Your soul is mine."

Antonio, awakened out of a sound sleep, initially thought it was his voice screaming, but soon identified the source. He rolled out of bed, his arthritic knees stiff, and sluggishly ambled to the pope's bedroom. He knocked, threw open the door, and saw the pope in a heap, kneeling, grasping a large crucifix. Saliva pooled around his lips, dripping onto the floor. He moaned, gasped, and collapsed.

Antonio rushed to clear his airways, felt his carotid artery, and immediately administered CPR. He reached for the phone and called for help, then resumed lifesaving maneuvers, pushing, pounding, desperately trying to jump-start his heart.

Ninety seconds later, emergency medical personnel rushed the pope to the special medical facility down the hall from his apartment. After heroic attempts to revive him, His Holiness died.

News of the pope's death soon spread, and by morning, the world knew. Pope John Paul III was dead. The world was shocked, the Catholic Church in mourning. Halfway around the world, locked down in separate facilities, the twins were elated.

Chapter Fifty-Five

Doc had returned home, conflicted, relieved over the twins' arrest, but feeling incomplete. He agreed with the Ghostbusters; the pope had dodged the critical question. How had he known where the Gospel of Mary was buried?

As he opened the morning edition of the *LA Times*, expecting to see more articles on the twins, he nearly choked on his coffee. There in enlarged letters was a stunner: "The Pope is Dead."

He scanned the article, barely able to contain himself. He phoned Father Gallagher, but there was no answer. He dialed Gypsy but hung up before the call went through. He needed to talk to someone. He gulped down some orange juice, a slice of buttered toast, and headed for his office. It was an hour before his first appointment. He closed shop and hustled over to Waldo's. The bookstore opened at nine. It was five after by the time he dashed by the checkout, shouting, "Where's Wally?"

"Back room," said Alice, not looking up.

"Wally! Thank God you're here."

"Where'd you think I'd be, the Bahamas?"

Waldo had the front page spread out, coffee stains dotting the headline. "You've seen it," Doc said.

"Seen what?"

"The pope's dead."

"Yeah. Happens to the best of us."

"But the twins are in custody." Doc's eyes darted about, nervous, frustrated with Waldo's cavalier attitude.

291

"They weren't the pope's only problem." Waldo stirred his coffee, banging the spoon against the side of the cup. "The pope was a political animal, made enemies."

"You think he was murdered?" Doc shot back, tiring of Waldo's untimely cynicism.

"Not necessarily. Maybe the stress of the job got to him." Waldo slurped his coffee, leaving a dark moustache on his upper lip.

"I got up this morning looking forward to more coverage of the twins; I wasn't expecting this."

"Now that's a story, two loonies shadowing the pope. I'm not Catholic, not even religious, but that's a hoot." Waldo folded the front page once, then again. "Check this out. A psychiatrist is quoted as seeing a classical philosophical problem at the heart of the twins' incarceration. Van Gogh is locked up in a psychiatric facility, unfit to stand trial, while his identical twin faces criminal charges: same genes, same parents. What gives?" Waldo leaned back, sipping his coffee, proud of his observation.

"Maybe the twins have fooled us all. Maybe they're not only crazy but demonic. I think they're connected to something primordial. Perhaps the devil himself." Doc got up and bid good-bye. "I got a nine o'clock."

"Say hello to Gypsy for me." Waldo put down the front page and checked out the sports page.

* * *

Fred Thompson finished an early morning meeting, congratulating members of the special task force for their excellent work. The pope's visit had been a success. He stared at his office clock, mentally reviewing highlights of the past month. Mildred had been apprehended, caught sneaking into her parlor. He'd had her spiritual practice on Reseda staked out for weeks. It had paid off. With the help of William Preston of Shamrock Investigations, they had linked her to the twins and the murder of Leonard "Ike" Eisenhower. The evidence was solid. *Lock her up and throw away the key.* Ike's snooping got too close to the truth. She'd hired him to locate Van Gogh. The P.I. had thought she feared the fugitive. But he'd uncovered too much. She couldn't risk disclosure of her relationship with the twins, so she got rid of him, for good.

It was a good month. He had nailed the bitch, the twins were under lock and key, and the pope had survived his California visit. Unfortunately he didn't fare as well in Rome.

The office phone sliced through his thoughts, causing him to flinch. He picked up on the third ring. "Detective Thompson."

"Are you sitting down?" the watch commander barked.

"What's up?"

"Vincent Salabrini is missing."

"What?"

"Early this morning, he suffered an apparent seizure and was rushed to the hospital. On the way over, a FedEx truck rammed the ambulance."

"How'd he get away?"

"The attending officer and medic were knocked unconscious. The ambulance driver was stunned but caught a glimpse of Vincent ducking into an alley near Spring and Seventh."

"Fuck!"

"My sentiments. Get on it now!"

Detective Thompson sprang into action and within an hour had put together a ten-man task force. He loved a challenge, but this was dicey. *He's not only crazy. He's evil.*

* * *

Amadeus ran through the alley, dodging trash bins and parked trucks. He came upon a cardboard encampment draped with colorful assortment of rags. Inside, he found a bum kneeling, combing his beard. He swung a short metal pipe, catching the dazed man on the chin, knocking him back. "Lights out," Amadeus whispered with glee. He stripped the man of his pants, tattered corduroy coat, and sneakers.

As he walked out on Spring Street, he heard something jingling in his coat pocket. He reached in and pulled out seventy-five cents in change and six dollar bills. *It's my day.*

After coffee at McDonald's, he rode the MTD to Ventura and Reseda. From there, it was a short two blocks to his PO box and freedom. He picked up five hundred dollars in twenties, an unused ID, a Lady Derringer, 38, and headed over to Mildred's parlor. *No way they'll look for me there. She's in jail, poor thing.*

He went around back, found a bathroom window unlocked, pushed it up, and with some difficulty slid through the small opening, twisting his shoulder. "Damn it!" he yelped. In the kitchen, he spotted a small black and white TV, turned it on, and caught the noon news. His mug was on every station. He switched to CNN. *Bingo! I'm the talk of the town.*

In the bathroom, he found scissors, hair dye, and a razor. Thirty minutes later, he stared in the mirror with amazement.

He found an extra set of keys, but left by the back door. *First stop, the thrift shop three blocks north.*

Chapter Fifty-Six

Doc's last client left with a smile, happy with his second smokeless week. The client had been addicted to nicotine for twenty years, tried quitting a dozen times, but finally hit the jackpot. Doc had perfected his magic bullet—*just a pinch of guided imagery and a dash of hypnosis.*

He turned off the desk lamp, preparing to leave, when the buzzer shattered the silence. He glanced at his appointment book; he had nothing after seven. *I'll wait it out.* The buzzer sounded again, this time for much longer. As he reluctantly opened up, a man brushed past him, demanding an appointment.

"You'll have to contact me tomorrow. The office is closed." Doc squinted, trying to get a read on the intruder.

The stranger whirled around, his long black coat fanning out like a cape. "Doc, don't you recognize me?" The intruder removed his brimmed hat, bowing gracefully like a magician.

Doc approached, looked into his eyes, and instantly knew. "Vincent," he said.

"I've missed you."

"Why me?" Doc's heart was in his throat.

"Did you like my escape?"

He hesitated, then nervously said, "I caught the news. Never thought you'd look me up."

"I need a favor." Amadeus plopped down on the sofa. "Have a seat."

Doc moved to his desk, sitting nervously on the edge, ready for the worst. *If I have to, I'll fight him.* "I'm fresh out of favors."

"I need a place to hang my hat, cool my heels. Get my drift?"

"No way! I'll not be an accomplice."

"This says you will." Schizzy flashed the Derringer. "Light, compact, and deadly accurate. So you were saying?"

"I'm not budging." Doc folded his arms defiantly.

"Gypsy will be devastated."

"What?"

"Don't test me. If I must, I'll use it."

"You'll never get away with it."

"Perhaps not. But you'll be dead."

"I can't get involved."

"Just provide me cover for a couple of days. You've a ready excuse. I'm armed and dangerous." Schizzy paused, waving the Derringer. "Some say I'm mad. So let's go. I don't want to make Gypsy a widow."

"We're not married."

"Maybe not legally. But I've seen the look in her eyes. Let's not let her down. So do we do this quietly or make a scene?"

Doc weighed his options and reluctantly acquiesced. In less than twenty minutes, they were at his hillside home, sharing a glass of wine. Schizzy's Derringer rested next to his drink, pointed at Doc.

"Great view." Schizzy motioned to the vista, now dotted by the city lights below.

"It was my parents' place. I was raised here."

"Nothing like home."

Doc's phone rang, piercing the still night.

"Answer it." Schizzy picked up the Derringer, waving it.

Doc picked up on the fifth ring. "Hello."

"Doc, why didn't you stop by? I've only been back for three days. I miss you."

"I had a late appointment. Just got home."

"I'm scared. Vincent's escaped. I don't want to be alone."

"Do you want me to drop by?"

"No! I'm coming over. See you in a few." Before Doc could protest, Gypsy signed off.

"Who was it?" Schizzy again waved the pistol, frowning suspiciously.

"Gypsy. She's on her way."

"Here?"

"There was no time to put her off."

"This should be fun." Schizzy sipped his wine, casually wagging the Derringer. "Drink up, Doc. The night's young."

Twenty minutes later, Gypsy entered the front door, calling Doc's name.

"Out here, on the deck." He was seated alone. Schizzy was concealed behind a potted fern, next to the french doors. As Gypsy walked toward Doc, he sprang forward, yelling, "Surprise!"

Gypsy turned abruptly, nearly collapsing at the sight of Schizzy. She screamed, retreated a step, and then fainted, collapsing into Doc. He caught her, cradling her fall.

Doc pulled her up, sliding her into a cushioned chair. He doused a napkin with water, gently wiping her brow. She stirred, blinking.

"It's okay. I'll take care of you." Doc continued stroking her, reintroducing her to their shared nightmare.

"Sorry for the fright. I mean no harm." Schizzy sipped his wine, still gripping the Derringer. "Doc, fix her a drink."

Unknown to the reluctant partygoers, and undetected by Schizzy, Alan Workman hid below the deck, eavesdropping. He had just left Wally's Emporium after buying a book by the Dalai Lama when he spotted Schizzy and Doc. At first he didn't recognize the fugitive, but when they pulled out on to Ventura Boulevard in Doc's car, a streetlight lit up Schizzy's face. There was no doubt. He had tailed them, hid, and now waited patiently.

"Gypsy, please forgive me." Schizzy smiled as Doc handed a merlot to Gypsy. "Take a sip. It'll clear your head."

With trembling hands, she took a sip. She wasn't much of a drinker, but the wine hit the spot. "Why are you here?" she said, this time taking a healthy swig.

"I need cover. But since you're here, a Tarot reading is in order. I need to know my immediate future. Doc, have you a deck?" Schizzy pointed the pistol at Doc.

"I don't know."

"I've a deck in my purse. It's in the living room."

"Stay here where I can see you. I'll get it." Schizzy walked cautiously through the french doors, looking back, eyes locked on his captives.

He located her purse on the sofa, opened it, and took out the deck. It was new, the packaging unopened.

"Doc, you and Gypsy sit together across from me. Let's do this." He threw the deck to Gypsy as the Lady Derringer held court despite its diminutive size. The single shot 38-caliber revolver was Schizzy's favorite ace in the hole. Not quite five inches in length and weighing only fifteen ounces, it was versatile. "How do you like the cameo grip?"

"What?" Doc frowned, confused.

"The pistol grip."

Doc and Gypsy remained silent, staring down the barrel of the pistol. As Gypsy spread out a Celtic cross, a booming voice interrupted Schizzy's game. "Vincent, we know you're in there. The house is surrounded. You've no options."

Schizzy moved to the edge of the deck, spotting Detective Fred Thompson, bullhorn in hand. Beside him were two uniformed LAPD officers, guns drawn. Down the hill, partially obscured by the orange trees was a police cruiser blocking the driveway. Two more patrolmen stood by the car. Schizzy was outnumbered ten to one. He displayed his Derringer and shouted, "Back off or I'll use this on Doc and Gypsy!"

"It's no good. Our marksmen have you in their sights." Detective Thompson paused, and then added, "The house is surrounded."

Schizzy grabbed Gypsy, put the gun to her head, and marched her to the deck railing. "Back off or she's dead!"

At that moment, Vincent Amadeus Salabrini's head snapped back, blood spurting from his forehead, eyes frozen with surprise. Gypsy collapsed, unconscious but unhurt. It had been Schizzy's last performance.

Chapter Fifty-Seven

Van Gogh, heavily medicated, depressed, and lethargic, gazed at the cross-section of crazies. The day room crawled with pathetic creatures drugged into submission. Mutt and Jeff leaned against the far wall, eyes glazed, tongues dangling uselessly, drooling. Their spit dripped to the linoleum floor like a pair of leaky faucets. The tall, lanky guy wore diapers, his vertically challenged friend a bib. Van Gogh's worst nightmare had come true. He was back at Patton State.

A zombie sat down next to him, babbling, gesturing to no one in particular. Van Gogh pushed himself away from the table, sliding slowly, the plastic chair screeching against the slick floor. He staggered to his feet, plodding toward a nineteen-inch TV at the front of the room. A semicircle of chairs provided a makeshift amphitheater for a ragtag group pretending to watch the evening news. He slumped down between two inmates. The balding man on his right snored loudly, the other, a disheveled redhead, farted, fouling the air.

A news alert flashed on the screen. "The LAPD has shot and killed an escapee a little after eight-thirty this evening. A fugitive, responsible for the recent bombing of Saint Vincent's, had been holding two people hostage at a hillside home in Encino." His heart nearly stopped when the reporter said the name of the victim. "A SWAT team was forced to kill Vincent Amadeus Salabrini as he held a gun to the female hostage. Officials at the scene reported that he was caught in the crossfire of three LAPD sharpshooters."

Van Gogh opened his mouth to scream, but nothing came out. He was too choked up. He could neither protest nor cry. His world had come to an end. Van Gogh stared off, lost, forever disconnected from his better self. Amadeus was the only thing that kept him sane and connected to reality.

Sally Overstreet, the head psychiatric nurse, leaned down, gently tapping Van Gogh on the shoulder. "Mr. Salabrini, I'm sure you heard the terrible news. I've arranged for you to meet with Dr. Oliver Sachs tomorrow morning. Here's something to help you sleep."

Van Gogh accepted the sedative. "I'm already numb."

"This will help." Nurse Overstreet handed him the water, looking on attentively, watching him swallow the tranquilizer. She walked him to his room, staying until he was asleep. He was out cold in less than five minutes. She didn't want a repeat—he burned her once, but not again. During his previous escape, he had boldly walked out the front door. Even nodded and tipped his cap at the security camera.

The next morning, shortly after eight, Van Gogh sat across from Dr. Sachs, a middle-aged man with a pencil thin mustache, staring at his mug. The shrink reminded him of a weasel, with his lean features, hollow cheeks, and pathetic moustache.

The weasel looked up, pursing his lips, nose twitching. "Mr. Salabrini, I understand you heard the news."

"News?"

"Your brother's death. How does that make you feel?"

"What the fuck do you know about feelings?"

The shrink paused and craned his neck. "Why the hostility?"

"I'm in a bad mood."

"That's understandable. Look, I have a treatment plan." The weasel looked down at his notes, nose still twitching.

"I don't think there's a treatment plan for what I feel."

"I think I can help you with both your recent loss and your delusions."

"What delusions?"

"Your obsession with the devil."

"Are you denigrating my faith? Maybe I should whip up a treatment plan for *your* obsession."

Dr. Oliver's eyes widened. "I think you have the roles reversed."

"I'm tired of the psychobabble. I want to go back to my room."

"As you wish." Dr. Oliver Sachs stood and called for the nurse.

"I've prescribed some new meds."

"Fuck you, Doc!"

* * *

It was the dead of night; the ward was silent. Van Gogh bolted upright, screaming. Before him loomed Satan, hovering above, eyes glowing red. "I beseech you to avenge your brother's death. Evil forces have broken our sacred bond." Van Gogh tried to smother the voice, squeezing a pillow to his ears, but the voice persisted, louder than before. "You must kill the doctor!"

"What?" Van Gogh shook his head, rubbing his eyes, more confused than terrified.

"Dr. Oliver Sachs has subverted our plans. Kill him!"

As the room's overhead light flashed on, two psychiatric techs barged in. "Are you all right?"

Van Gogh slumped in bed, rubbing his eyes. "I'm, um, shit, I think I had a nightmare."

"Did you take your meds?" The first tech checked his bed stand.

"Yeah, sure."

"Okay then, if you need us, we're outside."

Van Gogh's night was long and sleepless. A collage of visions consumed him, devils leaping from the flames of hell, demanding their due. "Kill the bastard!"

A tech pressured him to clean up and have breakfast. "Dr. Sachs wants to see you right after breakfast."

"Why?"

"He heard about your nightmare, wants to see you. Come on, get crackin'."

Van Gogh went through the motions; he showered, dressed, and picked at some toast and scrambled eggs. The toast was like cardboard, the eggs watery and bland. He shoved the meal aside and checked the morning news. After a CNN report on the selection process for a new pope, a picture of his dead brother flashed on the screen. The sight of his face triggered a surge of emotions, welling up from the depths of his soul. He covered his eyes and ears, but it didn't help. He heard his name, repeated again and again. His shoulder shook, gently at first, then harder. He uncovered his eyes, confronted again with the bothersome tech.

"Dr. Sachs is in his office. Let's not keep him waiting." The tech extended his arm, helping Van Gogh up. They walked slowly to the rear of the ward. A nurse's station, busy with techs, took up half the area and was flanked by several offices. The head shrink had the corner office with a view of the garden below.

"Sit down. I'll get Dr. Sachs."

Van Gogh's head exploded with piercing sounds. Breathy voices urged the doctor's death; Gregorian chants echoed the message. The chants and voices became so loud, he thought his head would split open.

"Good morning. The techs said you had a nightmare."

Van Gogh stared at the weasel. But this time, his faced had morphed into a hideous snake, tongue flickering, head bobbing slowly, like a cobra ready to strike. He said nothing.

"I'm putting you on a new tranquillizer, one that guarantees sound sleep." Dr. Sachs flipped a chart, making several notations.

As Dr. Sachs looked up, Van Gogh rounded the desk and ripped the shrink from his chair, executing a perfect hammerlock. As he stood behind the short doctor, leverage and rage inflicted the force of an anaconda. The immense pressure not only cut off the doctor's air, it made yelling impossible. His larynx snapped and trachea collapsed. He was brain dead in less than eight minutes. Van Gogh would now join his brother. *His* will had been done.

Epilogue

Father Gallagher chuckled quietly as he and Father O'Neil watched Doc and Gypsy walk down the aisle. Organ music filled the nave, bringing tears of joy to all. Saint Vincent's had literally risen from the ashes, and like the phoenix, had taken flight, reborn, seeking immortality. It was the rebuilt church's first wedding. The tapestries and stained glass windows were more magnificent than ever. Father Gallagher's saints were back, Aquinas and Augustine smiling, blessing the joyous event. The restoration had taken only a year from start to finish. He'd missed the "smells and bells," but thanks to Pope John Paul III, God bless his eternal soul, the building project had been put on a fast track.

Today was indeed special. Michael "Doc" Mesmer and Maria "Gypsy" Dumitrescu were joined in holy matrimony. Fathers Gallagher and O'Neil had shed tears during the ceremony. Waldo and Alan Workman served as best men; Gypsy's mother and two younger cousins were bridesmaids. Gypsy thought she was too old for a traditional wedding, but Doc convinced her to invite her entire Romanian clan. The church was packed, the ceremony elegant, and the reception joyous. Everyone loved Doc and Gypsy.

After the reception, Fathers Gallagher and O'Neil retired to the priests' new study, bigger and better than ever. Memories still hung in the air as the lifelong friends reviewed their careers. Of course, they talked of earlier times, their youth, Thomas Aquinas College, but recent events over shadowed the distant past: meeting the twins, the pope's visit, the death of Amadeus, and Van Gogh's murderous attack of the shrink.

"The holy books have been rewritten." Father Gallagher smiled, knowing he had personally witnessed the Catholic Church's latest revolution.

"Indeed," Father O'Neil chuckled. "The Gospel of Mary is now church orthodoxy."

"Do you think it will last?" Father Gallagher asked.

Father O'Neil appeared puzzled. "The Gospel of Mary?"

"No. Doc and Gypsy."

"Forever. God has made them one."

* * *

After the wedding and honeymoon, the newlyweds returned to their life's work, Gypsy reading Tarot cards and Doc making people feel better through hypnotism. Alan Workman and Doc remained close, the common love of Buddhism cementing their friendship for life. One evening, Alan dropped by Doc's office for a chat. He was surprised by the décor. The office had endured a facelift, revealing a more mature and honest hypnotist. Gone were the phony certificates and minister's license, replaced by tranquil pictures of snowcapped mountains and evergreen forests.

"I love the new feel." Alan walked around admiring the new motif, instantly feeling centered, drinking in the tranquility. "The waterfall is a touch of genius."

"Thanks. It projects how I feel." Doc smiled, appreciating Alan's sensitivity.

"What happened to the certificates? It gave you an aura of authority." Alan smiled, glad they were gone.

"Trappings of a former self, a self lacking substance." Doc grinned, proud of his openness.

"I liked the old Doc. But I love the new hypnotist."

"'Doc' is no longer a title. It's just a nickname."

Doc and Alan left the office. They had a dinner date with Gypsy.

* * *

Years later, at a cemetery high in the hills overlooking the San Fernando Valley, a mother and her young daughter placed flowers on two graves. The headstone on the first read Maria "Gypsy" Dumitrescu, the beloved wife of Doc. A second headstone, adjoining the first, read Michael "Doc" Mesmer, the beloved husband of Gypsy.

"Mommy, what kind of doctor was grandpa?"

The woman smiled, hugging her daughter. "He wasn't a real doctor. He was a hypnotist."

"What's a hypnotist?" The little girl clung tightly to her mother, feeling loved.

"When you're older, I'll show you."

The mother tilted her head, smiling. A soft voice called out to her. I love you. "Mom, it's you," she said aloud.

"Mommy, who was that?" The little girl looked about.

"It was your grandma."

The mother and young daughter walked away from the gravesite, holding hands, smiling.